I0627586

Also by Joan Byrd

From Indigo Sea Press

The All My Tomorrows Series:

A New Beginning

Love Finds a Way

Today, Tomorrow and Always

Lost Stories of Jesus

The Box in the Attic

The Good Seed—the Bad Seed

indigoseapress.com

Sunset Over Dixie

By

Joan Byrd

Deep Indigo Books

Published by Indigo Sea Press
Winston-Salem

Deep Indigo Books
Indigo Sea Press
PO Box 26701
Winston-Salem, NC 27114

This book is a work of fiction. Names, characters,
locations and events are either a product of the author's
imagination, fictitious or used fictitiously. Any resemblance
to any event, locale or person, living or dead, is purely
coincidental.

Copyright 2020 by Joan Byrd
All rights reserved, including the right of reproduction in
whole or part in any format.
First Deep Indigo Books edition published
November, 2020
Deep Indigo Books, Moon Sailor and all production design
are trademarks of Indigo Sea Press, used under license.

For information regarding bulk purchases of this book,
digital purchase and special discounts, please contact the
publisher at indigoseapress@gmail.com

Cover illustration by Joan Byrd
Cover design by Pan Morelli
Manufactured in the United States of America
ISBN 978-1-63066-509-8

To be able to live in this great nation, we, as individuals, should always feel blessed; and to uphold the sacred constitution written by our forefathers, stating, all men are created equal, and in our heavenly Creator's heart, every child is His and every child is created equal. If the Almighty God can love the greatest to the least of these the exact same way, should we not love our earthly brothers and sisters in the same exact way.

I dedicate this historic fiction to all my American family.

—Joan Byrd

Zachary Dawson

All the ladies caught the extremely handsome young man standing at the far end of the oval room. His features captivated their attention. The long black hair, deeply tanned skin and alluring blue eyes

that matched the royal blue shirt under the black suit. The young gentleman from Boston came down south for one purpose, to find the young nine-year-old red head he gave his heart to seven years ago, when he was ten.

Autumn Rose Forrest

Zachary's attention was frozen on the stairs and the last young lady with her beautiful red hair swept up into a cascade of curls to frame her incredibly beautiful face. He smiled into Autumn's emerald green eyes and she returned his smile brightly. The very proper southern belle had great love in her heart for everyone, but her greatest love and devotion was to Zachary Dawson, the young man she gave her heart to when she was nine years old.

"Autumn Rose's Dream Cream Cake" Recipe

1800's Recipe	Modern Description
1 chunk butter	1 cup butter, softened
1/2 cup lard	1/2 cup shortening
1 lb sugar-molasses mixture	16 oz brown sugar
1/2 cup sugar	1/2 cup sugar
5 large eggs	5 large eggs
1/2 tsp rising powder	1/2 tsp baking powder
3 cups sifted plain flour	3 cups all-purpose flour sifted
1 vanilla bean, split open & scraped out	1 rounded tbsp vanilla extract
1 cup chopped pecans	1 cup chopped pecans
1 cup milk	1 cup milk
1 cup raisins soaked in 1 cup rum for 1 hour	1 cup raisins soaked in 1 cup rum for 1 hour
Drain and reserved rum to drizzle over warm cake	Drain and reserved rum to drizzle over warm cake

- Cream butter and shortening in large mixing bowl; gradually add sugars, beating until light and fluffy.
- Add eggs, one at a time, beating well after each addition.
- Combine baking powder and flour, add to creamed mixture alternating with milk, beginning and ending with flour, beating well after each addition.
- Stir in vanilla, pecans, and raisins.
- Pour batter into a greased and floured 10-inch tube pan.
- Bake 350° for 1 hour and 10 minutes or until a wooden pick inserted into center comes out clean.
- Cool pan 10 minutes.
- Remove onto cake dish and drizzle with reserved cup of rum.

"Autumn's Secret Topping"

1800's Recipe	Modern Description
Chunk of butter	1 1/2 sticks of butter
1/3 cup of milk	1/3 cup of milk
1 1/2 cups of sugar-molasses mixture	1 1/2 cups of brown sugar

1 vanilla bean, split open &
scraped out

1 1/2 tsp vanilla extract

1 lb of sugar, pounded down
to a fine powder

1 lb confectioners sugar

- Combine butter, milk, brown sugar; bring to a boil and cook for 2 minutes, stirring constantly.
- Remove from heat and beat in confectioners sugar and vanilla.
- While it is still warm and creamy, ice cake immediately before it gets too stiff.

Chapter 1

Sunrise was a favorite time for the sixteen-year-old girl who made her way early in the morning to her special secret place to watch the sun coming up over her childhood home. The white pillared mansion glowed brightly when the first rays of sunlight captured its magnificent Southern charm and grace.

Her long red hair, braided in a single pigtail, hung down her back, adorned with a white ribbon to match her long white night gown, covered by a soft brown robe to ward off the morning chill. Even though the summers were hot at her family's South Carolina plantation, the head-strong girl always experienced the chill that came with the morning just before the sun rose in the Eastern sky. She was extra careful not to be seen by anyone working on the plantation, especially her parents. To be caught outside with just a nightgown on was not respectable for a southern belle and Autumn Rose would simply die from embarrassment being seen un-lady like.

Autumn Rose never felt afraid when she slipped out of her big bedroom window on the second-floor gallery and hurried quickly down the wide steps that led to the garden path. Autumn's faithful golden collie, Jack, would be waiting to make the trip with his beautiful owner, just as he had ever since the loving girl found him lying beside the road, beaten and abandon by some uncaring individual. Jack's sole purpose was to protect his best friend from any unwanted predator, four legged or two.

Autumn Rose Forrest was the only child born to Katherine and Frederick Forrest, who had inherited the 3,000-acre plantation called Laurel Grove, located between Charleston and Hilton Head, South Carolina. The sparling plantation boosted about having the best property in the state of South Carolina. Its rich fertile soil could produce two of the South's biggest crops, cotton and sugar cane, so there was never a shortage of income.

Like all wealthy landowners in the South, the Forrest owned slaves, over 400. The difference that set them apart from many other plantation owners was how they treated each slave. Both Katherine and Frederick had strong Christian beliefs, which they install in their little girl, and believed in the sight of God all men, women and

1

children where equal. By keeping families together and giving them a home which set on a half-acre of land for growing their own garden, it gave the slaves a since of belonging. They felt happy and secure working for this good family who made sure 'their family', as the Forrest family called them, never worked more than eight hours a day, with a lunch break in the middle of the day. Their children under fifteen, went to a small school room during the day, to learn reading and writing. Katherine thought fifteen was old enough to work in the fields and the young ones needed to learn lessons. Frederick strictly forbid any slave call him master Forrest or "massa," but make it simply Mr. Forrest or better still, Frederick.

Sunday was a day of rest for everyone living at Laurel Grove and the large chapel that set in a grove of Laurel brushes was built plenty big to accommodate the three Forrest members, one minister, and four hundred born again slaves, who felt more-free than when they struggled on the African plains. The plantation minister, Reverend Timothy Hollman, would begin each service with these words: "The Sabbath is a day of rest and rest is good for the soul and the fields!"

A few of the slaves worked solely around the plantation house and the stables. Big Ben, short for Benjamin, was in charge of the grounds which included the black smith shop, the stables and barns, the livestock, horses, and cattle, pigs, chickens and turkeys. Big Ben had twenty men working under him and taking orders from one of their own instead of a white foreman, made the work a pleasure, knowing they would be treated with dignity and respect, even though their big boss ran a tight ship and expected the very best from each man.

The staff in the big house consisted of Nora, the head cook. Her cooking skills was probably the best in the entire state, winning almost every blue ribbon for Mrs. Katherine in the county fair held ever October. Her assistants in the kitchen were mostly family members, Mallie, her youngest sister, Cora, her twin sister who was gifted herself in the kitchen with her culinary skills in making desserts. Nora's daughters also assisted in the kitchen as well as serving the food to the Forrest's. Florence, Elsa, and sixteen-year-old Nellie, Nora's youngest child and Autumn Rose's best friend and personal maid.

There was a staff of ten house servants that kept the big mansion sparkling clean. Erlene was Katherine's personal maid and Oscar was Frederick Forrest's groom. Nora's husband, Willy Henry, was the head butler and in charge of the house staff.

It always did Autumn's heart good to hear her black family either singing or talking freely among themselves as they did their chores. Even as a child, the girl with red hair and emerald green eyes could not understand how anyone, especially good Christian folks like her parents, own slaves, even though they treated them like family. So, at the age of ten, Autumn brought the subject up to their preacher, Reverend Hollman, without her parent's knowledge.

"Reverend Hollman, why aren't black people welcome at other churches? You said in your sermon this morning, all God's children are welcome in the Lord's house. Aren't all church's God's house?"

"Yes child, it is the place we go to worship Him. If you recall, I said brother Sims from Piney Ridge Baptist just down the way, told me he had went by to visit a new family in our neighborhood and invite them to church. He also said he ask his congregation to pay them a visit and..." before the minister could finish the ten-year-old Autumn interrupted.

"That's all well and good sir, but black people are God's children too and many of them have been our neighbors for many years and except for our large family attending here every sabbath, the neighboring blacks have not one time been ask to worship their God in the churches near them!"

"Autumn, your heart is in the right place child and if it were up to me, I would gladly open up the doors for them." The small girl could tell even at her young age that the preacher's statement was sincere as he continued. "Those other church members would not see things the same way as you and I. They would never permit their slaves to come inside their church, much less worship alongside them."

"Perhaps you could ask your fellow ministers to speak to them. The people respect their minister's words of wisdom. Please sir, you can even tell them it was I who suggested letting then attend." Autumn had looked up with her big green eyes full of hope.

"If they should except this proposal, the group would insist the slaves sit in the balcony." Reverend Hollman patted Autumn's red head. "Could you except that?"

Autumn had remembered her reply six-years ago. "I suppose I must Reverend, but at least they can enter into the house of God, hear the word and be filled with the spirit." She had giggled, remembering hearing the many voices lifting up within their chapel, praising God through spirituals "I know those white folks will be blessed by the singing from the balcony. Their little churches will come to life with all those joyful voices!" To the ten-year-old's delight, the church members agreed after their ministers made them feel like hypocrites if they refused the black man's rights to worship his Lord.

The sunlight lifted high above the pillared mansion and Autumn's faithful companion gave a little yap as he always did when he noticed the beautiful girl sat up, smiling at the heavenly sight.

"Oh, Jack! I never grow tired of watching the sunrise over Dixie! It makes my heart sing!"

"And if you do not get yourself back to the big house and in your room Miss Autumn, before your mama gets up, you'll get a talking to again!" The pretty petite black girl pulled at her mistress's arm as Autumn looked on in devilish delight. Now, red in the face from tugging, the young woman stomped her foot in aggravation. "I'm not joking missy! Remember what happen the last time your mama found you outside in your gown?"

"Relax Nellie and calm yourself down before you burst that pretty little vein in your neck." Autumn stood up with Nellie's strong tug. "Mama uses the same feeble threat every time she disapproves of my behavior." As she walked back down the path, Jack at her heels, she lowered her voice to resemble her mother speaking. "Young lady, you know better than to prance around in the mornings with only your gown on! One of the workers could attack you and have his way with you! Your life would be ruined! No respectful southern gentleman would want to marry you and God forbid if you find yourself pregnant with a slave's bastard!"

"Miss Autumn, your mama is right! You can't be trusting every black man on this plantation! I sees the way they looks at you, Miss Autumn, and put in the right circumstances, I would not rule out them, few though they be, gets out of hand, if-n the chance arrived!" Nellie opened the big window to Autumn's bedroom and pulled her inside. "You best listen to your mama girl; she is a wise woman."

"Then if mama is so wise Nellie, why on earth does she always threaten to take away my trip to Natchez and make me miss my coming out party at Aunt Isabell's, and share the spotlight with my two delightful cousins when she is the one who keeps insisting I attend?"

"Christina and Polly Anne are not the friendliest cousins you have Miss Autumn, only because they jealous of you! But, missy, that coming out party is about the grandest party in all Natchez and that's why your mama threatens to take it away!" Nellie eyes grew wide as she declared. "Why, you just might meet your future husband right then and there!"

"Heaven forbid I miss that big event in my short lifetime!" Autumn began unbuttoning the top of her nightgown and the maid rushed over to assist her as she pulled it over her flaming red hair, then took it to fold and lay on top of the folded robe before shutting the chest. Autumn walked over to her wardrobe and pulled out a simple blue dress, while chatting to her friend. "Nellie, I just as soon miss that ridiculous party where a bunch of strange men stand around staring at you all evening until they grow the courage to ask if you care to dance the next waltz. Christina and sweet Polly Anne will pretend to like me in front of the men, say they admire my dress while moving around to show off their expensive new gowns and sparkling jewels. All the while they gather around their stuck-up friends so they can gossip about their red-headed cousin with every available opportunity."

"Now Miss Autumn, listen how you go on and on! Why, you make the whole thing sound terrible! It is true Miss Christine and Miss Polly Anne are spoiled to the core and green with envy over your natural beauty, but all their gossip won't help them none. You will be the talk of the ball my friend, and there ain't no gentlemen in his right mind that won't desire your fair hand in marriage." Nellie pulled the blue dress down over the petticoats and commenced to fastening the row of small buttons as she gave a little snicker. "While you dance the night away with every man in attendance, those two wall flowers will have to settle for your rejects and them pretty dresses they done went and spent a year's living wages for and their dull hair done up with fancy little ribbons, will not do them any good."

"I cannot imagine finding the man of my dreams at that party, Nellie, but should he show up it will most likely be with one of the invited guest." Autumn Rose took a seat at the vanity and picked up her brush, waving the black girl's offer away and began brushing her own long hair. "Dear friend, pull a chair up and hear me out. I know ever since my daddy gave me the blue silk gown on my fifteenth birthday, my pretty, shy companion has admired it. If I must attend this coming out party, I insist that you except the blue silk gown, my gift to you, and accompany me to the dance. You shall stand next to me and dance if you are asked by a gentleman." Autumn stopped brushing her hair when the young woman let out a gasp and turned to look into her dark brown eyes. "Nellie, do not be pretending you do not know how to dance a waltz, as many times as we've pretended to waltz around in the ballroom downstairs."

"That was just play acting, Miss Autumn! Lordy me, missy, you know I can't go prancing around in that big house, pretending I be a debutant like yourself!" Nellie's eyes grew wide. "Why, your mama and pappy would never hear of sech a thing and God knows my mama will tan my hide if n I ever mention getting myself all dressed up to stand next to you! I would be going out alright, to the woodshed!"

"Goodness, how you take on, Nellie! I know how foolish everyone feels about black people staying in their place and I find the entire thing appalling!" Autumn slammed down the brush as she struggled with braiding her hair until her best friend brushed her fingers aside and took control of the thick single braid. "I swear Nellie, if it takes the rest of my life on this earth, I will do whatever I can to free as many slaves as possible!" Autumn reached up and touched Nellie's hand. "Nellie, you know you are more to me than just my dearest friend in the entire world, you are more like a sister to me." Noticing tears gathering in the girl's brown eyes, Autumn stood up and gathered her friend into a sisterly embrace. "Nellie, except for my parents, there is no one I love more, except of course my heavenly Lord. You and I have been together all our lives. We are merely months apart and we have grown up side-by-side and I truly do see you like a sister."

"Miss Autumn, you must know I love you just as deeply, and in my heart, you are nearer to me than my own flesh and blood sisters, and that's a fact! You took me with you when you learned to read and write and how to work with numbers! Now, even though I be born a slave, I too have the same knowledge and can be a big help to my family and all the black people here on the plantation." Nellie took her friend by the hand, squeezing it lovingly. "Miss Autumn, your big heart opened the doors to God's house and now when all those other black brothers and sisters commence to singing, I feels mighty proud when I sit in Laurel Grove Chapel, knowing my heart sister done helped me learn how to read, so I can follow along when preacher Hollman reads the scriptures, from the pretty white bible you gave me for my tenth birthday."

"I just regret that my dearest friend cannot openly sit next to me in church." The sound of footsteps made their way down the hallway toward them and both girls turned toward the door, waiting the coming knock as Autumn smiled down at her friend. "As far as the coming out ball, you will be standing beside me, one way or the other!"

"But, Miss…" Autumn cut her off before she could continue.

"Nellie, how many times must I have to tell you to call me Autumn and stop calling me Miss Autumn?" Before Nellie could respond, a soft knock fell on the door. "Yes, who is it? "

"It's the chamber maid, Miss Autumn. Breakfast has been prepared and set out. Your parents await your arrival."

"Thank you, Cassie. You may tell them I am on my way down." Autumn turned to her friend. "No more talk now Nellie, it is time to join mama and daddy in the breakfast room where I am certain we shall be discussing the Natchez trip!"

Chapter 2

"Good morning papa!" Autumn bent over to give her father a big hug around his neck, then turned and kissed her mother's cheek, alive with fresh make-up. "Good morning mama. You are looking very lovely this morning. Another trip to Charleston?" the young beautiful redhead gave her father a knowing wink when he smiled up at her remark.

"Your mother does have big plans for a shopping trip to the big city to purchase a few things for one beautiful special girl." Frederick Forrest reached over to pat his daughter's hand.

Autumn laughed softly and pulled out her chair. "Let me guess! A new gown to wear for my coming out party at Chatham Hall in beautiful Natchez, Mississippi." A beautiful smile graced Katherine's face as she reached for a silver bell and gave it a ring, drawing a servant girl waiting just inside the kitchen door.

"Not just the most beautiful gown in all of Charleston, my dear, but a new outfit for every occasion while you are at my dear sister's mansion in Natchez." The glamorous elegant lady glanced over at her husband, who watched her closely. "I just regret your dear father cannot join us and see how beautiful you will be dressed like a princess. Poor Christina and Polly Anne will be beside themselves with jealousy."

"The dear girls had the misfortune to take after their father. Elvin Chatham never was blessed with looks." Frederick watched as two servants came out from the kitchen carrying silver trays, laden with scrambled eyes, country ham with red-eye gravy, grits covered with fresh churn butter. The other tray featured a basket, filled with piping hot buttermilk biscuits, peach preserves and a big chunk of real butter.

The lady of the house watched as the oldest black woman refilled her coffee cup. "Thank you Mallie, everything looks splendid as always. Do give Nora our heart felt thanks for another lovely meal."

Mallie watched the mistress of Laurel Grove reached for the freshly ironed napkin and place it gracefully in her lap. "Thank you, ma'am. I will pass the compliment along to the head cook. Mrs. Nora will be please." After refilling the master of the house's cup, she made her way around the table to the smiling red head. "Coffee, Miss Autumn?"

"Mallie, I would love some of that great smelling coffee." Autumn reached up and patted the servant's arm. "Your bread smells wonderful as well. I can almost hear it calling for fresh churned butter and some of Cora's homemade preserves!"

"You hears it calling! You know how to make a soul feel real, good, Miss Autumn." Mallie giggled and reached for the peach preserves and butter to set it in front of the green-eye beauty. "Here you go Miss Autumn. It does me and my sisters, Cora and Nora proud to see you folks enjoining our cooking!"

"You three have earned the praises you receive, my dear." Mr. Forrest smiled up at the blushing servant. "Your men folk are indeed lucky to have you ladies for their wives."

"Why, thank you sir and I agree, cause when those men of ours sat down to eat, they don't utter a sound of talk, cause those mouths are too busy chewing and chomping!" the servant laughed out as she excused herself.

Autumn chuckled, then dropped her eyes on her bread as she spread on some butter, trying to avoid direct contact with Katherine. "Mama, since you will be buying things for the Natchez trip, could you get Nellie a couple of dresses for all the activities as well, since she will be accompanying me. I want her to feel pretty too."

Frederick observed his wife's instant disapproval when her eyebrow arched up and eyes grew cloudy but giving herself time to form her words correctly for her head-strong daughter, she said with total authority. "Autumn, not so much butter and preserves! You know that stuff packs on extra pounds, not to mention inches on your waist! Trust me, your corset will feel a whole lot more comfortable if you do not gain weight!"

Frederick gave his daughter a wink when she glanced up at him. "Mother is right, sweet girl, so pass me that fatting duet so I may join you."

"Frederick, do not patronize your daughter! You know she must look absolutely perfect for all those gentlemen!" Katherine sat up as she watched her smiling husband spread butter over his biscuit, then preserves and took a big bite, giving her a wink. "Very cute Frederick! I do not wish to have a 'fat' husband next to me in bed either!" The series woman's face grew red when father and daughter began laughing. Katherine cleared her throat and turned to face her daughter. "Autumn Rose, I was in hopes that you would leave Nellie at home this trip. You are older now and I cannot see any reason why you would need a companion to hold your hand! It's not becoming for a grown woman to have or need a nanny!"

"Nellie is hardly a nanny, mother!" Frederick knew by his daughter's tone and how she addressed his wife that she was ready for self-defense, a trait she inherited from her uncle, Nathan Bedford Forrest. "Nellie is my dearest friend and as you well know, she is only a few months older than me! I am telling you right now, I WILL NOT set foot in Natchez if Nellie is not by my side and that's final!"

"Oh, yes you will, young lady! I am your mother and you WILL listen to me! My sister and your cousins are expecting us and have been planning this big gala for over a month! It has become the talk around the old city and you will not let them down!" Katherine rose to her feet, eyes still on her outspoken daughter.

"Let them down, mother? Do not you mean, disappoint you, so you cannot show me off to a bunch of strangers who mean absolutely nothing to me!" Autumn pushed herself up to face her mother. "If you wish for me to go with you, then Nellie comes with me!"

"Then it's, no Nellie, no you? You refuse to go without that girl?" Katherine looked helplessly over at her husband, who had been observing their battle. "Frederick, she's your daughter, do something! Speak some sense into her stubborn head!"

Frederick stood up and walked between mother and daughter, taking his wife's shoulders, turned her toward the door. "Katherine darling, get your things for Charleston and I will have Ben send the carriage around for us while I have a word with Autumn." He reached over and gave her a kiss and his handsome smile. "Stop fretting now, things will work out. We have raised a smart girl, my dear. Autumn Rose pretty much knows things better than most men I am acquainted with. If she wants Nellie to accompany her to Chatham Hall, I see no harm in it and as for buying new clothes for the girl, I will speak to our daughter about that." He gave her a little push. "Do as I say now and off with you." He watched her leave and held his arms out for his only child.

"Thank you, papa, at least you understand." Autumn always felt safe in her father's arms.

"Autumn, my precious child, I cannot say I have ever understood you fully. You are much too like my brother Nathan, but at least I understand your devotion for Nellie. She has been by your side longer than anyone, including me and your mother. I will see that Nellie gets two new dresses for the trip."

Autumn threw her arms around her father's neck as she laughed with happiness. "Oh papa, whatever would I do without you! Thank you!"

"Well, just remember, Nellie can go along with you Autumn, but your mother is right about one thing. The night of the coming out party is strictly planned for you and your two cousins. Nellie must remain in your bedchamber while the ball is going on so I will not be purchasing a ball gown for her."

Autumn smiled, a certain mischief filled her emerald green eyes as she walked to the door and turned to face her father. "Thank you for buying Nellie two dresses papa and as far as the ball gown, there would have been no need to purchase one for her anyway. Nellie will be wearing my blue silk gown I got last year to wear at the county ball. See you papa! Have fun shopping!" he followed her to the stairs and watched her ascend, calling over her shoulder. "And do not worry about the work getting done while you're away in Charleston. You taught me well how to run a plantation papa, so it's in good hands. Ta-ta!" Autumn disappeared up the steps, leaving Frederick Forrest smiling.

Chapter 3

It was exciting times at West Point Military Academy for the staff as well as the cadets. The two-week event was held to choose the most outstanding student in the Calvary games and after the first week, twenty cadets remained until the final two days. The competitive group was now narrowed down to three young men. Two senior cadets from the class of 1856 along with an unexpected freshman. Cocky and ready to win the title for a second time, was George A. Custer, who was up against another champion, Fitzhugh Lee. Custer considered him his only arrival. Both Custer and Lee had competed in the games ever since their freshman year at West Point. It appeared their first year was a disappointment and turned out badly. Fitzhugh was caught sneaking out with his drinking buddies to a local pub and got thrown out of the games for misconduct by Robert E. Lee, the superintendent of the academy and Fitzhugh's uncle. George had taken a bad spill from his horse two days before the games showing off for a group of young women who was there on visiting day by trying a risky theatrical stunt while galloping at full speed, sword drawn for an attack. It cost him the games.

Their sophomore year gave George Custer the title and his rival came in second, only to claim first place the following year. So, now they stood tied and this would be their final year to prove which man was the best. Neither man considered the young freshman cadet might claim victory and beat them both. After all, he was still green behind the ears, a mere boy, which they both called him. Custer bragged to all his friends that this boy was not a threat and could be easy whooped when he poured on everything he had.

Feeling sure of himself and cocky as usual, George rode up on his fine steed, adorned with a fancy saddle to match his elaborate uniform and expensive hat atop his blonde locks. He smiled across at his competitor who sat even higher in his shiny black saddle, adorned with silver. Wearing his first-year cadet uniform and a great looking black western hat. His dark black shoulder length hair fell rich and full around his handsome face, which he kept shaved clean except for a neatly groomed mustache.

Zachary Dawson was not new to his horse-riding skills and the tall handsome young man was second to none when it came to fancy moves on his black stallion, Midnight. Since his childhood, Zachary had trained with the best, to learn tricks that other riders only dreamed about. Not being there to see the award-winning events this young cadet had been in, both Custer and Lee had no knowledge of the young man's skills, except what they had witness in the previous games just held. Like his senior competitors, Zachary Dawson was holding his best stunts for the final competition, but the two seniors did not see him as a threat. He was the new man on the team and as Fitzhugh Lee put it, that boy don't stand a snowballs chance in hell. George gave Zachary a mocking smile.

"Hey boy! Ready to get your ass whipped? Or, had you rather save face and bow out and spare yourself and those friends of yours the embarrassment of losing?"

"Don't start shining that trophy yet Custer! I'm not one to give up! I'm here to win these games same as you and Lee!" Zachary stared back seriously. "I might be just a freshman in your eyes Custer, but you senior cadets better not count me out so soon!"

"I like your spirit boy! When we graduate and leave the Point, you just might win one of these games, perhaps all of them, but you will find keeping up with me and Lee in these games will prove you are not up to winning the top prize! You have been warned boy!"

"The name is Zackary, not boy! You best remember that George Custer! That attitude might win you some enemies one day!" Zackary Dawson wasn't one to be ran over as the brass twenty-year-old Custer would soon find out.

Seventeen-year-old Zachary Dawson had been born to Irene and Jacob Dawson in the spring of 1839. Being an only child had not been easy for the handsome shy boy. Growing up on a two-hundred-acre farm just outside of Boston, Massachusetts, was the perfect place for a solitude young fellow like Zachary. He had made a few friends in school, but his closest friend was his first cousin, Reid Dawson. The cousins had grown up near each other, both living on big farmland where brothers Jacob and Henry Dawson inherited their family estate and divided the property after both men got married. Having family get togethers such as birthday picnics, corn shucking harvest and bar-b-q's made the cousins closer. They had always planned to go to West Point together as soon as they were old enough and become soldiers in the United States Calvary. Both boys were fairly good horseback riders but that was as far as any soldiering skills went until young Zachary turned ten.

One summer changed the shy young man forever. Around his tenth birthday, his Uncle David Hastings, his mother's oldest brother, ask to take young Zachary with him on a trip to Mississippi, down South, to visit a close friend of his. The year was 1849 and late spring had brought in yet another snow to the state of Massachusetts, so going South made young Zachary excited about finding a place where the sun was shining and he could shed his heavy winter coat. Not having any children of his own and losing his wife to yellow fever a year prier, David Hastings needed a traveling companion. Irene was totally against the ideal of sending her only child away for an entire month, especially down to the hot South. After all Summer would arrive while they were gone and she had heard how humid the deep south could become. To Irene's dismay, Jacob Dawson thought this was exactly what the young boy needed. To finally get off the farm for a while and learn about other places and people. Irene was finally convinced after being reminded how Zachary had become moody and would saddle their old farm horse, Jake, and disappear for hours.

So, Zachary set off with Uncle David, to visit a man name, Nathan Bedford Forrest, who would capture the young man's heart and give him a bright new spirit.

Chapter 4

Zachary and Uncle David had arrived at Hernando, Mississippi, by railroad and rented a carriage to take them out to the Crooked Creek Plantation, a sparling 2000-acre track of fertile farmland. Arriving late at Hernando station, the two tired travelers needed a place to stay the night and the only available place was a room at Sadie's Saloon and Inn. Not exactly suitable for a young boy like Zachary but Uncle David assumed beggars could not be choosers when no other places were available.

The owner and madam of the prostitutes known simply as Miss Sadie, was extremely polite and showed young Zac that she could act like a mother if she so chose. Her long blonde hair was swept up in cascading curls and her red velvet dress was cut extremely low reveling very large breasts. Despite her age of 62, under her heavy make-up, Sadie was very attractive and obviously wealthy, featuring six highly trained prostitutes who all took an instant liking to the handsome young ten-year-old. So, when they didn't have a client, they would chat with the young boy, finding him very intelligent for his young age.

It was due to all the attention the ladies in the saloon were paying his nephew, Uncle David took the boy to a small café opened across the street and then gave him orders to stay in their room until morning where it would be safe while he went down to the bar for a nightcap before turning in.

Most nights brought in the gamblers and no one could outwit the famous Jax Tyndall. Dressed in a rich black suit and his signature wide rim black hat featuring a single red feather, he was set apart from all the other henny-penny gamblers who won a little and loss a lot. Tyndall was slick, smooth, well dressed, well-educated and a ruthless card shark who could rob his unsuspecting opponent out of everything he had, including his very life if he gave him a challenge and accused him of cheating. Those who knew the man that smoked only the fineness, most expensive cigars, carried a solid gold cane with an ivory handle and had solid gold rings on six of his fingers, was someone to look out for. After emptying many pockets in neighboring towns, the bold man would be asked to leave and the local sheriff would run him out or risk being locked up.

Tyndall never traveled alone. Besides his four tough bodyguards, his very attractive and well-dressed mistress, Miss Melody Marigold was never far from his sight. Miss Marigold was a stage actress from New York City and the gamblers greatest asset. With her acting skills and her good looks, the petite blonde could charm any red-blooded gentleman into falling for her bate where she would set them up in a card game against her boyfriend and lover, who, in her act was her cheating, two timing, boyfriend.

David Hastings was to be her next target and he had not been just picked at random. The truth was none of his marks had been casually chosen. Jax Tyndall had done his homework and like his other marks, Hastings had all the qualifications. Not only was he rich, owned his big mansion and estate in Boston, he was an outsider, new to the town, and more important, David Hastings was a lonely widower.

After getting his nephew settled in their up-stairs room, David went down to the saloon for a couple of beers before turning in for the night. Not wishing to sit near the local rowdy men at the bar, the only man in the establishment who did not have a southern accent, found a quiet table in the corner of the large room. Hastings was enjoying his cold beer as he watched with amusement the barmaids slapping hands away from their revealing breast and their back sides, when Miss Marigold stepped through the double doors, dressed in a modest high neck blouse covered gracefully with a black jacket to match her long skirt. The charming lady wore a rather plain bonnet that sat atop her long blonde hair. David Hastings thought she looked like an angel, holding tightly to a single piece of luggage. He could hear her asking the receptionist if there were any rooms available for the night. She glanced briefly over at the drunken customers who were making rude remarks, blushed and turned back to the man behind the desk who was still checking the room situation. Looking around the room, her eyes locked with David's and smiles were shared between them. The clerk cleared his throat for her attention.

"You are in luck Miss Russell; we have one small room left. Although the size isn't much, the room is very clean and neat."

"That will do fine for me, Mr. Ross. It's just for one night and all I intend to do is sleep anyway." She smiled down at his name plate, then ask modestly. "Would it be an inconvenience if I had a cup of coffee. It's been a long trip and I haven't had a bite to eat since breakfast."

16

"Excuse me miss, I do not wish to interfere, but I too am traveling, along with my young nephew, who has turned in for the night." David Hastings tilted his hat politely. "You may join me at my table if you like. A bar is no place for a lady to be alone and I can assure you, you will be perfectly safe with me."

That is most generous of you sir," Melody held out her gloved hand. "Melody Russell, but if we are to have a drink together as friends, please call me Melody."

"I would be delighted and you may call me David, as in David Hastings, from Boston. Now that we consider ourselves friends, may I buy you something to eat from the kitchen here? There is a fine menu on the table and I insist that you let me treat you to a meal. I did overhear you tell that clerk you hadn't eaten since breakfast, so I know you must be starving." David gave her a genuine smile. He had not counted on meeting such a beautiful lady on this journey, but his heart jumped a beat when she had walked inside. She smiled shyly and gave him a nod, then they made their way to his table where she ordered a small vegetable plate and cornbread. With a little light coaching, David convinced her to change the coffee for a glass of sherry.

The new-found friends were making small talk when Jax Tyndall made a grand entrance into the saloon, accompanied by his muscular body guards, and ran a group of men away from the table he preferred, then ordered a round of beer for his men and a bottle of the bar's best brandy for himself.

"Did you see that? Who does that man think he is, asking...no, telling someone to get up from 'his' table!" David had never witnessed such arrogant behavior before, being only around true gentlemen all his life.

"It does not surprise me David! That low life is the great Jax Tyndall, a creep and a gambler, what's more, one sorry cheating boyfriend!" the actress turned her back on the man in black and lifted her glass in front of David. "I offer a toast to you David, for bringing back my trust in men."

"So, that rude man is your ex?" David studied the older man sitting several tables away, and despite his expensive attire, he wasn't much to look at. David's gaze turned back on the pretty women "It may not be none of my business Melody, but, that man is too old for such a pretty girl like you. I would guess my age would even put me out of the running, where you are concern, and I'm at least ten-years younger that this Tyndall, my dear."

"And that just goes to show you know absolutely nothing about my taste in men, David." Melony gave him a beautiful smile. "I happen to find you extremely charming, quite handsome and very much in the running. I dare say, after we grow more acquainted, we could become very close, if I could close that chapter in my tortured life with that man. All I want is to get my money back that crook stole from me." The pretty young woman nodded her head toward the gambler, who was busy stacking and shuffling his deck of cards as he waited for a man willing to take a chance and risk all his money."

"How much did he get and how?" David knew he was falling for this sweet young woman, who had felt safe enough to tell him about her deep secret concerning this gambler.

"Tyndall didn't exactly take my money from me. I was far too smart to ever play cards with him, although I could have easily beaten him, had he not been a cheater." Melony drank down her sherry, then turned to look at her so-call ex-boyfriend. "Jax always had me picking up things for him, those expensive cigars he is smoking, expensive booze to drink after a successful game of cards, money and titles to property sticking from his fat pockets. He always promised to pay me back, double for my trouble, but I never saw one red cent! The obnoxious creep left me almost broke, spending all my hard earn savings."

"He seems like a real slob Melony. How could a sweet girl like you stay with a man like that?" David questioned her reasoning. "Did you stay because you loved him and hoped he would change?"

"I had no one, David and Jax took me in and treated me good. He gave me a home, pretty clothes and servants serving great dishes, treating me like I was a princess. Now, that I look back on our life together, I realize Jax kept me for his sex pleasures and to use me for his gofer, knowing I had a little money saved." Melony turned back to David and took his hand. "Oh David, if only I could think of some way to get back what was mine. To get even with the lying, two-face bastard!"

"I wished I could help you, Melony." He held on to her soft hand and thought he really wished he could be her hero. Up until that moment, David did not realize how much he needed another woman in his lonely life.

"Do you want to help me David?" Melony caressed his fingers.

"Tell me, have you ever gambled? Do you play poker?"

David smiled broadly. "You just happen to be looking at Boston's county club champion poker player, but my friends and I only played for small winnings, the cost of our meal and wine."

"I think I should like your friends David, good, honest men, like yourself."

"And up until now, that has been enough." David stared over at the rude man who had stolen even from this sweet young woman who put her trust in him. "I think my betting just got bigger."

Her blue eyes lit up with hope. "David, are you saying you will take on that heartless man, for me?" Tears came easily to the actress as she touched his face and whispered softly "For us?"

"If you help me know what to look for so he cannot pull a fast one on me." David felt confident in his skills and knew he was good enough at poker to beat this cheater and do it legally. "Melody, do you know how Tyndall cheats at cards?"

"Every little detail." She smiled and lend in to whisper in his ear everything to look for and how to twist the outcome in their favor. Then the actress sat back and continued to speak softly, just for David's ears. "The first two games are rigged so the mark will win both games. This strategy leaves his opponent thinking he can beat him in every game, especially when Jax pretends to want to quit, before he loses more. The last mark felt so sure of himself he beat his entire estate for Tyndall's East to West Railroad line, which is worth millions, David!" Melody glanced over at the gambler, trying to convince an elderly gentleman to play him in a game of poker. "David, if we could win that railroad he prizes so much, it would really show that devil he cannot get by cheating honest people."

"What about those bodyguards? Would they let someone just beat their boss out of such wealth and permit them to just walk away?" David had noticed how the four serious men paid close attention to the old gentleman trying to make excuses for not playing.

"They won't cause trouble in a public place and too many witnesses will see you beat him fairly, so, unless the bastard wishes to go to jail along with his four goons, he will lick his wounds and leave for the next town."

Young Zachary Dawson had slipped from his room earlier after being bored with nothing to do, except sleep and he did not feel tired anymore after eating the big supper in that little café across the street. He felt sure he was missing some action down below in the bar like drunks getting in to fist fights or maybe even a shoot-out. Being young and impressible, he hid himself between two large potted plants and he had witnessed the pretty blonde lady walk in and go to the clerk's desk. He observed his Uncle David walking over to talk to her and Zac could hear their conversation very good from his high hiding place. He had watched them go to his uncle's table and watched him buy her supper, then he offered to help the pretty woman and it made Zachary feel extra proud of his uncle David. Although Zachary was young, he was well educated in adult matters and after hearing this woman named Melody speak about the gambler in black, he could not understand how such a smart girl had gotten into such a mess with the devil in the big black hat topped with a red feather.

Zachary watched nervously as his uncle easily beat the card shark in the first two games, then, seeing his uncle tell the gambler he would make a big wager if he agreed to play one more game and put up a bet to match his own. Zachary moved closer to the rail to hear what his uncle would be risking to an obvious long shark who was obviously stalling, pretending to consider his opponent's request.

"What is your wager, Mr. Hastings?" Jax Tyndall swallowed down the contents in his glass and refilled it. "What do you have to offer, sir?"

"I will put up my entire estate in Boston which includes a mansion, manicured grounds, stables with the finest horses in Boston, carriages and expensive furniture which decorate thirty large rooms." David watched the gambler closely, as did all the interested customers who had gathered around the gambler's table to watch the games.

"And you want me to put up my East to West Railroad, which is worth millions, for that little bit?" Mr. Tyndall sat back and looked thoughtful, pretending to compare what he might win verses what he could lose. David saw through the act and waited for his next comment. "Tell me Mr. Hastings, is there anything else you can throw in to make my risk a little more less painful? Say, cash on hand, bonds, savings, a life insurance policy, perhaps?"

Earlier at the table, Melody had warned David to keep his eyes on Jax because he would try to distract him, then slipped a set of Aces up his sleeve and exchange the winning set for the set he draws. She told David to watch Tyndall's moves and if he caught him cheating call him out secretly, giving the cheater a chance to save face with the large crowd he always draws. Then he would have to play an honest game, you would win, being the better player and Jax Tyndall would get what he had coming to him.

David lend up toward the gambler and said proudly, "Done! Cash, bonds, savings, and a huge life insurance policy, everything I have, Mr. Tyndall."

The crowd grew loud with whispers as Mr. Tyndall looked up over his glasses. "I'll take that gamble, Mr. Hastings, against my better judgement, but..." he looked around the room and saw the interested spectators waiting with bated breath. "I will bet with you!" the gambler held out his steady hand and David shook it, sealing the deal.

Zachary sat up, excited about watching his uncle actually win a railroad and take it away from the cheater, putting him in his place. The young boy hated anyone who cheated, lied, and stole from innocent people. This man name Jax was all three and now he had the nerve to ask his Uncle David to show him proof of all his holdings.

"Hastings, I have the title to my railroad line right here!" the shifty gambler held up a legal looking document. "I need some proof that you actually own an estate along with all this wealth you are bragging about."

"Mr. Tyndall, I just happen to carry an extra copy of my deed everywhere I go, just in case I have the misfortune of a fire destroying everything I own. My lawyer thought it was a good ideal for insurance purposes." David smiled across with confidence. "As for my finances, I have papers with me concerning them also. I will go and get them from my room and return to resume the game."

Melody met him at the stairs, smiling with satisfying joy. "We've almost won, darling and we shall leave here happier and a whole lot wealthier!" she reached up and kissed him. "I will go to the bar and get us a bottle of champagne. We need to celebrate the beginning of our long friendship!"

Zachary watched his uncle make his way up the stairs and knew he would find him missing, so he started to leave his hiding space and race back to the room before his uncle got there, but something below drew his attention. He could see the pretty blonde pick up the champagne, then slip one of the bodyguards a note, who carried it over to the gambler. Zachary watched Mr. Tyndall read the message, then look up at the blonde, tilted his hat and gave her a wink, as she held up the bottle of champagne and blew him a kiss. There was no doubt in young Zachary's head, his uncle David had been set up, and to keep him from losing everything to these crooks, he had to stop him somehow!

Chapter 5

David Hastings walked confidently back to the gambler's table waving the legal document and took his seat. Unaware of the setup, David smiled over at Jax Tyndall. "Are you really for the third game Tyndall?"

Before the cheater could respond, Zachary walked up quickly and grabbed his uncle by the arm. "Excuse me Uncle David, but I need to talk to you! It's very important!"

"Zachary, what are you doing down here son. This is no place for a kid. Go on back up and I promise to be up soon" David started to pick up his cards the dealer gave him when the youth pushed them aside.

"It cannot wait Uncle David, please, you must give me a few minutes of your time before you start this card game!" The boy's eyes went up to the frowning gambler, then fell back on his uncle. "I promise it will be worth your time sir." Seeing concern on the young man's face, David thought it best to hear him out.

"Alright Zachary, if it's that important to you. I will give you five minutes. I mustn't keep the gentleman waiting." David slid his chair away from the table and two of Jax's beefy bodyguards gathered on either side of him, staring down mincingly. Unsure of their action, David looked down at the card shark and found him staring at his nephew, pure evil dripping from his gaze. "Look, Tyndall, this boy is my responsibility on this trip, so I will see that he gets to his room and be right back."

"See that you do, Mr. Hastings! I haven't got all evening! I came to play poker with a serious opponent, not some nanny!" Tyndall's eyebrow arched upward. "Take the spoiled brat upstairs, put him to bed then get back down here before I pack up my cards and take my leave!"

Being called a nanny in front of all the spectators, especially Melody, David grew upset with his nephew and pulled him over to a quiet place and grabbed hold of his shoulders. "Zac, this had better be important young man! I'm only minutes away from fixing that low-life cheat and get his precious railroad to boot!"

"You have been set up Uncle David! That low life cheat is about to take everything you own!" Zachary glanced over at the gambler, who was still observing him closely, then his attention went on the blonde who had set up his uncle and saw she too was watching him as well. David had not taken his attention off of his nephew as he asked

"Zachary, how do you know this? Did you see something or perhaps hear someone talking while I was getting my documents? When I found you gone, I assume you had gone to the outhouse, but that wasn't where you were, was it?"

"No sir, I did not go to the outhouse. I was hiding in the hallway upstairs between to giant plants! I could see and hear everything going on down in the bar room." Zachary knew he had his uncle's full attention. "I saw you make friends with that beautiful blonde lady, the same lady I saw pass a note to one of the guards who took it to that cheating gambler. After he read the note, he tilted his black hat at her and gave her a wink. In return, she blew him a kiss." The young man could read the sadness in his uncle's eyes and he knew he had grown attached to the traitor. "That blonde is working for Tyndall, Uncle David! She was just using you, setting you up so her lover could rob you of everything!" tears came to Zachary's eyes seeing his uncle's hurt. "Please Uncle David, you got to believe me!"

"I believe you Zachary. Thank you for warning me son. I don't know how easy this is to get out of, so listen to me, I want you to go back to our room and stay there." David hugged his nephew, who had been keeping one eye on the evil gambler and his thugs. "Zachary, there could be trouble and I promised your dear mother that you would be safe with me. Now, go up to the room and wait!"

"No way Uncle David! I am not going to leave you alone with those men! They're dangerous!" Zachary reached for his hand. "Maybe they will not try anything with a kid around, but if they start something, I will put up such a good fight it will draw everyone's attention and they might give up and leave to avoid the law."

"Sounds like a good plan son, but let me do the talking. I might convince them that you're not feeling well and I need to see to you." David gave him an assuring wink before they made their way back to the card table.

"Mr. Tyndall, I am terribly sorry, but it appears my nephew Zachary has taken ill and I must drop out of the game." David pulled out his two previous winnings and laid them down on the table, then gathered up the small stack of documents he had laid down before his nephew interrupted the game. "I gladly return my previous winning tonight, Mr. Tyndall, to show good faith for quitting before you had a chance to win. Being, the honest man I am, that seemed only fair." David looped his arm around the young man's shoulder. "So, if you will excuse us, I will take this sick boy upstairs."

"No sir, you may not be excuse!" Jax Tyndall gave a nod to the two bodyguards seating closer to Hastings and within seconds they had stopped uncle and nephew from stepping away. "We sealed the deal with a handshake and gentlemen of high standing, does not weasel out of that sir!"

"You said gentlemen of high standing?" Zachary did not like the arrogant man's behavior and he could no longer keep quiet. "I only see one gentleman of high standing sir and it would not be you! It is my uncle David, who has got more decency in his little finger than you have in your entire body!"

"Just what are you implying, you little game breaker?" the angry man's face turned to stone, hate dripping from his tongue. "Speak up boy!"

"I think you know what you are Mr. Tyndall without my spelling it out for you!" Zachary held his ground, unafraid of the big giants standing over him. He felt like David, facing the mighty Goliath, knowing God was with him just as he had been for the young shepherd, David.

"You talk big, boy and for a little worm who is about to get quashed!" the gambler sneered.

"If that is a threat sir, warning me about your two big goons here, then I can assure you Tyndall, fear is far from my thoughts and I am not worried one bit!" Zachary smiled up at the frowning men. "The big ones just fall the hardiest!"

"Big goon?" one of the rough men yanked Zachary off the floor and lifted him up to his starling face while Jax Tyndall pulled out a small pistol from his vest pocket. But, before he could use it, without warning, a tall black boot sat down on his hand causing the small gun to slide to the floor. Tyndall grunted in pain as he looked up angrily into the cold stare of a man dressed also in black.

"Who the hell are you?" Jax stormed out. "This is no concern of yours mister! Stay out of it!"

"But it does concern me Tyndall." The stranger's voice came smooth and calm as he swiftly kicked his free foot into the big man's side, causing him to drop the boy, then gave him a stronger kick into his fat gut, sending him across the room. Before the other standing guard could grab him, the man in black was waiting for him with his fist, which left him sprawled out on the hard floor.

The stranger's dark eyes stared into the gambler's as his foot mashed down a little harder. "Tyndall, if you do not call off your hounds, I will break ever bone in your cheating hand!" he smiled over a David, who was grinning from ear to ear as he watched his good friend in action. It had been one year since he had seen him, but he was still the same tough guy. "What's it going to be Tyndall? Are you going to call off your dogs or do we start hearing the lovely sound of breaking bones?"

"Alright, damn it! You are hurting my playing hand! I'll call my men off, just get your foot off my hand!" the gambler cried in pain, then ordered his men to take a seat. The stranger laughed and called for the sheriff to come inside the saloon, then reached down for the pistol and placed it inside his pocket. "The young boy might need this one day if he runs out of stones for his sling-shot!" dark eyes turned to Zachary and gave him a smile.

Zachary had watched in astonishment at this man's heroic actions and how he had taken down the two big guards after stopping Tyndall from firing his weapon, single handed. "Uncle David, who is that man?"

"That man, my young, brave nephew, is none other than Nathan Bedford Forrest!" David said proudly.

"The...man we are going to visit for one whole month?" Zachary's excited face melted into a big smile, knowing this visit wasn't going to be boring after all. Then he saw movement coming toward the gambler's table, recognizing one as the sheriff and the two behind him were his deputies.

"Here's your man Baker! Jax, fast hands, Tyndall, the big cheat himself, caught by this kid!" Nathan winked at Zachary. "I was waiting in the shadows over by the hooker's door, trying to catch Mr. Tyndall cheating when Mr. Hastings, my good friend, and his nephew walked my way and I overheard their conversation."

"You have got nothing on me, you spying scoundrel!" Jax Tyndall gathered his cards and put them inside his pouch. "Witnesses could attest to seeing our game of cards, played fairly, I guarantee! Why, Mr. Hastings happen to win both sets! Just ask him?" He casually stood up and put on his black sport coat. "Mere gossip between these two morons will not stand up in a court of law! I say, I should sue this town for trying to ruin my good name and reputation!"

"Trust me Mr. Tyndall, we know the law and as of yet no one has mention locking your sorry ass up. "the sheriff whispered for one of the deputies to get the girl. "Even though we have witnesses to the conversation as to what the boy saw and heard, it's not enough to prosecute you at this moment, but I do have the authority to make you and your friends here, get out of our town! You may retrieve your things from your rooms and my deputies will escort you out! I must advise you to never come back to Hernando or you will be arrested and locked behind bars! Do I make myself clear sir?"

"We shall go, the sooner the better. There is nothing for us in this no-account town anyway!" the angry man stepped in front of Zachary and placed a hand on his shoulder, then stared coldly into his blue eyes. "I will not be forgetting you boy!! You'll be very sorry you crossed my path!"

Nathan Forrest knocked the gambler's hand away and stepped up between the boy and the irate man

"If you know what's good for you Tyndall, you will forget you ever saw this boy. I would hate to have to waste good time tracking your ass down, but believe me, I would gladly if I ever hear you've been bothering my young friend here!"

A creepy smile fell on his lips as he sneered. "We shall see about that sir! It appears there is a rumor of a war between the North and the South, so I should think you will be busy protecting your own family." Jax Tyndall turned to stare a Zachary. "I shall be headed North, where the towns are more civilize. I believe you are from the north, boy. Near Boston, perhaps?" he smiled sarcastically left the barroom with his group, escorted by the sheriff and his men.

Nathan walked over and laid his big hand on Zachary's shoulder. "Don't you go fretting about that street scum, boy or worrying about a war breaking out against the North and the South. Rumors have been few and most by drunken hotheads." Zachary smiled up into his dark eyes and he knew right away there was something special about this lad. "My old friend David tells me you got your heart set on going to West Point to be a Calvary man. If you like, I could teach you a lot of self-defense in two months-time, Zac. What do you say?"

"Yes sir, if Uncle David can stay that long! I have been practicing my horse riding and sword skills…well sir, to be honest, it's kind of hard to fence with a stick sir." Zachary dropped his eyes, feeling embarrassed.

"Sticks are a good safe start for learning your moves Zac. It's nothing to be ashamed of kid and please, stop calling me sir, call me Bedford, that's what my close friends call me!" Nathan laughed softly. "Since you are going to be with my family down here in Mississippi, I am going to treat you like my boy, William. He'll like having another fellow around and sharing me will not bother him one bit. I dare say, Will may sit out some of our teaching sessions. As for horseback riding skills, I'm sure we can improve on them. I can show you some tricks no one else has ever tried because I made them up, and up until now Will has not wanted to learn them."

"I do sir! I want to be the best at everything and I'm a good learner, right Uncle David?" Zachary felt like he just won the biggest prize in his life meeting this exciting man with the dark eyes and strong muscles.

"A perfect student alright, straight A's in every subject." David ran his hand through the boy's thick black hair. "But, maybe that's because Zac has not noticed girls yet and can concentrate on his studies."

"He just hasn't met the right girl yet, David and someone as serious as Zachary has to find that someone as special as he is." Nathan smiled when the boy blushed and cleared his throat.

"A soldier does not have time for romance!" Zachary stood straight "I am ready to learn anything you teach me sir, I mean Bedford. Will you be teaching me how to sword fight?"

"We will start by throwing away that damn stick so you can learn the skill proper, with a real sword. A used one at the start, but you show me you are serious Zac, I will award you with your very own sword, engraved with your name, Zachary Dawson! How does that sound, buddy?"

"Golly gee! That's about the greatest thing that's ever happen to me Bedford!" Zachary smiled up at his uncle. "Please say we can stay two months, Uncle David. I'm sure mother won't mind if she knows I'm being taught military skills by Mr. Forrest!" The excited boy threw his arms around his Uncle's waist. "Thank you for bringing me with you to Mississippi! This is going to be the best summer ever!"

Chapter 6

Zachary got settled in at Nathan's big three-thousand-acre plantation. He had always thought the family farm back home in Massachusetts was large, but after seeing his hero's place, the old farm looked pretty pitiful to the young ten-year-old. The grand plantation house suited the Forrest family perfectly and Zachary really like Bedford's wife, who reminded him a great deal like his own loving mother. Her name, although commonly used, fit her pretty face. Mary Ann Montgomery had married Nathan Bedford Forrest on September 25th in 1845 and they soon had two children. One son, William, born 1846 and their daughter Frances was born the following year. Zachary was glad he did not have to share a room with three-year-old William, who Zac had assumed would be closer to his age from Bedford's speech about them learning together the skills of battle. Two-year-old Frances, nicknamed Fanny, was kept in her room by a personal black nanny and even though both children were very young, they were very well behaved.

Zachary sat down at the large old vanity to comb through his long black hair, as he thought about the many things he might be learning on his first full day with his hero and new friend, Bedford. A soft knock on his door, brought him out of his daydreaming and laying the comb down, the young man went over to see who wanted him so early in the morning. Opening the door, a thin black man around eighteen, stood smiling in the hallway. He tilted his head politely, and looking over the young man, noticed he was already dressed for the day.

"Good morning, Master Zachary! I be coming up here to helps you with your clothes, but I's can see you be already fitted up! How is it that you already gone and get yourself dress?"

"I always dress myself, sir. I've been taking care of myself since I was three." Zachary frowned when he noticed the big toothy grin on the young man's face. "Care to tell me what is so funny?"

"Well, Master Zachary, fer starters, you just went and called me sir. Now, there ain't nobody called me sir, afer!" he shook his head and gave a chuckle. "Dang if it didn't sound real pretty. Now, I suppose the mister is alright, but to be's on the safe side, jest call me

Theodore, causing that be my name."

"Where did you learn to speak English, Theodore? That is about the worse attempt to speak I have ever heard!" Zachary walked out pass the smiling servant and started down the hallway, the young black man trailing behind him. Zachary made a sudden stop causing Theodore to bump into him. "Why are you walking behind me? Get up here next to me so I can talk to you, Theodore."

The black servant looked around nervously to make sure no one was watching, then he slid up next to the young boy. "Master Zachary, I ain't had no lessons in the ways I talk. Why, according to most black folks, I speaks the English language better than most slaves. So, you be thinking I speaks it pretty fairly?"

"You speak terrible English, my friend, but you are in luck." Zachary gave him a reassuring smile as he patted his back. "I make straight A's in school and English is my favorite subject!"

"Is that so? Well now, I be dern!" the black servant stepped off the bottom step and looked around to find the big hall clear.

"For starters Theodore, you said: Well now, I be dern and the correct English is: Well I be."

"It does sound a mite better, Master Zachary." Theodore chuckled softly. "You is new down here in the South, aint you boy?" the black man led him down the hall to a bright room with a table adorned with matching china on a white tablecloth.

"The correct word is, aren't, not ain't and yes, I am new to these parts, Theodore." Zachary walked inside the airy room, where the aroma of fried bacon filled the air and looked around. "Where is everyone? Am I the only one up around here this morning, besides you, of course and ever who is making that fine smell?"

"Master Forrest had his breakfast an hour ago, young Zachary. Now the Mrs. will be a joining you right soon!" The servant walked over to the table and pulled a chair out for the young man. "Will this seat do for you, master Zachary?"

"Theodore, why on earth are you calling me and Mr. Forrest master? I can see why the twelve disciples called Jesus Lord and Master, but isn't that a name used for a king?" Zachary had never known a slave before, so this lifestyle was brand new to the boy and what he would learn would put his friendship with Bedford on shaky ground for a short while until he learned of other owners and the cruel way they treated their people in bondage.

"I's calls him my master, young Zachary, cause, that is what he is. He up and bought us so we's work for him "Theodore jumped when a stout black woman smacked him across the back of his head with her free hand, while her right hand balanced a tray filled with dishes of bacon, eggs, grits and gravy.

"Theo, you' foolish man, get yourself out of the way!" The cook spooned some eggs, grits and gravy in Zachary's plate before giving him as serious look. "Boy, why you go talking to slaves liken they be your best friend? Ain't no good come of it! The master and mistress won't hear of it, no sir! Now eat your breakfast, no need to wait for the lady of the house. She won'ts come down till the clock strikes nine!" She turned, and with slow, sliding steps started toward the kitchen, calling back. "Leave off talking to my Theo, mind what I say, young'un!"

Zachary watched her walk away before turning to see if Theodore was still in the room. He spotted him quietly wiping out one of the big open window seals. "Theodore, care to join me? I don't enjoy eating alone and my guess is that you are hungry, since I heard your stomach growl coming down the hallway." Zachary stared down at the pile of white, taking up a third of his big plate, that wore a big chunk of butter. "And tell me what this strange white stuff is in my plate?"

Cautiously the nervous man looked around to find the room empty, except the boy staring at his actions.

"The coast is clear, my friend, so get over here and tell me what this unusual stuff is that resembles a very sick oatmeal." Zachary watched him move slowly over, keeping one eye on the kitchen door, the other on the hall door. Reaching the table, the thin slave looked down and smiled.

"Oh, that be only grits, boy. They be real, good for you, made from crushed corn and mum, they makes a mouth water!" Theodore gave him his toothy grin and stiffed the air. "Smells good too!"

Zachary pushed his plate over in front of the black man and pulled the chair out beside him. as the slave stared down perplexed. "You like grits, so you eat them, my friend, plus everything on my plate, please, I insist. I'm really not hungry and this milk is all I need, with…" Zac reached over to pick out an apple from a tempting fruit bowl, then tossed it in the air. "this big apple!"

"I really shouldn't be eating yourn food. It could get me in a heap of trouble with the master, not to mention big mama, if'n she was to sees me." Theodore licked his lips just looking at the tempting plate of food."

"I insist!" Zachary patted the chair and waved the nervous young man to sit. "Theodore, if Bedford is your master and you work for him, as you claim, do you take orders from him?"

"Oh, yes sir, Master Zachary, I's always taking orders from Master Forrest or his Mrs." His fingers trembled when he touched the chair, staring down.

"Then since you are always calling me Master Zachary, I should have the same rights as they do." Zachary picked up his fork and held it up to him. "Would you not agree, Theo?"

"Well…" the black slave rolled his eyes toward the kitchen as sweat trickled down his face. "You is white, Master Zachary and you be guest in this house, so I suppose you might tell me what to do, if'n you a mind."

"Then, I order you to take this seat and eat with me, if you would oblige." Zachary waved the fork over the plate of food, "Please."

"I guess you did give me the order to join you." His eyes once again fell on the kitchen door, afraid his big mama would catch him sitting at his master's table, eating the food meant for the master's special guest.

"Stop worrying about that cook, Theodore. I will tell her I made you eat my food so it would not go to waste." Zachary grabbed his thin arm and pulled him down in the chair, handing him the fork. "Now, enjoy that good breakfast."

Theodore laughed softly as he gave the young man another toothy grin. "You beat all, you know that Master Zachary. Yes sir." He folded his hands together to pray as the ten-year-old listened. "Dear Jesus, thank you most kindly for this food and the kind heart of my generous friend here. May you sees to his blessings, filled with happiness always, Amen."

"Amen! Now, dig in while its hot and I will enjoy this great apple." Zachary smiled as he watched his new friend enjoy the best food he probably ever had. Suddenly the quiet meal was interrupted by a loud voice behind them.

"Theo, just what do you think you are doing?" The upset woman had peeked out to check on the young boy eating and saw her thin son devouring young Zachary's food. Slapping him on the side of his face, she grabbed his arm and yanked at him to get up. "Theo, takes your leave before Mrs. Mary comes down!"

"Leave him be, ma'am! I order Theo to eat that delicious meal for me because I was not hungry and I do not wish to waste food or eat alone." Zachary stood up and gently brushed her hand away, then checked the red mark on his friend's face where he had been struck. "Do you always strike your son on his head, ma'am? You might damage something inside his brain."

"What brain, young man? This boy is going to get the whip from Master Forrest for doing the wrong thing! Slaves are not allowed to sit or eat from this table, and my Theo knows better." Instead of showing anger as before, the cook looked around nervously. "We's not like you, boy. We's got to stay in our place and..." her eyes fell on her nervous boy. "take orders only from the master of this plantation, not some young fool that don'ts know anything about a slave's life!"

"Who are you calling a fool, Maude?" Mary Ann had walked in and overheard the conversation between young Zachary and her cook.

"I's apologize for my tongue, Mrs. Mary, but I's was upset with my Theo here!" the cook shook nervously, getting caught by the master's wife. "I's be sorry master Zachary. I's be the fool here, me and my boy."

"No ma'am, you are not a fool. You are just a mother worried about her boy getting into trouble and if he does, it would be my fought, not yours or your son's." Zachary walked over and took Maude's trembling hand. "I will explain everything to Mrs. Mary Ann and she won't judge you or your son when I tell her what happen and why Theo was sitting here eating my breakfast."

"You heard the boy, Maude. Now stop fretting about Theodore getting himself into trouble with my husband." The gentle woman smiled lovingly over at her house guest. "Take your leave and fix my usual breakfast and you may fix Zachary another plate, leaving off the grits this time." Mary Ann noticed the instant relief on the young man's face as he watched the cook and her son disappear into the kitchen.

"Please forgive my self-authority, Mary Ann, but I never thought for one second I could get Theo in trouble by offering my food." The lovely woman couldn't help but smiled at the sincerity in the young boy's face. "I merely felt he needed to eat far worse than I. He appears so frail and thin, the poor fellows stomach growled frequently as we made our way down the stairs and to this breakfast room." His eyes grew wide as he recalled what happened. "Theo did not want to sit down and eat that food, Ma'am, even though I could see his mouth watering, so, I simply ordered him to have a seat, eat my breakfast for me, and give me some company." Zachary lend forward, eyes pleading. "You see, it was all my ideal, Mary Ann and dear lady, you should have heard the grateful prayer he lifted up. I swear, it almost made tears come to my eyes. You got to believe me!"

"I do believe you, dear, sweet, boy." Mary Ann reached over and caressed his handsome young face. "You've got a generous heart Zachary and I can see you haven't been told about the slaves and their role on all the southern plantations."

"No ma'am, I guess Uncle David skipped that part." Zachary watched as Theodore came out carrying a tray with two plates of hot food, a fresh glass of milk for his friend and hot coffee for the lady of the house. "Thank you, Theo, I guess I finally got hungry."

"Yes sir, Master Zachary, you's got yourself a busy day ahead, what with Master Forrest teaching you all those new tricks!"

"Bedford can really cram a lot of teaching in a day's time, but you seem to be a lot more excited about learning than our young son, Will. I think the boy rather play with his wooden toys his father made him this past Christmas." Mary Ann noticed a question on the young black man's face. "Theodore, is there a problem?"

"Nothing that can't be cleared up, Mrs. Mary. I's just confused a mite. I's be thinking old Santa Clause went and made them wooded blocks and soldiers ups at the North Poll, then brung them to young Will, where he's and I's stuck excitedly down them steps in yonder, and gots down on our knees under that big cider tree covered with white candles, waiting to be lit on Christmas morning."

"Santa Clause? Do you believe in Santa Clause Theo?" the serious look on young Zachary's face never shown one hint of mockery, a sign of a true friend, Mary Ann thought as she smiled, knowing most ten-year-old would laugh at an eighteen-year-old still believing in Santa Clause.

"I sure do Master Zachary! Just watching young Will's excitement fills me with real Christmas spirit and I praises the Lord for giving little children sech joy on His birthday, every December 25th! Theo gave his new friend his big toothy grin.

"Well, that's just swell Theo, because Santa Clause can bring the magic of Christmas to anyone young at heart, just like you and me!" Zachary knew to take away the magic feeling from his friend would be cruel, when having just this little bit of belief could bring someone in bondage such love and joy. "And to clear up your question about Mary Ann saying Will's daddy making those wooden toys, she just meant, Santa brings them in pieces so the children's parents won't feel left out. They get up when they hear him leave and put them together!" Zac smiled when Theodore's eyes crinkled in a big smile.

"Zachary is right Theodore. Santa has so many children to make toys for, he needs all the help he can get!" Mary Ann winked at Zachary when the tall thin black man laughed out.

"Yes'um! I guess you's right about that. Mrs. Mary." Theodore sat the tray down and took a slight bow. "Enjoy them fettles! I's off to check on little Will and gets him ready fer his breakfast!" he almost danced out whistling.

"You know Mary Ann, even though Theo is a slave, he seems to be pretty darn happy." Zachary had noticed the servants stirring around, working and humming or simply talking and laughing with one another. "Everyone here seems very content, almost like they enjoy doing their jobs for you."

"That's because we treat them like family, Zachary." The pretty woman sipped on her coffee. "Many plantation owners are like us, never separating families."

"How do families get separated, Mary Ann?" Zachary could see the slaves living at Crooked Creek Plantation lived in their own small cabins and the overseer was a kindly old man who got respect from the slaves working under him. Maybe, he thought, he had not been there long enough to see one of the slaves punished. "Is being separated a form of punishment?"

"There are plantation owners who let their overseer have full control over the slaves they own. When one of the slaves get out of hand, do something they're not suppose, to do, like Theodore taking a seat at the master's table, much less eating the food meant for us, they are punished severely by the overseer. There are some really cruel men that whip their slaves badly, tie them down and burn them with a hot ember or coal." Mary Ann could tell the young boy was feeling anxiety over her hurtful words, but he needed to know slaves must stay in their place, regardless to how good or bad they are treated by their owners. "Zachary, it is the way of life down here. It is the only thing we have ever known, since our birth. The black souls were round up in Africa by their own people, for the love of money. Brought over on big slave ships, bought and paid for by the British, when they established the first colonies in America. Then, both the north and the south had slaves, but later the northern people didn't have need for slave labor, so they sold off their slaves to the plantation owners in the south. The number of plantations has grown considerably and so has the demand for labors, so, unfortunately the slave market is thriving."

"And how do families get separated?" Zachary re-ask the question, the need to know weighing on his young mind.

"Mind you, Bedford would never hear of separating a single-family member from one another. No matter how irate or mad he gets over a slave that gets out of control, he has a way of punishing him or her without raising a hand." Mary buttered her biscuit before spooning on some freshly made jam. "Young Zachary, you might find out for yourself just how my husband can speak to you, once irritated by some foolish thing you do, but he only does it to help you learn, much like he does for the slave he is taking to task. Now, some owners, unlike Bedford, have absolutely no attachment to their slaves, see then more like work animals instead of people, so pulling a son or a daughter out and selling them to another owner, even perhaps a mother or a father, a young husband or his wife, pregnant with their first child. Selling, buying and trading go on with no thought of the sorrow they are putting those dear people through." Zachary could read real hurt in her brown eyes, even before her tears began to build up and roll down her cheeks. "Yes, my young friend, it is a sad thing to witness and I just thank the good Lord that I have a husband whose as passionate and caring toward our black family as I am."

"Then bless you ma'am! Bless you both, but I pray, that someday God will pull his black children out of their captivity just like he did the Israelites when He brought them out of Egypt!" Zachary stood up, lifted her soft hand then kiss it. "You, madam, are a loving person and I do not wish you anything bad. I only pray that one day, all will be free in our great nation!" the young boy walked silently out the back door.

Chapter 7

It had been a busy two weeks for Zachary Dawson, but he was thrilled to have such a fine teacher as his friend, Nathan Bedford Forrest. Already his horse-riding skills had improved a hundred percent to the delight of Forrest. He had dreamed of such a student as young Zachary and secretly wished he had been his son, instead of his friend David's nephew. It did not matter that Zachary was a northerner. He had the heart of a southerner and the makings of a great Calvary man when he grew a little older. Nathan thought his young student could already do the stunts in the saddle as good as himself and his sword fighting was growing stronger with each passing day. Nathan had planned target shooting for the days practice and he could tell by his anxious face his young student was eager to get started.

"Now Zachary, I will teach you with a musket, since this is the weapon you will be using should you need to shoot instead of swing your sword." Nathan Bedford handed his student the long firearm and pick up his own. "I have set up several targets at different distances. Since this is your first day of practice I have them in plain sight but on the next lesson, each target will be hidden and you must walk around to find the enemy hiding. You will have one chance per target tomorrow, if you miss, we must assume you have gotten hit. Any questions before we began."

"I can see ten targets, some close and others further away. Do I move toward then today or shoot from here, Bedford?" Zachary hadn't dreamed the musket would be so heavy. It would take some getting used to.

"Today is target shooting, so you shoot from here. Your gun must be loaded before you can fire it, so watch me closely, then you try it." Nathan made fast work at loading the long musket, then waited for Zachary to try. "Take your time until you learn how boy, then it is important to remember, the faster you reload your weapon the quicker you can shoot, instead of being a fumbling idiot and become the perfect target yourself."

Zachary was a fast learner and had his musket loaded under a minute. "I'll get faster Bedford, as fast as you." There was a twinkle in his blue eyes. "Maybe, I will get faster than you!"

"I like your enthusiasm Zachary, but don't get to cocky or you will screw up." A rider coming toward them in a gallop, her long red hair blowing wildly behind her, had drawn their attention, and Zachary watched his big friend lay his musket aside and laugh out.

"Well now, I'll be damn! Look who's coming out to see us!" Nathan almost ran up to the white horse and caught the rider when she jumped off in his waiting arms. "Autumn Rose! What a wonderful surprise! We were expecting you tomorrow evening!" Nathan set down his niece and looked her over. "I swear girl, you have grown two more feet since you were last here."

"It's not good to swear, Uncle Bedford!" she reached up on her tiptoes and kissed his cheek. "My favorite uncle is as handsome as ever."

"And, my favorite niece is more beautiful with each passing year!" Nathan chuckled and lifted her up and swung her around, causing her to laugh. Zachary could not take his eyes off of the beautiful girl with the long red hair and the most incredible emerald green eyes he had ever seen. He was so caught up in her beauty, he had not heard his big friend speak to him.

"Zachary, can't you hear me boy?" Finely getting the young man's attention, Nathan waved him over.

"Get over here and meet my niece, my brother Frederick's only child."

"It really nice to meet you Zachary. Aunt Mary says you will be visiting them for two months, with your Uncle David." Autumn was glad her voice did not reflect how nervous she felt speaking to this handsome fellow with alluring blue eyes.

"Yes ma'am, although two of our weeks has swiftly past and I have so much more to learn from your uncle before I leave Mississippi." Zachary swallowed back his fear and continued. "Is your home in Mississippi too, Autumn?"

"We have a plantation in South Carolina called Laurel Grove." Autumn had never had so many butterflies fluttering around in her stomach before as she did that very day, looking into the young stranger's eyes. Autumn knew she had fallen in love at nine-years-old. "You are not from the south are you Zachary?"

"I am from Massachusetts, Autumn Rose, near the old town of Boston." Zachary couldn't understand why he was having such unusual feelings in his body. He had never been interested in girls before, at least, he thought, before Autumn Rose Forrest. "I am the only son of Jacob and Irene Dawson and we have a farm about twenty miles from town."

"Then I guess we have something in common Zachary. A farm is very similar to a plantation, isn't it?" Autumn could feel her uncle watching them and wondered why he remained so quiet when he usually dominated the conversations with the family.

"I suppose you might say they're somewhat alike, only our farm is very small compared to the plantation way of life." Zachary wondered how her family treated their slaves, but knew it would be unpolite to ask, so he simply stated "We have no need to own slaves with such a small place, but should we have needed the help of laborers, we would never put another human in bondage, instead, we would have saw fit to hire them!"

"This may surprise you Zachary, but I too am against slavery. It's wrong and immoral and one day those beautiful souls will be set free to live the American dream they deserve as children of God." Autumn had noticed the boy's serious anger turn to respect by her loving words. They both believed the same thing and this made Autumn feel happiness in her heart.

"Children, no one likes slavery, but it has been a way of life in America for so many years, I guess we've just grown to comfortable with it and try to make excuses." Nathan knew this was a touchy subject, especially for the youth, but when they grew older they could either except it like most southerners did, or do something about it, and change the old ways to a newer, better America.

"Uncle Bedford, why is so hard to simply hire workers to work in the fields, instead of make someone do it for free?" Autumn couldn't understand why things couldn't be worked out.

"I suppose one day we will have to make a change, grow fewer crops, have fewer workers and make ends meet, but until that day comes, I promise I will never treat my workers bad." Nathan draped an arm over each of their shoulders and gave a cheerful laugh. "But for now, we have to get back to target practice. Autumn, if you wish to stay around and watch, you may, or you can take off back to the house and we'll see you later."

"I think I will stay, if that is alright with you, Uncle Bedford. All there is to do at the house is sit around and watch mama and Aunt Mary work on their needle point and talk about the latest fashion, neither of which interest me." Autumn looked around and notice some bales of straw stake up, so she climbed up for a seat. "What type of gun will you be using, Uncle Bedford?"

"The kind Zachary will be using when he becomes a soldier in the Calvary, a musket." He winked at his niece when she made a face, then pulled off her riding scarf and climbed back down. "What are you going to do with the scarf girl?"

"I am going to help save Zachary's ears, that's what!" Autumn marched over and started to place the scarf over his black locks, when he grabbed her hands.

"Hey, what are you doing, Autumn? Boys don't wear girl's scarfs around their head!"

"They do if they wish to save their hearing! Have you ever heard a musket go off, Zachary Dawson?" Autumn narrowed her eyes at her uncle when he laughed. "I am serious here, Uncle Bedford. I've already had to repeat things back to you and daddy and it's all because of loud mucket fire!"

"Let the boy hear my musket fire before you tie him up like some sissy." He motioned her to stand back and noticed her hands moving swiftly over her ears and chuckling softly, turned to Zachary. "I will shoot the third target at my end. You line your man up by the sight at the end of your gun and that order from your officer will be aim, then fire, like so." Nathan aimed his musket and fired. Smoke rose from the loud gun as Zachary jumped back. "I will give you that jump boy, but build up your endurance if you wish to be a soldier."

"Yes sir. It just caught me by surprise, that's all. My daddy just had a regular shotgun, so I guess Autumn was right about the loud noise." Autumn walked over smiling at her uncle and tied the scarf over Zachary's head. "This will only be for training Autumn. I wouldn't be caught dead wearing a girl's scarf over my head around guys!"

"I never would expect you to Zachary, but there must be something we could put in your ears to muffle that loud old musket fire." Autumn bit her lip, trying not to laugh at the funny sight of such a handsome boy wearing her scarf, and hearing her uncle laughing softly, she slapped his arm playfully. "Behave Uncle Bedford, I just wish for Zachary to be able to hear me when we're old and grey, that's all."

"You are already planning that far ahead, little lady?" Nathan laughed as her face blushed, turned and climbed back on the straw and he heard her mumble, "Just practice."

Zachary, still blushing from Autumn's comment about them growing old together, was glad to finally shoot at the target. "Third target on my side." Aiming carefully, and preparing for the loud bang filled with thick smoke, Zachary fired the musket and hit his target. "Got it!" he called out excitedly, then started reloading his gun to Nathan's delight. "Now what teacher?"

"Enthusiasm, that's what I like to see in my students!" the tall strong man turned to wink at a smiling Autumn, then gave a whistle, a sign for the targets to start moving. "The targets are moving now more like a person would be doing when you are shooting at them. Aim high!"

"Is there some purpose for aiming high at those moving targets?" Zachary couldn't figure out what made the wooden faces start moving, as if by magic, then a young black boy stood up behind the target on the end. "Hey, where did you come from?"

"Been back here all the while, Master Zachary, jest waiting for the master to give that thar whistle." The black boy smiled nervously. "Me and the other nine boys, we's the dummy movers."

"So, aim high! Now I get it." Zachary smiled over at his big friend. "Shoot the dummies not the movers."

"You learn fast boy. Now, listen and learn." Nathan trained his musket on the moving target. "This time, take aim on your man and follow his movement with your gun, then shoot." The loud musket went off, hitting the wooden head. "Now, your turn."

Zachary aim the gun, and moved slowly with it, whispering, aim high, aim high." He shot at his man and after the smoke cleared, the target had been blown away" I got him!"

"Dang if you didn't kid!" Nathan slapped his back, a sign of approval from the touch guy. "Best shot of the day!"

After eating the late meal with all the family, Autumn took Zachary outside to sit on the swing and watch the stars come out.

"I never like to sit around hearing adult's talk after supper until bedtime. It's much nicer coming outside to hear the first whippoorwill sing or the cricket's chirp, do not you agree Zachary?"

"My cousin Reid and I used to camp out in the front yard, just to enjoy those very things, and more." Zachary gazed up at the rising moon, creeping slowly over the big trees that filled the big yard. "We would hear an owl call its mate and in the distance, he would answer her call. Bull frogs bellowing out from the old pond and the growing

41

darkness bringing out thousands of lighting bugs along with a million stars." Zachary looked down and saw her gazing up at him, her alluring green eyes reflecting the moon. "You were looking up at those same stars, weren't you, only I never dreamed I would meet such a beautiful fascinating girl the very next summer."

"Uncle Bedford has to leave tomorrow to go sell his early summer produce to neighboring towns and I was wondering if he asked you to go with him." Autumn crossed her fingers behind her, hoping the answer would be no, but afraid it was yes.

"He asked me to stay behind and keep you busy." Zachary swallowed "That is, if you want to spend some time with me while he's away."

"I'd love nothing more, Zachary. There are lots of things to do on the plantation. Ride horses, go for a swim in the big pond, or just fish, if you're into fishing." Autumn smiled down, blushing.

"Uncle David did have me pack something to swim in. Back home, Reid and I just jumped in our pond butt naked, but then, we were the only two boys around." Zachary noticed Autumn blushing. "Gosh Autumn, I never meant to embarrass you. I keep forgetting girls are more delicate than us fellows."

"That's alright Zachary, you did say you were never around many girls before." She smiled up shyly. "I suppose Adam and Eve must have swam around without bathing attire on before Eve ate that apple that changed everything for all God's children. I guess I will never know what it feels like to swim 'butt naked'!" she giggled.

"I just bet when you become a young woman and find the right beau to call your own, you may take that plunge just like Adam and Eve." Zachary's alluring blue eyes locked with hers and for a silent moment, they both were thinking the same thought. I already have found the right one. The moment was shattered when Katherine Forrest called for her daughter.

"Autumn Rose, say goodnight to your friend and come inside. It's growing late and you must prepare for bed."

"Alright mama, I'll be in shortly, after I tell Zachary goodnight." Autumn waved at her mother as she got out of the double swing, Zachary jumping up beside her. "I best be saying goodnight now."

"You sure have to turn in early. I'm too keyed up to go to sleep." He kicked at a stone. "I'll stay up with the men folk a spell, then go up and read."

"Read? That's real swell, Zachary, because I like nothing better than reading a good book!" Autumn heard the back door open and saw her mother look out. "I better go in. Will I see you for breakfast?"

"If you come down at seven, I'll see you. If not, I'll be waiting in my bathing suit on our swing at ten." Zachary did not think girls could get up and dressed as fast as boys, so he just assumed he would be eating breakfast alone again.

"Tell cook to make my eggs scrambled, bacon crisp, and lots of grits and biscuits!" she waved over her head. "See you at seven, sleepy head! Good night!"

"Sleepy head?" Zachary mumbled and called out. "Good night Autumn Rose!"

Chapter 8

Having a big breakfast together was a great start to a new day. Zachary was glad he did not have to eat alone and without all the drama of the first morning. They ate their meal with few words, knowing they were being watched by David and Bedford who had loaded up his wagons before eating. The kids sat quietly until both men said their farewells and walked out discussing the day's events.

"I'm glad Uncle David is traveling with Bedford. He has been spending far too much time alone or with Mary and the children." Zachary lend back so the black servant could collect his empty plate. "I guess I have taken up most of Bedford's time with all my practicing. He seems to enjoy teaching me what he knows."

"Uncle Bedford thrives on knowing everything there is to know about soldiering. He is great at everything and all self-taught." Autumn lend up on her elbows. "Why, I just bet Uncle Bedford could lead a Calvary as good as any West Point graduate!"

"I must agree with you there Autumn and I would be proud to serve under his leadership any day!" Zachary could not take his eyes off his pretty companion. "I feel lucky he took me under his wing. I'm going to be way ahead of all the other freshman when I enter West Point."

"I can tell Uncle Bedford likes you better than your cousin he tried to teach last summer." Autumn noticed Zachary sat up and stare down at her. "Didn't you know your Uncle David brought your cousin Bradley Hastings last summer?"

"Aunt Charlotte was still alive last summer, battling cancer. She was much too sick to travel." Zachary showed real concern, and Autumn wondered was it because David left his sick wife at home to visit his friend or was the reason Zachary had grown upset, because he knew his cousin Bradly had a reputation with girls. "I bet Bradley wasn't really interested in learning how to fight. He's not the soldier type! He will be working at his father's steel mill when he gets out of school in a couple of years."

"Bradley is five years older than you, because he would be fifteen this year. He kept bragging he was the oldest grandson of Henry Hastings and his little cousin Zachary just turned nine."

Autumn wanted to tell Zachary he had nothing to worry about as far as her feeling went, but that wouldn't be lady like.

"Cousin Bradley always like to brag about being five years older than me, but the truth was, he always acted five years younger! He was afraid of his shadow, wouldn't ride a horse because he got thrown off once, waves a gun away like he's afraid it might bite him, and all that happen when he was ten and I was five!" Zachary stood up and walked over to the window and looked out. "It was me that showed him the shadow was only a porch post, A gun is safe if you know how to use it and I showed him, and horses could be rode without fear once you learned how to handle them." He turned around laughing. "Would you believe the big baby cried on my shoulder?"

"I guess that why he didn't want to go horseback riding and ask if we could just go on a picnic "Autumn walked over to Zachary and laughed softly. "Poor Bradley, he tried so hard to impress me with his harmonica playing and fancy words."

"You were not impressed with the older cousin?"

"Let me just say, I much prefer the company of the younger cousin, anytime, any day!" Autumn smiled at Zachary's happy face. "I best get ready for our swim. See you at our swing."

"Autumn, before you go up, why did you call be sleepy head when I said I ate at seven? Most females prefer a later time." Zachary had been curious about her comment and assumed she was picking with him.

"If you promise you won't tell a living soul, I will tell you." She glanced around to make sure they were alone.

"I promise never to say a word to anyone. This sounds like a big dark secret." He moved in close. "Do tell me."

"Every morning I get up before dawn, sneak out of the house to my favorite secret place to watch the sunrise over Dixie! It's like a never-ending gift from heaven seeing the first rays of sunlight rising over the trees and the river, sparkling with brilliant red glows!" Autumn closed her eyes and she could see the sky filling with swirls of pink clouds as the filtering rays spread out and God Himself was shining down calling out softly, good morning Autumn Rose.

"Just how long have you been sneaking out in the dark, Autumn? Aren't you afraid?" Zachary suddenly felt the need to protect the girl he thought so much of.

"Not as long as Jack was with me." Autumn noticed Zachary

frowned at the sound of a boy's name, causing the beautiful redhead to laugh softly. "Jack is my collie I raised from a pup. He is very protective of me and would scare any intruder away just by growling." Seeing Zachary's smile and relaxed face, she waved and left to get ready for their swim.

"This is a beautiful pond." Zachary threw down the big blanket and looked around at the trees lining the far side of the huge pond, obviously spring fed by the fullness of the clear water. A small flock of geese flew down, honking their arrival, causing the young couple to laugh. "It's very peaceful down here and we seem to be the only two people around." Zachary set down a big basket he had waiting beside him at the swing. Autumn had assumed it was a picnic since he carried no fishing poles, therefore, needed no hooks or bait.

"Somedays it is lined up with servant men fishing, food for everyone's supper." Autumn had remembered to bring a couple of towels, knowing most boys did not think of such things, so she laid them next to the picnic basket. "I see you had a picnic made for us. That was most thoughtful Zachary."

"I was hoping we could spend the day out here together, if that is alright with you." Zachary pulled off the white shirt he wore, reviling his tan chest. Autumn recalled seeing only one other male chest in her life, and Zachary's won hands down over his older cousin, Bradley.

"Spending the day alone with you sounds wonderful! We've only got three more days before I must leave for home, so I want to know everything about you, at least what you might share with a new friend who is a girl."

"I hate the thought of your leaving Autumn. Things just won't be the same around here without you." Zachary could not draw his eyes away from the young girl. He suddenly wished they were older so he could kiss her and ask her to be his forever, but a ten-year-old boy could never confess his love to a nine-year-old girl.

Autumn pulled off her long wrap that covered her long-ruffled bathing suit with full length sleeves and a high laces collar. Zachary quickly turned his head to keep from laughing at her ridiculous outfit meant for swimming. Being the attentive girl that she was, Autumn could see the handsome boy was fighting laughter.

"Tell me Zachary, does my outfit amuse you?" the clever girl smiled down knowing by his blushing cheeks he had indeed thought she looked funny as he pretended to busy himself by removing his pants, revealing knee long shorts.

"It's just that I have never seen a bathing suit quite like yours before." He finally glanced up and seeing her smile, felt relieved. "It's hard to picture you swimming in such a wrapped-up garment, that's all. It looks...well...very unconvertable."

"It's even more unconvertable when I get into the water, but it's only proper for a lady to cover up herself until she is old enough to dress more mature." Autumn pulled a swimming bonnet from her small bag and placed it on her head, tucking her long pigtail inside. "Now I am ready to dive in."

"And you're sure the weight of that outfit won't pull you under?" Zachary teased as he limbered up his young muscular arms. "Then I would have to dive down to save you and give you mouth to mouth."

"Mouth to mouth?" Autumn's eyes twinkled with happiness. "That's almost like a...kiss. I think I should like that...from you, Zachary."

"A...are you ready to go swimming?" Zachary was stunned by her words, as if she could read his mind and knew just how bad he wanted to kiss her. He grabbed her hand and walked to the edge of the pond and studied the water below. "This spot looks perfect for diving in. The bottom is not visible so it should be deep enough."

"It alright here Zachary, but the best place is up there on that long straight tree limb that grows out over the middle." Autumn stood pointing to the massive tree that held the perfect diving off place. She watched her swimming partner closer, sizing him up and wondering if Zachary would take the safest way out like his cousin Bradley, or climb out on the high limb and jump. "What's it going to be Zachary? Here, on the bank or from the high tree limb?"

"What a neat place to make a dive! I say we make the climb up that big River Birch and jump off its long branch!" Zachary was glad the conversation was switched to diving, because no matter how much he would have loved to let the first girl he ever kissed be Autumn Rose Forrest, he knew he would never have the nerve to carry it through.

Running to the big birch, the two-young people climbed up unafraid and made perfect dives into the big pond and swam until they grew tired. Climbing out dripping wet, Autumn and Zachary could not contain their laughter as they remembered the family of mud turtles moving slowly past them and the funny frogs they saw sunning on flowering Lilly pads that floated gently on the service of the clear water. Their day past by quickly as they let their hair dry in the wind when they ate the picnic lunch the cook had prepared them that morning. They talked about school, their parents and home places. What they enjoyed doing on their spare time. Zachary found out that the beautiful green-eye redhead, love to write poems and short stories, draw landscapes, flowers, and people. Outdoors, Autumn was good at a lot of things. She was an expert horse rider, thanks to her Uncle Bedford. She had a green thumb for planting, whether helping the slaves plant their family garden or growing beautiful flowers around the big house and in the gardens behind the big mansion. Autumn learned how to throw horseshoes with Big Ben and some of his closer friends, Leroy, Sammie and Carmine. Young Zac admired Autumn's sweet sincere love for all their slaves and they all love that little girl the very same way. Autumn Rose was the one bright spot on Laurel Grove Plantation and now in Zachary Dawson's heart.

Autumn sat back, swatting the flies away as Zachary spoke about things he personally enjoyed, most of which were soldiering related. He told her how bored he had become working on the family farm and meeting her uncle was one of the greatest things that could have happened to him, besides of course, meeting Autumn herself. Nothing could top her. When he finished speaking, Autumn knew Zachary would not stop until he was the very best Calvary man in the entire army. All Autumn wanted was for Zachary to be safe with her, away from all the fighting, but in her heart, she knew this handsome boy she loved so much would never be happy without all his dream.

The days flew past and Autumn and her parents had packed their last bundles on the carriage. As the grown-ups were saying their goodbyes, Autumn was looking desperately round for Zachary and could see no sign of him. As tears formed in her big eyes, she never seen her uncle walk up behind her, placing a tender hand on her shoulder.

"You are looking for the boy, aren't you sweet girl?" Even at nine-years-old, Autumn was light as a feather for her big strong uncle to lift up in his arms and give her a hug. "Zachary ask me to tell you goodbye child. He just couldn't bear to see you drive away."

"Oh, Uncle Bedford, please, tell me where to find him!" Autumn could not control her tears as she buried her face in his big chest. "He might not wish to tell me goodbye personally, but I need to tell him

I will see him someday and this is not goodbye forever!" she looked into his serious eyes. "Please...please tell me where I can find my friend."

"Zachary is down by the pond Autumn." The usually tough guy had tears of his own as he added. "Leaving someone you've grown to love is never easy. Do not worry about your parents, I will take care of them for you, Autumn Rose." His big hand ran over her beautiful red hair. "You have grown up right before my eyes and even though the little girl is still here, I can see the change in you. I understand Autumn, I love Zachary too. Run along and make your farewells. Katherine and Frederick can wait." Autumn wrapped her arms around Nathan's waist and gave him a long hug and whispered.

"Thank you, Uncle Bedford. I shall miss you too!" Autumn turned and raced away as her parents started to call her back, but was stopped by the big man of Crooked Creek Plantation.

Chapter 9

Autumn reached the spot where they had had their picnic and she could see no sign of the boy she loved so deeply. Shading her eyes with her gloved hand, she scanned the big lake for Zachary, but with disappointment she lowered her hand and her tears floated down her cheeks.

"Zachary, where are you hiding?" Autumn choked out the words. "This plantation is too big for me to find you if you do not wish to be found! I came to tell you this is not goodbye! We shall be together again, one day, we must! I cannot live without you in my life, Zachary." Autumn sank down on the grass, shaking her head in defeat. "Zachary, how can I leave without seeing your face one more time, how can I leave without telling you, I love you."

"You love me, Autumn?" she twirled around and looked up into Zachary's tear-stain blue eyes. He got down on the grass next to her and gave her a hug as he finally got the words out he had been wanting to say before she had to leave. "Autumn Rose Forrest, I have loved you from the moment I saw you, but I couldn't bring myself to tell you because of your young age."

"Zachary, I'm but one-year younger than yourself and I too fell in love with you at first sight." Autumn could not contain her mixed emotions, to laugh and cry at the same time.

"Do you truly believe we will see each other again? Oh Autumn, that would make my going home in a few weeks a lot easier if we could believe this."

"I feel when God brings two people together in real love Zachary, He will see that we are indeed united when we grow into adults, which isn't all that long away, although it will seem like an eternity." Autumn took his tan hand. "I think if we are meant to be together, we will and that will be my greatest wish and prayer.:

"And mine, dear Autumn." He touched her face and looked into her green eyes. "Do you think your mother will permit you to write me?"

"Mother can be very strict when enforcing discipline and observing her rules and she may think writing a boy at this age is forbidden, but I shall do my best to persuade her what great friends we have become and we just wish to keep in touch." Autumn let Zachary help her up when she glanced up the hill toward the house.

"I know your parents must be wondering what is keeping you, so I guess you must leave soon." Once again Zachary's arms were around the girl he gave his heart to. "I shall miss you dreadfully! How can I get you my address?"

"See to it that you give it to Uncle Bedford. He is the only one that knows how we truly feel and he won't share that information with anyone else, not even Aunt Mary." Autumn looked deeply into Zachary's blue eyes. "Are you going to kiss me goodbye before walking me back up the hill where we will have to act like childhood friends?"

"I have been wanting to kiss you for a very long time, Autumn." His fingers trace her sweet lips. "I have never kissed a girl before, but I've watched grown-ups do it."

"I am sure when our lips meet Zachary, you won't need to remember what those other couples did, we will be showing our own new love through our first kiss." Autumn lifted her head and closed her eyes as Zachary finally found the courage to give his girl that first kiss.

"Hey boy, what's on that mind of yours?" George Custer's husky voice snapped Zachary from his beautiful thoughts, and he looked up from the bench where he had been waiting for the games to start. "Let me guess!" George smiled down, still sure of himself. "You were reconsidering challenging me and old Fitz over there, right boy?"

"The name is Zachary, I told you! I have no intention of quitting these games, George, so you and Fitz can cut out the cute remarks and get ready to lose!" Zachary walked over to his black stallion and slung himself up in the saddle and rode over to the starting point, George Custer close behind on his fine horse.

"Don't say I did not warn you bo…Zachary!" George tipped his hat and smiled over at the man in charge of the games, the superintendent of West Point, Robert E. Lee. The handsome man checked out the two rivals he had been observing carefully and stepped up on a platform to announce the next round of games.

"Gentlemen, there are two more games to be played before we find this year's best soldier. As in the previous games, I expect each man to use self-control at all times and show respect and dignity to your fellow opponent. If at any time I see you are playing unfairly or over-reaching the challenge before you, you will be immediately eliminated from these games." Lee looked at each man sternly as he added. "Are we clear cadets?"

Both soldiers respectfully saluted and said loudly, "Yes, sir!"

"Then I shall turn the games over to Mr. Hancock." Robert E. Lee stepped away and found his seat in the observation platform as Winfield Scott Hancock stepped up and raise his sword to begin the long hard game.

"Men, as before, you will start by showing us your riding skills, which includes jumping off your horse and remounting. How well you perform in the saddle and have complete control of both your horse and your moves. We will start with George Custer and you have ten minutes to perform." Hancock held up his sword. "At the drop of my sword, your time will begin!" As soon as the sword dropped, Custer was off his horse, then on in a flash to continue his exciting ten-minute routine while Zachary watched, not impressed. "Time!" the signal for stop. "Good work Custer. Now the judges will see what you got Dawson." Zachary rode out in front and gave his judges a salute just as Hancock dropped his sword. Doing a back flip off the horse and diving on from its backside, the young man caused the excited group to sat up as he continued doing fancy, yet very hard stunts until the last minute when he overwhelmed them even more by standing up in the stirrups as he pulled out his sword and swung it around, then quickly slid it back inside its sleeve before his horse gave them a gallant bow.

The spectators rose to their feet whistling and clapping loudly for the young freshman from Boston, when the judges held up a row of perfect 10's. Zachary was ahead but instead of rubbing it in to his boastful opponent he got of Midnight to shake his hand and offer a word of praise.

"Good riding George! I knew I had my work cut out after seeing your great performance."

"Zachary, that was the darn best riding I have ever witness!" George Custer patted his back. "You deserve those perfect 10's." he scratched his long blonde curls. "I cannot recollect anyone ever getting straight 10's for anything, except Robert E. Lee."

"Then, I consider myself in very good company." Zachary finally gave Custer a smile. "He is one of my two most admired men ever to carry a sword."

"Who is the other man that holds such a high place that he's equal to Robert E. Lee?" Custer knew their rest time was almost over but he needed to know who this special young cadet held so highly. "Some man here at West Point?"

"No sir, my teacher-trainer is a true southerner, from Mississippi. He is self-trained in all his skills and I dare say, one day everyone will know the name, Nathan Bedford Forrest." Zachary slipped on his white glove as he watched the judges sitting back down on the observation platform. "The judges look ready. Good luck George."

"You are the one that will need luck this round Zachary." George gave him a cocky smile. "I am the best in my class, four-years counting, at sword fighting and this southern farmer could not know much about sword fighting!"

"Live and learn, my friend." Zachary pulled his sword from its sleeve and gave an officer's bow. "Who do you think gave me my own engraved sword after I passed his strict lessons?"

"Forrest?" Custer asked softly, almost afraid to hear the answer.

"It will do you well to remember that name, my friend and pray if a war does break out between the states, my friend doesn't decide to take up arms." Zachary turned when he heard Hancock give the order to ride forward.

Getting on their horses, both cadets rode back to the starting place to wait for orders. "This next game is to display your skills at sword fighting. Each of you are in training to join the United States Calvary. To be good at horseback riding is a must and the officers here have already seen how Dawson can be a big help in our Calvary. After the enemy sees him doing back flips on and off the saddle, jumping on and off from side to side, as well as all the other fancy almost impossible tricks this one can perform, those soldiers will be so transfixed by all those skills they leave themselves open to attack by our waiting Calvary." Hancock winked at the young soldier as they listened once again to the roar of the men watching. "Gentlemen, I see each man have followed safety rules and placed guards at the end of your deadly weapons. This will give you full advantage to fight your opponent to win without hurting them, except maybe their pride should they be the one to receive the pretend final blow or get knocked off his mount in the battle." The young officer reached out to shake each man's hand. "Good luck to you both and may the best man win to play again tomorrow for the title: Best Soldier of the Year! Now, separate, Custer to the far left and Dawson to the far right, then wait for my pistol to fire before you advance to fight this battle."

Riding out to the long stretch of ground, Zachary thought once more of his friend Bedford telling him, "Never rush your opponent son. Travel toward him at a slow, deliberate gallop, looking into his eyes the entire time. This will rattle his nerves enough to make him less sure of his skills, then you hit and hit hard with everything you got. My boy, you will then find the victory is yours to get! Trust me, Zachary, trust me son."

"This day, I will put your training to the test, my good friend and have confidence I will have the victory!" Zachary rode up to the far end and turned his horse around, giving him a pat on his long smooth neck. "Midnight, the battles before were mere children games, but today, we must fight to win, so tomorrow, we can claim the title I've worked so hard to win." He perked his ears, waiting for the pistol to fire. "This win is for you, Bedford! Tomorrow's win will be for my girl, my Autumn Rose." Zachary shook the tears from his blue eyes, longing to see the nine-year-old girl that he had watched until she went from his sight, looking back and waving her sad farewell.

Chapter 10

The gun went off and Zachary watched George Custer take off at a fast speed toward him. With deliberate slowness, he began his gallop across the wide space, blue eyes clued on his 'enemy'. George had watched the younger cadet's slow approach and how his stare never swayed away from his own eyes. Sweat began to trickle down the senior's face as he grew closer to Zachary Dawson. Both swords went up, striking out heavy blows. Never taking his attention away from his attacker, Zachary willed his sword around as he impelled forward, thrusting his weapon closer to his victim's chest until at long last he struck him and George Custer felt himself falling, knowing he had loss to this kid.

The loud roar from the group of cadets watching grew deafening as Winfield Scott Hancock called out, "Game is over! Zachary Dawson has won the chance to play against Fitzhugh Lee tomorrow afternoon at 2:00 p.m. Congratulations Zachary!"

"Thank you, sir." Zachary smiled down at George Custer as he got off Midnight and held out his hand to assist him stand. "I had a great opponent and I am sure one day this man will be leading his own group of men."

"Why, thank you young Zachary. Perhaps you will be apart of my fine group." George shook the winner's hand, proving not to be a sore loser.

"Perhaps George, if I don't have my own Calvary army to lead." Zachary laughed along with Custer and both men turned to see who was shouting across the playing field.

"Lieutenant Hancock, sir, a message has just been delivered for Cadet Dawson, sir." He gave the lieutenant a salute, glanced at the young man that just won the next to the last game, then handed Hancock the telegram.

"Dawson, I believe this is for you. Son. It looks very urgent." Hancock waited for a somber Zachary to walked up slowly to retrieve his mail. "It looks important son. Maybe you best read it here."

Zachary slowly opened the telegram, feeling a since of dread. He read the words and swallowed, then re-read them. Only moments before Zachary was overflowing with happiness for winning against his strong opponent, and now, he had gotten bad news that would change his life forever. Zachary crumbled up the letter and tossed it down and not looking up ask permission to be dismissed.

Not wishing to pry, the lieutenant dismissed him and watched him lead the big black stallion away as George Custer picked up the discarded letter. A frown creased his forehead as he read the words and shaking his head, he looked around at the silent group.

"Damn! What kind of bad luck can one boy have!" George watched Reid Dawson rush off the stands and grab the letter to read. "I feel real, bad for your cousin Reid."

"Would someone tell us what the shit is going on?" Fitzhugh Lee walked up to the small group. "Maybe we could help if we knew what is wrong."

"Zachary's father has been killed in a duel over some card game. It appears he had bet the entire Dawson estate to this gambler and lost everything." George spoke up as Reid kept staring at the paper. Lee touched the young man's back as he read the letter over his shoulder.

"Reid, does your cousin have anything left?" Fitzhugh asked. "How can he pay for his West Point dues?"

"Zachary had everything tied up in the Dawson farm. What little money he had made working small jobs, he spent on farm supplies." Reid glanced up toward the barracks, wondering what Zachary was thinking, doing. "Don't get me wrong, the farm was doing good and the Dawson's had a sizeable bank account. That's how Zachary was able to enroll here at West Point." Sadness laced the cousin's eyes as he recalled the day Jacob Dawson changed. "Zachary was fifteen when his mother passed away, leaving Uncle Jacob depressed. He had assured his son that he would be fine when he went off to West Point. It had been two years since Aunt Irene died and his father seem to have gotten over his deep depression. He hired two extra men to help on the farm so Zac could achieve the career he always dreamed of." Reid placed the letter in his pocket and moved about nervously. "Now, my best friends dream is gone and all he has left is Midnight, the clothes he brought, and his prize possessions, the sword Bedford gave him and some girl's scarf he carries with him everywhere."

"Dawson, go to your friend. I am sure he needs you son." Hancock had been listening and the silent group watched the sad young man walked slowly away. Hancock looked over at George

Custer, whose attention was still on Zachary's cousin. "Custer, looks like you are still in the game. I am sure cadet Dawson is packing as we speak. Dues are set for the first of each month and that is tomorrow."

But sir, could not Zachary …" Hancock cut off the junior cadet

"Son, if we let every poor boy in for free, this place would be running over." Hancock looked up at the barracks sadly. "Zachary is a special young man and he would have made an outstanding officer, but rules are made for a purpose, and they cannot be broken. Not even for someone as talented as Zachary Dawson."

"Then sir, could we at least give him the one thing he has been working for all week?" George Custer stepped up. "I could never live with myself if I just stepped in where he would have been, sir. Zachary has earned a chance to be Soldier of the Year. Could we not at least give him that much." George glanced over at his classmate and smiled. "That is, give him a chance to beat Lee here, fair and square."

A roar went up in agreement from the surrounding cadets, all in favor of Custer's ideal. Hancock turned when he heard Robert E. Lee speaking.

"Hancock, I believe we can bend the rules this time, seeing as to how young Zachary has already proven his good soldering." The gallant man nodded to the smiling men around him. "The kid has earned a chance to win. At least we can give him that much."

"What are you going to do Zac? You have nothing to go back to! Some damn gambler has taken everything you own, except what you have with you." Reid had watched Zachary slowly packing his duffle bag, never saying a word. "Zac, say something? What about your Uncle David? Surely, he would take you in and help you. I would suggest moving in with us, but the house is already filled with my two sister's families, plus mother and father. That's one other reason I came here without you, I could not move around the house with bumping into a family member."

"I will be fine, Reid. I can get a job and find a little place to live until I find Jax Tyndall, the son of a bitch, and kill the murdering bastard!" Zachary walked over and looked out at the growing darkness. "He found his chance to get even by tricking my daddy with the same damn trick he used on Uncle David in the town of Hernando, Mississippi." Zachary turned to look at his cousin and best friend. "Jax swore he would get even with me for ruining his

57

crooked bet to get everything David had. I saw the woman who lured Uncle David into the fixed game, pretending to like him. David was a lonely widower and she took full advantage of his loneliness by befriending him, flirting with the pretense of caring for him. I am certain the same blonde whore used my father in the same way and in his drunken state, felt the need for a companion again after her superb acting!"

"Zac, you do not intend to go straight to the farm and confront this evil man!" Reid walked over to join him at the window and looked out, seeing most of the cadets had already left the playing field, that a short hour ago had everyone jeering for his cousin. "It is probably a part of his plan, to wait for you with a trap, then brag about getting the last laugh before shooting you."

"Then the lying devil would tell the sheriff I rode in causing trouble and demanding a duel and he had no other choice but to defend himself!" Zachary walked back to the bed and dropped down, only to stare up at the ceiling. "I shall wait until I have come up with a plan, and that will require money, lots of money to win back what he stole from me!"

"How do you plan to get a lot of money my friend. I know robbing a bank is against your morals and no bank will loan a man who has only a horse and saddle for collateral!" Reid could tell his brilliant friend was coming up with a strategy when he suddenly sat up and twirled around until his feet hit the floor.

"Tomorrow, I shall turn in my uniform and resign from West Point. There is not enough money left in the allowance daddy sent me to cover my dues." Zachary finally looked over at his worried cousin and best friend. "There's no need talking about this matter, Reid, I have got to quit and get a job."

"Maybe Uncle Jacob got your allowance mailed before this mad man tricked him and it will arrive in the morning mail." Zachary's cousin looked hopeful. "You know how slow the mail runs and the academy, is good to give us cadets a few extra days to pay the month's payment."

"Look Reid, even if the money arrives tomorrow, it would be foolish to waste it just to stay one more month. It won't make me a soldier and that money spent would be same as throwing it away when I can start saving it instead for my plan."

"Where will you go?" Reid looked down at his hands, sorrow spreading with the thought of losing his best friend and spending three more years at the academy without him by his side. "It won't be the same here without you Zac."

"You'll make new friends Reid. This place is crawling with great cadets, besides, you and I will always be friends, no matter where we are." Zachary got up to hug his favorite cousin. "If it makes you feel better, my plans are to pay Uncle Hastings a visit and ask for work. Surely there's something in that big steel mill I can do."

"Mill work is a far cry from being a soldier, my friend." Reid fought the tears forming in his brown eyes. "I only wish I had twice the allowance I usually get so both of us can train to be soldiers like we always dreamed."

"It looks like you will be carrying that dream for the two of us, Reid." Zachary forced out a smile. "Do not worry about me, my friend, I promise not to do anything stupid."

"What about the first place in the games you worked so hard at winning?" Reid and Zachary turned toward the knock on the door, then Zac got up to answer it. "God, I hope that's not more bad news! We never get visitors after barrack turn-in."

Zachary opened the door and was surprised to find Lieutenant Hancock and Robert E. Lee waiting on the other side. "Gentlemen, do come in, sirs."

"We are truly sorry for the loss of your father son. It is times like these your leaders feel your great pain and offer our condolences and offer our aid in making your departure from the point as painless as possible. "Lee's kind eyes and warm words made the heartbroken cadet feel cared for and Zachary nodded politely. "One day you will make a great soldier, Zachary, with or without military training. It is obvious you already know far more than most of the senior cadets and your courage of steel will help you rise in the ranks." Lee touched his arm as a loving father. "Believe me son, I know a good officer when I see him in action."

"Yes sir, thank you sir." Zachary could feel his emotions building, but he had trained himself not to show them, especially in front of his leaders.

"We know how hard you fought to win soldier of the year and your chances to fulfill that title was just in reach for you when the unthinkable happen." Hancock stood proudly beside the well-known superintendent as he thought, this news I soon will share with this poor lad might help make the hurt he feels, less painful. "Dawson, we have rules, as you well know, and one of the game rules state, to participate in Soldier of the year, you must attend West Point Academy and entries must be year-round students."

"Yes sir, I am aware of the rules and I know I must give up my place in the games." Zachary spoke politely, knowing his chances were gone forever. "Tell George, he has been blessed with a second chance to prove he is the better man." Zachary gave Lee a real smile. "But Custer has his work cut out for him battling Fitzhugh Lee."

"Son, Custer will not be playing that last game, he plainly refused and made the case that you should be the one playing against Lee!" Hancock laughed softly watching the handsome cadet's face light up. "I was just about to overrule his declaration, knowing I had sworn to uphold all the academy's rules when Superintendent Lee stepped in and made the decision to let you play tomorrow's games against Fitzhugh Lee."

"You want me to continue the games, sir?" this time Zachary could not control his tears, his heart bursting with the chance of walking away with the greatest title any Calvary cadet could ever dream of, West Point's Soldier of the year!

"What do you say Zachary? Can we count on you being there tomorrow?" Robert E. Lee hated to see this young man leave the academy and would have paid his way himself if he did not have to set an example for all the leaders working under him by following his own rules.

"It would be an honor to finish the games, sir! It shall make leaving a little better, knowing I have accomplished at least one of my goals, therefore making my trainer as a youth, proud of his student!"

"You would make any teacher proud, young man, and thank you for excepting the final game, I know all the cadets will be very happy you stayed to play." Lee smiled. "I too look forward to tomorrow's games."

Chapter 11

As before, Zachary was ahead of his competitor and by the end of the sword game, he had beat Fitzhugh Lee by making straight 10's again. The spectating cadets went wild in their applause from their mixed emotions. First, from a freshman cadet beating out the unbeaten two best seniors at West Point and the sad fact that Zachary had to leave the academe, even before his first year was up.

Standing proudly on the platform in front of all his classmates and the entire school staff, Zachary was awarded the prestigious metal for West Point's Soldier of the Year award by Robert E. Lee, their most respected leader.

"Zachary Dawson, it is with great honor I award this soldier of the year award to you and on behalf of the military instructors and staff, we have included a diploma for completing your first year at West Point." Lee smiled at his confused expression. "Together, we agreed that you have proved to know everything required of a freshman and it was only befitting to give you yours early. This way if you ever decide to return to the academe, you will automatically go up to sophomore class."

"Thank you, sir and all the academe instructors and staff for believing in my abilities. To get both the metal for soldier of the year and my freshman diploma means a lot to me. It is something I have been working toward all my life, to become a soldier in the Calvary." Zachary looked around at all the serious faces. "It would appear, my dream has been altered by some cruel fate, but this let down will never stop me from finding my dream again. My faith has taught me that I am never alone and I know the loving Lord I so lovingly serve, will lead my footsteps down the right path." His attention fell on his fellow cadets. "My brothers, my advice to you is, always listen to your military instructors and follow all their rules. To be good soldiers you must learn to take orders without question, defend America with a full heart and love your fellow man as you love yourself." Knowing he wouldn't see most of these men again, Zachary had sad feeling as he added. "Please stay safe on the battlefield and be sure your first duty is to the Almighty God. Farewell, my brothers." Without looking back, Zachary walked swiftly to his horse, took his duffle bag from his cousin Reid, who had already given him his tearstain goodbyes, then tied on his things, and rode away from the place he had dreamed of attending to become a soldier.

Zachary had finally reached his uncle's steel mill just outside of Boston and looked around at all the excited commotion. Climbing off his black stallion, he tied him carefully to a hitching post and stopped one of the town spectators who watched big strong men guide the steel across a heavy wagon.

"Is it always this much activity in the loading yard?" Zachary was amazed by the muscles bulging from the mill workers as they loaded the wagons with more steel sheets.

"Haven't you heard, boy? The mill got a big contract from Uncle Sam needing all the strong steel they could send their weapon's department." The older gentleman grew excited. "The war department has ordered all their steel to be sent to Harpers Ferry, the site of a U.S. Army armory, arsenal, and rifle works!" his weathered lips crewed excitedly on a stub of a cigar. "It's them rumors of war that's got everyone on edge."

"Perhaps our new candidate for president can calm everyone's anxiety and worked things out with the south." Zachary had heard the cadets talking about a possible war with the south over state's rights, and he, for one, had hope it was only nervous whispers of war. Zachary knew in his heart, he could never raise his sword against his friend Bedford Forrest, the man who had taught him how to fight and ride a horse better than anyone else, nor could he bring himself to hurt the one girl that lived in his heart and would not escape his mind, Autumn Rose. The old man broke into his thoughts by laughing.

"I'm not too sure Mr. Lincoln can stopped them hot heads in the south. They don't like a bunch of men sitting around in that unfinished chamber in Washington, telling them how to live their lives."

"I suppose most states feel they have the right to run their state in a lot of areas. No two are exactly alike, in size or industry." Zachary looked around for what looked like an office. "I do not wish to cut our conversation off, but could you point me in the direction of Mr. Hasting's office?"

"Are you looking for a job here, young man?" the old man sized him up. "You strike me more as a military man or rancher, perhaps."

"My uncle owns the mill and as a matter of fact, I did come in hopes of employment." Zachary did not wish to share any more personal information with the elderly gentleman. "So, if you could just tell me where I might find him, I would be grateful."

"Down yonder, on the end." He stuck a shaky finger down to a small brick building. "You will find Hastings in there, cause that's his fancy carriage out front." Zachary thought he caught a hint of sympathy when he added "Good luck son."

Zachary knocked gently on the oak door and waited until a thin man, around 5'6 wearing wire rim glasses opened the door. His nasal voice came out slow and dry.

"May I be of some help sir? We are quite busy here, so state your business and depart."

"Could you tell Mr. Hastings that Zachary Dawson would like a word with him?" he watched the man's eyebrow rise in distaste.

"It is quite impossible to disturb Mr. Hastings at this time. Perhaps you can make an appointment for, let's say, day after tomorrow?"

"I have just traveled many miles to come straight here to speak with my uncle, sir!" Zachary spoke up, in hopes his uncle was listening and come out. "I assure you I will not take too much of his valuable time."

"But sir..." before the little nervous man could finish his response, he heard his employers booming voice.

"Mr. Tittle, show my nephew in immediately and go back to your filing!"

"This way Mr. Dawson, I believe." He hurried over to the closed door and opened it, giving his boss a shaky smile. "Begging your pardon sir, I merely thought it was your orders not to be disturbed."

"Just go back to work and reframe from any dramatics before you give me a migraine." He watched him twitch and straighten the glasses on his nose. "And close the door so I can have some privacy with my nephew." Seeing the door close quietly, Horus Hastings waved toward the leather-bound chair in front of his large oak desk. "Zachary, it saddens my heart to learn about your father's demise. Poor boy, and to think his depression has left you penniless. I knew poor Jacob was devoted to my saintly sister, Irene, your dear, departed mother. Being an only child has left you an orphan and I can understand why you felt the need to come to me, what with brother David away traveling with his new wife, Margaret. We are the only family you have left."

"It was a tragic thing to learn of daddy's murder, Uncle Horus. I shall not stop until I find the man who tricked and killed him, stealing everything we owned, but I must wait until I have saved enough money to pay him back." Zachary felt uncomfortable speaking to this man, who always regarded him as a mere farmer's boy, while his son, Bradley was a steel mill owner's son.

"Zachary, don't be foolish son. You cannot expect to make enough money to buy back your family farm from an experience gambler." The robust man chuckled at the ideal. "Gamblers only know one way to deal, and that is through cards. They do not sell their assets, they just keep collecting them."

"Uncle Horus, I never intended to buy the land back, I plan to WIN it back, the same way he stole it." Zachary stood up and stared down at his mother's younger brother. "I did not expect you to take me into your home sir, I came to ask for a job, if not for me, then for the memory of your saintly sister, my dear mother, who always loved you."

"Sweet Irene, the angel in our family." Zachary saw real emotions from his uncle he rarely saw and watched him rise from his chair and walk over to a small family tin portrait, hanging on the wall. "She always had love in her pure heart for everyone and when she married your father, I think that was one of the happiest days of her short life." Horus Hastings walked over to the dark hair young man and looked up into his radiant blue eyes. "I can see your mother in you Zachary. Same beautiful black hair and eyes of an angel." His beefy hand touched Zachary's face as a tear drift down his cheek. "She once told me her happiest moment ever was the day you were born. What kind of man would I be if I did not honor her memory, by giving her son a job."

"Thank you, Uncle Horus. I promise to work hard in the mill, any job, any amount, of hours and days except the sabbath." Zachary put out his hand for a handshake and watched Hastings shaking his head.

"Not the mill son, it's no place for you." Horus Hastings looked up at a painting of one of his prize stallions and a broad smile covered his fat cheeks. "Of course, why did I not think of that before!"

"Think of what sir?" Zachary had watched him admiring the horse painting and knew it must have something to do with him. "You need me to care for your horses? A stable hand?"

"Not just a stable hand, Zachary. My head trainer just up and quit two weeks ago, family problems or something, and I had left hiring a replacement with Bradley. As of yesterday, he has had no success in getting a replacement." Hastings laughed out. "Its an omen from God! You need a job and we need someone who knows horses and can train them. With you as my man, I should win all the blue ribbons at the state fair and horse shows!"

"I can start right away Uncle Horus, if Bradley hasn't already hired someone else for the job." Zachary felt relieved to have a job he knew and loved instead of starting out in something new and obviously strenuous "I am well suited for this job since it's what I have done for most of my life."

"I say, you get the job and if my son has hired someone else, we shall find that person another position." Draping his arm around his nephew's shoulder, the mill owner walked him to the door. "I'll have my driver escort you to the stables and show you your rooms, then come to the big house at seven for dinner with the family. Dear Geraldine has been asking about your welfare, now she can see for herself. Bradley will be happy to see you and know he can stop looking for a horse trainer." He opened the door and waved to his groom, waiting by the fancy carriage. "Do not be surprise if your cousin asked you to accompany him to Natchez, Mississippi, to attend some party he's been ask to attend."

"I'm really not good at parties, Uncle Horus, perhaps Bradley will ask one of his many friends." Zachary had no desire to go sit around some fancy rich mansion and watch other couples dance and make small talk. It made him uncomfortable. "I'm sure he'd rather not be stuck with me as his partner."

"It would appear the dear boy can't find any of his friends available and he is beside himself with worry over the situation. He really wants to attend and should he ask you Zachary, I would personally find it a good sign that you wish to make your employer happy he hired you." The groom had been listening and felt the tension between the young man and his boss, so he thought best to intervene

"Would you like me to escort the young man to the estate sir?"

"Yes Stewart, show my nephew where the trainer's rooms are located and introduce him to the stable boys." Horus patted Zachary on the back. "Go bring your mare around and follow my groom. We shall see you at seven." He turned and disappeared back in the brick building.

65

Joan Byrd

"I have my horse tied up over there Mr. Stewart if you wish to go ahead. I'll catch up." Zachary walked away, shaking his head. "That uncle of mine, thinking all this poor boy has is an old mare. I'm surprise he didn't say mule!" Untying the stallion, the young man swung up into the saddle and galloped off to catch the fancy carriage.

Chapter 12

"Autumn Rose! Now where is that girl? How long does it take to fetch a book to Miss Hilda Mae?" Nellie shaded her eyes from the evening sun and looked down at the slave's quarters. "There is no sign of that girl and knowing her mama soon will be home looking for her! Why, she cannot stay out of trouble, always wondering down to the stables to shower all those men folk with her funny tales, and they lap it up like starved pups!" Hearing her friend's bright laughter, Nellie lifted her skirt tail and ran toward the sound, finding the beautiful redhead patting big Ben on his broad back.

"I finally beat you at horseshoes and there you boasted I could never beat a man at the game!" Hearing his booming laugh as he shook his head in surprise, Nellie could not help but to cheer her best friend on.

"Lordy me, Big Ben, you none went and let this little biddy girl beat you at horseshoe and you the champion of Laurel Grove!" Nellie grabbed Autumn's hand and held it tight. "We best leave you so you can practice. This girl's mama will be home any old time now and she will be looking for her wondering daughter!"

"Is it that late already? It seems like that carriage just left for Mrs. Patterson's alteration shop. I just knew that beautiful white dress trimmed in yellow silk Mama purchased in Charleston, would be a perfect fit this time." Autumn made her way up the wide steps to the big front porch, surrounded by massive round pillars.

"It's that tiny waist you have Autumn. Why, them cousins of yours would kill for such tiny waist like you have, yes ma'am!" Nellie giggled, remembering how Christina and Polly Anne's personal maids had to place their knees in the girls back to tie their corsets tight enough for a tiny waist. "Why, them girls faces went red, trying to breathe while you looked just as relaxed as if you be in your nightgown, ready for bed!"

"I guess I'm just lucky to have a tiny waist, despite mama's constant worrying about me eating hot biscuits, loaded with butter and preserves." Autumn stopped and turned toward the kitchen, to Nellie's dismay. "I just remembered, I promised your mama I would show her a new recipe I made up after watching Uncle Bedford mixing up molasses with sugar."

"Molasses…and sugar? Now, why on earth would Mr. Forrest want to go and ruin perfectly good sugar with more sweet molasses?" Nellie made a face before adding. "It sounds real horrible. I think I will pass on your cooking, Autumn."

"And miss out on cake squares, loaded with raisins, pecans, soaked in rum and topped with my creamy new topping, made with the molasses sugar, butter and rum, for flavoring." Autumn smiled when Nellie licked her lips and followed close behind in a daze. Grabbing a bowl off the shelf, Autumn instructed Cora and Nora what to do. As they stirred up the flour milk and eggs, the happy redhead mixed the sugar with the right amount of molasses, keeping it dry. She threw a hunk of butter in a saucepan and hung it over the fire. After measuring the right amount of sugar mixture, brown sugar, as she added it to the melted butter and stirred slowly, a she enjoyed the aroma of the cake baking. With the cake pulled out of the oven, Nora set it on the window seal to cool while Autumn added the rum and one vanilla bean, stirring it in. Knowing her creamy new topping might grow hard quickly, she had the cake brought over then poured the smooth thick topping over the raisin-pecan-rum cake and watched it magically set up as her audience watched with hungry smiles.

"Mumm, Miss Autumn, what you be naming this delightful cake of yours?" Nora scraped off the crumbs in her plate and licked the sweet spoon. "I do declare, that is the best cake I have ever had the privilege to eat."

Autumn had insisted that the kitchen staff be the first to sample her new recipe and give their true opinions, she promised not to get her feelings hurt if they choose not to approve of it. After watching all the satisfying faces enjoying the rich dessert, Autumn felt relieved.

"To be honest, I haven't thought up a name yet and the only name near and dear to my heart just doesn't sound like a cake, Zachary Dawson."

"Is that boy still running through that mind of yours, Miss Autumn?" Cora licked the sweet caramel off her lips. "I thought your mama done went and ran his memory clear out of that pretty head of yours."

"When you are in love with someone Cora, they will live in your heart forever." Autumn stood up and looked out of the big kitchen window. Even though most plantations had their kitchens separate from the main house, Laurel Grove did not. Adding the big kitchen to the far end of the south side had been approved by the builder after the owner ask for double brick walls to separate it in case of fire. Mr. Forrest had insisted that a doublewide back door be added for easy escape, not wanting any soul to parish in some horrible fire. "My mother might have forbidden me to write him letters when I was nine, but she had no right to stop me when I reached fourteen by forcing Willy Henry to hand them over to her after he promised to mail them for me, along with the other house mail. The only reason I held my tongue was merely out of respect for her being the woman who gave me life."

"You don't go blaming Willy Henry for not carrying out your request to mail those precious love letters, do you, Autumn Rose?" Nora felt bad for the love stroke girl.

"Dear Nora, Willy Henry was just obeying the mistress of the house, knowing mother far outweighed the child." Autumn, despite argument from Cora, started gathering the dirty plates and carried them to the big wash sink as she continued to talk, drowning out the servant's request for her to sit down and let them do the work. "Mother might have had her way concerning all my letters, but she cannot stop fate. If the Lord wants Zachary to have a life together with me, then my beautiful dream will come true."

"That's it! Autumn Rose I have got the perfect name for your very special cake!" Nellie jumped up and raced over to her friend's side. "Autumn's Dream Cream Cake!"

"Dream Cream Cake! That is perfect Nellie, and Nora..." Autumn pumped water over the plates to the kitchen staff's dismay, as they kept glancing over their shoulder for Katherine Forrest. "serve a big piece to my parents this evening at supper but let them think you made it, then I can see if they really like it instead of pretending. If daddy knew I made it, he would go on and on about how delicious it was even if he hated it. Daddy is always showering me with praise to build up my confidence where mama on the other hand, tries to keep a tight rein on her only daughter. If she had her way, I would end up an old maid."

Erline, Mrs. Forrest lady's maid, had stepped inside the kitchen un-observed, on an errand to find Miss Autumn for Lady Katherine when she stopped to listen to the young woman speaking. Everyone in the kitchen jumped when the maid cleared her throat loudly to get their attention.

"Good Lord Erline, you 'bout gave me an attack of the heart, sneaking up on us like that." Nora let out a breath of relief, glad it was not Mrs. Forrest. "Is there some purpose you are invading my kitchen? More hot water perhaps, to wash the dust off, Mrs. Forrest's shoes."

"The fine lady of the house does not require water at this time, Cora." Erline proudly lifted her head, feeling a higher rank, being the lady of the house's personal maid. "Madam Forrest has asked me to find her daughter and bring her to the master bedchamber without delay."

"The dress?" Autumn reached for a towel to dry her wet hands, then passed it to Cora's oldest girl and went over to place a heavy bowl over the remainder of the yummy cake. "Tell Mother I shall be right up as soon as I've finish down here."

"Begging your pardon, Miss Autumn, but you mother told me, no…ordered me to make sure I brought you right up." Walking to the door, she pushed it open and stood waiting. "Come along now and let these women do their own jobs."

Autumn noticed their worried expressions at the maid's statement. Would she tell Autumn's mother her daughter was down in the kitchen doing the servants work for them while they ate cake and watched her? Autumn walked by them slowly and turn to whisper.

"Stop worrying! I'll have a word with Erline on the way up. I am sure we will see eye to eye once she hears what I have to say." Autumn gave the relieved faces a wink and followed the obnoxious woman down the hall to the stairs. Before Autumn could speak to the brazen maid, Erline stopped and stared down into Autumn's emerald green eyes.

"You are very mistaken about your mother's good intentions for you, young lady! It is not a companion she desires in her old age by making you an old maid as you proclaimed to the kitchen help. She is looking for the proper mate for you, Autumn Rose, three of which will be present at your coming out party in Natchez."

"Thank you for the warning, although I am sure you never meant to give me a heads-up on possible suitors showing their advances toward me because mother had led them to believe they might be the 'lucky one for her daughter'!"

"You'll say naught to your mother about our conversation, missy!" the maid's eyebrow flew up. "I have plenty of sour news of my own about how the kitchen servants sat around eating cake and watched you taking care of them when it was their responsibility to care for you!"

"If you must know, Miss Erline, I ask them to try my new recipe and let me know if it passed their professional test! They are the cooks and bakers around here, and very good at what they do! On my own, I took care of the dishes and I do not need you or anyone else to tell me I cannot do things for 'my friends'!" Autumn's hands went to her hips. "One word about what took place in that kitchen to my mother and I will fill her in on a certain personal maid who made flirty advances to my father when she thought no one was watching!"

"Who would spread such lies about me? That person should be horse-whipped and ran from this house and given a manual job in the fields!" Erline's face grew red with anger as her fingers bit into Autumn's arms. "Tell me girl! Who is the liar? Nellie?"

"No, it was not my dear friend, Erline! I saw you with my own eyes and how father pushed you away, when you wouldn't relent to his warning to stop and go to your room!" Now it was Autumn staring in the maid's nervous dark brown eyes. "What's it to be Erline? Do we keep what we have seen to ourselves or shall we tell my mother everything?"

"Very well, Autumn Rose, we must not worry your mother over these things." The chamber maid took the young woman by the hand and pulled her up the stairs to the master bedchamber and knocked lightly on the solid oak door. "Madam Katherine, I have your daughter with me, as you wished."

"Thank you Erline. Please have her come in and fetch Nellie to help you with the new dress." Katherine motioned her daughter over while her personal maid went back out, closing the door. "The seamstress has done a wonderful job with your dress, darling. It's even more beautiful than it was before." Standing, Autumn's mother lifted the large lid off the box and pulled out the exquisite ball gown, fit for a princess and laid it on the bed. "I think it is the loveliest gown you have had so far. I know you shall be the prettiest young debutant at the coming out ball!"

"I'm not so sure your nieces, Christina and Polly Anne will agree, nor your beloved sister, Isabelle." Autumn would never admit to her natural beauty, even though she admired her reflection in the mirror when she dressed in such a fancy gown as the beauty lying before her on her mother's bed. "I do agree mother, that it is the prettiest gown I've ever had, but then you are the perfect shopper and that is why I leave buying such things to you."

"We shall get some ideal what it will look like when Erline returns with Nellie. She could not have been far away from where Erline found you, my dear." Katherine let her hand run down the full skirt. "Surely Nellie is not outside in the rose garden."

"Not even close mother. Nellie was down in the kitchen helping her mother clean up my mess!" Autumn laughed when her mother looked over surprised. "I was going to let it be a surprise for you and daddy at supper, but since you were wondering about my friend's disappearance from my side, I might as well tell you."

"What sort of mess did you make in Nora's kitchen that it would require so much help to clean it up, Autumn Rose?"

"The mess wasn't so great that Nellie's help was really needed, but your personal maid insisted I come with her to see you, so, here I am." Autumn lifted up the ball gown and held it at a safe distance from her soiled dress. "I made up a cake recipe after watching Uncle Bedford making that strange sugar mixture and Cora and Nora helped me put it to the test. It was judged by the kitchen staff and Nellie gave it the perfect name!"

"You let the kitchen servants eat a piece of your cake?" Katherine narrowed her eyes. "Why on earth would you go against tradition and permit our help to sit down to something you made?"

"Mother, would you have preferred to be the one to test my cake first?" Autumn smiled at her mother's sour face. "Just as I thought. I needed to know if the recipe would be a success or a failure."

"And, did it pass the expert baker's test?" Katherine gave her a weak smile.

"I can proudly say Autumn's Dream Cream Cake was a 100% approved by the entire kitchen staff!" Autumn beamed proudly "It will be served tonight for dessert, for your and daddy's approval, but please, Mama, don't tell daddy I made it. I want it to be a secret surprise for him."

"I can see what you are referring to darling. If Frederick knew his little girl came up with this recipe, he would swear it was the very best cake in the entire world, even if it tasted like Big Ben's horseshoes." Katherine joined her daughter in laughter as a soft knock fell on the door.

The maids where there and everyone agreed, Autumn Rose would be the queen of the coming out ball and the Dream Cream

Cake got a perfect score from both of Autumn's parents.

In one short week, The Forrest family, along with the women's personal maids and Frederick's personal groom, would be on their way to Chatham Hall, in Natchez, Mississippi. The coming out ball was two weeks away and everyone was growing excited, except Autumn Rose. Autumn had convinced her father to go with them to give her support.

Chapter 13

"Cousin, is that what you plan to wear at the ball?" Bradley Hastings made a distasteful face after asking Zachary to show him what he planned to wear. "I cannot possibly let you wear that worn out old suit to this exquisite party. The place will be draped with beautiful young ladies, all available and ripe for the taking."

"Like it or not, Bradley, it is the only suit I own, so if you prefer, find yourself a better dresser." Zachary casually put away his suit.

"You are aware of my dilemma, Zachary! There is no one else I can ask and I simply cannot go by myself!" Zachary's rich cousin paced the floor in the stable room. "What I prefer is for you to get something more appropriate to wear and I have the solution "He looked around at Zachary's poor surroundings and brushed off a worn sofa, then sat down. "It is obvious you cannot afford to buy a new suit, unless you, sale your horse. It's the only thing you have that is worth enough to buy the perfect suit."

"Bradley, I will say this one time, I will never sell Midnight, not now, not ever!" Zachary's eyes shot fire at his insensitive Cousin. "He is the only thing I have left and if you have a problem with that, then run tell your father! But I warn you, if you want me to go with you to this stupid ball, you can just come up with another solution!"

"Very well, cousin. I shall send you my own personal tailor and he will sew you up the perfect suit for a fine northern gentleman, such as we are." He held up his hand. "And before you ask about the cost, consider it a gift from me to you, for going with me. The only thing I require from you Zachary, is to at least pretend to be having a good time. Be sociable and ask the ladies for a dance occasionally." He gave a sarcastic laugh. "You need not worry about any of the ladies falling for you when they have me in their presence. I suppose they all will be after me and choosing the right girl might prove impossible."

"Why is that, Bradley? Do you consider yourself too good for a southern belle or won't any woman match your perfect self-image?" Zachary was growing tired of his cousin's constant bragging on himself.

"I deserve the very best, Cousin Zachary unlike men like you.

You are satisfied with the first girl who gives you any attention." He mocked.

"How can you claim to know what I care about, Bradley? It's obvious all you care about is your own interest. I know what I want in a woman and when I see her, I will claim her for my own!" Zachary could vision Autumn Rose's beautiful face as she declared her love to him and he to her. She is the true love of his heart and he knew one day they would cross paths again and rekindle the flame that burned inside them when they were younger.

"Perhaps she will be at the coming out party, this perfect woman you are looking for." Bradley laughed. "Good luck prying her eyes away from me, cousin. My good friend in Natchez who sent me the invitation, has told me the beautiful southern bells are all pure and sweet and he had his eye on one particular redhead with emerald green eyes." Bradley turned to see what made Zachary gasped. "See there, the mansion will be filled with beauties such as this." Bradley gazed into space as recalled seeing some girl with that very description. "I once traveled with Uncle David on this super boring trip to some plantation in Mississippi. It was named after some sort of branch or river."

"It was the name of a creek Bradley, the Crooked Creek Plantation." Zachary remembered everything about his long visit to Mississippi, and it was anything but boring.

"Oh yes, that's right, I remember now. Uncle David took you the following year because I just did not want to go back to that old would be soldier's house!" Bradley gave a sarcastic laugh. "The man was a real smart ass, thinking I cared to learn how to ride a stupid horse or fool around with weapons. It was pretty pitiful that all I had to occupy my time was playing babysitter to this little kid with red pigtails and green eyes. I think her name had something to do with the seasons. Summer? No…"

"Her name is Autumn and I'm pretty sure she didn't need you to be her babysitter." Zachary stared at his cousin, dismissing any chance that Bradley had intentions to go after his girl who had told Zachary she did not like his older cousin.

"I'm sure you might think that, since you and her were about the same age." Bradley looked thoughtful for a moment, trying to add up the years. "I cannot remember how old she was then. I wonder, how old would she be now?"

"Autumn Rose would be sixteen this year, but the chances of her being there might be slim, since she lives in South Carolina." Zachary sat down and picked up his leather strap and starting buffing up the bridles on the floor. His mind was on the girl he loved and, in his heart, Zachary secretly hoped the girl with the red hair and emerald green eyes was his Autumn Rose.

"Shit kid, you remember a lot about that old plantation visit." Bradley laughed out. "Did that old tough guy try to show you how to shoot his guns?" he continued laughing as Zachary slammed down the bridle he had finished and picked up the next one on the pile. Bradley stared over at him and stood up. "What's with you cousin? Don't tell me you liked that old man!"

"Nathan Bedford Forrest is a far better man than you are cousin and one of the best friends I have ever had!" Zachary looked up at his obnoxious cousin. "Bedford taught me how to be the best Calvary man in West Point! I have the proof right here, on my chest! The West Point medal for soldier of the year! Bradley, you can talk all you like about me, but cousin, I never want to hear you say anything wrong against my friend Bedford again!"

"Hey, calm down little cousin, I was just fooling around with you." The 5ft 11" Bradley gave his 6ft 3" cousin a cocky grin. "Just keep buffing up those bridles until my man comes down to measure you up." He started for the door and turned to add. "Remember, you eat with the stable hands from now on. They fix enough grub for you too. Enjoy!" he laughed mockingly and walked out as Zachary threw the bridle up against the door.

"I would prefer their company over yours, Cousin Bradley, any day!"

"I see you fellows have everything packed on your horses." Horus Hastings admired the big black stallion belonging to his nephew. "That's one fine horse, Zachary. If you ever need to sale him, let me know. I could breed an animal like that and get paid plenty."

"My horse will never go up for sale, Uncle Horus. He and I belong together." Zachary swung up into the saddle with ease. "If I feel the need for extra money, perhaps I could breed Midnight myself." he glanced at his cousin making a feeble attempt to climb on his gentle mare. Trying hard not to laugh, Zachary climbed back down to offer him help. He cupped his hands together to form a lift and told Bradley to place his left foot inside. "Now, reach up and grab the saddle horn and I will give you a boost up in the saddle.

Bradley stared down at Zachary's hands for a moment, his face red with embarrassment until he heard his father tell him to do it. So, without hesitation, the cocky young man followed Zachary's orders and rose up swiftly to the waiting saddle and grabbed on.

"I cannot believe I agreed with you to go all the way to Natchez, Mississippi on horseback!" Bradley stared nervously down at the ground and suddenly felt dizzy. "I'm not sure this is the way I wish to travel, father. Couldn't we take one of the smaller carriages and tie these horses on the back, in case we need them."

"Would you feel safer son?" Horus gave Zachary a doubtful look. "Zachary, I know you tried to help Bradley learn to ride all week and I really appreciate all your effort, but that childhood accident still haunts poor Bradley, no fault of his own. He has always been a sensitive child and I'm sure he really did try."

"There's no need to explain Bradley to me sir. The fact is we will be taking a carriage to suit your son. He will never outgrow his fear of horses if he doesn't learn to respect them and show he is not afraid." Zachary jumped back into the saddle. "I will see the carriage is made ready and bring it around. The faster I go the faster we can depart on our long journey." Bradley had bragged to Zachary earlier how they would be stopping early to find a decent place to spend the night and hopefully find a nearby pub or bar, where the prostitutes hung out. Now with slower travel, Zachary must change his mind.

When Zachary pulled the carriage up, he got off to tie the mare next to Midnight on the back of the carriage. "Climb in Bradley, we will let our things ride on our horses today and switch them to the carriage early in the morning."

"Not too early, cousin!" Bradley waved goodbye to his parents as Zachary pulled the horses away in a trot. "Now, that we are away from my dear folks, this is what we will do! Stop early, just as I have said, find a room, then a bar with some extras! I will get up when I'm good and ready!"

"Your fun will have to wait until we reach Natchez, Cousin." Zachary stared at the road in front of him as he continued. "You insisted on a carriage and carriages travel a lot slower than horseback riding. If you want to reach our destination on time, we stop when I say stop and get up early when I give you the call! If you have a problem with that, you may take over driving the carriage and I will ride Midnight and wait for you in Natchez!"

"Me? Drive a carriage, with two horses pulling and the mare tied behind me?" Bradley looked over nervously. "I … I have never taken the reins before Zachary! I have always had a driver to take me wherever I needed to go!" he reached over and took a nervous hold of his arm. "Zachary, I insist that you drive! You…you work for us and if I tell daddy…"

Zachary laughed and interrupted his spoiled cousin threating speech. "I have no doubt you will run to your daddy, hoping to get me fired, if I do not drive this carriage to Natchez."

"Zachary, you did promise to take me! I even bought you a suit so you would look presentable setting next to me at the ball." Bradley pulled his hand away and stared nervously up at the horses. "Aren't you the lease bit grateful for that fine suit of clothes?"

"I recall thanking you when you brought them to me, Bradley." Zachary smiled. "I am surprised you did not ask me to try them on so you could have a change of heart if I looked too handsome in it and the ladies would be staring at me instead of you."

Bradley gave a sarcastic laugh. "Don't be ridiculous cousin! You could never hold a candle sitting next to me! The ladies find me irresistible, dashing and charming!" he looked over and sized up the handsome man sitting beside him, but in his vain eyes he only saw a poor farm boy. "I am afraid you do not fit any of those traits, cousin."

"I agree Bradley. I would describe myself as, gallant, romantic, a gentleman and the perfect soldier!" Zachary smiled when he heard his cousin grunt. "We shall let the ladies decide Bradley and if they find you too hard to resist, I will be happy with the one young lady that chooses me."

"Then, I shall be offering my I told you so, dear cousin, when I am surrounded by all the beautiful women in the room." Bradley ran his fingers through his curly blonde hair and patted Zachary on the back. "If it makes you feel better cousin, you will be the ladies second choice. Those southern hillbillies will never stack up to a northern gentleman, right Zachary?"

"Just close your eyes and keep dreaming Bradley." Zachary had enough of his cousin's bragging and throwing off on everyone else. "And you can relax about having to take over these reins. I would not want to be the one responsible for giving you worry lines on that irresistible, dashing, charming face."

"Very funny, Zachary." Bradley placed his hat down over his eyes. "I think I will take you up on that little nap. Try not to hit any bumps in the road."

"Just go to sleep!" Zachary welcomed the sound of the wheels rolling over the rough packed dirt instead of hearing his spoiled vain cousin flatter himself for one more second. Zachary would spend this time remembering his beautiful memories with Autumn Rose, seven year ago.

Chapter 14

"Dear cousin Autumn, I am simply beside myself with joy! I thought this night would never arrive and now that it's finally here, I'm as nervous as a kitten up a tree!" Polly Anne stood holding on to the bedpost while her lady's maid tightened her corset around her waist. "How do they expect us to enjoy our coming out party when we cannot even breathe?" she whined.

"Sister dear, mother has been trying the entire year to make you stop eating such large portions on your plate." Christina shook her curls in make-believe pity. "You just insisted on having that second piece of pie every night.

"Christina dear, with the way your face is turning a bright red, I would say you have put on a few pounds yourself!" Polly Anne turned to slap the maid's hand away. "That will be quite enough, Bertha Joyce! One more pull and I shall faint right out!"

"You both look lovely and I think those waists are small enough to pass the fashion lookers." Autumn had been observing her cousins being fitted into their corsets and she tried hard not to laugh at their dilemma. "I bet once you put those beautiful gowns on, you both will be the bells of the ball."

"Do you really think so, Autumn Rose?" Polly Anne flopped down on the fainting couch and ask for a Mint Julip. "I need something to calm these nerves! Mother has invited some very wealthy men here tonight, all available bachelors. Cousin Drake has asked his northern friend to come as his guest. They met at Harvard and graduated the same year with a business degree. Dear Drake tells us, Mr. Hastings' family owns a steel mill in Boston."

"Hastings? From Boston and they own a steel mill?" Autumn knew this could not be a co-incident. "His name wouldn't be Bradley, would it?"

"Why yes, it is!" Christina sent her maid away and walked over by Autumn. "Now how would you know Bradley Hastings, dear cousin, him living way up there in Boston and you on that big plantation in South Carolina?"

"I met Bradley when I was eight-years-old, while visiting my Uncle Bedford." Autumn wondered if he knew any news of his cousin Zachary. She made a mental note to ask him. "I remember he wanted to hang out with me because he was afraid of my uncle and wanted no part of him."

"What did he look like Autumn?" Polly Anne sat up, wanting to hear more about the complete stranger coming from Boston. "Was he handsome?"

"I don't know if I would call him exactly handsome, Polly Anne. To be perfectly honest, his looks have faded from my mind. He just wasn't my type." She could see disappointment on her cousin's faces. "Don't get me wrong, He had blonde hair and I recall it was curly but nice. He was older than me by a few years and I remember him bragging a lot. I guess you could say, he was cute." Still long faces from both cousins. "I am certain by now, he has become a man, and has grown more handsome than he was at fourteen, or was it fifteen, I just cannot remember."

"I'm certain of it!" Christina produced a fake smile and walked to her mirror. "Cousin Drake has been bragging about how handsome his friend Bradley is and I for one, believe dear Cousin Drake."

"Then I am sure he must have turned into a swan!" Autumn smiled at her friend Nellie when she walked in obviously with exciting news by her bright anxious face. "If you ladies will excuse me. I think it time to get into my dress and have my hair done up. I will meet you both at the top of the stairs, I believe your mother said, seven."

"That's right Cousin Autumn. I do hope you can be on time, what with dear Nellie working with that red hair of yours." Christina forced another smile at her beautiful cousin. "See you at seven, dear Autumn Rose."

"I will be there waiting." She gave them a real smile and dashed off behind her excited friend. When they were inside Autumn's guest room, she felt her friend grab her shoulders. "Do tell me Nellie, what has you jumping with news!"

"I just heard your cousin Drake Chatham welcome his friend Bradley and the.one who came with him from Boston!" Nellie nearly jumped out of her skin with the good news. "It's him, Autumn! He is here, downstairs at this very moment!"

"He?" Autumn's heart was pounding as she wondered, could it really be him, she thought. "Zachary, are you saying...Zachary is here?"

"I heard it with my own ears Autumn! That cocky cousin of his you met was introducing him to Mr. Chatham, his college friend." Nellie laughed at Autumn's big smile. "That Bradley boy still sounds vain, trying to make your Zachary sound like a loser."

"Just what did that stuck-up, bragging bully, say about Zachary?" Autumn held up her arms for Nellie to remove her day dress and replace the petty coat with a much fuller petty coat and two wide grenadines. Picking up the beautiful white ball gown, Nellie lifted it over her best friend's head and started fastening the many buttons down the back of the dress.

"After introducing Zachary as his cousin, he made a point to add, Nellie lowered her voice to mock the obnoxious young man. "Poor Cousin Zachary has lost everything he had for an inheritance after his depressed father was shot in a duel over his gambling loss. The poor boy had to resign from attending West Point Military Academy and never even finish his freshman year."

"That Bradley Hastings is the epitome of deceit! To put his own flesh and blood down in front of a perfect stranger is as low down as one person could get!" Autumn slipped into her white shoes and propped them up on a shoe rest so Nellie to fasten them up. "Did Zachary say anything?"

"I could not hear all his words, but he remained civil and soft spoken, even though there was a slight edge in his tone. I can already tell from each man's voice that your Zachary is ten times the gentleman than Bradley is."

"Poor daring, losing his father in such a tragic way, not to mention their farm." Autumn swirled around to face the mirror for her hair to be fixed. "Oh Nellie, I wonder how his dear mother took losing both her husband and home, to some crooked gambler." Autumn sat up, remembering Zachary telling her about some gambler who tried to scam his Uncle David out of everything he owned and how scared he felt when the same gambler threatened to get even with young Zachary for spoiling his game. Autumn spoke at a whisper, mostly for herself. "Could it have been the same gambler who threatened a ten-year-old boy for catching him cheating and ruin his chance to win big, then being thrown out of the small town by the local sheriff?"

"Are you saying that Mr. Dawson was set up to lose everything he had, just to get even with something that happened seven years ago?" Nellie placed the ribbon through the upswept curls and gave the long curls around Autumn's beautiful face and on her soft silk neck a light fluff. "It takes a devil of a man to hold on to revenge for seven years to get even with a child! To take another life as though he were just rolling the dice, and pretend it was Zachary's father fault for insisting on a duel!" Nellie stood back to admire her work, her heart still feeling anger over this heartless gambler that thought more about money than he did a human life. "Why, I think the man should be caught and hung on the nearest Pine tree!"

"Why a Pine tree Nellie? Why not an Oak or Chestnut?" Autumn couldn't help but laugh at the ideal of someone hanging from a spindling Pine, with branches mostly at the top.

"Cause, the Pine's branches are higher and weaker than most trees, that's why! The lawmen might have to put more effort in getting his sorry ass up on that limb, but, once the noose is on and they let him dropped, that skinny old limb will snap and send the cheating weasel all the way back down to the hard ground!" Nellie gave a chuckle. "That way, if the hanging does not kill the cheat, the fall will do the trick!"

"Nellie, I would not be planning for that bad man's hanging just yet. I also recall Zachary telling me if that man ever tried to get even with him, he would take matters into his own hand and see that he was put away forever. Either under the jail or under the ground, one way or the other." Autumn turned to look at her reflection in the big mirror and saw a fairy tale princess looking back.

"Dear sweet Jesus, Miss Autumn, I was so bent up with anger over that horrible man that killed young Mr. Dawson's daddy, I was blinded to your enchanting beauty." Nellie stared at her friend's reflection in the big floor length mirror after she rose to her feet and looked for the first time at her own reflection. "There is no question as to who will be the bell of this ball, dear friend and land sakes alive, your cousins will be seeing green jealousy for sure!"

"I can only thank the good Lord for bestowing me with these good graces and for you, dear Nellie, for creating a miracle with this hair of mine." Autumn looked around laughing happily. "I do think Zachary shall be totally surprised to see me here and no longer the little girl wearing pigtails with a flat chest."

"I agree, dearest friend, hardly the flat chested little girl with the love-struck green eyes." Nellie peeked out in the hall at the big grandfather clock and said softly. "6:45!" She gave her nervous friend a big smile. "It looks like your boring night has done went and

83

changed for an exciting night, Autumn. In less than 15 minutes, you will see Zachary again. It would appear a greater power has brought you two together."

"And why aren't you in your dress Nellie? You are supposed to be standing next to me, or have you conveniently forgotten?" Autumn made her way to the open door. "You cannot let mother and my cousin's maids, warning you to stay in your place, stop you from having a good time."

"Look Miss Autumn, we have discussed this, many a time. I knows I a free woman, because of your good kindness by buying my freedom papers for me, and as your birthday present instead of that new horse you had your eye on." Nellie walked over and gave her a gentle push out the door. "I'm not going downstairs with all them white folk. I have made up my mind and that is that! Now, you get over there before them cousins come out first and gloat because you be late! Just you get down there and claim your handsome fellow before he's spotted by a wondering eye flirty gal."

"Alright, I am going now, but if you have a change of heart, feel free to join me downstairs." Autumn waited until Nellie closed the door and the pretty redhead knew she would not see her best friend until she went up for bed, much later.

Tiptoeing slowly over to the rail, she looked down into the ballroom for any sign of Zachary. From her viewing point, Autumn could not make out any guest. Only staff members, mostly waiters, standing up against the enter wall, waiting until it was time to serve everyone invited. On the east wing of Chatham Hall Mansion, the red-carpeted grand staircase was the perfect place for the southern ladies to make their entrance. Each lady, the oldest to the youngest, was decked in their finest evening gowns and jewels. Each beautiful head was adorned with the perfect up-do, laden with soft curls or smooth buns with sparkling diamonds or rubies. The approach of the women was supposed to draw the gentlemen's attention and see them rise to their feet in respect and admiration. Wives kept their husbands in the dark about the gown they would be wearing so she could sweep him away once more, like when he first saw his mate waltz down the wide stairs. But all the silk, all the lace, all the exquisite gowns and jewelry, could not equal the beauty and grace of the redhead with the alluring green eyes.

Christina and Polly Anne, walked out proudly, feeling pretty enough to draw all the men's attention away from their cousin from

South Carolina, and stopped short when they spotted her, looking like an angel.

"Autumn, I see you chose white for this ball. I guess you didn't want to clash with mother's wallpaper again!" Polly Anne chuckled and tapped her sister's back, who had joined her in the laughter. "You do remember don't you cousin? How your yellow gown made you blend right in the wallpaper?"

"What I recall, Polly Anne, darling, is deliberately moving as close to the wall with the flowered wall paper in hopes of blending in, so all those men, old and young, would get their attention on someone else instead of circling me like a pack of hungry wolves." Autumn was happy to recognize a lot of familiar faces as the women filed out from guest rooms all down the hallway. Glad not to be alone with her two hateful cousins, Autumn found her mother talking to Isabelle and Mary Ann Forrest, and went over to see what they were wearing. Katherine, Autumn's mother, had on a ruby-red velvet gown with a one carat diamond around her neck. Christina and Polly Anne's mother wore a rich royal blue gown with an incredible neckless filled with both diamonds and emeralds. Mary Ann's dress was a simple but charming green gown and she wore a single ruby brooch right above her bosom. They all stopped speaking to admire the beautiful vision standing there.

"Ladies, you look very glamorous this evening and I am certain that daddy, Uncle Stanley, and Uncle Bedford will be at a loss for words when they see you make your graceful walk down those stairs."

"I am just glad the older ladies go first, my dear." Autumn's Aunt Isabelle could not get over her niece's perfect beauty and figure. "Your girl Nellie doesn't have to pull your corset too tight, does she dear?"

"Dear sister, Autumn Rose does not wear a corset." Katherine smiled at her sister's drop jaw. "She has no need of one, having such a tiny waist."

"Your proportions are perfect, sweet girl." Mary Ann gave her niece a hug. "Like you, I have always been well endowed with a large bosom, but I cannot boast to having such a tiny waist and such smooth shapely hips like you, dear Autumn Rose. You can have your pick of all the available young men in attendance tonight."

"I have narrowed down her choices to three eligible gentlemen, dear Mary Ann." Katherine checked the big clock as it struck seven.

"I will be introducing her to them, separate of course, to make it fair."

"I will gladly meet your gentlemen friends, mother, but I am very capable of choosing my own husband." Autumn Rose gave her a knowing smile. "Perhaps he is here tonight!" she smiled at Isabelle "We still go down by age, right Aunt Isabelle?"

"Yes darling, so that makes you last. Polly Anne is two months older than you dear." She faked a smile and made her way to the start of the line while Mary Ann took her niece by the hand.

"Isabelle is just jealous over your beauty child. No amount of make-up, high fashion, or fancy hairstyles can make those daughters of hers match your natural beauty, inside or out." She watched Katherine smile and walked to her place in line. "And as for finding the man you are meant to love, I hear Zachary is downstairs and hoping the redheaded, green-eye young woman coming tonight is his Autumn Rose."

Chapter 15

As the ladies made their way down the elegant steps, the men stopped all their conversations and stood to admire their beauty and choice of gowns. All thirty men watching remained respectful and silent, no sudden outburst of clapping or wolf whistles, just true gentlemen, taking in and admiring every woman descending the red staircase.

The married ladies spotted their husbands immediately, as they stepped up to offer their hand for the last step. Each woman looked around the room at the nice-looking group of eligible men, who might be interested in their daughters. All caught the extremely handsome young man standing at the far end of the oval room. His features captivated their attention. The long black hair, deep tan skin, and alluring blue eyes to match the royal blue shirt under the black suit.

Zachary's attention was frozen on the stairs and the last young lady with her beautiful red hair swept up into a cascade of curls to frame her incredibly beautiful face. He didn't think his girl could get any prettier than she was when he last saw her, but Autumn had grown into an angel.

Searching the room of staring men, Autumn found the one she was hoping to see. How handsome he had become from the good-looking boy she had dreamed about and longed for. Now that they found one another again, would Zachary ask her to marry him and take her away from Dixie? Autumn knew she would be happy wherever she was, as long as Zachary was there.

Without hesitation he started to walk to meet her, working his way through the moving group of available men, who had the same motive as him, to reach out to the girl with the beautiful green eyes. The group of single young ladies grew excited watching the men walking swiftly their way and thinking they were the reason for their excited advancing. Before the men could swoop in on the girls, Mr. Chatham stepped in front of them, holding out his hands and giving a soft chuckle.

"Gentlemen, I realize you are transfixed by all these beautiful young ladies, but must I remind you, this is their coming out party, a chance to show the world that they are eligible and ready to start courting. As parents, we attend the ball to make sure all gentlemen act like true gentlemen, and wait for an introduction. Then, you may ask any girl if she cares to dance with you when the music starts playing waltzes." He waved his hand around the big ballroom. "So, if you would go back to your seats, we will begin the introductions."

Zachary and Autumn smiled at each other before he walked back to the far corner, hoping he would be with her soon. The need to take her into his arms and kiss her sweet lips would have to wait until he could find a way to sneak the girl he had longed for, outside, someplace private.

Bradley lend over and whispered loudly. "What a looker! She keeps looking this way! What did I tell you, the girls just fall for me and my great looks!" he laughed. "Damn, she is about the prettiest girl I have ever seen! My friend was right, that's some hot redhead and those eyes, I could look into those eyes every second of the day.: he punched Zachary on the arm. "Especially the nights!"

"Perhaps it is me she watches and not you at all, Bradley." Zachary smiled into Autumn's green eyes and she returned his smile brightly. "You must stop assuming every pretty girl in this world thinks you are God given, just for them."

"One way or the other, dear cousin, we shall soon find out." Bradley sat up and straightened his shiny silk vest, that matched his expensive tucks. "The fair damsel just pointed this way to her mother who has been speaking in her ear for some time. They must be discussing me?" Bradley gave a soft sure laugh as Zachary thought

"There's no talking to that conceded man! He will just have to find out the hard way he is not her choice at all."

Across the large oval room, Katherine and Autumn had been in a heated conversation about which man would get the first interview. Autumn, in love and determine to speak to the man she loved, insisted it be the gentleman with the long black hair and mustache seated at the end of the room.

"Darling, I can see why you are drawn to that incredibly handsome young man with the most alluring blue eyes I have ever witnessed, but he was not one of the gentlemen I had sent an invitation too." Katherine looked around and spotted the three successful businessmen she had hoped might interest her head-strong daughter and noticed her sister Isabelle had already beat her to the banker, Cameron Wilks, along with Christina, wearing a frozen smile. "Now, just look at that! My dear sister invited five available gentlemen and she is pouncing on one of mine!"

Autumn followed her mother's eyes over to the man she and her sister seem to have an interest in and tried not to laugh. Being a good Christian girl, Autumn tried to never judge another person's looks or personal habits shown around others, but the short, nervous, balding man acted a though he was in front of a firing squad as he looked from daughter to mother, as she gabbed away about her daughter's qualities. Autumn shook her head in pity.

"That poor man, I'm not sure he realized what he was getting into. Poor Mr. Wilks might flee the first chance he gets." Autumn glance over at Zachary and noticed Mrs. Creekmur had taken her daughter over to meet him and Bradley. She had no doubt of Zachary's intentions and she knew he had no interest in Pattie Creekmur or any other available young lady there. "Mother, I am going across the room, with or without you, before someone has the chance to receive the first dance with the blue-eyed vision!"

"Autumn, we just don't know anything about that young man." Katherine felt like she was losing the battle with her determined daughter. "He could be just a traveling companion with that Bradley Hastings! Mr. Hastings would make a better match for you." Noticing the sour look on her daughter's face she said. "So, he isn't your type either? Bradley Hastings is the only child of a rich steel mill owner, Autumn, he will inherit everything and you would be set for life."

"With a man I detest and do not love? Really mother, don't you recognize those two young men?" Autumn had played along with her mother not remembering the two boys she had met seven and eight years ago.

"Do we know those two gentlemen? I am sure Isabelle said they were from Boston, Massachusetts." Katherine lifted her fancy glasses to her eyes to try and see them better. "Are you quite certain, darling? Why would we know Northern boys?"

"Because we met them while visiting Uncle Bedford and Aunt Mary's. We met Bradley eight years ago, when I was eight, and…" Autumn looked over and saw the man she loved smiling back. "we met Zachary when I was nine and he was ten, seven long years ago."

Katherine stood stun for a moment, then swallowed back the obvious. "Zachary? I guess I had planted that memory deep down inside and hoped you had forgotten him as well."

"Mother, I know you stopped my letters to Zachary after I reached fourteen, so I just had the faith that God would bring us back together, and He has." Autumn gave her mother a quick smile as she took her hand. "You cannot fight destiny mother. We are meant to be together, poor or rich, we will and can make it work, because of the great love we share." Her smooth fingers brushed her mother's tears away. "First, we shall go over to see the man I chose and love, then out of respect for those three men coming, I shall go to make their acquaintance, but only briefly. I shall not dance with either gentlemen because I shall hold all my waltzes for my Zachary."

Autumn led her mother over to the far corner of the oval ballroom and stopped in front of the two cousins from Boston, waiting for the Creekmur's to finish. Mrs. Creekmur laid a gloved hand on both men's hands as she concluded her bragging.

"I can assure you gentlemen, my Pattie will make you a lovely mate, what with her motherly charm and cooking skills. What man isn't looking for the perfect mother for their children or the perfect woman who can cook as good as the best chef's in good old Paris."

Bradley had been sizing up the well-stock girl with a chubby face and shy smile. "We can see she is an excellent cook, no doubt enjoys her own cooking a bit too much." Never a man to hide his feelings, Bradley merely gave the shocked mother his cocky smile and turned to his cousin, who had been listening to him degrading the sweet shy girl. "Would you not agree, Cousin Zachary?"

"Ma'am, I find your daughter charming and sweet. Except for my cousin here, most men would appreciate having a wife who was both a great cook in the kitchen and a loving mother to his children." Zachary reached for the mother's hand and gave it a kiss, then took Pattie's hand and kissed it. "Although I am already spoken for, I know there is just the right man here for you Pattie. Looking around at the choices, my guess would be Cameron Wilks, the banker. With both of you being shy, you would make the perfect couple."

Autumn lend over to whisper in her mother's ear. "See there, mother, Zachary is ten times the man as his outspoken cousin, Bradley Hastings."

"He certainly is more thoughtful, that is true, but darling, Zachary did say he was already spoken for." Katherine had been listening to the brash comment by Mr. Hastings, and how kind Mr. Dawson was in comparison. All was going well for her daughter's choice until he spoke of possibly being married or at the most, engaged to another. Katherine watched Pattie tearfully thanking him for promising to introduce her to Mr. Wilks. "Autumn, surely you're not still pursuing a man that is spoken for!"

"Mother, Zachary was speaking of me." Autumn watched the Creekmur's walk away. "Didn't I tell you we are meant to be together." She continued to whisper. "Now, stay quiet about this."

"I was hoping you would come over to speak to me, my dear lady." Bradley stood there admiring Autumn's beautiful face, then as he spoke to Katherine his eyes dropped to her low cup dress and a smile of approval fell on his lips. "I would love to be the first to dance with your daughter. Just looking at her as lifted my joy to greater heights "

Zachary had to hide his smile when Autumn moved closer to him. "Why Bradley Hastings, you have not changed a bit."

"I am confused, my dear, but have we met before?" Bradley gave an uncertain laugh. "I know I would remember a woman as beautiful as you."

"Would you now?" Autumn reached her hand out for Zachary's as he clutched it lovingly. "It is wonderful to see you again, Zachary."

"I have been longing for the time to come when I would once again be with you, dearest Autumn." Zachary's heartbeat totally for this girl and her mother standing close and listening to his words of devotion did not bother him. Their reunion was interrupted by Bradley's loud outburst.

"Autumn Forrest? That little girl with the red pigtail. The same dirty little kid I had to lift out of that mud?"

"The mud you pushed me in when you came running from that pasture?" Autumn laugh remembering the funny event.

"It was an accident..." Bradley looked around nervously, trying to make light of his cowardly actions. "Autumn and I were pitching a small tire back and forth, and she threw it over my head and it sailed into the pasture behind me. We had taken it off Mr. Forrest's big wooden wheel barrel and had planned to put it back when we finished our game." He tried to laugh. "I had to retrieve the silly thing before that big man found it missing." Bradley narrowed his eyes at the smiling girl "If you had not whirled it so hard it would not have flown over my head!"

"Dear Bradley, if you would not have ducked, you could have easily caught it."

"Had I not ducked, that hard wheel would have scared my perfect face!" he stated loudly.

"And if you had not been so afraid of Uncle Bedford's big bull, you would not have rushed out the gate I was holding open for you and knock me out of your way, right into the pig's mud." Autumn couldn't help but smile at Bradley's red face.

"Autumn, are you speaking about Tank, Bedford's prize breeding bull with the brass ring through its nose?" Zachary gave a chuckle, picturing his cousin running from the angry bull. "Tell me Bradley, didn't you realize Autumn's uncle had that gate close for a purpose?"

"You, Zachary, are the farm boy, not I! My dealings with livestock are limited to horses and only for carriage use! That mean bull was out to get me and if you had been in my shoes, cousin, you would have run too!" Bradley's face was fused with embarrassment and anger. "Just admit it!"

"Bradley, Zachary did have to go inside that pasture with that bull but not to retrieve a wheel, he went in to get Tank and take him to the barn." Autumn remembered watching how brave Zachary had been and could tell he had deal with animals before.

"My beautiful niece is right there, young man." Nathan Bedford Forrest had joined the interested party. "I stood back watching, proud as a peacock, wishing the lad belonged to me as he walked straight up to old tank, grabbed his ring and led him to his stable before the storm hit." He smiled over to the young man he had been waiting to speak to, then turned to Katherine who had been taking the conversation in. "Katherine, you ladies would not know what happen that night because you were all in the drawing room having after dinner tea." Nathan recalled the stormy night. "I had stepped out on the front porch with David and brother Frederick to have smokes and brandy, since the night air had a cooling breeze in it. We heard thunder in the distance and I could tell by the pink sunset and darken skies, this storm would bring with it hail and dangerous lightening. Excusing myself, I raced to the back pasture to get old Tank, the other animals had been put up already, but the bull preferred to remain out in the night air. When I reached the gate, I spotted your little girl, standing there bravely as the thunder grew closer. That's when I saw the boy, there…" he gave Zachary a pat on his strong back. "walking out to that bull, standing there pawing at the earth, threating the boy with its snorts of anger. Not for a single moment did Zachary's stare leave that bull's eyes and just like an enemy on a battlefield, the bull began to grow weak and yield to the boy's command to follow once he took a strong hold of his ring." He laughed out. "It was brilliant!"

"You are right Bradley, to call me a farm boy, because I can proudly say that I was before I decided to become a soldier." Zachary heard Autumn's mother gasp at the word soldier. He looked at her, knowing she had doubts of her daughter marring a soldier who would be gone most of the time and even get killed, while fighting. "Mrs. Forrest, there are many devoted husbands that are soldiers and find they can do both successfully. I regret that I must wait though before I can continue my military career."

"Yes, it would appear dear cousin Zachary is penniless." Bradley smiled at the love-struck couple, knowing his words hit hard with Autumn's mother. "At the present time, my family gives Zachary employment as our horse trainer. Tis a sad affair when one's father is shot in a duel over a gambling debt and loses everything he has."

"Bradley, you are the barer of bad tidings, that's plain to see!" Autumn detested this man for trying to degrade a better man than himself. "I believe its ill to make light over another man's misfortune. Can you not for one moment think about someone besides yourself, Bradley Hastings! If perchance Zachary broke his leg at this very moment and could not dance a single dance with me, I would take root as a wall flower before I took one step around that ballroom with the likes of you!"

Zachary looked down smiling as Bradley searched for the correct words to say. No one had ever spoken to the spoiled brat like his Autumn had. Hearing his cousin clear his throat, Zachary glance up.

"I guess this means I have no chance to win your fair hand, Autumn." Bradley faked a smile at her mother. "Dear lady, I am certain you must be upset over the fact that my cousin is poor as a church mouse, but perhaps you, at lease, might consider me for your daughter's hand in marriage. I can see that she is well taken care of, and…" he smiled over at the couple "give her a mansion to call home instead of a stable room."

Autumn Rose stepped up and stared into his face. "You arrogant, conceded man, I would rather live in an outhouse with Zachary than in the largest castle in England with you!"

"You heard my woman Bradley, go find yourself someone who can match your standards! Perhaps…" Zachary tilted his head apologetic to Katherine, "forgive the one I suggest, dear lady, no reflection on your sister, I assure you, but I think you should check out Miss Christina. She strikes me as more your type, cousin, always flattering herself with her words."

"You've had a chance to speak with my cousin already Zachary?" Autumn did not feel the least bit jealous; she was curious as to when Christina could have spoken to any man in attendance, seeing as how the women had to remain upstairs until seven o'clock. "Did the silly flirt finds means to find you before the ball begun?"

"I do not wish to bring disgrace to any lady, but yes, Miss Christina did show up at my room and request a word." Zachary knew he had everyone's attention, even his usual outspoken cousin remained quiet to listen, perhaps hoping Autumn would get mad with jealousy and storm away. To Bradley's dismay, she remained by Zachary's side faithfully.

"I knew she was up to something when she slipped from the room while we were supposed to be resting up for the night's events." Autumn touched his arm lovingly. "Did she knock on your door or did my charming cousin just walk in."

"I never knew women could be so impudent before, not the trait of a virtuous lady, to walk so boldly into a man's bedchamber without knocking." Zachary showed no sign of being guilty of any wrongdoing. "After I got over my shock from her shameless entrance, I tried to make it easy on her before she advanced further into my room by asking her if she mistook my room for hers. She merely laughed and said she just wanted a word with me."

"Did my niece remain in the doorway Mr. Dawson or did Christina make her way inside?" Katherine felt her face flush with embarrassment over the rash action of her sister's daughter.

"I could tell your niece was about to close the door when I walked over and held it open." Zachary looked down at the girl he loved, knowing she trusted him with all her heart. He squeezed her hand gently. "You are right, dearest one. Your cousin Christina is a big flirt. She batted her eyelashes while asking if I would dance with her first at the ball. She grew upset when I told her, I would be dancing with my woman every dance, so it would be impossible for me to spare one dance for her."

"I guess that's when poor Christina flew back inside the door, her face flushed with anger." Autumn dared not look in her cousin's direction, for she knew Christina had been watching her ever since she had walked over to Zachary. "She is bound to know by now that I am the girl you were speaking about, Zachary and if you hear a cat fight on the third floor tonight, you can bet it will be me and my unhappy cousin having it out!"

Chapter 16

"Autumn, Mr. Harold Davenport has a big plantation outside of Charleston. He is a lonely 45-year-old widower and looking for a wife to bare him children" Katherine had persuaded her daughter to at least meet the gentlemen who had come at her request. "I know your heart is set on Zachary and I must admit you both make the perfect couple, although I have trouble seeing my only child living in some stable room."

"Mother, Zachary has informed me that he would like nothing more than to make me his bride, but due to the fact that he is working to save enough money to regain back his family's estate in Massachusetts, he asked me to become his fiancé and wait until he can carry me over the threshold of our splendid farmhouse after we are wed." Autumn stopped and sized up the widower she was about to meet. She noticed he had a gentle face and a warm smile as he spoke with Pattie Anne, while eyeing her waiting to meet him. She could tell, even though his words were kind to her cousin, that he was not interested in making her his wife. Knowing all the available girls at the party, she could help him find the perfect match he was seeking.

After Pattie moved on to the next man, Katherine led her beautiful daughter up for introductions. "Harold, may I introduce my daughter Autumn Rose."

"It is a pleasure to finally meet such an outstanding young lady." Mr. Davenport lifted her gloved hand and kissed it. "To ever have thought I might have a chance in making you my bride was short lived when I saw you with young Dawson." No malice showed on his face as he turned to the lady who had sent him the invitation. "Katherine, the young have the advantage over us, especially when the love was already there waiting to be rekindled."

"It came as a surprise to me as well." Katherine touched her daughter's face. "Autumn Rose is a very determine young woman and when her mind is made up, no amount of talking can change it."

"Love that looks that blissful should never be stopped." Harold Davenport proved to be the perfect gentleman and Autumn knew whose company he would enjoy the most. "Perhaps I will take my leave after I have spoken to the other ladies."

"Mr. Davenport, I don't think you've met Margaret Chatham yet. Margaret is a lovely young woman, smart and soft spoken and one of my dearest cousins." Spotting her pretty cousin at the punch bowl pouring the spiked drink in crystal cups for some guest, Autumn gathered the friendly man's hand in hers and took him over for introductions. "Margaret, I don't believe you have met my mother's friend, Harold Davenport yet."

The pretty blonde handed him a glass of punch and smiled, receiving his smile in return. "It is a pleasure meeting you sir. I must admit, I was hoping to meet you, Harold, is it?"

"That's right, Margaret." He sipped on the tasty punch. "Why would a pretty girl like you hope to meet a widower of 45?"

"I find you very charming Harold and to be honest, I much rather entertain an older wiser man than a younger foolish man, like my brother Drake and his friend, Bradley Hastings."

"Margaret, would you care to join me in some of your fabulous punch over on that love seat, so we can get more acquainted?" Harold gave Autumn a wink and led the pretty blonde away as the clever redhead smiled at her mother.

"One guest happy, now to the next one."

"Autumn darling, Clint Reynolds might be a little harder to convince Zachary Dawson is the right bachelor for you." Nodding his way as not to draw his attention away from Christina, Katherine showed her daughter the dashing plantation owner dressed in a white tux. Standing a short distance away, mother and daughter could hear every word spoken by Christina.

"I do declare Clint darling, that is about the most charming thing any man has ever said to little biddy me." She gave a soft laugh. "I do believe you are flirting with me, sir. Perhaps we can be the first to waltz around our ballroom."

"Perhaps, we might, lovely Christina, if I have the chance to meet the other prospects first." Clint Reynolds flashed a big smile. "I have been a happy bachelor all my adult life and have made the acquaintances with a great many charming ladies, such as yourself. I am searching for the perfect mate to finally settle down with and if I cannot find such a beautiful woman, then, my choices of charming ladies are many."

"Oh, but Clint darling, I just know with my perfect looks and the incredible charm I possess, we could make beautiful babies together." Christina batted her eyelashes as she moved her fancy fan swiftly in front of her hot cheeks.

"Christina, my dear girl, you must not get your hopes up until I decide who this perfect..." Clint Reynolds spotted Autumn Rose standing in the open door with her mother and closed his eyes as a smile fell on his handsome lips. "the perfect woman will have a body like a goddess, a face like an angel, the hair the color of soft flames and the eyes, as green as an emerald."

"You describe Autumn Rose?" Anger fell over Christina's flirty eyes. "Why must every man drool over my overbearing cousin? Unless the wonderful, marvelous Autumn Rose starts collecting men like Mohammedans collect harems, you and every Tom, Dick, and Harry can forget wedding bliss with her!" she stomped her foot and marched away as Autumn and her mother tried not to laugh at Christina's raging.

"Clint, I am truly sorry for my niece's behavior." Katherine forced a smile at the man who had his full attention on her daughter. "I am afraid dear Christina's jealousy over my daughter is starting to get the best of her and reveal the worse."

"Yes Katherine, you are very correct about the spoiled girl who wants her way at others expense." Clint Reynolds lifted Autumn's hand and gave it a long kiss. "I'd much prefer kissing the lips of one as beautiful as you, Autumn Rose."

"Mr. Reynolds, that is a bold statement to make to a young lady who is yet to know you." Autumn could well understand why the ladies thought this plantation owner handsome, because, in truth he was, but not as handsome or gentle as her Zachary. "Mother tells me you have a plantation on the outskirts of Natchez, so I would assume you have met my cousins Christina, Polly Anne, Margaret and Drake before."

"I have indeed had the pleasure of their acquaintance before, Autumn Rose." His eyes remained locked on her. "But that is not the reason for my presence at the ball tonight."

"Oh, and what brings such a devoted bachelor to a gathering swelling with young single women looking for the proper beau to court?" Autumn knew her mother had sent him a special invitation in hopes she would choose him to marry, never knowing Autumn had already picked her life mate.

"Sweet, darling girl, I came for one purpose." Clint lifted her hand. "To meet you and sweep you off your feet, to make you my wife and to start a family at long last." His face grew serious. "Last year in Charleston, I saw you for the first time, standing across the ballroom at the Mills Hotel. I could not draw my eyes away from your beautiful face. Your radiant hair seemed to come alive with lights under the crystal chandelier and those alluring green eyes captivated my imagination like never before." Clint's hand touched her hair. "I did not see you at first while entertaining my charming date and when finally, you caught my eye and I could not pull away. I tried with haste to make it across the long ballroom through the crowd, leaving my confused date behind. I had to reach you but when I finally arrived where you were, you had disappeared."

"It had grown late and we left, needing to return home to the planation which was several hours away." Autumn remembered the ball and how she had wished Zachary would just appear and sweep her away. "Mr. Reynolds, I pray you have not been thinking about me ever since that night. I too remember that night and how I was wishing the man I loved would show up and take me away from there."

"Perhaps the man you wished for was me, Autumn Rose." Clint Reynolds said hopeful.

"Perhaps if I had not already met the man that stole my heart six years before that ball, Clint Reynolds, but I did, and I am completely devoted to him." Autumn could see the color drain from his face as she confessed loving someone else. "Clint, I am certain there is the right girl for you someplace out there, but it won't be me."

"Tell me then, who is this lucky man that has captivated you so?" Clint Reynolds raised his voice. "Surely you cannot mean someone here tonight, Autumn. I am sure it's not the little nervous banker or Harold Davenport, the other men your mother invited."

"It is neither Mr. Wilks or Mr. Davenport, if you must know, Clint, but the man I love with all my heart is here tonight." Autumn raised her eyebrow in defiance. "His name is Zachary Dawson, from Boston, Massachusetts."

"A Yankee! Tell me you are kidding, sweet Autumn Rose!" Clint Reynolds obvious hate flashed on his dashing face as he looked around, trying to pick out this Zachary Dawson, he had heard women around him whispering as the most handsome man in the room. "A southern belle like you my dear have no business being around a man who could easily be our enemy!"

"I can assure you, sir, Zachary Dawson is no enemy of the

south." Autumn felt the need to defend the man she was to marry one day. "His attachment to a great many friends down here will always keep him loyal, if it's the war that keeps being rumored by all you men, that you refer to!"

"Dear girl, I fear it is much more than just a rumor! "Clint drew in close in case a northern spy may be among them. "Even now cannons have been sent to the Charleston Harbor and are lined up along the Battery facing Fort Sumter. The military cadets from the Citadel have been sent to Fort Wagner on Morris Island across the Cooper River and are presently building a wall out of Palmetto Trees to protect the cannons, set ready to fire on the fort out in the Harbor when the order is called!" Reynolds grew serious. "Autumn Rose, it's just a matter of time before Beauregard gives his men the order to fire on Fort Sumter, then we will be at war with the North!" he took hold of her arm, knowing it would not be easy to convince this determined young lady he knew he must have for himself. "Can't you see the division between the north and the south? They fight to takes our rights and tell us how to live in the name of preserving the union! We fight to save our states' rights, still united, yet individual!"

"Sir, I must ask you to release my fiancé's arm immediately!" Zachary had seen the wealthy plantation owner speaking to Autumn Rose and knowing she had promised her mother to give them a courteous greeting for attending the ball at her invitation, he had stepped out briefly for some fresh air to give her time. Bradley had found his cousin outside and informed him of the brash man's behavior toward Autumn. Without hesitation, Zachary had rushed back inside and to his loves rescue.

"Your fiancé?" Clint Reynold's stared up at the handsome young man with the piecing blue eyes and noticed he wore a regular black suit with a royal blue shirt that matched his eyes perfectly. He was the only man in attendance who was not wearing a tuxedo, but it never bothered the chattering women, who couldn't seem to stop watching the tall man with the long black hair. "How old are you, young man?"

"Not that it's any of your business sir, but I am seventeen and old enough to get married now whenever I choose." Zachary pulled Autumn away from his hand and took her hand. "We plan to be married when I regain that which is mine."

"If I have my math correct Autumn, you said you had met the man who stole your heart, now it would be seven years ago, so that means you were only nine and this fellow was only ten, correct?" Clint laughed. "Kids? How would kids know what real love was like?"

"Like Zachary told you Clint, we owe you no explanation and I'm not really sure we could describe such a feeling to someone like you." Autumn looked up into Zachary's eyes and that beautiful feeling flooded her heart. "It is so special you just know in your heart this is the one the Lord wants you to be with forever."

"The most incredible feeling that swept through us when we were together, the overwhelming sadness when our goodbyes came and for seven years a longing to see, hear and hold my Autumn Rose close to me." Zachary finally broke away and stared down at his new enemy. "Autumn Rose is the reason I breathe and war or no war, I will never lift my sword against her Dixie. For as long as I breathe, Autumn can continue to find that secret place and watch her sunrise come up over Dixie and when I take her to our home, together we will find our own secret place and watched from a distanced, the sunset over Dixie."

Autumn's heart was bursting with love for this man who had declared his undying love for her, and all she wanted was to be in his arms, away from this 'southern gentleman' who obviously hated Zachary, not just for being a Yankee, as he called him, but the fact that he was the man she had given her heart to and not Clint Reynolds.

"Now, if you will excuse us Mr. Reynolds, the music has started and I promised my fiancé I would give him every dance tonight."

Chapter 17

The men had watched with envy and all the ladies waiting to be asked to dance, could only dream of being in this handsome man's arms as they watched Zachary and Autumn waltz around the oval ballroom as the music played. Knowing the night would soon be over, Zachary whispered, pulling her ever closer to his lips.

"Dearest Autumn, we are near the garden doors. How easy it would be for us to dance right out under the stars so I can give you a proper goodnight kiss, away from all the watchful eyes."

"Tis a bold move you request, dear Zachary." Autumn squeezed his hand lovingly. "And yet, I have dreamed about dancing under a starry sky with the man I love."

"The doors have been opened to let in the evening air and as the last waltz has been announced by our host, everyone has found a partner in which to whirl around the room." Zachary's eyes sparkled with romance. "With the ballroom alive with dancing, no one will notice the young in love slip away for some privacy."

"Then sweep me away my darling, to have our final dance under a canopy of stars." Escaping without being seen by all the previous watchful guest, Zachary finally pulled his true love in a warm embrace, his attention on her luscious lips he had been longing to kiss since he was ten.

"Autumn, do you know how long I have wanted to hold you like this, to at last kiss your beautiful lips?"

"Dear sweet Zachary, do you think I have not longed for this moment as well? Oh yes, my love, with every waking moment and in my dreams alone would it happen." Autumn's slender finger touched his lips. "Dearest Zachary, let me feel your lips upon mine again before the music ends and all the gossiping women start their frantic search for us."

"Then to the last strands of the violin, our lips will join again as one" As he drew just a breath away, he spoke softly. "but with the desire and passion of a man and woman, no more two children just learning with their first kiss." Their lips met and the love that spread through their bodies was like the flames of an unstoppable forest fire. Zachary and Autumn were so caught up in their continuing kisses, they almost missed the music ending and the clinking of glasses, toasting the couples who had found that perfect someone.

Smiling at one another, the love-starved couple slipped back through the open doors and grabbed a glass of champagne, hoping no had witness their disappearance. Autumn's father, Frederick, and his brother Nathan Bedford, had been near the doors, trying to cool down from the long waltz when they spotted the couple.

"There you are darling, I lost sight of the two of you dancing when your mother insisted we dance the last waltz." Frederick was still breathless from the rousing waltz.

"I'm surprise any father could have found their daughter and escort as crowded as that dance floor was." Nathan held his glass over to the server for a refill then smiled over at Zachary and Autumn giving them a knowing wink. "If I had just met my Mary Ann, I would have waltzed that little gal right out of those open doors and danced under the stars with her." He gave them a sneaky smile and added. "Then gave her a little kiss if no one was watching."

"Would you now, dear brother?" Frederick gave a chuckle, remembering being with his older brother when he met his wife, Mary Ann. "I'm not so sure you could have survived that unhappy father when he caught you with his darling daughter." Frederick smiled back a Zachary, who had caught on to his friend Bedford's spotting their escape and no doubt had found the means to slip away from Mary to make sure they were behaving proper. "I can trust young Zachary here, brother. It is a fact that all northern gentlemen raised in Boston, know how to properly court a virtuous young woman like my Autumn Rose."

Bedford's eyes twinkled with mischief. "I could not agree with you more. Brother Frederick." He draped his arms around the couple's shoulders. "Besides, is Zachary not a student of mine? Did I not teach him that a great soldier must at all times respect the fairer sex and treat them with upmost dignity and gentleness?"

"That's right, you did have him for your student, I believe you called him, your prize student?" Frederick waited for his brother to shake his head and smile. "And it was you who taught him about soldiering, to shoot, sword fight and ride a horse with style and daring acts." Frederick looked from teacher to student. "Zachary, my brother taught you also about women?" he asked somewhat worried.

"Mr. Forrest, I can assure you, your brother taught me only the best of what life has to offer. I would never do anything to hurt your daughter sir. I am in love with Autumn and you may rest assured I will respect her virtue and save myself for her until we are wed, and only show my love for her through my arms and my lips."

"Damn boy, you are brutally honest!" Nathan Bedford Forrest chuckled at his brother's dropped jaw. "Little brother, I have wished this boy could have been mine ever since he stepped into my world, and with that declaration, I'm not so sure he ain't!"

"I can understand the need for wanting to give my daughter a kiss, Zachary, and I am sure once you both have been courting for some time, a small kiss might prove harmless, but son..." Autumn reached up and gave her father a sweet kiss.

"Daddy, my dear daddy, you need not worry about me whenever I am with Zachary. I feel as safe with the man I love as much as I do in your loving arms." She gave him a bright smile. "I see nothing wrong with a kiss, when both of us desire it. It seems quite natural for a couple that is engaged to be married, not just meeting and courting."

"Then my darling girl, be sure that no one witnesses such a kiss or the wagging tongues will spread the gossip all over the south and your prefect reputation will be ruined.

"Not to worry sir, I would never do anything in the public eye to degrade my darling Autumn." Zachary noticed the guest were beginning to leave and saw his cousin Bradley headed his way. "I must be going soon." He felt Autumn grab his hand and look up, tears starting to fill her eyes. "I promise to visit Laurel Grove in the near future, if that is alright by you sir."

"It is perfectly alright by my father, Zachary." Her voice trembled. "Why must we always have to say goodbye, dearest Zachary?"

"I can assure you it will not be another seven years before I hold you again, my darling." Blocking out the interested party standing nearby, Zachary pulled his girl into his arms and whispered for her ears only. "I love you Autumn Rose."

Declaring her love in a whisper, she added, "I will love you forever, dearest Zachary."

"I shall see that father gives my cousin some off time to accompany me back to the balmy south with such fair southern ladies." Bradley had escorted Christina over with him to collect his cousin Zachary. He lifted her gloved hand for one last kiss. "I shall call on you again, dear Christina. Your cousin Drake has invited me back for the fall harvest festival. I hope I might be your escort to such a happy affair. Perhaps your cousin Autumn might attend and partner up with Zachary."

"I would like that very much, Christina, if you have room for one more." Autumn was aware that the fall festival, was a joyful celebration to commemorate the final harvested crops of the season, with elaborate celebrations throughout Natchez and surrounding plantations. Each year the celebration was held at a different place and the party host would send out invitations to neighbors and friends. Unbeknown by Autumn and Zachary, this year's host would be, the Belmont Plantation, owned by Clint Reynolds. Autumn's trust of family and friends, no matter how jealous they were of her, gave them her trust and family loyalty. On the other hand, Zachary was not as trusting where his cousin Bradley was concern and he had witnessed Christina's anger over his loving Autumn. He had guessed it was some kind of set up, but as long as he was with Autumn, Zachary knew he could protect her from what trap lay ahead.

"But of course, cousin Autumn Rose, you are more than welcome, darling." Christina smeared on her phony smile "We do love having you visit and always have such a gay time!"

"Thank you, Christina and please have Aunt Isabelle send my mother a message with the date and time." Autumn held tight to Zachary's hand, not wanting the moment to end, but knowing she would see him in a few short months helped the pain somewhat. Hearing everyone say their farewells, Autumn smiled up at the face she loved so dearly. "I promise to write dearest Zachary, and this time, you shall receive all my letters."

"You wrote me before, my love?" Zachary fought back his tears. "I never received a single letter. After five years, I just stopped looking."

"Mother! At nine, she refused to let me write you, then when I reached fourteen, I tried again and got as far as giving them to Willy Henry to mail with the other out-going mail he was delivering to the postal, then later I found out mother had been collecting all my letters from the head butler before he even left the house." Autumn looked at her beautiful mother telling other guest goodbye. "Willy would have helped me if mother had not threatened to demote his position to the fields."

"I would have loved to have read them, darling Autumn." Now it was Zachary who was looking at the woman that stood in their way, hoping they would forget one another. "I too wrote you letters. Autumn, but I am certain you never received my letters either."

"Had I received such a lovely gift, I would have already thanked you and told you about yours." Autumn heard Bradley call for Zachary. "Dearest Zachary, until we meet again, do not forget you are taking the very best of me with you, my love and my heart."

"And I leave mine with you, darling Autumn," Zachary felt Bradley's hand on his arm.

"Come along cousin, the servants have gathered our things from our rooms here and placed them on the carriage. We must leave for the hotel so these fine people can retire for the night." Bradley lifted Autumn's hand for a kiss goodbye. "Fare Autumn Rose, rest assured, you will see Zachary in the near future." He gave her a big smile. "I will personally see to it. Father lets me have my fun and he won't deny my request to bring Zachary with me."

"That is indeed reassuring Bradley. I hope you both have a safe journey to Massachusetts." With one last squeeze of her hand, Zachary forced himself away and looking back, walked out the door.

Autumn tearfully watched the door close behind them then rushed off to her bedchamber. Quietly entering the dimly lit room, Autumn noticed Nellie lay sleeping peacefully and dared not to awaken her, just to aid her in getting ready for bed. With care not to awaken her friend, she gathered her gown and slippers and walked quietly inside the dressing closet, carrying the single candle Nellie had left burning for her. Autumn knew she could not sleep anyway, thinking about Zachary and already missing him dreadfully. Stepping out of all her dancing garments, the sad girl draped them over the clothes stand and pulled the gown over her upswept hair and carried the candle to the dressing table and started taking down her hair. In her dream-like state she did not see the girl stepping up behind her to take the brush from her hand.

"Autumn Rose, you let me brush out your hair!" Nellie spoke softly, as not to wake anyone that may be sleeping. "You are late coming up girl, so you must be exhausted from all that dancing tonight." In the candlelight Nellie's eyes sparkled as she shook her head. "Now, how come you did not wake me up Autumn? Why, if Erline slept through your mama's changing, she would find herself working those cotton fields the next morning. Yes ma'am, right there beside mister Oscar, your daddy's groom, if'n he was sleeping instead of grooming!"

Autumn could not help herself from laughing at Nellie carrying on so. "I do declare Nellie, can you just one time to something that is good for yourself. I came in, all sad and sorrowful for having to tell Zachary goodbye again and saw you lying there, so peaceful, not a care in the world, so I did not have the heart to wake you from what looked like a beautiful dream." Autumn smiled up when Nellie grunted. "A man perhaps was among your dream?"

"Go on now, Miss Autumn, how come you think I was even having a dream?" Nellie blushed, remembering her very real dream about that plantation owner, Clint Reynolds and she dared not share that dream even with her best friend. "To be honest, I do not remember what I was dreaming about, but I can tell you, it wasn't no man, no sir re."

"Maybe not, in your dream Nellie, but when you came in the room where Christina and Polly Anne where, all excited about your good news about Zachary being here, you seemed overly flushed, the same way I get when I am around Zachary." Autumn turned around and took her hands. "Did something happen out it that hallway I should know dear friend?"

"Promise you won't tell a living soul, Autumn Rose. I could gets in big trouble if'n your folks found out what happen." Nellie looked nervous about telling her friend, but deep down, knew Autumn would believe she was innocent of what happened.

"Nellie, you know you can trust me with your secret. I can see whatever happened has got you upset, so maybe I can help." Autumn did not like anyone hurting her lifelong friend and she would take matters in her own hands to help Nellie if something did happen.

"I guess I might as well tell you if there's going to be any sleep for us tonight." Nellie took her friend's hand and led her to the small sofa next to the big bed. After sitting down, Nellie began to tell what had happened in the hallway.

"I was waiting for you out in the wide hallway so you could visit some with your cousins and was joined by Christina's personal maid, Ester Sue, where we talked about the big ball to be held downstairs. It wasn't long when Bertha Joyce, Polly Anne's maid, came out of the room all flustered and trying to catch her breath.

"Lordy me, that girl can't stand still and I swear she gets fatter every day!" she flopped down exhausted. "I pull and pull on them corset strings and she balers like a cow in labor!" Bertha Joyce pulled out a handkerchief to wipe the sweat off her face. "Now, your Miss

Autumn is so petite, I bet you get her tied up in no time a tall."

"I could say it takes me no time at all and mean every word of it." Nellie chuckled at their confused faces. "Miss Autumn does not wear a corset, ladies. She has got such a tiny waist and a shapely body to boot, my friend has the gift of natural beauty."

"Why, she is the prettiest little thing I have ever seen." Ester Sue lend against the wall with her eyes closed. "That precious girl is about the sweetest white person I have ever met."

"You are right there, Ester! Miss Autumn treats us like equals, always showering us with love and praise for our fine work, unlike Miss Polly Anne and Miss Christina, who throw orders around and expect us to obey, without so much as a thank you."

"Them spoiled girls say mean things about Miss Autumn too, causing they be jealous of her beauty." Bertha rose to her feet and stretched. "Why, if I knew I wouldn't get horse whipped by the master, I would tell those mama's babies what's what!"

"I'm with you sister, put those two complaining busybodies in their place." Ester joined her working companion. "We are off to help those charming sisters get ready for the big dance as soon as we go up to our room and roll back the covers for a long nap later, until the party is over."

"Aren't you afraid you might oversleep and get into trouble by not being at their beck-in-call when they return?" Nellie knew Autumn would not be mad with her for sleeping, but Christina and Polly Anne would demand punishment if they had to wait on themselves.

"We have that covered, but thank you for your concern over our welfare. It is obvious you know our ladies well." Ester Sue chuckled. "One of the servers at the party, comes up to wake us when the last waltz is being play. Master Stanley always announces the last waltz, a reminder that the party will soon be over."

"Then, you both enjoy your rest. I'm sure you are going to need it, what with getting Miss Christina and Miss Polly Anne ready for bed."

"We said our goodnights and I was just about to come fetch you so you could get ready yourself and perhaps save you from those jealous cousins of yours when everything took a change for the worse!"

"Please tell me Nellie! Did someone do something to hurt you, molest you, right out there in that empty hallway?" fire shot from her beautiful eyes. "Why, if any man ever hurt you, I would shoot him myself!"

Autumn could read her friend well and knew her mind was reliving what had taken place hours ago. "Who is it you're thinking about Nellie? Tell me!"

"Mr. Clint Reynolds, that's who my thoughts are about." Nellie looked far away in thought but quickly snapped out when Autumn jumped up, ready to do battle.

"I'll kill the bastard! Does that overly pompous jackass think he can just take any woman he desires without permission!" Autumn's small hand went into a tight fist. "The big flirt!"

"No, no Autumn Rose, you have it all wrong! Mr. Reynolds did not molest me, nor touch me inappropriate! The gallant man came to my rescue and saved me from Bradley Hastings advances toward me!" Nellie pulled Autumn back on the sofa before she went into another display of outrage.

"Just what did Bradley do to you, Nellie?" Autumn's eyebrow went up in anger, knowing Zachary's cousin was a big flirt and had the bad habit of touching girls in delicate places, like he had tried on her when she was just eight, when she slapped him away and swore if he touched her again, she would first push him in the big pond, then tell her Uncle Bedford. Knowing she meant business, he backed off and behaved. "Nellie, what happen?"

"Let me go back to when I was coming to get you. Just as I started to move, I heard Bradley's guestroom door come open. I knew it was his because earlier Miss Christina bragged about walking him up to the end room, just down the hall from her bedchamber." Nellie rolled her eyes up with discuss. "I started to leave when I heard Bradley speaking to someone in the room, then I heard him say,

"Hurry on down Zachary, I'll go get us some good seats to watch the stairs and then ask for a drink."

"Then I heard Zachary tell him he would be down shortly when Bradley mentioned the beautiful redhead with green eyes. Seeing him step out I quickly turned and started down the hall when Bradley grabbed my arm.

Earlier:

"Hold on there, pretty girl." Bradley turned Nellie around to face him "You're about the prettiest darky I have ever seen. Who do you belong to, honey?"

"I belong to no one, if you mean, who owns me! I am a free

woman, thanks to my missis!" Nellie tried to pull her arm free from Bradley's grip. "Please sir, let me be! I got to get my lady ready for her coming out ball! She is waiting for me, so let go!"

"I thought you said you were a free black! Are you lying to me, little darling?" Bradley ran his hand over her face. "Maybe I will just wait for my friend to leave our room and take you there so we can get to know one another better. I never had a dark skin woman next to me before." Bradley pulled her close to him. "Would you like that sweetheart?"

"No sir, Mr. Bradley, I would not!" Nellie fought against him, trying to free herself. "Please turn me loose now or my lady will come out here and give you what for!"

"Now, isn't that cute talk, what for." Bradley chuckled. "I am a guest here missy and I can take any servant I choose to my bed and I choose you!"

"You heard the young lady. Hastings! Get your Yankee hands off Miss Nellie now or I'll smash you in your pretty boy face!" Clint Reynolds had stepped from his room across the hall and noticed the commotion between Nellie and Bradley Hastings.

"Just stay out of this, Reynolds!" Bradley tried to sound tough although he was nervous about the man's threat to hit him in the face. "This has nothing to do with you!"

"That is where you are mistaken boy! You are mistreating this lady and she ask to be released so I had better see you backing away if you wish to keep those pearly whites that you like to flash to all the ladies!" Clint Reynolds took a step toward Zachary's cousin, causing him to let go and hold up his hands laughing.

"Who needs the darky anyway, when there is so many beautiful white ladies about to make my acquaintance." Bradley bowed slightly for Nellie. "Go about your servant duties, sweet Nell and dream about the one that got away." Bradley gave the plantation owner a cocky smile and dashed down the steps laughing.

Nellie closed her eyes, still shaken from the incident and whispered "Thank you sir. You are truly a fine gentleman."

"Will you be alright Nellie?" Clint ask with real concern, knowing how the young black women on his plantation reacted to white men's advances.

"Yes, thanks to you, Mr. Reynolds." Nellie finally opened her eyes where she had been reliving the event to her friend Autumn. "He just smiled and excused himself as he went down the stairs to join the other men."

"Well, maybe I have misjudged Clint Reynolds." Autumn hugged her dear friend. "As far as Bradley Hastings goes, we will make sure you are never alone with that man." She took Nellie by the hand and lifted her up. "Time for bed and if you dream about Clint Reynolds, I will let it pass this time." Autumn smiled as she stretched, finally feeling tired and sleepy. "I know you see him as your hero now Nellie, but remember, Mr. Reynolds has a thing for pretty women also, so I'll be watching. But for now, I hope to dream about those romantic kisses Zachary was giving me tonight."

"He found a place to give you a kiss?" Nellie yawned as she climbed under her sheets. "With all those people down there?"

"He found just the perfect place Nellie. Under the stars and we did not stop with one kiss." Autumn heard her friend breathing peacefully and knew she had fallen asleep. "Sleep well, my darling friend, as we both have our own prince charming to dream about." With those words, Autumn too drifted off into a peaceful sleep, filled with dreams of her Zachary.

Chapter 18

Time had seemed to drag by for Autumn Rose as she waited for fall to come so she could finally see Zachary again. In one short week she would be on her way to Natchez, to stay with her Aunt Isabelle and her cousins. Standing at her wardrobe, she pondered what she might take to wear, not knowing exactly what events were planned. Her cousin Christina had promised to send her a schedule of the four-day celebration and some ideals as to what to wear each day, but, just a week away before leaving, she had heard nothing.

"Boy, Miss Autumn, that mail sure does get slower coming, but Willy Henry just this minute came in from his trip to Charleston with all them supplies your mama sent him after. He made a stop by the postal clerk and praise the good Lord, that cousin of yours finally sent you this here letter." Nellie smiled at her friend's happy face as she snatched the envelope out of her hand. "Could you read it aloud so your friend here might know what to pack as well?"

"Gladly Nellie, if it is indeed from Cousin Christina and not Zachary." Autumn gave her friend a friendly wink. "Dearest Cousin, forgive my delay in getting this schedule out to you and what you might bring to wear for all the events relating to the festival. The first day is spent relaxing and getting acquainted with all those in attendance. Many are local people and will travel back and forth from their homes each day, during the festival. There are those who are fortunate to have an invitation to stay at the host's mansion for the entire festival, and lucky us are included. So, day one, just wear a lovely dress for daytime and a smarter looking dress for evening dining and cocktails." Autumn looked at Nellie's worried face. "Why the worried look, dear friend, already fretting that you haven't enough clothes for all the events?"

"Don't be silly Autumn, you know I won't be in attendance for any of those events." Nellie shook her long pigtails. "I shall be sitting upstairs with the other servants waiting to help you whenever you need help in changing."

"Not according to Christina." Autumn smiled when her friend moved over close to see the statement written about her as her best friend pointed at the next line. "My sweet cousin, I do hope your girl

Nellie has the proper attire to wear when she joins you for all the events. It would appear the host wishes for her to be a part of all the festivities. He is just the most caring man I have ever met." Autumn rolled her eyes up in discuss at her cousin's next statement. "Dear Christina is not as caring as our nice host as it would appear by her next statement. Please Nellie, do not take it personal. Why the selfish little snob feels the same way about me, when she is penning a letter to someone else. She says, Personally, I think a maid's place is in the servant quarters instead of pretending to be a southern belle like the two of us. Why, I would just be beside myself if that dear man asked me to have Ester Sue attend the festival with me. I can just say my prayers of thanks that it is your girl and not mine, standing there, looking completely out of place."

"I say you will fit right in with all us southern belles." Autumn reached over to give her friend a hug. "Why with your olive skin and long smooth hair, I swear you could pass as a southern belle, Nellie. You already speak with a charming draw, same as me. I shall help you with your wardrobe and make you ten times prettier than Miss Christina or Miss Polly Anne. What do you say…sister?"

Nellie looked at their reflection in the mirror and smiled. "What with that summer tan you got working in the garden and playing horseshoes with Big Ben, we do look a lot alike, you and me. You think it's true what most folks say about being around someone so long you tend to start looking and acting alike?"

"Now that you mention it Nellie, we do favor. It's true, my hair is red and yours is black, my eyes are green and your eyes are a beautiful brown with a hint of green, but our cheek bones are both high and our lips are very similar." Autumn was thoughtful for a moment, but decided to keep any suspicions to herself for the present until she did some thinking. Her eyes scanned over the words from her cousin and folded the letter. "I do believe you and I must go into Charleston and buy a few more suitable outfits for some of the events. I am certain mother will want to join us so I will check on it first thing in the morning."

"I could have made my dresses for the events had I got longer noticed from Christina." Nellie moved her hands nervously. "I do not think your mama will agree to buy us both outfits to wear. Maybe its best if I let you attend alone. That should please your cousin."

"We are not trying to please Christina, Nellie. Besides, the host has gracefully asked you to attend, so I think it's only right to do so."

Autumn stood up and walked to the door, then extended her hand for her friend. "If you are standing beside me when I ask mama, I feel sure she cannot refuse helping both us."

Just as Autumn predicted, Katherine Forrest agreed they both needed proper attire to wear for every event during the big celebration. The fact that the host had invited Nellie to join them had been one of Katherine's reasons for buying the girl an outfit for each day's activity, including a matching riding attire for the day of horseback riding.

"Nellie slipped the riding boots over her shapely leg and giggled. "Never in my born days did I dream I would own a pair of such fine boots." Her brown-green eyes fell on the riding derby as she reached for it and placed it a top her head. "I almost look like a southern belle for sure now, Autumn Rose."

"What do you mean, almost? Why Nellie Forrest, you are as much a southern belle as any one of those fancy dressed Mississippi ladies who will be in attendance at that plantation, wherever it is." Autumn smiled up at her mother who had been watching the girls try on their new outfits. "Mama, I just cannot for the life of me figure out why no one has mentioned our dear host's name. You wouldn't be knowing who he is, would you now?"

"I haven't the slightest ideal, darling." Katherine walked over to help Nellie fix her hat on correctly, then stood back admiring her striking beauty. "I swear Nellie, you will have all those eligible men's hearts just melting when they look at you."

"Thank you, mother for that true observation! I have been telling Nellie how beautiful she is, but up until today she refused to believe me." Autumn picked up her cousin's letter and tapped it lightly on her dresser, trying to reason with the big secret over their host. Then it suddenly dawned on the smart redhead. "Of course! I know exactly who this mysterious host is! It has to be him!"

"Darling, are you going to share your discovery with me and Nellie, or do you expect us to figure it out for ourselves?" Katherine walked over and took the tapping letter away from her daughter's hand. "Who is the mysterious host? Is it someone we know or perhaps met at your outing?"

"Yes Autumn, please tell us." Nellie took off the derby and twirled around, hoping it was her hero.

"Clint Reynolds!" Autumn stood up and looked down at Nellie

who had suddenly grown interested in the conversation. "I may be wrong, but from the wording of Christina's letter, I believe this is the first time our guest host has invited them to be his guest at the plantation's manor house during the festival." Her green eyes caught Nellie's big eyes. "Remember, in her letter she said those living nearby left for home and returned the following day. According to Mr. Reynolds his place was not far from Natchez."

"I suppose Mr. Reynolds has not given up on you yet, Autumn darling." Katherine absent minded rub her hand over Nellie's smooth hair while she thought. "You don't suppose Clint Reynolds has ask your cousin Drake to stay over with his two northern friends, Bradley and your Zachary, do you?"

"My guess would be no, mother. I do not think Clint Reynolds desires to compete with rivals in his own home." Autumn joined her quiet friend on the vanity bench. "But to answer your question mother, I am not sure if Clint has his eye still on me when it could certainly be another beautiful girl in our mist." She smiled over at her friend as her mother laughed softly and ask who could compete with Autumn Rose Forrest.

Nellie started shaking her head in a negative when Katherine stopped laughing and stared down at the blushing girl. "No ma'am, Mrs. Katherine, I would never compete with Autumn Rose. She is just teasing with you. She knows that wealthy plantation gentleman has no interest in the likes of me."

"Autumn, I know you would not claim something like this unless something happened the night of the ball I am not aware of." Katherine pulled up at chair in front of the two friends. "Would either of you care to fill me in on what took place to make you believe Mr. Reynolds has ideals about our Nellie?"

"Nellie, would you like to give mother a short version what happen right before the men went downstairs to wait on the ladies?" Autumn draped her arm around Nellie's smooth shoulders.

"When Autumn was visiting with her two cousins, I needed some fresh air, so I found a nice quiet chair in the large hallway. I was soon joined by Ester Sue and Bertha, the cousin's lady's maids. We chatted awhile, then they left and I was fixing to return back to fetch Autumn Rose, when I heard this here door open down the hall. Bradley Hastings was talking to his roommate, who turned out to be Zachary." Nellie grew nervous remembering what happen next. "Autumn's Zachary was not ready to go down, so that Bradley fellow came out and spotted me. He got a hold of me, ma'am, and I tried real hard to get away, but that man was too strong for me." Her eyes got big as she recalled the anger on the handsome plantation's owners face when he stepped up. "That's when Mr. Reynolds walked up and ordered the young man to let me go! He was…amazing!" "Nellie, did Mr. Reynolds show any interest in you as a woman, besides of course helping out a young lady in distress?" Katherine pondered the notion of this highly educated man being interest in this simple girl. "Did you, perhaps, overreact by hugging him or something physical?"

"Oh, no ma'am! I could never do anything so bold as to hug a complete stranger, no matter how grateful I felt." Nellie blushed, remembering how she felt when he touched her and their eyes locked for a few moments. "I told him how grateful I was for his help and answered his few questions, like who I worked for and my name."

"Then later, he insisted you be a part of all the events, my dear friend." Autumn stood up and stretched.

"I think good old Clint just might be that first eligible man you were speaking about earlier, mother. Why, the gallant southern gentleman just looked down into those alluring soft brown eyes of our Nellie, and his heart melted."

Nellie could still see him looking down at her and how it made her heart speed up. She tried to cover up her true feelings by laughing at her friend's outrageous statement, but still hoping in secret it was true. "Autumn Rose, you are too funny! That handsome gentleman has his eyes totally on you, my friend and he is still hoping for a chance to win you over."

"Then tell me, my adorable girlfriend, why did Clint Reynolds insist you be at each event? "Autumn held up her hand to stop her from answering. "Nellie, do not say it is because he wanted you to be there to help me. So, besides being there to help do your maid services, which you do by your own free will, because I am very capable of doing for myself, what other reason can you think of?"

"You know there is no reason for that fine white gentleman to be interested in a slave girl, Autumn?" Nellie looked down shyly. "I cannot possibly know his reason for inviting me to all the festivities."

"For starters Nellie Forrest, you are not a slave girl, so kindly stop referring to yourself as one!" Autumn touched her chin and lifted up her pretty face. "If Clint Reynolds is interested in you, then he will treat you like any southern belle and not someone he decides to have an affair with!"

"Autumn, you must not give Nellie any false hopes where Mr. Reynolds is concern." Katherine knew the situation would be torn apart by gossips if a white gentleman was seen courting a woman of color. "Our Nellie has a good reputation right now but if a romance were to blossom between these two, it could be devastating!"

Autumn had been looking at the color of her mother's hair next to her friends. The same shade of black, just like her father's hair. Autumn had taken her hair color after her grandmother Rose Chadwell, who had Irish blood. Could there be some kind of connection with Nellie and one of her parents. Autumn had heard how some plantation owners had affairs with their slaves, but she could never see her loving father doing anything like that, nor hurting Katherine. That would mean it had to be with Nora, but the loyal daughter just could not fandom anything remotely like that happing She glanced at her very proper mother and shook off any affairs Katherine could have committed, but why did Nellie look so much like her and have more white features than her older sisters, Florene or Elsa?

"Mama, I would never give Nellie false hopes, especially where love is concerned. My heart tells me if there is a way for everyone to be happy, then a new truth will arise to save this distressing situation!" Autumn thought she noticed her mother tremble from her words, so she added "Nellie deserves happiness, mother, just as much as you or me. If you can think of any reason that can assure her of this happiness, please let me know." Her attention fell on her friend's tears. "Please let both me and Nellie know."

Chapter 19

Big Ben drove the carriage up to the entrance of Chatham Hall Manion in Natchez, Mississippi and was instantly greeted by Autumn's Aunt Isabelle. She stood waiting on the big pillared porch, a welcoming smile stretched on her face as her footman helped both young ladies off the carriage before speaking with their driver.

"Autumn darling, it is so good to see you again. I do hope your journey here was uneventful, as there has been some reports of highwaymen along the roads between here and South Carolina."

"Nothing that Big Benjamin could not handle, auntie. "Autumn peered over her aunt's shoulder, expecting to see her two cousins but found the grand hall empty, except for them. "Christina sounded excited in her letter about us staying with our host, but failed to mention the dear man's name. Is there a big secret for keeping us in the dark?"

"Nothing for you to worry about Autumn darling." Isabelle waited for the footman to stop in front of her. "Jackson, please take these two boxes out and place them on the carriage. It is my gift to the owner of Belmont Plantation for having my daughters and my niece and servants stay at his lovely home during the festival." After Mr. Jackson took the parcels outside, Isabelle turned and smiled at the two young women. "Now, let's see, you were asking about the owner of Belmont. I think he wishes to surprise you both with a special welcome, so he has asked everyone living close by to arrive early. Christina and Polly Anne left for Belmont early this morning and that is why I've asked Jackson to inform your driver to take you straight-way there. I am truly sorry we could not visit a while longer, my dear, but I know your host is dying for you to arrive."

Autumn and Nellie followed Isabelle to the front door and stepped back outside where the beautiful redhead handed her aunt a box she had brought in. "Mother sent you some peach preserves she helped Cora put up. She remembered how much you loved them."

"Katherine is so thoughtful and never forgets what we enjoyed when growing up." Isabelle's attention was on Nellie when she climbed up into the carriage behind her friend. "Nellie dear, I swear you just keep getting prettier every time Autumn brings you here and your dress is quite stunning." She smiled over at her niece. "Autumn, you are most thoughtful to give Nellie your hand-me-downs so she can feel special too."

"My dear aunt, that dress on my dear friend is no hand-me-down, I assure you. Mama bought both of us new outfits to wear for this four-day festival." Autumn smiled at her aunt's dropped jaw.

"Well, why on earth did my dear sister get your slave girl so many new dresses when she will be just waiting with the other servants." Isabelle noticed Nellie watching her and listening to her hateful words. "Nothing against you personally, Nellie, but it will be a long time coming before I spend good money on a lot of outfits for slaves."

"Isabelle, for starters, Nellie is not a slave, she is as free as you or me. Second, mother got my friend clothes to wear because she was personally invited by our mysterious host, who I believe is Clint Reynolds, to attend all the events of the four-day festival!" Autumn heard the big black driver grunt, obviously irritated over the rich woman's lack of charity toward the black community.

"I have nothing against the black race child. I just feel they need to be kept in their place." Isabelle forced a faux smile up at the seven-foot driver, then smiled at the two women as they returned her smile with a real one. "Just have fun at the festival, my dears and please do not let on to Clint that you guessed his identity. Let him think it is one big surprise, alright Autumn darling?"

"Why Aunt Isabelle, no actress on stage could act that part any better than me and Nellie will." Autumn winked at her friend. "Dear Mr. Reynolds will be patting himself on the back and the only ones knowing we knew all along will be the three of us, me, Nellie, and big Ben!" the girls waved as Benjamin laughed and gave the horses his signal to move and they headed out of town toward Belmont Plantation.

"I done went and talked to Mr. Jackson back there, like you ask me to Miss Autumn." Ben gave a soft chuckle. "He more than happy to help a brother in knowing what is going on."

"So, he knew about Zachary?" Autumn had asked her big friend to see if he could find out any news on Zachary and his cousin, Bradley. She was certain her aunt would be no help concerning Zachary, due to the fact that Christina like him herself and informed her mother to say nothing.

"Oh, your sweetheart is here in Natchez, Miss Autumn, both he and that bad seed cousin of his." Benjamin looked over his shoulder as he drove the two horses out of town and onto a country road. "My brother Jackson says he is staying at your cousin Drake Chatham's plantation, about ten miles west of Mr. Clint's big spread. Jackson said he done went and heard that sassy Miss Christina bragging about those three gents coming later this evening 'cause Mr. Clint wants to spend some time with you before that hound comes around sniffing."

"Hound?" Autumn sat up, ready to defend her man. "Well, I'd rather be with the handsome hound than that rapid fox any day!"

"The way I hear it Miss Autumn, your cousin's place is not far out of our way, so if'n you ask me to go by there first on the way to Mr. Clint's place, I would be more than happy to oblige you." Ben looked around and gave her a big wink.

"What a lovely ideal Big Ben!" Autumn felt relieved to know she would be seeing Zachary first, maybe even persuade him to ride with them to Belmont Plantation. "Why, I just cannot remember the last time I was at cousin Drake's home. I bet Aunt Vera would love to see me after so many years have passed and the poor dear does not get out much herself. I dare say the sad reclus has never stepped beyond the gate of Willow Creek Plantation."

"Then I think that is the perfect reason to drop by there first, Autumn Rose." Nellie gave a soft chuckle. "And even though you have grown up since your last visit there some ten years ago, I just know she would remember you by that incredibly beautiful long red hair of yours. Wouldn't you agree Big Ben?"

"Yes indeed! I just bet your visit will help bring a smile on Miss Vera's lips and I just know it will bring one on Mister Zachary!" Benjamin gave a big toothy grin as he turned the horses down a narrow road. "We got just one mile down this here road to Willow Creek and you will be in that boy's arms before you know it."

"And just how do you know the way to cousin Drake's house, Ben?" Autumn ran her hand through her hair to get out the tangles. "It might have been ten years ago when I came here with my parents, but you were not driving the carriage, daddy was."

"No ma'am, Miss Autumn, you are correct about my not being with you then. I was needed on the plantation due to it being planting time and Mister Forrest up and made me the over seer, or grounds keeper as I's calls it, since he up and fired Mr. Tar for whipping Jamie Joe." Ben pointed to the massive gate ahead. "I learn the way here from my black brother, Miss Autumn. Jackson says he likes you cause you are good to all the servants, treat us real fine and he knows love when he sees it and watching the two of you at that ball, he could tell you loved one another real strong. Johnson could read the sadness in both your eyes when you had to say goodbye. He just wants you to be together again."

"I knew there was something about Mr. Jackson I liked." Autumn recalled the friendly waiter. "He had genuine love in his eyes every time he spoke to me. Remember Nellie, how he helped us when we arrived at Aunt Isabelle and Uncle Stanley's big house the weekend of the coming out party."

"I sure do, Autumn Rose. He insisted on carrying up our bags after telling two other footmen to assist your mama and daddy with their things and let Erline and Oscar fend for themselves." Nellie reflected back to how the head footman had taken them under his wing.

"I wonder if Clint Reynold's footman will be as polite and helpful when we arrive at Belmont?" Autumn felt butterflies invade her stomach when she spotted the big white porch and saw Zachary sitting in a big rocker having a drink with his cousin Bradley and her cousin Drake. "It's Zachary! How…do I look?"

"Beautiful as ever Miss Autumn!" Benjamin let out a chuckle when Zachary spotted the carriage and the girl in the back with the glorious red hair. Sitting the glass down on the small table next to him, the tall handsome man stood up and raced down the steps toward them. "From the looks of your man, Miss Autumn, I would say he thinks he has just spotted his angel!"

When the carriage came to a stop, Zachary was there, arms up to receive the woman he loved. Before she could take the first step down from the fancy carriage, Zachary had her lifted up into his arms and twirled her around laughing.

"Autumn, my beloved, I had thought I must wait until this evening's dinner before I could see you again! Yet, here you are and it is still morning!"

"My darling, when Big Ben informed me that you were staying at Willow Creek Plantation, the home of my relatives, I could not just pass it by! You are the reason I agreed to attend the Fall Festival in the first place." Autumn could not control the kisses between them for they had hungered for far too long. "Perhaps you have figured out the reason why your invitation was for dinner this evening, Zachary."

"I can now Autumn, what with you here early and obviously on your way to Belmont." Zachary felt everyone watching them, so he gently sat her down and took her hand. "The mysterious host wanted some alone time with my love, am I correct?"

"Very correct darling. I see your 'friends' have not told you who owns Belmont Plantation yet?" Autumn let Zachary lead her into the rose garden for some privacy.

"There was no need for them to Autumn." Zachary pulled her into his arms, longing to keep her right there forever. "I could tell something was up between our cousins, some kind of big secret so when your sweet aunt said she heard her niece was arriving in Natchez this morning, I put two and two together and came up with their scheme to keep us apart so Clint Reynolds could win you over from me."

"Mr. Reynolds is wasting his time if he thinks for one minute I will give him the time of day!" Autumn reached up to touch Zachary's face. "No one can or will ever replace you in my heart Zachary."

"Nor you in my heart, dearest Autumn." His blue eyes fell on her waiting lips. "I suppose our cousins were hoping you might be swayed by Reynold's wealth and his large plantation."

"Money could never buy my love Zachary. I have had everything I have always wanted, beautiful dresses, select jewelry, the finest horses, a grand manor house and servants to wait on me day and night, but I would quickly give all that up to be with you darling. You are all I want or need."

"I won't always be penniless Autumn. I will win back everything that was stolen from my father and when I have saved up enough money to put my plan into action, I can finally take care of you properly my darling." Zachary heard his cousin call them to the house. "Thank you for coming by to see me first Autumn. But for now, out of respect for our host, I will come when invited. I know I can trust the woman I love to see through any charming things Reynolds might try."

He took her hand and walked slowly to where the others were waiting. "I suppose you are right for waiting, although I would prefer you coming with me now." Autumn noticed her fragile aunt waiting on the porch and waved as she ran up the steps, Zachary right behind her.

"Aunt Vera, it is so good to see you up and about." Autumn went into the smiling woman's waiting arms.

"I cannot believe it has been ten long years since I saw you child. You were just a little thing." Vera had asked a servant to bring out small glasses of Madeira for her guest. "Drake tells me you are on your way to Mr. Reynold's Belmont Plantation dear, so I just wanted to share a toast with you and this fine fellow you seem to have fallen in love with before you leave."

"Thank you, Aunt Vera, that is very gracious of you." Autumn picked up a glass and handed it to Zachary, then another to her friend Nellie before getting her own glass. "Aunt Vera, you remember my friend Nellie, don't you? She was with us when we came for that visit with you."

"That little girl with the big brown eyes who clung to you like you were joined together?" Vera gave Nellie her own hug. "Having you two little girls here was one of my best memories." A hint of sadness showed on her sweet face. "It just about breaks my heart that you won't be staying here with me while you're visiting Mississippi."

"If you feel like having us a few days after the festival Aunt Vera, I could wire my parents and informed them I will be spending some time with my favorite aunt." Autumn felt Zachary's hand touch her shoulder as he slipped it around her. Perhaps, you might even have Zachary's room available for him if you feel like having company." Autumn heard Bradley clear his throat. "As well as dear Bradley. What fun could we possibly have without him and his witty jokes!"

"That's right, my dear Vera!" Bradley gave her a gentlemanly bow. "You know you have enjoyed my entertaining company, have you not madam?"

Vera chuckled, suddenly feeling happy to have a house full of young people to liven up her lonely days with her son Drake being away a good part of the time. "Praise the Lord! How could I not want such a fine group under my roof, making this old house come alive again! You all are invited to stay for as long as you like!" the grey hair lady set her glass down and hugged her niece tightly. "Thank you, Autumn, for making me feel needed again."

"I am just sorry it took me so long to come back, sweet Vera." Autumn gave her aunt another loving hug before getting back on the carriage. "We will return in four days and spend some time with you before we head back to Laurel Grove. I do wish you would consider making the trip to South Carolina with us, Aunt Vera, we would love to have you and Drake come for a nice long visit. I know mother would love having you."

"That sounds like a wonderful ideal mother!" Drake lit up, hoping his mother would finally go somewhere to get away. He felt sure it was what she needed to help her cope with the death of Walter, his father and her beloved husband of thirty years.

"Darling, there is the harvest to get in and the pounds of fruit and vegetables that will need canning for the winter season." Vera began to ring her hands, fretting the ideal of leaving her home where all her memories where. "You could not be away for long Drake, you have some kind of big meeting that will keep you away for at least a month. You told me so just last week! Someplace out of town, I cannot remember now where."

"Charleston, mother! That is why this is an answer to prayer. Autumn has given us a wonderful invitation to be with family. How many times have I heard you say, I would love to see my sister Katherine again?" Drake took his mother's hands. "Almost every day, mother! I can see your face light up when you recall childhood memories with her, how close you were, sharing secrets. Aunt Isabelle lives just a few miles away, but she has never one time paid us a visit, even when father died. Who was here, standing next to you, holding your hand at the graveyard? Katherine!" he looked at her pleadingly. "Please mother, you have grieved father long enough. It is time for you to start living again! Not for me, but for yourself!"

"Drake is right, Aunt Vera, your sister needs you just as much as you need her." Autumn lovingly touched her face. "I know mother worries about you, for I have heard her praying every morning asking the Lord to keep watch over you and make you happy again." Autumn watched Vera drop her head and she touched her hand. "Promise to think about it while we are at Belmont and please do not go through a lot of trouble for the three of us when we visit with you. I love you, my dear aunt."

Autumn started to leave when her aunt took her arm to stop her. "I do not need any time to think about your beautiful invitation, my dear, after how quickly you accepted mine and relit the flame inside my soul." Tears filled her eyes. "I have suffered enough grief and sorrow." Vera wiped her eyes and smiled. "Autumn darling, you have done what my loving son has tried to do for all these years, make me want to live again!" She wrapped Autumn in a bear-hug.

"God bless you, sweet child! Now get going before my neighbor sends out a search party for his prettiest two guest!" the suddenly spry woman ushered them down the steps, bringing out chuckles from the menfolk. "And as for not over doing my planned festivities when you return, I have four long days to plan! You two just have fun. Maybe I will see the fellows over a slight bit early." She winked at her niece.

"You do that, Aunt Vera, and I will take a peek at the seating arrangements for dinner and move a few cards around if needed." Autumn blew Zachary a kiss. "I am looking forward to dinner."

"I shall count the moments until we are together again, dearest Autumn." Zachary reached for her hand and kissed it before patting the horse's rear. "Get going now. Drive careful, Ben."

Chapter 20

"There it is Miss Autumn, the grand entrance to the Belmont Plantation!" Benjamin pulled the horses to a stop when the massive gates rose high in front of them. "Now, how come this Mister Reynolds has his gate closed, him a knowing your arrival?"

"Maybe Miss Christina or Polly Anne closed it behind them when they arrived, hoping the owner of Belmont wouldn't think we were coming and give up on us." Nellie looked disappointed as she frowned at the closed gate holding them back.

"Now Miss Autumn, if'n you want, I could get off and swing that big fancy gate open and take you on in." Ben had turned around to speak to his beautiful friend and owner's daughter when she patted his arm smiling.

"It appears that won't be necessary, Big Ben. I do believe our gallant owner has come to our aid."

Ben turned back around to see a man dressed in a white suit and matching wide brim hat was galloping toward them, accompanied by two black servants. Clint Reynolds' men jump from their mounts and opened back the heavy gates as the owner of Belmont removed his hat and swept it in front of him.

"Ladies, welcome to Belmont! I trust your trip was without troubles." A slight hint of concern was on his face as he added. "I was expecting you a couple of hours ago, according to your cousins."

"The trip from South Carolina was uneventful Clint, but if we are somewhat late, it is due to a short visit with my Aunt Vera, whom I had not seen for ten long years. I was only six at the time of that visit and my dear aunt truly enjoyed our dropping by to see her."

"Yes, my neighbor, Vera and her son Drake." Clint motioned down the long drive. "Please have your driver come behind me and my men will follow your carriage." He led the way down a long tree lined road until finally his big white mansion came into view. Autumn was used to the big houses, but Nellie looked on, eyes wide and her jaw slightly dropped.

"Autumn?" Nellie whispered, not wishing the owner to hear. "I know Laurel Grove is large, as is Chatham Hall and Willow Creek, but this is the biggest mansion I have ever seen!"

"That is because Mr. Reynolds inherited a substantial amount of wealth from his parents when they passed away." Autumn whispered in Nellie's ear. "He is a clever businessman and got his education at Harvard."

"Autumn, Nellie, what do you ladies think of my little home?" Clint gave them his handsome smile.as he nodded for the servant girl. "Drinks Glenda."

"I would hardly call your mansion little, Clint." Autumn took his hand when he helped her off the carriage, then assisted Nellie. "Nellie and I were just admiring its southern charm and elegance, wasn't we Nellie?"

"Yes, we were, Mr. Reynolds." Nellie felt butterflies swirling in her stomach when he smiled down at her. "I declare, it is the grandest home I have ever had the pleasure to see."

"That makes me very glad to hear that you like it Nellie." He touched her face, causing her to take a deep breath, "And please, call me Clint, my dear."

"Lordy me, Miss Nellie, you just gone and went high society. You just gone hobnobbing with the rich folks!" Big Benjamin chuckled when Nellie frowned up at him. "Yes, ma'am Miss Autumn, you best be keeping a close eye on that one!"

"Big Ben, why don't you make yourself useful and start unloading our bags before you stick your big foot in that big mouth of yours." Nellie pulled off a small parcel and handed it to the owner of Belmont, who listened with a smile, as the two went on. "Misses Isabelle sent you these things for having us, sir"

"Now, brush down those swan feathers little Nellie. Big Ben is just fooling with you girl." The big black man climbed down and started handing bags to the waiting servants, still laughing. "Be careful with them bags boys. Our little princess's crown might get damaged if'n you get too rough."

Autumn tried hard not to laugh as she patted the servant on his big arm. "Big Ben, have these fine gentlemen show you where to take the carriage and horses, then find your quarters and if you need anything, do not hesitate to ask for me."

"Thank you, Miss Autumn." Benjamin climbed his big frame back on the carriage and followed the two men on horseback down to the stables.

"My dear, you are very thoughtful to your darkies, perhaps a little too familiar." Clint led the girls on the long porch to three chairs. "Does your father know you treat them so friendly?"

"Why shouldn't I treat them friendly Clint. They are my friends as well as a big part of our family." Autumn smiled up at the serious maid as she held out a tray of mint julips. "Thank you, Glenda. This is exactly what I need after traveling all those miles from Charleston." The shy girl gave her a weak smile, feeling her master watching her closely.

"You are quite welcome Miss Autumn. It is a pleasure to finally meet you ma'am."

"Thank you for bringing out the drinks Glenda." Clint Reynolds took a big sip as he noticed the girl still standing in front of his guest, admiration on her face. "That's all Glenda. You may go back to your other duties."

The young servant jumped back and hurried into the house. Clint shook his head as he heard the front door shut.

"I truly am sorry for Glenda's behavior. Autumn. It would appear she is hypnotized by your beauty and grace."

"Or maybe Glenda felt there is someone white who actually respects her as a person instead of a mere slave." Autumn took a small sip of the strong drink. "I take it, this is your own recipe for mint julip, Clint. Your three-parts bourbon is a wee bit more."

"You have a smooth way of changing the subject my dear." The host glanced over at Nellie who was staring down at the fancy drink. "Why, Nellie, you have not even touched your julip, sweetheart. I promise it will not bite."

"I ain't, I mean, I haven't ever had but one small an alcoholic drink before, Mr. Clint. Mostly just mama's lemonade for special occasions." Nellie blushed, feeling completely out of place. "I guess I am just a mite afraid of how this pretty drink might affect me."

"Just do what I do Nellie and that little old drink will last all evening." Autumn gave her friend a big smile. "Remember now, if you get caught up with excitement, never start taking bigger sips and that includes your wine at dinner."

"My dear Autumn, you sound just like a mother hen, looking after her baby chick." Clint Reynolds laughed.

"That's right Clint, exactly like a mother hen guarding her young innocent chick from the sly fox!" Autumn stood up and stretched. "Where is everyone? I heard this place would be swarming with friends and neighbors this afternoon. Isn't this get acquainted day?"

"I just wanted some along time with my two-special guests so I sent the group around back in the rose garden where games are set up along with plenty of mint julips." Clint let his eyes wonder to her low-cut dress. Nellie sat up as she watched him admiring her friend. She felt a pain of envy as she spoke up.

"Mr. Clint, what sort of games are they playing, croquette, perhaps?"

"Christina and a few women are playing the game, yes, and please Nellie, drop the mister and just call me Clint." He lifted his glass in a toast and waited. Nellie glanced over at Autumn who lifted her glass to show her, so she did likewise. "To my two beautiful new friends. May these four days together prove prosperous."

"I am sure mine will Clint, knowing Zachary is coming." Autumn smiled down at his serious face. What other games are being played in the back? Perhaps we can join in."

"The men are playing horseshoes, the ladies, croquette." Clint stood up next to Autumn. "Looks like it's croquette for you, if you play the game."

"Are you kidding, croquette is a piece of cake, compared to horseshoes." Autumn's eyes twinkled with mischief. "I do hope the fellows have room for one more player."

The day quickly past and Autumn proved to be the best at horseshoes, even though it took some time to convince the group of players that she could even lift a heavy horseshoe, much less throw it the games distance. Excusing herself and Nellie so they could prepare themselves for the fancy dinner, Autumn and her friend walked in the quiet airy house laughing.

"Did you see the look on Clint's face when you actually approached those men to join them at horseshoes?" Nellie continued to chuckle, never knowing they had a quiet observer waiting just inside the large dining room. "Big Ben would really be proud with his prize student today!"

"Big Ben is the best at horseshoes and he did teach me everything he knows about the game." Autumn looked around to see if they were alone and nodded with her head to the open door leading into the dining room. "I promised Zachary I would check the seating arrangement for dinner and switch them to suit us." She laughed softly as she slipped inside the dining hall and found the big table set for, ten-guest. "Either someone cannot count or everyone in the garden won't be staying for dinner!"

129

"You are right Autumn. I counted fifteen of us out in the garden and Zachary, Bradley and Drake make eighteen." Nellie frowned. "You don't suppose…"

"That Mr. Reynolds is seating some of his guest in the smaller dining room?" Glenda, the shy maid, stepped from the shadows and gave a polite curtsy in front of the two well-dressed young women. "Begging your pardon Miss Autumn, Miss Nellie, for listening to your conversation, but I may be of some service to you." She gave a sly smile. "After all, you are our guest and must be treated with up-most respect, so you have a right to know why there is only ten table settings in the main dining hall."

"Let me take a guess Glenda." Autumn had been doing the count in her head and had concluded what Clint Reynolds' motives were. "There are exactly nine women present on the estate and Clint, our lovely host makes the tenth one to dine among us. The other eight gentlemen will dine together in the smaller room, to enjoy men talk about hunting, fishing, the talk of that dreaded war still raging in men's minds and how they are going to bravely join the new confederate army to fight for 'the cause'!"

"Yes ma'am. That is what Mr. Reynolds has done." Glenda rolled her big dark eyes toward the door to make sure her master hadn't slipped in and was listening. It would mean a whipping for her if he caught her, so she kept her voice down. "I's know you got a good heart, Miss Autumn, causing I heard black folks talk about it and then I sees it for myself!" Glenda felt good when she received a beautiful smile from the girl with hair the color of red maple leaves in the fall. "I be glad to help you if I can."

"Glenda, first, I would like to thank you for your kind words and to tell you Nellie or I do not expect you to bow for us. We are your friends and we genuinely love you for who you are, a child of the Almighty God and our Christian sister." Without hesitation, Autumn walked over and pulled Glenda into her arms as tears filled the girl's brown eyes. "Thank you for offering your help as well but if you can just point out the other room, Nellie and I can manage the swap. You mustn't get into trouble with your boss and we can handle our dear host."

Knowing the new table arrangements were more pleasing to Autumn, she had a radiant smile when she made her grand entrance, along with Nellie, down the wide staircase. Her smile grew even brighter when she saw who was waiting for her at the bottom.

Zachary had on all black, which seem to highlight his raven black long hair and his smile brought out his radiant white teeth, which obviously proved he never smoked. Lifting her hand in his, he gave it a long kiss as he spoke softly.

"If we were not standing in a room filled with interested people, I would have greeted my dearest Autumn with a passionate kiss."

"And that would have please me greatly, my darling Zachary." Autumn smiled down at his offered arm and took it smiling up into his alluring blue eyes. "Have you had a chance to check out the dinning arrangements yet?"

"I was told when I first arrived the gentlemen would be dinning in the adjacent dining hall, to assure everyone had plenty of room and that the men could openly speak without women's interruption." Zachary frowned at the thought. "Then overhearing the conversation, a sweet little maiden handing out before dinner drinks told me some beautiful redhead did not like the arrangements and took the liberty to change them." Zachary smiled and touched her soft red curls. "I must find this clever redhead and thank her properly."

"She will gladly except those exciting thanks, good sir." Autumn heard the clang of the dinner bell and watched husbands kiss their wives and started moving down the hall toward the other dining room following the other men. Clint Reynolds unaware of the change as well, stood talking to a group of women when Autumn and Zachary casually strolled by toward the main dining room.

Christina snickered, thinking her poor cousin wasn't aware of the seating arrangements and that poor Zachary would be marching back out disappointed and upset. After waiting a few minutes, she began to worry and punched Clint's arm.

"Christina is getting hungry ladies so shall we go into the dining Hall for dinner?" Clint caught Christina's eyebrow arch as she shook her head. "Darling girl, if you are not hungry, then what is your problem?"

"I just saw Autumn and Zachary go inside the main dining hall five minutes ago and he has not come out!"

"That cannot be good Clint! Maybe Zachary is waiting inside to let you have it, then take Autumn back to Aunt Vera's!" Polly Anne said dramatic. "You better call your bodyguard!"

"For heaven sakes, Polly Anne!" Clint narrowed his eyes. "I do not need a bodyguard to take down that poor young man! I will go in there and—" Clint stopped speaking when he saw the other seven men walking into the main dining hall. "Hey! What the devil is going on here?" The owner of Belmont moved swiftly down the hall and into the dining room, stopping short when he noticed the extensions had been placed on the massive table to accompany all the guest.

The women came in smiling and found their places as they looked up at the quiet host.

"Clint, darling, you did have us going there for a minute, making us believe we could not celebrate this marvelous meal with our men." Mrs. Stephenson said gracefully. "You are such a darling man."

"Yes, he is Dorothy, darling and thoughtful!" a relative visiting from New York City gave Clint a wink. "Now I know why the family thinks so highly of you, Cousin Clint. For a southerner, you are very considerate."

"Well, dear friends, I do not know if I should be getting all the credit for the latest table arrangements, but should I know who helped make this evening a success, I would thank them." Clint's attention fell on the smiling redhead and his eyes locked with hers as he said, "To have this person forever by my side might prove a very prosperous move."

"With the looks of this overwhelming change Clint, my guess is that it took more than one intelligent person." Autumn felt Zachary squeeze her hand gently under the table. "They did know which couples went together and who was single. It would also appear they were brilliant for placing you in between two beautiful single ladies, Christina and Nellie. Would you not agree Mr. Reynolds?"

Clint looked across the table and noticed the empty seat between the two women, who had turned around to face him as he walked over and took his seat. "This seat is perfect Autumn. I could not have placed myself at a better spot." Looking directly in front of him, the happy host gave the beautiful redhead his grateful nod as he rang the silver bell for the servers to bring the first course.

Chapter 21

The four-day festival went by quickly with so many activities packed in such a short period of time. Clint Reynolds had tried to find some alone time with Autumn, but she was intent on spending every waking moment with Zachary, so the gallant southerner turned his attention on Nellie and before long, they were enjoying each other's company. This led Autumn to stay close by to be sure Mr. Reynolds would remain a gentleman with her best friend, and to her delight he had been.

At long last the carriages were heading out, guest promising to return to Natchez and whomever decided to be the next year's host for the Fall Festival. Autumn's group was among the last to depart due to Nellie's reluctance to leave the man she had fallen in love with.

"Why did the time fly by so swiftly, Autumn?" she asked with unhappy tears in her brownish-green eyes. "Why does love have to hurt so bad when you have to say goodbye?"

"It is because your heart is not complete without that one special person Nellie. I know! I have had to say goodbye to my Zachary far too many times and I long for the day we can be together forever." Autumn gave her best friend an understanding hug. "Cheer up, my friend. Aunt Vera is just a few miles down the road and I just bet your Mr. Reynolds will want to pay you a visit before we return to South Carolina."

"Oh, Autumn, do you think Clint could really love me the same as I do him?" Nellie looked hopeful. "Do you think he suspects I am a darkie same as Glenda?"

"Nellie, I would not be sharing that information with Clint right now." Autumn watched the subject of their conversation glance their way as he bid his friends goodbye. "I feel certain you are not anything like that sweet Glenda and I believe you have felt it too. I think there is more, white in you than there is African and I will not rest until I find out what secret my mama is hiding!" she dropped the subject when Zachary stepped up and hugged her. "I see you're packed and ready to head back to Willow Creek."

"I am." Zachary looked over at Nellie who could not pull her eyes off their host. "Sweetheart, Nellie is in love with Clint, isn't she?"

"Nellie is head over heels in love with that man, darling." Autumn followed her friend's attention. "I just wonder how Clint feels about Nellie. I will not allow that man or any man to hurt her!"

"If it makes you feel better, Clint did ask Drake if he could call on Nellie while she stayed with them." Zachary enjoyed Autumn's smile.

"That does make me feel better and if he does not say something to Nellie about it, would you tell her darling." Autumn reached up and gave him a kiss. "Coming from you would mean a lot."

Zachary noticed the rich man heading their way and whispered "We shall soon find out what his intentions are darling. Clint is coming our way."

"I see you are all packed up and ready for your visit with your family." Clint handed Benjamin a shiny new horseshoe. "This is for your next game with your student. You will learn she beat the pants off six grown men in horseshoe on her first day here. Nellie told me you taught her all about the game."

"Yes sir, that I did!" Big Ben gave a toothy grin. "Why, that little gal up and beat her teacher just a few weeks back! Yes, that one is a quick learner."

"Clint, I guess it will seem quiet around here now that everyone is leaving." Autumn gave him a gracious smile. "Or, perhaps you will be happy for a little time to yourself."

"Not necessarily, Autumn." His attention fell on the quiet young woman watching him with her big brownish-green eyes. "I will miss one very pretty young lady and those long walks we had in the rose garden."

"I shall miss those beautiful walks as well Clint." Nellie's heart was fluttering with love. "More than you know."

"Sweet girl, I pretty much know." He reached for her hand. "Nellie, would it be alright if I came to see you while you are at Willow Creek? I cannot let you simply step out of my life now that I have finally found you."

"Nor I yours Clint. I would love to have you visit me, every day of my life if I could manage it." Nellie smiled, feeling relieved over his feelings for her. "I fear the miles may keep us a part but you shall never be completely away from me, for my constant thoughts will be of you."

"I travel often to Charleston Nellie, so perhaps I can visit you at Laurel Grove if you cannot make it to Charleston." Clint did not care if he had an audience watching them, he had to plan ahead.

"I am sure Mr. Frederick will approve your visit." Nellie looked hopeful at her friend. "Wouldn't he Autumn?"

"We would love for you to visit Nellie, Clint. Just drop us a telegram when to expect you." Autumn still did not exactly trust this latest situation, but she did not wish to upset Nellie. "In the meantime, we look forward to your visit at Aunt Vera's." Zachary helped Autumn up on the carriage and waited for Clint to give Nellie a hug before lifting her up. He climbed in next to his love.

"Thank you for your hospitality Clint and allowing me to attend, even if I put a damper on your plans with my woman!" Zachary reached out his hand and Clint laughed and shook it. "You still got your leading lady Clint. Nellie is a great girl so treat her right."

"You do not need to worry about that Zachary. I know when to give up on one dream and follow another." Clint lifted his hat politely to the ladies. "I shall see you tomorrow evening for dinner. Drake said he would inform his mother of my visit. Until then, good day ladies, Zachary."

Benjamin pulled the horses away from the massive mansion and made his way back to Willow Creek.

Chapter 22

Autumn had instantly noticed the change in her Aunt Vera and she thought the happier version looked a lot younger than the sad, stay at home recuse she had become after her husband had died. Autumn wondered how she would react if anything happened to her Zachary. She had no doubts that she would mourn for him for the rest of her life and even if she found another partner, no one could ever replace Zachary in her heart.

As promised, Aunt Vera had kept the small group busy from the moment they stepped off the carriage. A small luncheon had been set up in the flower garden, then horseback riding before dinner. The following evening after a day of fishing on the lake, Nellie took special care to look her absolute best for Clint Reynolds, who would be arriving any moment.

"Oh Autumn, I am as nervous as a cat in a lot filled with hound dogs!" Nellie checked her reflection after her friend helped her fix her long dark hair in cascading curls. "Why, I really do look like you now, Autumn Rose, except your hair is red! Do you think Clint will think I am pretty?"

"I think Mr. Clint Reynolds is in for a night of admiring his beautiful date instead of filling up his belly with Aunt Vera's big ham roast." Autumn gave her friend a big hug. "Do not forget to sip all those drinks that go with dinner, Nellie. We would not want Mr. Reynolds to take advantage of your innocence if you got tipsy. Do you understand what I mean?"

"Yes ma'am, Miss Autumn!" Nellie withdrew to her old self when she got nervous, even if it was just a possibility something might happen, but not necessary a given. "You are worried that he might try and lay with me?"

"We just do not want to take any chances Nellie." Autumn took her hand. "I believe Clint Reynolds is a real gentleman and he would never take advantage of an inexperience young lady like you." Nellie smiled when her friend frowned at the door, knowing an angry statement was coming next. "And if Mr. Reynolds knows what's good for him, he will NEVER force himself on you, EVER!"

"Why, Nellie Forrest, you are about the prettiest young lady I have ever seen!" Bradley stopped his bragging about catching the biggest fish, when Nellie walked down the stairs, then Autumn came out and followed behind her friend. "And, of course Autumn Rose can never be replaced in the beautiful column!"

Zachary pushed his cousin to one side as he assisted Autumn down the last step. "I must, at long last, agree with my cousin Bradley. You ladies look adorable tonight and I am sure Clint will agree once Vera stops greeting her long-loss neighbor."

"Did I hear someone speak my name?" Clint came through the parlor doors and stopped short when he spotted the two southern ladies, looking almost like twins. "Never have I seen a prettier pair of angels." He walked over and lifted Nellie's hand to kiss. "My dear, just when I think you cannot get any fairer, you appear like a vision."

"I thank you sir." Nellie laughed softly. "I never knew Autumn could fix hair as well as I until I looked in the looking glass at my reflection." She patted the silky curls. "Do you like it Clint?"

"I find both your hairstyles very striking." He turned and offered his arm "May I escort you to the dining hall my dear. Mrs. Chatham announced dinner as soon as everyone is seated."

Everyone had found their places and the food had been served. Small talk drifted around the table and everyone stopped to hear what Clint was going to ask their hostess when he said her name.

"Vera, I have been wondering for sometime why your name has never changed from Vera Chatham to Vera Chatham." The rich plantation man gave her a handsome smile. "It seems unusual to have two different Chatham families living in one area."

"My late husband was my second cousin, Clint." Being the gracious hostess, Vera gave him a lovely smile, understanding why this sounded confusing. "Cousin Dooly, that was my nickname for him, and I, his little Rosebud, were always sweet on each other growing up and never outgrew our love for one another, so our parents blessed us with their approval and we got married."

"Falling in love with a childhood sweetheart can grow into the most beautiful relationship two people will find, Aunt Vera." Autumn felt Zachary take her hand under the table. "We were not exactly cousins, but we both loved and admired Uncle Bedford."

"We knew the moment we looked at each other, God had brought us together and our love just blossomed between us." Zachary and Autumn hadn't taken their eyes off each other as they spoke. "Our hearts beat as one and when we are apart, my heart remains behind with my one and only love and I take hers inside me until we can at last be together again."

"That is so beautiful Zachary, Autumn." Vera touched her chest, feeling her one love near her. "I pray that the two of you can be together for far more years than me and my Dooly."

"I hope we can have that same closeness sweet Nellie." Clint lifted his glass toward their kind hostess. "Vera, may your sorrows be replaced with beautiful memories and may you live the remainder of your life with the gift of friends, like me, and family, like your loving niece, Autumn Rose."

"Why, thank you, Clint. What a lovely thing to say." She rang for dessert. "I intend to do just that! Starting with my visit to Laurel Grove to see my devoted sister Katherine."

Leaving those we love is never easy, but knowing Aunt Vera would be paying them a visit sooner than she had planned due to her good neighbor, Clint Reynolds offering to take her in the spring, the following year, 1861, Autumn Rose could at lease hold back her tears when she said her farewells. Clint Reynolds had been a frequent guest after the dinner party, so he was on hand to say his goodbyes, and this time planned to kiss Nellie before watching her drive away again.

Zachary and Bradley had also packed their things, and waited for the girls to hug their sweet hostess goodbye. Vera pulled them to one side to offer some wisdom and advice after witnessing Nellie's attachment to a white man.

"Girls, you know how very much I love you both and I am only saying these words in hopes of saving Nellie from getting hurt. I have watched you and Clint get closer to one another and I fear you are falling in love with a man you could never have."

"Is it because I am the daughter of a slave woman, Misses Vera?" Tears started forming in Nellie's eyes.

"Aunt Vera, I know you mean well and I too never wish to see Nellie hurt, but I feel there may be some hope for their love." Autumn drew close to her aunt. "Do you know the secret of why Nellie is almost as white as me and why we could almost pass as twins, except for our eyes and hair?"

"I promised your mama I would never tell her story she told me in secret." Vera glanced over at the men, still waiting for the ladies to finish their conversation. "You will have to ask your mama child.

I gave her my promise and I will take it with me to my grave."

"Then, I will not ask you to divulge her secret, Aunt Vera, but can you at least tell us if there could be some hope for her happiness?" Autumn looked hopeful. "Is there anything, please, just tell us that much?"

"There might be some hope for Nellie if what your mama told me was 100% accurate." Vera gave them one last hug, afraid the men would start wondering what they were discussing and require about it. "I pray it will be what you need child." The loving woman touched Nellie's face. "I shall see you both in the spring. Now, go say goodbye to those loved-ones."

Autumn had her arms around the man she loved, not wanting to let him go and knowing his Uncle Horus needed him to return to his job for a big horse show coming up, the Massachusetts' state champion for 1860.

"I have no doubt your uncle's horse will win the competition and your man you have been referring to as our new president will finally become just that in November's election!" Autumn waved her hand around as if writing in toward the sky. "The 16th president of these United States, Abraham Lincoln!"

"And may he remain our president, once elected, for two terms and hopefully put an end to the rebellion down here in the south and the hateful talk up north about killing a few rebels!"

"I can assure you my friends, Abraham Lincoln is not the right choice for our president if we hold this dwindling country together!" Clint Reynolds had been telling Nellie goodbye with a long kiss when he overheard the conversation between Autumn and Zachary. "We need the candidate who believes in state's rights above government-controlled rights!" he gathered Nellie's hand in his and made his way beside them. "Cooler heads prevailed the last time Beauregard had order guns placed on the battery and the island fort across the Cooper River. They were aimed at Fort Sumter in the Charleston Harbor and the strike was called off at the last moment. Now Jefferson Davis is being voted in to be the president of the southern states and the guns have been ordered to be replaced on both points and will be set to fire very soon, unless someone in Washington writes an amendment for States to have their own rights which will enable state government to make their own rules."

"My fertile prayer is that our men of Christian brotherhood can work these problems out with constant prayer to the Almighty God!"

Autumn never understood why men always kept things stirred up and couldn't just abide by the rules of their elected congressmen. Did not each state's male citizens vote in their choice to represent their state in Washington, to bring up their request concerning commerce?

"My dearest, I believe the poor farmers are led to believe State rights are under attack by the federal government when the main purpose for the land holders' decision is they are afraid of government interfering with their slave trade." Zachary looked out at the Chatham's few slaves toiling in the hot fall sun. "I believe slavery is wrong Autumn, but I know you think so too and would personally free every man, woman and child if you could. Since visiting the south, I know most all plantation owners are genuinely good to the slaves and many are freeing them daily, like your father and you, dear one." Zachary could feel Clint and the Chatham's watching him closely as he spoke so he guarded his words carefully. "I am also aware the north once had their own slave population and when they no longer needed free labor, they made money by selling their slaves through the south's slave market making them just as misled by their ancestors as you southerners."

"And their ancestors were misled by the English who brought the first slaves over in the first place and like your northern hypocrites the British hypocrites call our slavery deplorable!" Clint arched his eyebrow, irritated that slavery had been brought up as a reason for breaking away from the union. "I can assure you Zachary, slavery is not Mississippi's reason for choosing to break away from the union, nor would I dare say any southern states reason!" the plantation owner's voice grew tense. "We merely wish to have control over our own states and there is nothing more but that!"

"You have to admit Mr. Reynolds there is some plantation owners who are worried about men in Washington and up north talking about abolishing slavery." Bradley had listened all he could and he had to speak up. "Many fear they have been multiplying so fast it would be up to working men to keep them up if we didn't send them back to their home land. Can you imagine the slums growing in every town!"

"Send those dear men, women, and children back across those dangerous seas to Africa where the same greedy black slave dealers chased down their ancestors in the first place and will recapture them to sale to other trade markets?" Autumn could not hold back her anger. These were her family he was casually speaking about and it

140

cut her to the core. Watching the solemn look fall on the usual jolly face of her big friend, Benjamin and the tears forming in Nellie's sad eyes, Autumn's hands flew to her hips. "Can you not for one time have a little compassion for someone who has less than you do, Bradley Hastings! These dear people have the same feelings, the same dreams, the same hopes for a better tomorrow, as you or I! The families living today only know America as their homeland! They have never been to Africa, they were born here in America, THE HOME OF THE FREE!"

Zachary took Autumn's hand and led her a few steps away from the group. "Sweetheart, you must not let my overbearing cousin upset you dearest. I shall be sad to leave with you so hurt and troubled about all this talk of war and Bradley's bad mouthing your black family. I respect your compassion for them and like you, I too pray for their freedom, but I also believe that someone who is free should be able to choose whether they stay or go." Zachary gently touched her lips when she started to disagree with him. "Autumn, each person has his or her rights to decide what's best for them. If they ask for guidance then by all means, give them good advice, but if they should choose to follow their own heart and wish to return to their homeland, then it should be up to all of us to send them safely to their homeland and into a safer door." He lifted his finger to find her beautiful smile. Pulling her up into his arms, he kissed her with loving passion.

"My darling Zachary is as wise as he is handsome and fantastic at kissing." She laughed softly when he moved his eyebrows up and down. "I shall miss you dreadfully my love. Not knowing when we shall meet again is breaking my heart into."

"I fear war is closer than we had hoped darling Autumn." Zachary pulled her into a tight embrace, dreading having to step away from the one thing in life in loved beyond words. "It may be difficult to travel if the north and south are fighting against each other. Right now, no one considers me a Yankee but when that war breaks out, any one from the north will be viewed as the enemy, weather they are loyal to the south or not."

"Dearest Zachary, I would die if I put your life in danger by wanting to see you again! If I could perhaps come up North to be with you instead." She buried her face in his white shirt, breathing in his handsome scent so she would remember it.

"You must never come north after the war has started, dear Autumn. That precious little southern accent of yours would alert the northern spies and they could catch us before I got you safely away." Zachary pulled away to look into her beautiful green eyes. "Darling, if one of us must risk our being together, let it be me. With my skills on horseback I can easily escape any advancing Rebels."

"Perhaps it would be best to be apart as long as this hateful war is raging, but I will continue to pray for an early end so we can be together as soon as it is safe." Autumn looked up at him with the one unanswered question neither had wanted to bring up, but she must know where the one she gave her heart to stood when it came to fighting and choosing sides. "Zachary, answer me honest, if you must fight in this war, will you join the Union and fight us?"

"Autumn, my dearest love, could I ever draw my sword against the woman I love most? Could I lift up my rifle against my southern brothers I have grown to love? Could I do battle against the one man I admire and love." He ran his fingers over her lips. "Not for all the metals in the army! I will never raise my sword against the south, Autumn Rose Forrest, so help me God!"

Autumn was smiling through tears when Bradley walked up and spoke softly. "I would not be speaking these words around your fellow workman once we get home, dear cousin. They might get offended and think to turn you in as a southern sympathizer! It could prove dangerous for you, even the family."

"Cousin, I know who I can trust and those men I cannot." Zachary felt Bradley's hand on his arm and looked down at his gripping fingers. "I won't be long Bradley, just get on the carriage and wait!" he watched his cousin walk over and climb on the fancy carriage before taking Autumn into his arms for one last kiss. "This kiss will have to last us for some time, I fear. I will wait until I find safe travel, then rush to Laurel Grove to be in your arms again, dearest Autumn." He kissed her with passion, needing more but excepting the wonderful gift that was theirs alone. "I shall see you soon, my love. If not for spring, then hopefully fall, but most certain at Christmas!"

"Then if spring and fall should pass without your presence, surely the season of the Christ child's birth, I will find you at my door!" Autumn held him tightly, "I need no other presents, dearest Zachary, just you and your wonderful love!"

Through her tears, the beautiful girl with the flaming red hair and the alluring green eyes, watched her Zachary disappear down the long drive from Willow Creek Plantation and without anymore words, Autumn climbed up on their carriage and headed for home.

Chapter 23

Charleston: April 12, 1861 The Mills Hotel

The Mills was crowded with spring travelers and the Forrest family had drove into the big town early for brunch before going to the courthouse to sign the final papers for each slave's freedom at Laurel Grove. Autumn was in high spirits and feeling overjoyed that at last her mother and father had finally took the hard step to go up against the other local plantation owners and decide to free every single slave they owned. They had offered them the choice of leaving or staying on as hired help, owning their own home and plot of land. All but three slaves decided staying with the family that showed them love and respect was their easy choice. The family had planned a big celebration for the next day. A big bar-b-q would be set up in the rose garden and a day with absolutely no working, except of course milking the cows, feeding the livestock and chickens, plus gathering eggs.

Nellie and Autumn were chatting away about how the table would be decorated. Nora and Cora had out done themselves with all the pies and cakes they were making and Big Ben would get up earlier than usual to start roasting the pork for the bar-b-q. Their talk was interrupted when everyone grew excited about a very distinguish man walking in wearing a General's uniform, with white hair and a beard. There were other officers with him, but the only one Autumn recognized was, P G T Beauregard. Autumn bent toward her father and whispered, "Daddy, who is that handsome man in the highly decorated uniform?"

"That, my dear, is one of our military heroes who has fought in many American wars." Frederick Forrest gazed over at the general with admiration "I heard the north wanted him as their number one general but his loyalty to his state, Virginia made him decline their generous offer. I hear he was President Lincoln's first choice but now President Davis has stuck our best man doing office work for him instead of putting him in charge of the Confederate Army."

"Then that is Robert E. Lee?" Autumn sat up for a better look. "He looks so much older than I had pictured, yet he is still a very handsome man."

"Yes, he is darling." Katherine sipped on her coffee as she admired the man sitting straight in his chair, speaking softly to the gentlemen around the table. Her attention fell on the tall man with his back to them. "That gentleman sitting with General Lee, he seems so familiar, yet different in the uniform." She glanced back at the girls. "I do believe it was someone attending the ball in Natchez. Do either of you recognize him?"

Nellie had watched the group of officers walk in and had felt something familiar with the man trailing the rest. It was true he was in a completely different outfit from what she was use to seeing him in, but those brown curls on the back of his head were the same ones she had ran her fingers through as they had made love after everyone else had gone to sleep. As she watched him casually having coffee while listening to the men around him, her mind drifted back to Belmont Plantation and the night before they had to leave for Willow Creek.

Nellie and Autumn had gone up to bed early due to departing the next morning and had chatted a while about the days events before blowing out the candles. Listening and counting the doors closing by other guest and the house growing silent, Nellie slipped from her bed and out the door, where the moonlight reflected through the big windows at each end of the great hallway. Clint had told her his room was the one on the west end and the door would be left unlocked for her. Hearing his door opening, Nellie jumped next to the wall and hid herself in the shadows as she watched the servant girl Glenda come from Clint's room carrying a tray in one hand and a candle in the other and slipped down the back stairs. Nellie closed her eyes, hoping she was doing the right thing, then slipped back out and moved quickly down to the master bedchamber.

Knowing the door would be unlock, Nellie opened it slowly and stepped inside. Her hand went to her chest as she took in the romantic room lined with flickering candles, a bottle of champagne waiting with two glasses and a yellow rose, her favorite, lying on one of the pillows. She closed her eyes slowly when she felt Clint slipped his arms around her from behind and whispered in her ear.

"Does my Nellie like what I have done for the girl I adore?"

"Clint, this is the most wonderful surprise I have ever received." Nellie answered breathlessly. "And a yellow rose, how did you know that was my favorite and where did you get it this time of year?"

"So many questions, my darling. I found out by asking your best

144

friend and I grow them in my green house, the one place I did not show you." His voice came soft and romantic in her ear, causing her to grow warm. "You look lovely and very tempting in your soft white nightgown, sweet Nellie."

"And I am sure you must look as handsome and tempting in your..." she turned around and covered her eyes with her hands as her face blushed a bright red.

"My, birthday suit." Clint laughed softly as he touched her face and brushed her hands away from her eyes. "My girl blushes! Is this the first naked man you have seen darling?"

"No man has ever touched me Clint, except for a fatherly hug or innocent kiss." She tried to focus on his face, but her eyes kept straying to his perfect manly features. "You are the first."

"And do you like what you see, my beautiful Nellie or are you disappointed in the male body?" Clint let his fingers play along her buttons, then slowly he began to undo them.

"I am very satisfied with what I see standing before me Clint, because I have you in my heart." Nellie stood still as he unfastened the last button. "I just hope you will be please with my body, darling."

"My Nellie, I already am. With or without your clothes fair one, my heart beats the same for you." He took a hold of her gown and lifted it over her head and smiled down at her laced-up undergarments. "Why do woman insist on wearing so many clothes, even at bedtime?"

"It is the proper thing to do for a lady, Clint." Nellie laughed softly as he began undoing all the strings. "I think you are enjoying your task of undressing me, darling."

"Making love is just so much better when both partners are in their birthday suits, little darling." His hands finally encircled her breast as his lips melted over hers in a fiery kiss. He easily lifted her into his strong arms and carried her to the bed, never taking his lips away from hers. He stopped and looked down into her eyes, love swelling in his heart for this unusual girl. "Nellie, I will be gentle my love. All you need to do is just enjoy our moments together." She felt Clint take her virginity but it felt right for Nellie because she had never loved anyone like she did Clint Reynolds.

"Nellie, did you hear what I said?" Autumn rose punched her arm bringing her out of her beautiful memories. "You looked like you were a million miles away. I ask if you recognize that man with his back to us. He does seem familiar, like mother said."

"That was what I was just trying to figure out and then it hit me why we did not recognize Clint Reynolds. He is in a uniform instead of his white suit and matching white hat." Nellie smiled.

"Of course, that's who he is." Autumn titled her head. "I never would have thought Clint would enlist in the Confederate Army. Who will watch after his big plantation for him?"

"I am certain Mr. Reynolds has hired someone to oversee his plantation while he is away." Katherine shook her head, never understanding why men wanted to fight other men. "I guess he did not see us sitting here, for I am sure he would have acknowledged us when he past our table."

"Those men are discussing a matter of grave importance, dear." Frederick reached over and patted his wife's hand. "I am sure the young man has more serious things on his mind right now than noticing the casual dinners."

"I was in hope Clint would bring Vera with him, like he promised." Autumn noticed her friend's eyes drop sadly. "Perhaps he did bring her and hasn't had the opportunity to bring her out to Laurel Grove."

Nellie looked up, new hope lighting her eyes. "Yes, I just bet he will. Clint is a man of his word and I for one trust him."

"Nellie, you seem very familiar with Mr. Reynolds." Katherine sat up and looked back at the man they were discussing. "Is there something I need to know?"

"No mama, Nellie was referring to Clint's gentlemanly manners and genuine care for all his guest at the festival." Autumn took Nellie's hand under the table knowing the real reason her friend defended this man, she was in love with him. "Mr. Reynolds ask everyone there to call him Clint, so we all went on first name basis, nothing more to it."

Nellie watched the men rising from their meeting and sit up, wondering if Clint would look her way. To her happy surprise, Clint was left at the table to pay the bill, so when he got up to leave his eyes fell on Nellie. A big smile spread across his handsome face as he made his way over to the interested party. Stopping next to Nellie, Clint casually place a hand on her shoulder as he nodded respectfully to the older couple watching.

"What a lovely surprise to find my favorite family here in Charleston. I was hoping to pay you a visit later this evening and bring your dear sister, Mrs. Forrest." His hand continued to rest on the young woman's shoulder as though he was familiar with her and the happy smile on Nellie's face reflected his own.

"Vera is here, in Charleston?" Katherine looked around the crowded room, in hopes of seeing her. "Why did she not come with you for breakfast, Mr. Reynolds?"

"The dear lady was thoroughly exhausted after our long trip from Mississippi and after arriving late last evening, I let her sleep in this morning." Noticing Katherine and Frederick's attention was on his affection toward their Nellie, Clint pulled his hand down and gripped his hat with both hands. "I had an early morning meeting with some of the leaders, so I hired someone to sit with her until she roused, then give her some breakfast."

"That is most thoughtful Mr. Reynolds." Autumn felt Nellie nervously take her hand and squeeze it. "Would you like us to wait on Vera and take her back with us, then you may surely come later, when it is more convenient?"

Any other time I would take you up on your offer Autumn, but due to the situation, I think it is better if you finish your reasons for coming to Charleston quickly and leave for Laurel Grove as soon as possible." Clint had a very serious expression on his face as he continued. "After I have carried out my orders here, I will not be far behind with Vera."

"Son, you fear this might be the day Beauregard fires on Fort Sumter, don't you?" Frederick had seen the faces of the officers as they spoke softly, obviously planning something big. "He threatened before and changed his mind. Perhaps cooler heads will prevail and recognize the foolishness behind this attack."

"I hate to be the one to disappoint you Mr. Forrest, but foolish or not, Fort Sumter will be fired on this day at 4:00 sharp!" Clint kept his voice down as not to cause a panic. "My orders are to inform business's and hotel's such as the Mills here, to warn their staff and guest of the attack and to assure them all will be safe if they avoid the battery along the Ashley River and the island across the Cooper." Clint noticed their shocked faces, hearing the rumors but now the reality of it actually happening. "My men will spread out over the residents and warn them to remain inside their homes until the firing ceases."

"Clint, promise me you will be gone when the firing starts!" Nellie grabbed his hand, to upset to worry about the Forrest's, until she felt their sudden stares. "I mean, poor sweet Vera must be on her way to Laurel grove before the firing starts. You will have to take the Ashley River bridge to get there and I am sure the army will close the bridge long before 4:00!"

"Not to worry, pretty Nellie. I promise to have your Aunt Vera far away from the Charleston Harbor before the firing begins." Clint gently touched her soft face. "You are sweet to worry about dear Vera."

"And you Too Clint! You have become such a dear friend to us." Nellie turned nervously to her friend. "Right Autumn?"

"Absolutely!" Autumn reached over and patted his arm. "The world would never be the same without our fine friend from Belmont Plantation."

Clint gave both girls a knowing smile as he bowed. "I must be about my duties now. Time is ticking, my friends, and I urge you to get your business done quickly and leave Charleston while you can get out."

"Then, you will have time to carry out your orders and get Vera out of here before they shut down the exits, Mr. Reynolds?" Frederick pulled out his watch to check the time, 10:00 a.m. "We should be done by twelve. Will that give us long enough to wait for Vera and get out?"

"I am telling you sir, just get you and these ladies out as close to 12:00 as possible!" Clint looked down into Nellie's eyes. "I will see to it Vera and I will get out safely! Even if they shut the exits for civilians, I am a high-ranking officer and I will be permitted through. I will be long gone when the big guns start firing, this I promise you." With that, Clint Reynolds made his way up to the desk clerk to begin his warnings.

Chapter 24

Zachary got the news he had feared was coming. The Confederate's had fired on Fort Sumter, and guns firing from both the Charleston Harbor Battery and the old fort across the Cooper River, overtook Anderson and his men stationed at Fort Sumter. The Civil War had begun!

Staying busy with his uncle's horses, Zachary had planned to avoid joining the army until the day a soldier showed up at his uncle's big mansion looking for the young Calvary cadet from West Point that won soldier of the year.

"Zachary, there's a carrier here to see you. He said headquarters requested for you to come into the enlistment office to meet with a General George McClellan, Monday morning, 9:00." Bradley had walked in the stable where Zachary was grooming one of the prize stallions. His cocky cousin nodded toward the door with his head. "You're not going to join, are you Zac? It would dismiss what you told that pretty little gal of yours, besides, father might not take kindly to his main trainer going off to war right now. The business has picked up since the United States Army needs iron for weapons and we are known for the best!" Bradley got up close to his cousin as he watched him call one of the helpers to take over. "Look Zachary, we need every man here! We might have to put you in the mill too! That will mean a lot more money!"

"Out of respect to General McClellan, I need to keep that appointment, Bradley." Zachary stepped past his cousin to meet with the young carrier and gave him a salute. "You have orders for me soldier?"

"Yes sir, Mr. Dawson!" the young soldier looked with admiration at the tall man with the long black hair and incredible blue eyes. "It is a pleasure to finally meet you sir. You are a legend at the Point! The cadets who witness you win that best soldier award last year still cannot get over how you managed those hard maneuvers while riding that big stallion!"

"I had a great teacher, young fellow." Zachary knew he wasn't but a year older, but the young man seemed so intrigued by his fancy skills, he took the admiration with a smile, watching the soldier hold tight to the papers. Zachary held out his hand. "May I have those papers now?"

"Yes sir!" the soldier removed his hat before passing the papers to the man in black. "I will wait for you outside sir. I am to take you directly to headquarters. We should arrive early Monday morning."

"Very good son." Zachary smiled at Bradley's arched brow. "What's your name boy?"

"Randy, sir! Randy Sharp from Ohio!" he answered proudly. "I heard they want to put you in charge of a Calvary unit, starting you out as a senior lieutenant under General George Custer, who requested you for the position."

"Good old George! He said he hoped I would be under him!" Zachary laughed. "Well, I admit, he does deserve top billing since he actually graduated from West Point and I did not even finish my freshman year there."

"Too bad old Custer, whoever that pudding soldier is, will have to find himself another senior officer!" Bradley chuckled as the young carrier looked from Zachary to the outspoken cousin. "Do not look so dismal young man. There is a man around every corner waiting to put on the uniform and fight for our country. Just not Zachary. If he wishes to keep his position here, he cannot go off to war with the south, not that he would if he could."

"But, I do not understand?" the young man looked upset as he rung his hat with both hands.

"Randy, just take me to see General McClellan." Zachary patted the boy's back. "Give me a few minutes to pack a few things and saddle my horse." Without another word, Zachary walked swiftly to his living quarters to prepare for his trip to Washington.

At nine sharp, Zachary was standing in front of the general. "Zachary Dawson, reporting for an interview sir."

McClellan looked up from his papers and noticed the tall handsome man for the first time. He slipped from his leather-bound chair to shake hands, then motioned to the chair in front of him. "So, you are Cadet Dawson, the young soldier with magical skills unmatched by any other cadet from West Point." The general smiled as he pulled Zachary's record from his stack. "Straight A student, both in class and on the field with only one merit for your length of stay." George looked up from reading. "What did you do Dawson, to get that single merit?"

"I had missed the mail going out due to guard duty sir, so I made a quick trip to town to mail off my letter and to pick up the one they took back with them." Zachary continued to remain serious. "I was not on duty sir at the time and was not gone for more than one hour. Twenty-five minutes both ways, with only ten for waiting in line."

"Those letters must have been very important to you, young man, to risk getting your first merit." The general watched the young man closely, as he asked. "The letters, were they worth your penalty?"

"The one I went after was sir." Zachary did not always receive many letters from Laurel Grove until Nellie started writing him, telling him how much Autumn loved him and wrote him a letter every day. He could only assume her mother or father had stopped them from going out and now he knew after Autumn informed him they had been stopped by Katherine Forrest. "I would have walked to Hell sir to get all those other letters I missed!"

"I see. So, you had a girl back home?" George lifted up a frame and turned it around for Zachary to see. "Son, we all had to leave our girl back home. I know it is never easy to be a soldier, to be away for days unknown, worst yet, to be gone forever. War is not pretty, fun or gallant fighting like knights in some fairytale." George looked over serious. "War is like hell Zachary, it's a waste of time to make it sound less than it is." The general, lend back in his chair. "How soon can you join us Dawson? Custer spoke highly of you as does your record! You sir, are a leader, and we need good leaders! What do you say?"

"To be asked by such a distinguish general as yourself is an honor sir, but I cannot join the army, sir." Zachary did not blink as he watched General McClellan get up and walked around his desk. "I am sorry to disappoint you sir, but I do have my reasons for not fighting."

"Dawson, it was brought to my attention that you are a southern sympathizer. Is this true?"

"I do have friends in the south sir, many of which I have known since I was ten-years-old." Zachary showed no sign of being afraid, he was merely admitting the truth.

"This woman, whose letters you would go to hell for, is she a southern?" George crossed his arms.

"She is very much a southern lady, General McClellan. The prettiest, the smartest, and the best competitor I have ever been up against!" Zachary could vision Autumn's face in his mind. "Besides,

I have a job I am invested in. I am very sorry to disappoint you, but I must decline your offer sir,"

"The president is just calling for volunteers now Dawson, so I cannot make you join. Should the day arrive when President Lincoln demands a draft, you will be made to join Dawson and you might not receive such a high position, should that happen." The general showed a little disapproval with the smart man's decision. "You may look in on your cousin before you leave Dawson. It would appear Reid Dawson is a little more loyal to his country than you seem to be!"

"I'm sorry you feel that way sir." Zachary put on his black hat. "I do not wish to see our nation break apart any more than you sir, but I also do not wish to see my southern friends suffer because our government, cannot come to terms over state rights verses government rules! If the government would have just taken the time to listen to Southern states side without trying to push legislative ideals on them as law, we would have no need of soldiers to fight our southern brothers and Fort Sumter would not have been fired on in the first place!"

"Like it or not Dawson, what's done is done, and the south did fire on the fort, killing northern soldiers, some of which you probably called your classmates at West Point!" McClellan walked back behind his desk. "Visit your cousin Dawson, then leave, go back to your safe job! Just see to it that you do not go south! Do you understand that order?"

"I understand, sir!" Zachary suddenly had a distaste for this arrogant man in the crisp new uniform and wondered if he even had the guts to fight a war." I shall leave then!"

"You are excuse, Dawson!" George McClellan did not even look up for Zachary's salute, so he dropped his hand, smiled and walked out the door, never looking back at the man who was now staring at his back.

"Where can I find Captain Dawson?" Zachary had gone out on the practice field to find his cousin before leaving Washington. "I was told he was out here drilling his men."

"Captain Dawson, you got a visitor sir!" The young soldier called out and Reid turned around to see his tall cousin standing up on a small hill.

"Zachary!" he waved proudly and dashed up the embankment to

where his cousin stood smiling at the man dressed in a captain's uniform. "I heard you would be coming in this morning! You are looking sharp as ever, cousin!"

"I see you got promoted to captain, great position, and the war has just started." The cousins hug one another as Zachary laughed. "I guess it paid off to be taught at West Point."

"I hear McClellan is giving you senior Lieutenant under George Custer! Dang cousin, that's a heck of a jump for a freshman dropout!" Reid slapped Zachary as he picked with him. "Personally, I think you should have been Custer's general, man of the year!"

"That's real cute, Captain Dawson, a leader and a clown!" Zachary laughed, then grew serious. "Reid, do you know who told McClellan I was a friend of the south? Someone has been spying on me and I need to weed out the traitor!"

"I may be wrong, but that young carrier I saw bringing you in this morning, went inside while the general's guards were drilling you with questions, and he had what looked like a letter in his hand." Reid drew close as not to be heard by passing soldiers. "I couldn't approach you then, not when you were just outside the general's office. I was hoping to see you before you got fitted in your high-ranking uniform."

"Reid, I won't be enlisting in the army. This is one war I must sat out, for Autumn's sake! Her family, Bedford Forrest, and all my other southern acquaintances!" Zachary looked around at all the soldiers, picking with one another or playing cards. "Those innocent boys have no idea what they will be facing in a few days. Being a soldier is not as glamorous as we thought when small boys, playing with sticks for our guns and swords. War is killing another human being or getting killed or wounded and losing a leg or even both!" Zachary took a tight hold on his cousin. "Promise me, you will not take any stupid chances, Reid! I won't be there to save your butt!"

"Zachary, I can understand your reason for not wanting to fight and I respect you for it, but if there's a draft, dang man, they could put you up front out of spite!" Reid started to worry about his best friend. "If once you hear Lincoln has declare the draft, I think you may be safer to leave and go south, to Autumn, or better yet, Bedford Forrest! I know he would not see you as a traitor or a spy. He would hide you."

"You're right Reid, I could never stay up north and I would never put Autumn or her family in any danger." Zachary looked around again, trying to spot Randy Sharp. "Bedford would be my only hope. No one would expect me to be hiding at Crooked Creek. I'll find that kid and ask him who gave him that letter to give General McClellan, then I will guard my words and plans around them. It had to be someone at Uncle Hastings estate, and I will not rule out Cousin Bradley!"

Zachary had kept a close eye out for anyone capable of writing that letter to McClellan and decided not to put his trust in any man at his uncle's estate except Simon Hutchens, the big freed slave that was over the steel mill. Since the horse competitions were past and with Zachary' expert grooming and training, every single horse Horus Hastings entered into local contest, won first place, including the grand prize at the Massachusetts State Fair. With the horses put out to pasture until next season, Zachary's uncle placed his young nephew in the iron works mill and within days, Simon Hutchens saw his potential and advanced him to overseer. The mill workers liked their new boss and it showed in production. Unlike the previous overseer, who ordered everyone having lunch over fifteen minutes, they must work an extra thirty minutes to make up the lost time.

Finding the mill workers dragging around on their jobs due to lack of rest, Zachary gave each man thirty minutes for lunch and released them at seven p.m. instead of nine. Before his uncle could complain about the shorter hours with the same pay, Horus noticed the production picking up and within a week, the mill was putting out twice as much iron.

With summer came the overwhelming heat that the hot furnaces produced and the chance of an explosion was always in the mill workers minds, so Zachary and Simon paid close attention to any cracks or signs of heat damage building on either of the two massive burners.

Zachary was on the factory floor checking out the heavy steel moving steadily off the belt when one of the workers ran up, excited, eyes wide in terror, his face masked with black soot. "Sir, I think we got trouble on boiler one! I bent down for an armload of wood to stoke the fire when a large puff of smoke blew out on me!"

"Tag, show me the crack quickly!" Zachary ran behind the anxious worker as he yelled to the other wood stokers. "Boys, stop feeding that blaze! Grab the water buckets and put out this fire now!" Drawing the mill workers attention, every man began running to the rain barrels filling up large buckets to dash on the blazing fire.

Within seconds the blaze started dying down as the mill's manager ran out of his office to see what all the excitement was all about. "My God, Dawson, I just checked that old furnace this morning! How in God's name did I miss a crack that size?"

"It's not hard Simon, with furnaces this old!" Zachary shook his head in discuss. "I warned Uncle Horus that these old furnaces were getting too dangerous, but the greedy bastard refused to let me order new ones to replace them." Zachary turned to shout orders at the workers. "Boys, start putting burner B down and take a rest! I am going up to see my uncle and insist we order new furnaces at once before his mill goes under and he loses all the Union Army's contracts!"

"Zachary, it should be my job to ask the big boss about ordering new burners, but I agree this time with your going." Simon listened to the strange sound on the factory floor. The sound of complete silence. "After the men have took a break from that sweaty work, I'll have them start cleaning up the mill floor and empty the old furnaces."

"That's good Simon, then maybe I can weld the cracks so we can used them until we get our new ones." Zachary spoke as he washed the mill dust off him so he would be permitted into the owner's office.

"You can weld too Zachary?" Simon smiled at last, shaking his head in admiration over this young man's many talents. "Can you tell me first, what talent can you do the best, Zachary?"

"Without a doubt, I am certain my very best and favorite talent will be making love to my Autumn, the young lady who stole my heart when I was ten-years-old." Zachary winked at his new friend and headed for the main office.

Before Zachary drew nearer to the brick office building, he noticed the big fancy black carriage sitting out front, flanked by six soldiers, three for each side, sent here to protect whoever had came in the grand carriage. Taking a deep breath, Zachary continued to the front door and was stopped by another soldier, standing guard just outside.

"I am afraid you cannot disturb Mr. Hastings at this time. He has a most important visitor from Washington, here to check on the iron works production as well as the quality of the iron." The soldier glanced up at the handsome man waiting, then down to the factory from whence he came. "The big noise we heard coming from the mill moments before seems to have died away. Is there a purpose for the stillness? Break time, perhaps?"

"There is a reason for the stillness sir, but I can assure you my men are not resting!" Zachary would not bulge until he spoke with his ungrateful uncle and he knew he could not wait all day. He did not have the luxury of waiting when there was a contract to be filled. "Is the gentleman inside the office speaking the head of defense?"

"The gentleman inside is much higher than just a cabinet member, young man. He happens to be the president of the United States, Mr. Abraham Lincoln!" the officer stopped and watched the tall gallant looking man starring at the office. "Did you say Mr. Hastings is your uncle, boy?"

"That's right, Zachary Dawson!" he looked back with serious concern. "I could stand here all day in respect to President Lincoln if my reason for seeing Horus Hastings wasn't so darn important! We just shut down both our furnaces before they exploded and took half this town with them, including our president!"

"I guess we would have all went out with a bang then!" Abe Lincoln had raised the window in time to catch Zachary's statement after hearing him introduce himself to the guard. "Sargent Lamb, send that young man in here at once so Hastings and I can hear what he has come to say about exploding burners!"

Zachary walked through the open door straight to his uncle's office and looked over at the man he admired so deeply. Uncle Horus tried to keep his voice calm, but Zachary knew it was only for the president's benefit

"Zachary, why on earth are the burners shut down? Are you trying to make me look like an idiot in front of President Lincoln, son?"

"I do not need to do that when you are capable of doing it to yourself, sir." Zachary heard Lincoln chuckle. "I just thought it best not to burn down your business sir when it could be saved by replacing the old worn out furnaces with new ones, not to mention saving your life and everyone inside and outside this office."

The owner turned red as he tried to cover up the obvious truth his bright nephew was describing. "Forgive me President Lincoln, sir. My dear nephew can over exaggerate the facts when it comes to making life simpler for mere mill workers. They should feel grateful that I give them employment with fair wages."

"Fair now uncle, since Simon and I decided they could use a raise after the production load increased on them." Zachary could since Lincoln's attention was on him as he continued. "As for my over exaggerating, I believe large cracks billowing out huge puffs of smoke indicate danger and it is just a matter of time, something would have to blow. Forgive me if I decided to save the mill, order new furnaces, weld the old ones to use until we receive our order, then melt the old burners for even more steel."

"Well said, Zachary Dawson! By welding the old burners, production can resume, then just taking a few minutes to replace with the new ones, production will go twice as fast and this mill will be cranking out steel faster than before!" Lincoln declared. "Hastings, you better hang on to this young boy before I snatch him away to Washington as my aid." Lincoln stood up and smiled to find the young man the same height. "If I may have a word with you son before I leave for Washington?"

"It would an honor sir." Zachary gave the commander a soldier's salute "I will go make the order for new burners and be just inside the mill, welding the cracks safely shut."

"I will not be long, I promise. I am a man of my word." Lincoln sat back down as the interesting man walked toward the door.

"I have heard stories about your honesty sir, walking miles back to town to pay a store clerk one penny he handed you by mistake." Zachary smiled. "Most men would have just put it away in their pocket and counted themselves lucky for the man's mistake."

"But not you, young Zachary Dawson, like me, you would have returned it too." Lincoln looked down and chuckled. "Isn't it funny how people tell the same story so many times its completely different than the actual happening. I never turned right back around and went that great distance back to Butcher's store to return a single penny he overpaid me. I counted my change that night as I have grown accustomed to doing every night before changing into my sleep gown and found I had a penny extra. I did take it back, a week later when I returned to get staples, such as sugar and coffee, for Mary."

Zachary smiled at the cheerful man. "You are right about me Mr. President, I could never keep what doesn't belong to me, but the things that belong to me, I will guard with my life and challenge any man who tries to take them away from me."

"Especially his charming southern belle, Autumn Rose." Bradley had been waiting outside the door to see the president and felt the most important man in America, the president of the United States, was making over his cousin far too much for his liking. The jealous rich son never considered the fact that he could get his cousin in a lot of trouble with the government. Bradley's father had sent word to him with his office secretary informing his son of President Lincoln's surprise visit. Now Horus was having second thoughts about his son being in the same room with this remarkable nephew, who could do almost anything, while his playboy son only knew how to spend money, not make it."

"That's right cousin Bradley, that girl has my heart so you best stay clear of her." Zachary turned and stormed out the door.

"Bradley Hastings?" Abraham Lincoln sized him up. "Now I know why your name is so familiar. It was you who sent us that message about the young man, informing us of his ties to the south." Lincoln ignored the owner of Hastings iron works mumbling his son's name in a question. "I don't suppose you were hoping we would arrest young Dawson for treason because he had friends from the south. I grant you young Bradley, most everyone has known people on both sides, including me and Mary. You better be thankful your cousin was not sitting in some military prison when that crack was discovered in that furnace young man or you would have found yourself in line explaining to Saint Peter why you threw your innocent cousin in the lion's den."

"Bradley, just go on back to the house, boy!" Horus stepped over in front of his cocky son and escorted him from the room. "We'll have a little talk when I return home!" he whispered in his face. "I had better never hear you have gone behind my back and done anything as remotely stupid as that again! Like it or not, Zachary has turned things around here and we are getting more out of our workers than ever before and we have finally caught up on our orders, despite the temporary shut down!" Mr. Hastings called his secretary over. "Be sure Bradley gets home and see that he remains there!"

Zachary had just finished welding the last crack when the same soldier who was standing guard outside the office building stepped up to him and waited for him to order the fires restarted and work to commence until quitting time. Without a word, the soldier ushered Zachary outside, where the carriage sat waiting, inside, the tall man with the stovetop hat perched above his big ears.

"President Lincoln has requested an audience with you Dawson." Sargent Lamb opened the black door and stepped aside after checking the young man for any weapon.

"I am sorry about the body search, Zachary, but my security guards are super careful when it comes to my welfare." Lincoln crossed his long legs. "I was just forming a letter to General McClellan. I think you had the misfortune to meet up with the man, correct?"

"Yes sir, I did go in for a requested interview, but I do not think the general was very happy with my decision not to join the army." Zachary understood now why he had always admired this simple man. He was not only smart in politics, but he was a man of compassion and wit. "I feel certain if you ever call for a draft and that man is still in charge, he will try to make my life a living hell, sir."

"I cannot argue with you there, son, the general sometimes acts as though he outranks me." The president's eyes twinkled with mischief. "I have written the great general because he has been sitting firm, waiting for more troops, more weapons and cannons because he swears the enemy has more men. The truth is, McClellan can teach an army to fight but he does not have the slightness ideal how to lead an army to battle." Lincoln's long fingers waved the letter he had just written. "I simply told the great McClellan, if you are not going to use your army, may I borrow it for a while?" Lincoln chuckled.

Zachary laughed out at the obvious question. Lincoln was letting the cowardly general know to start fighting or step down. "I am sure General McClellan will not find it as funny as we do sir. He'll, no doubt, have some unpleasant words to say about you, sir."

"Tell me young man, if you had not such a good reason for saying no to joining our army, what sort of action would you take if you had McClellan's place?" the president had heard many things about this good soldier and he had hoped he might convince him to change his mind and join.

"First of all, to be in the general's position, I would have had to finish all four years at the academy, but let's say I did and I had trained the army and sent out scouts to find out the real size of the enemy's army, then without hesitation, I would carry out an attack that I had planned carefully to the last detail."

"Zachary, you are meant to be a soldier and you would be a darn good soldier! It would appear by what I have heard about the young freshman cadet who won the soldier of the year award last year and was given a passing certificate for your complete first year, even though you still had half the year to go, that you could easily be promoted to general of the army." Abraham Lincoln would never push this young man into joining if his heart was really dead set against it, but at least he would try. "Hear me out Zachary before you answer. I feel this war is going to drag on for many months, even years. Our southern brothers are strong and determine men, especially when they are fighting for a cause. Right now, it started due to state rights, but my heart tells me before we see an end to this dreadful war, it will turn to slavery." Lincoln leaned forward. "We need good men Zachary, like you. Men who are brave and not afraid to fight for what they believe in. I know you are against slavery, other men in bondage and in a nation of free men." The president sat back, eyes gentle and understanding. "You gave me time to speak, now It's your time."

"President Lincoln, I appreciate everything you have said and I could not agree more with you about fighting for what one believes in, but I made a promise that cannot be broken, sir."

"It's that little southern belle who stole your heart, Autumn Rose, I believe." Lincoln's eyes remained tender and understanding.

"Sir, have you ever loved someone so much you feel like only half a man whenever you are apart?" Zachary closed his eyes and saw Autumn's beautiful face. "Whenever I leave her side, my heart remains behind with her. She is the very breath I take and I long for her night and day. I made her a promise that I would never raise my sword against the south and if it should mean losing my life over it, I will never break my promise to the woman I love most in this world."

"Then I will not hold anything against your choice son." The president laid his hand on Zachary's knee. "Love is a powerful thing and when God brings two people together, such as you and Autumn, nothing can come between it. I guess I'm not as good at keeping promises as you, Zachary."

"I'm sorry sir, I don't understand what promise you are referring to." Zachary hated to hurt this man, but he knew Abraham Lincoln felt his sincere reason for refusing to join the Union Army.

"I also promised the woman I love something, a long time back, but my Mary never lets me forget I broke that promise when I decided to run for president in the Republican party." Abe scratched his head after removing the tall hat. "I sincerely pray that I do not have to issue the draft Zachary. Right now, loyal northerners are joining by the thousands, but if the ones not yet to join, find the war harder to except due to soldiers dying on the battle fields or returning with limbs missing, then I would have no other choice but order the draft." The tall thin man moved over next to Zachary, who had been taking in every word silently. "Son, unless you find a way to get away, there's not much I can do for you. Do you know of any way that I might help you should you get brought in to join or go to prison, if hanging is not their choice?"

"President Lincoln, should I hear of a draft being posted, I am smart enough to know that the enlistment department will start with last names that began with A, then B and so down the alphabet. I would not have much time to escape the north since my name is Dawson. I would be near the top of the D list." Zachary leaned in and spoke softly, not wanting anyone outside the carriage to hear what he was about to ask the most important man in Washington, D.C. "Sir, if I came to see you for help, would it be against you conscious to help me?"

"Son, I believe in you and everything you have confessed to me, even knowing that I have the authority to have you arrested for siding with the enemy." The warm man had genuine feelings for the special young man and he knew he would listen to his plan and see if it would help him. "Zachary, my children are yet young, scooting around the white house as though it were a playground. My little boys like to play soldier and pretend with wooden guns and swords."

"My cousin Reid and I grew up playing soldier with wood guns and swords, mostly small limbs we scraped down smooth." Zachary remembered back to simpler days, scampering through the woods behind their old farmhouse, pretending to shoot small trees or squirrels dashing up the nearest tree. "Things are different now, sir. War is not glamorous! It's filled with anguish and killing, finding yourself trapped behind enemy lines after running from friendly lines because your own people is after you too!"

"I can see your dilemma Zachary and if there is anything I can do, as your friend and president, please tell me!" the fatherly figure placed his arm lovingly around Zachary's strong shoulders and listened carefully to the young man's ideal, nodding his head in agreement as Zachary's words flowed into his listeners ears. "Son, your plan is sound and very well thought out." Abraham Lincoln pulled out his pocket watch to check the time. "I must be on my way soon Zachary, but have no fear, things at my end will be all set and ready to put into action if the time arrives." He pulled out his calling card and slipped it in the young man's shirt. This will be your pass to get past my guards when entering the White House. I am afraid you will find an overrun cabinet when you arrive. It would appear everyone I am acquainted with has a brother, son or father-n-law looking for a position in my cabinet. Like I just told a friend of mine who ask me why I looked so worried, I simply told him: there are too many pigs for the teats!"

Zachary laughed along with the president as he placed his hand out to shake Lincoln's. "I cannot thank you enough for being there for me sir. Is there anything I can do for you, except join the army?"

"There is son!" with eyes bright and loving he stated: "Wait until this war is over so I can come to your wedding and hopefully be by your side, since your father cannot!"

"It will be an honor sir, to have you there and to fill..." tears filled Zachary's eyes as emotions swept through him by the sheer wonder that the president of the United States had offered to be his substitute father at his wedding to Autumn Rose. "fill in for my father."

"With all the little boys running around my feet, distracting me from my troubles, having a son like you will make a handsome addition to my big family." Without hesitation, Abraham Lincoln wrapped his long willowy arms around the young man. "With the way things are going son, I feel I shall be seeing you very soon." Lifting up a cane from the floorboard, the president wrapped on the door for the soldier to open it. With last farewells, Zachary climbed out and the black carriage pulled away.

Chapter 25

Clint Reynolds had made several visits out to the Laurel Grove Plantation ever since he had brought Katherine's older sister Vera there for what looked like a very long visit, due to the war breaking out. For the present, the main battles had been fought in Virginia, but the northern troops were moving future down south and it looked like Charleston might be one of their next targets. Reynolds had made the trip out this time to warn the family that their plantation was in the cross hairs of Charleston and Savannah and this made them easy targets. He had offered to escort the family to Mississippi, where they could take refuge at Belmont Plantation. It was out of reach for the northern army and his servants had orders to place a white flag with a red cross on it, at the entrance if they heard the Yankees where anywhere near. Vera's Willow Creek sat near the main roads and could easily be a target for Yankee cannons, but Clint's long driveway would give them safe haven.

"Even though you have the same situation here at Laurel Grove, Mr. Forrest, the gunners might reach parts of your plantation, although I pray not." Clint Reynolds had proved to be a loyal friend to the Forrest family as he had made sure they got provisions from Charleston whenever they ran out of needed items. Clint and Nellie had stolen a few precious minutes together, but never alone long enough to make love.

"Do you think by leaving my workers here they will remain safe?" Frederick Forrest could not bear to lose one of his loyal friends and if it meant losing the crops for the season, he would find a means to feed the lot.

"Couldn't we put out the white flag with the red cross too, then no man would dare take the risk of catching the yellow fever." Autumn knew the loyal blacks would never desert their work or homes, so she wanted assurances that they would be safe.

"Then I suggest you always have two of your workers stationed at the end of your driveway, taking turns. If they are there to warn the enemy that the fever has spread throughout the plantation, they will take their word for it, thinking they are slaves."

"Then we will tell my family not to let on they have been freed, if that's what they need to do to save our homes!" Nellie suddenly realized she had made herself one of the freed slaves in front of the man she loved as she watched him stare down at her and ask.

"Your family, Nellie?"

"Clint, that's what we call all our black brothers and sisters here at Laurel Grove." Katherine spoke up before Autumn had the chance. "It just comes natural for our family to call them our family."

Clint relaxed as he smiled down at Nellie. "I am sorry if I jumped to conclusions over your comment sweet Nellie. I guess it just set me back for a brief moment." He slipped his hat on. "I am sure everything will be safe for your black family, but I must insist you pack what things you need for a long stay at Belmont and I will return to escort you, along with four soldiers, to assist if we run into a scouting party from the north. We can never be too careful."

A week later, the small caravan left for Mississippi, leaving Laurel Grove in the care of their extended family. Finding no northern troops waiting for them, they made it safely to Mississippi, where Vera insisted on being dropped off at her home until Yankee's had been reported in the area. Finding many of her slaves gone and only a handful of loyal houseworkers, Vera was forced to leave with her family, leaving the house in the care of her small staff.

"I knew when Drake left to join the army, this place would fall to ruin." Vera wiped her eyes as Ester handed her a hot cup of tea to relax her. "Things will never be the same! I cannot just abandon my home when my dearest lies down in the old plantation cemetery, next to my little Sally."

"Aunt Vera, I promise to go by and check on your place as often as possible." Autumn reached over and patted her tear-stain face. "I am hopeful that one day when this horrible war is over, we can all go home and try to resume some type of normal life." Autumn got up and looked from the window at the falling rain. "I wonder how my Zachary is? What he must be doing and if he misses me as much as I do him?"

"Dearest friend, I can guarantee you, your Zachary is beside himself with worry for your welfare and misses you as much as you miss him." Nellie was worried about Clint's next assignment because he had never told her where he would be going when he left Belmont. "I have never seen any two people more in love than you and your Zachary. I know it cannot be easy never hearing from him, same as it must be for Zachary. But the mail going North has all but stopped and unless he can slip away down here and find you by some miracle, you must try to wait patiently, praying constantly for his welfare and safety."

"Darling, I know you said Zachary promised you that he would not raise his sword against the south, but sometimes situations change's a man's thinking and you must not hold it against your young man if he has joined the Union." Frederick pulled out his pipe and lit it as he watched his daughter, still facing the window.

"No daddy, Zachary would never break a promise he made to me." Autumn turned around. "And that is why I am worried about him. He could get in big trouble with the army for refusing to join and they would insist on knowing the reason. My darling Zachary would never back away from the truth, even if it meant…" Tears raced down her cheeks and she covered her face then ran up the steps to her room.

"I will go after her Katherine." Nellie started for the stairs when Clint stepped out and took her in his arms. "I must go see to Autumn. Her heart is torn with fear for Zachary."

"Then go to her, my darling, but tonight, come to me before I leave for Crooked Creek tomorrow morning." His hand swept through her hair. "I need to lie with the one I love most before I go off to battle with Nathan Bedford Forrest."

"Bedford? Autumn's favorite uncle?" Nellie held tight to him.

"The same! I am joining his Calvary. He has sent out word that he's looking for soldiers willing to kill Yankees!" Clint looked around to be sure they were alone. "I will leave my door unlock for you my darling Nellie.

Washington D.C.

"Mr. President, there is a Zachary Dawson outside." The secretary looked around at the group of men, discussing raising the taxes again to support the war effort. "Shall I make him return later, sir?"

"That will not be necessary Benton. This meeting is getting nowhere and I refuse to hear the word tax again, so as soon as I release these monkeys from their cage, you may send him in." Abraham Lincoln ordered the finance committee out of his office because he had an important meeting.

Zachary watched the irate group of men walk out of the

president's office mumbling under their breath as he followed the short man with wire rim glasses inside.

"Thank you, Benton. Will you see that I am not disturbed by anyone." Abraham rose up to shake the young man's hand as his personal secretary went around the room shutting the wooden shutters, to keep the public from pocking their head inside to ask a favor of the president. "That will be all Benton." After the door closed behind the secretary, Lincoln let out a sigh. "You got here just in time to save me from killing my finance committee!" he chuckled.

"That bad?" Zachary laughed, then grew serious. "President Lincoln, did you come up with anything to help my plan?"

"Does the pig squeal when you pull its tail?" Lincoln leaned up on the desk when the young man smiled.

"Yes sir, very loudly!"

"First, I had to think of a way to keep the army's enlistment group from coming after you, so I am making you my top aid." He waited for Zachary to respond.

"Your top aid? What does a top aid do sir?"

"They stay by my side at all times, unless I have a mission for them to perform "Lincoln smiled. "First of all, no one would ever insist that an aid to the president be enlisted in the army. Second, aids travel with the president when he goes out on the battlefield to converse with his commanding generals and they are all over the enemy lines."

Zachary sat up, starting to understand where this brilliant man was heading. "So, this will be my first step in getting south, Mr. President."

"Zachary, if you wish to make me happy, please stop calling me, Mr. President or President Lincoln. Simply call me, Abe!" he gave Zachary a big smile when the young man looked up surprised by the request. "It really would make me happy, son."

"Very well, Abe it is." Zachary suddenly was glad Benton had not heard him, in fear of getting thrown out by addressing the president of the United States, just plan Abe.

"You have no one to fear Zachary, I am the big man around here and I do not always feel so big. Sometimes I'd much rather be back in Kentucky reading the newspaper with some other man as president back here in Washington making big decisions about this terrible war with our southern friends." Lincoln reached over and patted Zachary on the back. "I too have friends in the south, Zachary. One in particular who has offered to help you get further down south. He owns a small business, delivering goods to various towns and states. I had him do some checking on your Autumn and he has found out that she has left her plantation with her family and was seen going into Mississippi. I guess they left their slaves in charge of looking after the plantation."

"Autumn's family do not own their slaves anymore, Abe, they bought every man, woman and child their freedom papers on the same day Fort Sumter was fired upon." Zachary had cherished that last letter from Autumn and carried it with him. "She managed one last letter to me and told me how the family had gone to Charleston that very morning, unaware of the plans to shell the fort." His eyes grew serious. "her words of affection have sustained my waking hours and my dreams are filled with her beautiful smile and sweet kisses."

"Do you know where she may be at in Mississippi, Zachary?" Lincoln knew the depths of this young man love for this girl and Abraham could only imagine how he would feel being away from his Mary for such a long length of time.

"I can think of one possibility, an uncle we both love and admire." Zachary thought back to his youth and learning to be a soldier by the man he spoke of. "Autumn could very well be there."

"Then, you must not tell me the name of this man. It is better that I do not know the names of anyone you love for fear of the wrong person finding out." The gentle man walked around the desk and took a seat next to the young man. "Zachary, you are like a son to me. A son that has gown up to manhood, handsome and a born soldier, afraid of no man." Abraham Lincoln seem to be far away as he stated: I have had dreams, disturbing dreams about being dead and never able to see my children grown. I find myself waking in a cold sweat, as if the angel of death is nearby and cannot do anything about it."

"Abe, have you told these dreams to anyone else?" Zachary suddenly felt heartbroken over the thought that this man with integrity and such a pure heart would die young. "Dreams can sometime seem so real you start believing in them until you grow sick with worry. You seem so healthy, Abe. A little thin maybe, but still young and vibrant."

"It's not my health that will take my life, Zachary. I cannot pinpoint what will happen to me, but as my dreams change, I can see things more clearly each time." Abraham took a big breath. "Enough gloom, let's go back to our plan. Next week, you and I shall travel, with my fleet of guards, to the battle field and on our return trip, we will meet up with my friend, who has staged a break down and I will leave you with him to assist him with his repairs, after giving you a fake assignment to remain with the troops until I send word. This order will be done in front of my guard, to witness why you did not return with us."

"Then I will leave with your friend instead of returning to the field." Zachary could see the plan unfolding. "I will stick with him until he tells me what I need to do to go to Mississippi and travel to Autumn's uncle's place."

"You catch on fast son." Lincoln stood up and stretched. "Dang if I'm not hungry!" he slapped Zachary's back playfully. "I bet mother has dinner ordered and she will love a handsome dinner guest to dine with us this evening. I won't take no for an answer, son."

"Then, how can I refuse such a wonderful invitation, Father Abe?" Zachary smiled when the president chuckled out and gave him a wink. "Come to think of it, dang if I'm not hungry myself!"

"Mustn't keep these stomachs growling. We have our marching orders! Dinner awaits!" Abraham Lincoln felt that for the first time in months, he could actually go to bed that night and fall to sleep without dreaming those morbid dreams.

Chapter 26

President Abraham Lincoln made a surprise visit to the camp of Ambrose Burnside, on the outskirts of Fredericksburg, Virginia. The Federals were waiting to launch the offensive on December 13, 1862, after the pontoon bridges arrived.

"What is the confederate's position, General Burnside?" Mr. Lincoln drew the arrogant man's attention away from the tall young soldier standing behind the president.

"Those rebels are waiting behind a stone wall at Marye's Heights. We plan to cross the Rappahannock River when the pontoon bridges arrive, Mr. President, and cross over in one impregnable force!"

"Sir, that plan sounds suicidal, sending your troops straight into enemy fire!" Zachary had listened to the general's plan and found it very disturbing. "Our boys will be mowed down and the Confederates will be safe behind the stone wall, losing very few men."

Abraham was looking up at his new friend and it was plain to him, they had the wrong man in charge again. "Burnside, maybe you had better come up with a new strategy. My aid is right, this plan will never work."

"Excuse me sir, but I believe I know a little more about leading troops than this West Point drop out! I personally graduated from the military academy with high grades and like General McClellan, the army leaders have been keeping a close eye on this young man." Burnside raised his eyebrow. "I hope he proves to be a better aid than he was a soldier."

"General Burnside, if you are through bragging on your accomplishments, and believing your brilliant plan is failproof, I can only think of one wise quote." President Lincoln crossed his arms and leaned back on the wooden camp stool. "The hen is the wisest of all God's creatures, she does not cackle until after the egg is laid!"

The soldiers standing around the tent started laughing over the president's funny quote. "May I suggest, it is the wise general who listens to sane advice over an obvious disaster about to happen, or carry through with this ridiculous plan and find yourself replaced like your buddy McClellan!" The president rose from his chair and motioned for Zachary to follow as he said for the general's benefit. "Zachary, even though I would hate to lose such a good aid, perhaps you best study up on the duties of a general, because I will be looking for a good replacement real soon!"

The small group headed out and had not gone far when they came upon the broken-down wagon. Two of the soldiers hung back to guard the president, while the others checked out the traveler's wagon, making sure enemy soldiers were not hiding under the tarp that covered the long trailer. Finding it only contained merchandise, the advancing guard waved the President forward.

"This is an honor, Mr. President, to meet you this far south." It was obvious to Zachary that this man was educated someplace up north, due to his lack of southern slang. "I travel around from state to state selling my general merchandise, mostly on street corners or empty lots. I knew by the squeaks in the axle I was headed for a break down sooner or later, I just didn't count on it breaking down in the middle of nowhere." The man nodded his white head. "The name is Anderson, Albert Anderson."

"I must return to Washington, Mr. Anderson, but I will leave my aid to assist you in tying up your broken axle rod long enough for you to reach another town, and I must warn you, it must not be Fredericksburg. There's going to be a lot of gunfire and cannon fire, shelling that town before long." Lincoln tilted his top hat to the man and ordered his guards to wait by a small grove of trees while he gave his young aid instructions. "Mr. Anderson, my aid, Mr. Dawson, will be over shortly to assist you after I have a word with him."

"Of course, I do not plan on going anywhere." The selling traveler chuckled. "I truly appreciate your stopping to help me sir. Thank you."

"Just like the Samaritan, I saw a need to help someone in trouble, even though he is a southerner." Abraham Lincoln smiled and rode over near the waiting soldiers, Zachary right behind him. Speaking loud enough for the men to hear him, he gave Zachary his pretend orders as he handed him what looked like an official letter with the seal of the president of the United States, pressed in wax.

"Dawson, after you have completed the repair on Mr. Anderson's wagon, then I want you to carry this letter to General Sherman." He handed him a map. "This should lead you straight to him." Lincoln looked down at the soldier's resting under the trees. "Stay put boys until I give my aid some private instructions." He led Zachary over to one side and climbed off the horse.

"It has been some time since I have ridden horseback." Abraham rubbed his back as they walked a little further away. "Zachary, I've been meaning to ask you how your Uncle Hastings took your leaving his employment."

Zachary laughed, as he recalled the day he received the final payment from his job, for getting the family farm back from Jax Tyndall. It had come at just the right time. Word spread that all young men capable of fighting would be drafted immediately. "I got up super early that morning and packed up what few clothes and personal items I had, Fed Midnight before saddling him, then rode out to the manor house, knowing I would find Uncle Horus having his breakfast and Bradley still in bed, fast asleep after a late night down a Darrel's bar, boozing and picking up some harlot." Zachary chuckled when he noticed the president was caught up in his story. "I walked right inside and to the breakfast room, ask for my wages, stuff them inside my pocket, then laid my resignation down, smiled, told my uncle to enjoy his breakfast, then walked away. I am certain he must have gotten strangled over his coffee while reading my farewell letter. I was halfway down the driveway when I heard his faint call from the porch."

"That poor fellow, let's hope he does not replace you with that son of his." Lincoln laughed, trying to picture the spoiled young man working in a dirty steel mill. A sad expression overtook the president as he reached over and took hold of Zachary. "It is never easy to let someone go you have grown so attach too, son. I was hoping I could ride away without the thoughts of never seeing your face again, at least, not on this earth, but I cannot shake that very ideal."

"This war cannot last forever Abe. Once over, travel will resume and my wedding day will be set. My flesh and blood father has been taken from me, but I still have you, Father Abe." Zachary tried hard not to cry, but seeing tears in the eyes of Abraham Lincoln, brought on his own. "These dreams, do they still haunt your nights?"

"Unusual dreams, like someone in the distance, acting. They are…saying words like in some act from a play, then somewhere overhead, a single gunshot." Knowing they could not be seen by anyone, the two friends hugged their farewells, wiped their tears away. And climbed back in the saddle. "Enough with this sad talk. I am sure these dreams are brought on by all the boys killed or wounded in this dreadful war. Once over I will resume back to my old self and life will take on a rosy existence God will mend the hurt and distrust and bring all states back to unite as one great nation under Him."

"What a blessing that will be and with much prayer, hopefully the southern plantation owners will follow Frederick Forrest's example and free their slaves, fully mending the black brothers hurt and make them one with us." Zachary could see the soldier guard rise up when they caught sight of the president and his aid. "Safe journeys President Lincoln and do take care of yourself as well as your guardian angel."

"Mum, guardian angels, that is a story for another time. Please, be careful Zachary. The south is a dangerous place for Yankees, and I would not want anything to happen to one so young and loved." Lincoln waited for the handsome young man to salute him before he returned his own salute, slow, with dignified honor. "Look forward to seeing you soon, son." Turning his horse, President Abraham Lincoln rode away, not looking back.

When Zachary rode back over to Mr. Anderson, the wagon was as good as new. "You fixed it?"

"It was never broken, young man. Hop aboard after you tie that beautiful creature on the back." He smiled up at the tall man before starting the two horses into a trot. "Son, you must be pretty special to my friend, Abe. He took a lot of risk doing this for you."

"Father Abe is a very special man and we have grown a close bond between us." Zachary kept looking around for any danger along the quiet road. "After this terrible war, Abe will stand in for my own father who was killed a few years back, when I get married to the woman I go to see."

"Sorry to hear about your father, but if Abe promised to be at your wedding the only thing that would stop him would be death." It was obvious to Zachary that this friend of Lincoln's did not know about the recurring bad dreams that pledged the president. "How was Mary? No more frantic attacks, I hope. The poor man has enough to worry about with all this war business."

"Mary was in good spirits when I was with them, as was Abe." Zachary remembered how all the family had taken an instant liking to him, making him feel like he was somehow, part of the Lincoln family. "My days with that family will be part of my best memories."

"Abe says you are headed for Mississippi. You are in luck kid. I am going as far Natchez myself and I have good friends there who can assist you to your destination." Albert Anderson reached over and slapped Zachary on his knee, causing him to jump. "Dawson, will you please relax and stop looking around every tree we come to along the road. I am just a working-class southern citizen and you are my mute helper, should we meet up with any soldiers looking for spies of the enemy.

"Why is your helper mute, Mr. Anderson?" Zachary wondered if he could refrain from speaking if someone started beggaring him.

"Because boy, anyone can tell by your speech that you are a damn Yankee." Before Zachary could talk, the smiling man held up his spare hand. "And before you ask why they would take me for a southerner when I speak a lot like you, is because, being from the south," he started speaking with a slang. "I know how to smear on a great southern accent, boy." He gave his smiling companion a wink. "Just sit back, relax and enjoy the ride. We have a long ride to my river boat that will take us up the Mississippi River until we reach Natchez."

Just before dawn, Autumn Rose made her way up a small hill with an open vista, behind Belmont Hall. As she walked, her thoughts turned to Laurel Grove as she wondered if Jack was missing his mistress as much as she missed his company on these quiet morning walks. She would have asked Nellie to make the climb with her to view the rising of the sun over the wide Mississippi River, but she had heard her coming into the room around 2:00 a.m. and knew by her breathing that she was in deep sleep.

"My dearest friend, just where did you go until 2:00 in the morning?" her soft voice cut through the morning stillness. "I suppose you could have awakened and were unable to return to sleep, slipped down to the kitchen for a glass of milk and another sugar cookie you enjoyed before going to bed." Reaching the vista, Autumn found a seat on a smooth rock and gazed out at the first rays of sunlight lifting up from the water. "My gracious Lord, the creation of your glorious sunrise never fails to make me sing your praises! Each sunrise is different, yet all somehow the same, weather they come over water or hillsides, like at home."

Autumn thought she saw movement on the river, so she leaned forward as the rays of sun flickered over the paddle wheels rotating around, moving the water in a rhythmical pattern. It appeared to be pulling into the banks of Natchez.

"Oh, to see who is traveling on that paddle boat!" her thoughts turned as usual to Zachary. "What a delight to think that my beloved was on that vessel. But alas, I dare not wish for something so remotely possible."

"And what seems impossible why up here, and might I add, all alone!" Nellie pulled her robe tight around her neck to ward off the winter wind and looked down on the spot her friend had been observing. "Mum, it seems a little early in the morning for a paddle boat to be traveling the Mississippi."

"It does not seem any earlier than my very best friend sneaking back inside our room at two in the morning, Nellie Forrest!" Autumn turned to look at her and found her looking down serious. "Nellie, were you with Clint Reynolds all that time?"

"Did you hear me slip out?" Nellie finally looked over at her friend. "Clint is leaving for war in the morning, Autumn, and we needed to be together before he left."

"Thank you for being honest with me Nellie." Autumn reached for her hand. "I know how much you love Clint sweetheart, but you have been taught about saving yourself for marriage! "Worry draped Autumn's face "Nellie, what will happen if you get pregnant? You will be considered a fallen woman if Clint refused to marry you."

"If Clint and I have a baby, I will be overjoyed!" Nellie stood up and walked over close to the edge to watch what looked like two men getting off the boat. "Everything is fine. I love Clint and he loves me."

"Nellie, how can you take this so lightly? "Autumn got up to join her friend and pulled her around to face her. "We need to be careful until mama tells us what secret she is hiding! If Clint finds out that Nora raise you for her own baby, he will consider you a slave and drop you, He would not marry you if he remotely thought you were black!"

"Autumn, I tell you, everything is alright!" Nellie stayed relaxed and Autumn could not help but think she was living a fantasy and when reality finally hit her, she would be devastated unlike anything she had ever known.

"Please Nellie, let us pray that you have not gotten pregnant and Clint is away long enough for us to convince mother to tell us her secret. I cannot help but believe that you are really somehow my sister and if that's true, how much African blood do you have and who really had you?"

Chapter 27

Zachary had to wait a few days until Albert's friends were ready to take him to the Crooked Creek Plantation, so the young man decided to wait in a boarding house instead of seeking refuge at Chatham Hall. The magnificent mansion belonging to Autumn's aunt. He had promised Mr. Anderson that he would meet him across the street at Tavern on the Mississippi, nestled in the lower part of Natchez, to get instructions from a Willy Perry and his side kick, Herbert C. Fawn, a couple of fur traders, who knew the land well.

Zachary had arrived early and had ordered himself a mug of beer when he noticed an interesting character seated at the bar talking to the bartender. Zachary quickly looked down when both men looked his way and he noticed the stranger slide a dollar bill over to the man behind the bar as he ordered two fresh beer, then made his way to Zachary's table.

"May I please join you, boy?" the voice was familiar, but the brown hair, beard and mustache were unfamiliar to Zachary as he studied the hidden eyes that remained dropped on the beer in his hands. "Another cold beer for a bit of your time, Mr. Dawson."

"Sir, I am at a disadvantage here. You appear to know who I am yet I cannot place your features." Zachary was leery of anyone in enemy territory asking him anything. "Do I know you?"

The stranger leaned forward, speaking just above a whisper. "You really do not recognize your old class mate, do you Dawson, even after whooping me at what I do best!" the familiar laugh fell on young Zachary's ears, bringing out both precaution and jubilant joy, as he slid his chair in as close to his old West Point classmate as he possibly could. George had already made a reputation for himself in the south and this was no place for a Northern hero.

"Dang it, George, what in the name of God are you doing down here? Trying to get yourself killed?"

"I could ask you that very same question my friend, but I overheard one of Lincoln's guards telling General McClellan the president sent you on an errand and you never returned." George Custer looked around to make sure no one else was interested in their conversation. "I could tell that soldier liked you because he was telling his army buddy that big shot McClellan paid Lincoln a visit to ask about your desertion and what he knew about it."

"Please tell me Abe did not get into trouble because he helped me?" Zachary checked the big ball and chain clock behind the bar for the time, knowing Albert and his two friends would be arriving soon. "Why does someone unimportant like me cause this high-ranking general go to such trouble to search me out?"

"He dreams of being the next president and replacing President Lincoln, while hunting you down like a wild dog and making sure you pay for him being released from his high position!" Custer grew in closer. "He and Burnside have a bounty out on your head, my friend! They have become desperate, They, seek to kill you, Zachary! "Custer looked worried. "Zachary, they had your Uncle David beaten because he refused to tell them where you might have fled. They threaten to beat his wife to a pulp if he did not share any information with them."

"Uncle David would have known where I was heading, since it was he who took me there when I was ten and met...Autumn!" Zachary 's heart started pounding with uncertain fear. "By now, they are sure to know my woman's name and maybe even where she has gone."

"The only thing your uncle managed to say before he blacked out was, Mississippi." George looked around at the door, hoping he could finish before every who Zachary was waiting on, came into the tavern. "Witnesses say, when your Uncle David finally came to, he saw his beloved wife lying beside him, beaten with an inch of her life and his beautiful old home and stables, just smothering embers."

"Those so call northern gentlemen hired some no-account lowlife and robbed my uncle of everything he possessed after all!" Zachary gritted his teeth angrily. "I am certain he will get no help from his brother Horus or sympathy from Cousin Bradley."

"I doubt anything good can come from either father or son, especially your cousin Bradley." George Custer looked over at the double doors when they opened and two men stepped in dressed like trappers from the past. "They seem safe enough, still living in the past, by the looks of it. Probably go by Crocket and Boone!" George finally found something to chuckle about.

"More like Perry and Fawn, fur traders by trade, guides for extra wages." He watched them walk up to the bar and order whisky. "They must be waiting on Anderson." Zachary drank down the beer before asking "Tell me what do you suspect about Bradley Hastings, besides sending that letter to McClellan with the Carrier when I went in for an interview."

"Bradley Hastings has been seen visiting both generals in a closed meeting, where it was said, they all came out shaking your cousin's hand and having an office uniform issued to him after promising him a big position." Custer made an angry face. "I am sure the little weasel squealed everything he knew about you Zachary, including the fact that your Uncle David knew the location of your destination and that he could draw them a map to the place. Your cousin had bragged on visiting the place but could not remember anything about the owner or the name of the plantation. He could name one pretty redhead, as he put it, his greedy hand out for more blood money!"

"Autumn!" Zachary's blue eyes grew dark with defiance. "Judas! The scared bastard pretended not to know Autumn's uncle's name because he fears the very sight of him and with good reason! No one messes with Nathan Bedford Forrest's family or close friends or they will live to regret it! That little coward deliberately sent those men to Uncle David and I can only pray he does not take his own life like my father did!" Zachary stared into space, fresh hate feeding his very soul. "Just let them send soldiers down here! With me fighting alongside of my personal teacher, we will win!"

"Nathan Bedford Forrest?" Custer's eyes grew wide. "There is not a general or a soldier who is not frightened by the mention of that gorilla's name. General Sherman said, Forrest was the only Cavalryman, North or South, whom he feared and he has ordered Maj. General Samuel Sturgis to search out and destroy Forrest's command, if it meant breaking the entire United States budget!"

"Bedford is a man to stay clear of if you are the enemy and Sherman is correct on one thing, Forrest is the very best Calvary man alive! He is smart and unafraid. The genus can ride circles around anyone!"

"So, that is why they call him the Wizard of the Saddle!" Custer watched the two men order another whisky. "I guess his young student will one day inherit that grand title from him. Zachary, your skills must match his to the letter!"

"Like student, like teacher!" Zachary noticed three Confederate soldiers walked in the tavern, glanced their way, then walked up to the bar to order beer. "George, who sent you down here to warn me?

It cannot be safe for you, should your true identity come out. There are no two men with long, curly blonde hair and that cocky smile. Should you lose your disguise, I will be saving your butt."

"The source of my visit must be kept secret because should I get caught before I make it back over the enemy line, he must not be traced to me, understand, and definitely not linked to you again!" Zachary's loyal friend spoke softly. "I have a gunner boat waiting on the banks of the Mississippi, just beyond town, so I will slip away in the darkness of night and hook up to Grant's bigger gunner boat, which is stabling my Calvary's horses. We are headed for Vicksburg, just upriver from here."

"George, be careful and do not tell General Grant that Nathan Bedford Forrest may be close by. I would hate to have to fight you, my friend." Both men stood up and shook hands. "If I do not see you again, keep safe George, keep happy. And tell my friend Abe, thank you for everything but please, do not try to help me anymore. McClellan will try anything to become president so he can put that loving, caring man down, anything, short of impeachment!"

"So long boy, stay safe" Custer watched the two traders buy another round. "May I suggest you wait until morning to travel with those two drunks! You might end up back at the northern border!"

"Sage advice George." Anderson walked inside the tavern and waved at Zachary. "It's 6:30, getting dark outside. Watch your back, friend."

"You too Zachary!" George Custer hurried out the door while the Rebel soldiers were ordering another round of beer, as Zachary motioned Albert Anderson over and pointed to the two drunks singing at the bar.

"My guides can at least carry a tune Albert, should they start to sing while we travel."

Chapter 28

Autumn knew it was time to face her mother and find out what secret she was harboring inside her, so she traced her to the rose garden, where she sat staring out into space. Joining her on the garden bench, Autumn reached over to give her a kiss.

"Here you are. I have been looking all over for you." Autumn looked around and noticed they were the only two out there, so she gave a silent prayer of thanks for the privacy. "Mother?"

"You are here to ask about Nellie." Katherine placed a loving arm around her daughter's shoulders. "Darling, I know you are concern over Nellie's affection for Clint Reynolds and worry about their secret affair."

"You know about Nellie and Clint?" Autumn sat up, new interest building up. "Nellie confided in you, didn't she?"

"Yes Autumn, after asking me point blank if I were her mother." Katherine waited for her daughter's reaction and found tears forming in her incredible green eyes. "You have always felt that closeness with Nellie, more a sister than a friend."

"Then...I was right!" Autumn smiled. "Nellie is my twin, isn't she?"

"Your unidentical twin, yes darling. Same mother but different fathers, conceived only hours apart." Katherine took her younger twin's hand. "Nellie was born September 10th at 8:00p.m. then you arrived an hour later at 9:00. Your father knew there was a possibility that the babies might not be his, but he was overjoyed to know we were having twins anyway."

"Your mother is right, sweet girl, and I never blamed Katherine for seeking love with another friend of the family after I let her down." Frederick was glad the truth was finally coming out and for two reasons, Nellie and Autumn.

"I cannot imagine either of you being disloyal to one another." Autumn respected her parents for being honest with her as she took their hand. "What happen to cause all this mistrust and heartache?"

"The mistake we both made started with my bad decision to seek out your mother's best friend for affection, instead of giving your mother time to grieve the loss of her first baby from an unfortunate miscarriage." Frederick reached over and caressed his wife's teary cheeks. "God knows I recredited the affair as soon as it happened and your dear mother walking in to catch us in the act."

"In my heated anger I ran them out of the house and told them I did not wish to see either of them ever again." Katherine gave her husband a weak smile, wishing this truth could have stayed buried from their beautiful daughter but new circumstances over their Nellie's falling in love with a white man changed everything. "After a few months, I began to miss Frederick and regretted my rash actions, but all looked hopeless as the months turned into two years and I knew in my heart he was not coming back. Doctor Lacy was a trusted friend and looked in on me often, especially after his wife died in childbirth. First, we just sought comfort from each other, but one night after sharing a bottle of wine, we made love." Katherine stood up and folded her arms to ward away her nerves. "As soon as Mark left I regretted the brief affair and when your father showed up on that same night, I confessed everything to him."

"How could I hold your dear mother to blame for needing someone to love when she thought that I had abandon her." Frederick walked over to comfort his wife. "After seeing your mother's hurt the night she found me in the arms of her best friend, I told Emma it was over and we went our separate ways. I stayed away to give Katherine time to release her pain and distrust, then I came home and begged her forgiveness."

"Your father and I made love that very night and you, our beautiful daughter, was conceived." Katherine smiled at Autumn. "We know you belong to Frederick because we both have Irish blood in our families and Mark doesn't. I found out after Nellie was born why her skin was a beautiful tan, her hair and eyes are like mine."

"Yes, I could always see that mama." Autumn stood up and stepped between her parents, giving them a daughter's loving hug. "Did Mark Lacy have African blood in his family then?"

"Doctor Lacy said his family had a small amount of Indian blood and it might affect the babies skin color. There might be gossips who might think she had blood of a slave, so in a private meeting with Doctor Lacy and Reverend Steelman, it was suggested that we give the first baby to Nora, who had just had a miscarriage and agreed to take Nellie for her own child."

"I see no reason why Clint Reynolds would need to know anything about that small amount of Indian blood or frankly why it should make that much difference to him." Autumn was wondering how Katherine and Frederick could reverse what they did and make Nellie the real daughter she was to them. "As far as Clint Reynolds is concerned, I believe he thinks Nellie is somehow connected to our family anyway so I will just come out and inform him that Nellie is my sister!"

"You are just going to bluntly put it out there, dear friend?" Nellie had been standing in the open doorway listening to the story all over again. "Why not just tell Clint the truth? He loves me! I know it will not make any difference to him if I have Indian blood in my family." Nellie walked over and was welcome in the circle. "If he will not except the truth, then he cannot truly love me with a pure heart and I need to find out now before we get married."

"Married? Nellie, did Clint ask you to be his bride?" Autumn grabbed her.

"Several times!" she laughed. "But I told Clint I must get my parents' permission and blessings from my beautiful sister!"

"This is as far as we can take you boy." The taller trapper had stopped the lead horse when they had reached a crossroad. "Perry and I will be taking this road but you must take the road going right and keep going until you reach Echo Pass. It would be wise to leave the road at that point and go through the forest until you reach the long drive into Crooked Creek."

"Mr. Fawn, is Nathan Bedford Forrest stationed nearby or has he moved elsewhere to fight the enemy?" Zachary was getting anxious to meet up with his old friend and teacher before some of his men stopped him and might take him for a Northern spy.

"We would not be knowing that sonny boy!" Short and missing a front tooth, Mr. Perry spoke with a slight whistle. "You just best take my old friend and partners advice and stay among the tall trees and to hide your Yankee self! Be thankful that we only shoot fox or bears! Not damn Yankee invaders!"

"I am not your enemy, Mr. Perry. My affection for the south is as great as yours, maybe greater!" Zachary looked down the long empty road he would be taking. "I only wish you both the best of luck during this troubling time!"

"Don't mind old Perry here boy, he's just cranky today." Fawn reached over to slap his friend's back. "He had a wee too much whisky last night and now his head is paying him back. Keep safe Dawson!"

"Yes, thank you and you both as well." Zachary watched his guides ride on down the road, then turned onto the long road looking for Echo Pass.

About ten miles down the long road, Zachary came to a stop and gazed up on either side of him at two high rocky hills that followed the road out of sight. "Echo pass." Speaking softly to himself as he strained to hear possible danger, the incredible blue eyes never stopped scanning his surrounding, a must for any soldier in enemy territory. A great hawk flew overhead and swirled down lazily into a big oak tree, letting out a loud squawk and the echo's reflected its call from every corner. Zachary smiled up at the interested prey when he cocked his head down at the young man's voice. "They chose the perfect name for this place, I agree with you my feathered friend. Thank you for the demonstration!" Quickly Zachary grew quiet and looked up the pass at a faint familiar sound. Horse hoofs, galloping toward him. With expert speed, the man dressed in black rode his black stallion up the hill and into the thickness of the forest to seek shelter for hiding.

As a group of ten soldiers galloped into view, the great hawk let out his cry and flew from the big oak, sweeping past the startled men. One young skittish soldier clumsily pulled out his gun, aiming up at the high-flying bird, letting off a shot.

"Dang it all, Billy, how many times must I tell you to stop shooting at no account hawks!" A rough looking man riding in front grabbed the young man's pistol away from him. "This is no child's play, boy, shooting birds and squirrels like back on the farm! You aim for damn Yankee's kid, you hear! Bullets are not wasted on the blue devils, so make every shot count!"

"Captains right Billy, you gotta stop being scared at everything that moves! Why, Yankee's aren't hard to recognize! You can smell those varmints ten miles away!" Zachary listened to the man with the uncombed hair bragging to the boy as he mumbled to himself.

"Smell a Yankee can you fellow?" the men had stopped just below his hiding place and Zachary felt safe about Midnight remaining still, knowing as well as him when danger was nearby and these men would just as soon shoot a stranger without finding out why he was there or what he wanted.

Looking around, the soldiers went on down the road out of sight, but to be cautious, Zachary sit still for another fifteen minutes, which paid off when three trailing soldiers rode slowly down through the woods. From his hiding place, Zachary could make out what each man looked like and what weapons that were carrying. Staying quiet and well hidden, the soldiers slowly rode by, stopping briefly to fire one shot off in the stillness. Zachary gently rubbed Midnight's neck, a sign for him to remain quiet, knowing the small group were trying to flush him out. Someone had obviously turned him in and warned Forrest's Calvary the time the Yankee would be arriving. Getting no response, one soldier was heard saying

"That Yankee spy must have got cold feet and turn tail! We will get word back to the colonel as soon as he returns to camp! Let's turn back!"

Zachary proved to be well worth the prize for West Point's soldier of the year, by fooling seasoned soldiers and slipping from his hiding place to follow at a short distance. He would now be assured of finding the camp where his mentor and teacher was stationed, then stay hidden until he saw "the Wizard of the Saddle" return from the battlefield.

Chapter 29

Zachary had found a good hiding place to watch the activities going on down in the quiet camp. Besides the thirteen men he had witness earlier at Echo Pass, the camp only consisted of six other men by Zachary's count. Smells from the camp cook filled the late evening air, bringing the handsome young Yankee another problem, food! Zachary had not eaten since the fur traders gave him a stick of beef jerky as they travel along, leading the young man as far as they could before, splitting up and going their separate way.

The whole time Zachary sat observing the men below, he tried to reason who could have set him up and he kept coming back to the short bawl headed fur trader who obviously did not trust Zachary's excuse for wanting to see their local hero. Thinking back to the customers that came in the tavern, Zachary remembered the Confederate soldiers that glanced his and Custer's way before moving up to the bar.

"Up to the bar, right beside my trusted guide, Perry." Zachary scanned the men below, priding himself as holding someone's face once seen, and as always, his training skills by Bedford paid off. "Now I remember where I saw those three scouts in the woods looking for us, Midnight. It was Perry! He was high on whisky and grew confident in his ability to be a spy! The little weasel, he had better hope I never see him again."

"And what exactly, do you plan to do with that old weasel? Stuff his candle out, my boy?" Zachary turned around startled to find his old friend and teacher standing over him.

"I might have known the one man capable of tracking me down was you, Bedford, but I did leave you some clues, did I not?" Zachary watched him closely, unsure by the seriousness on his strong face if he was glad to see his ten-year-old student or not. "You are glad to see me, aren't you, Bedford?" Still only silence and stone-cold eyes watching him. "I have come to fight alongside you Bedford, not fight you!" Zachary stood up, holding his on. "If you do not want my help because I am from the North, then just say the word and I will fight every man here, including you if need be, then go back up north and find a safe place until this stinking war is over!"

The big man laughed out and grabbed Zachary in a fatherly bear hug. "I am damn proud of you son! To stand up to me like that takes courage and believe me there is not one man down there in that camp that is as brave as you, Zachary!'

Zachary laughed, feeling relieved, knowing he had made the right choice after all. "Tell me Bedford, how did you track me down when your three scouts rode right past the tree I was hiding behind and never saw me."

"Yep, those good clues you left behind, just for me to find." Forrest slung his arm over Zachary's shoulders. "When the soldiers came back from Natchez, where I had sent them for some supplies, they decided to have a couple beers before traveling back to camp. Big mouth Perry was drunker than usual and told my men he had a good tip for them to make high marks with "the colonel", so he provided them with the information they needed to surprise you at Echo Pass, never knowing that I had taught you everything you know about the enemy." He laughed as he sat down on a rock and stretched out his legs. "After observing you in that tavern, the boys gave me a good description of the Yankee they had seen talking to a stranger, Perry did not know," his big hand reached over to flip Zachary's long hair. "I knew the instant they described the handsome young man with long dark hair and the bluest eyes they had ever seen. Nathan Bedford looked over at the beautiful black stallion waiting patiently for his master. "Dang if you didn't train your horse how to stand quietly and with patience when in enemy territory. Think you might have time to train mine before we head out again?" Nathan mumbled "If I can keep the damn Yankee's from shooting every horse I ride in to battle on, your training new horses may be a non-stop job for you! You would think the dumb bastards would learn to shoot straighter or realize that I shoot a Yankee for every horse shot out from under me! So far, I am ahead!"

"Sounds like you ride right upfront in a battle Bedford! It is easy to make light of their shooting but all it will take is one lucky shot! I can ride up front, we need our leader!" Zachary felt it was up to him to save the man who taught him how to win.

"I had planned on that, son. You and I will head up the front along with young Will, who just turned fifteen this year. Soon 1861 will be over and this war will run right into a new year." he looked over his boys below. "I started the tough group of men and so far, we have had few casualties and not many wounded. I have put up the cost for my entire Calvary and personally trained them." He watched two of his men arguing over a card game. "There is not one of them as smart as my young ten-year-old student." He gave a grunt. "Fighting over a stupid card game!"

"Have you heard any news from Uncle David?" Zachary got his old friend's attention. "No, I guess not. Your friend David is in a bad way, the way I hear of it. A bunch of northern rough neck soldiers where paid by higher ups to get information out of him about my whereabouts. He would not talk so they almost beat him and his wife to death, leaving them unconscious while they burned down everything he owned. Thankfully some neighbors saw the smoke and found them, barely breathing."

"After this war is over, we will hunt out those mad dogs and make them pay for what they have done to my friend!" Bedford gritted his teeth.

"Autumn, what do you know about my girl, Bedford?" Zachary had held back asking for as long as he could, but he could not wait another moment. "Tell me my dearest one is alright and safe from my northern brother's hands!"

"Autumn is safe, son and nearer than you think." Bedford smiled when the blue eyes glistened in the moonlight.

"She is at Crooked Creek?" he closed his eyes, picturing her smiling face.

"Not my place but somewhere just as safe. Your Autumn waits for you at a plantation, a few miles away." When the young man stood, Nathan joined him. "I shall send you to see her soon with the owner. He rides with me as well."

"Do I know this gentleman that has given my beloved a refuge from South Carolina?" Zachary had heard Autumn speak of many relatives he had never met yet and wondered if she was at one of their manor houses.

"You have met him Zachary and have even stayed at his beautiful plantation. The Harvest Festival I recall Autumn writing me all about your beautiful four days together."

"Belmont! Autumn is staying at Clint Reynold's place?" Zachary looked concerned. "Excuse my suspicions Bedford, but why would Reynolds invite my woman to stay at his home?"

"It would appear the family has become great friends with Captain Reynolds. He invited the entire family there for as long as Laurel Grove is unsafe ever since that devil Sherman captured and burnt down Atlanta. The blue coat continues his cruelty on the south as he headed for Savannah, just a few miles from Laurel Grove." Nathan's eyes shot fire. "Sherman may act tough around most people, but the little weasel is scared as a hare getting cornered by a pack of hounds when he hears my name!"

"Then I am grateful for Reynolds' kind hospitality. Knowing all the family is there with my girl, I can relax." Zachary grabbed his stomach when it growled loudly.

"Boy, when was the last time you had anything to eat?" Bedford untied his horse and motioned Zachary to Midnight.

"I would not exactly call the last thing I ate, a meal, but that strip of beef jerky I had around nine a.m. was it!" Zachary untied the big black horse and easily swung up in the saddle, then noticed his old friend smiling broadly.

"Pretty good mount kid! I see you have got even better since you left Crooked Creek in 1856." Bedford reached over and slapped his back. "We are going to make quite a pair on the battlefield Zachary! They already call me the Wizard of the Saddle! I cannot wait to hear what name they give my partner!" Forrest waved over his shoulder for Zachary to follow him as he called back. "Let's go and round that cook back up and feed my boy!"

All the soldiers in the camp sat up, a few jumping to their feet in shock when they saw their leader ride up with a young stranger, riding a black stallion.

"At ease men! This is the man you were tracking...let me rephrase that statement. The Yankee you were looking for, tracked you back to camp after he outwitted all thirteen of you fine boys!" Nathan got off his horse as a young boy ran up to take the reins and gazed over at the very tall, very handsome young man climbing down from the black horse.

"Willy? Has it been that long?" Zachary looked down at Bedford's oldest child. "The last time I saw you, you were playing with a twirl top with my friend Theo!"

"Is that you, Zachary?" William Forrest grabbed the young man around his waist. "We thought you done went and joined the Union Army and dreaded the day when we met up with you on some battleground! I know you would never run from your duties, you know, a traitor, so why are you here, this far south?"

"He's a damn Yankee, isn't he?" Jack Carter's eyes burned on him. "He's probably just a stinking spy! You cannot trust any damn Yankee, colonel!"

"I can and I do, Carter and if you say one more bad thing about my boy, I will personal beat the shit out of you! Is that clear?" Nathan Bedford yelled for the cook. "Trever, get your no-account butt out here and heat up me and the boy some fettles and make it snappy!"

"Yes sir, food coming up, along with two big mugs of beer, compliments of the fellows you sent to Natchez!" The fat cook race away in a frantic pace to please his scary leader.

"At least you fellows did one thing right. Saving some of your hidden treasure for the boss!" Nathan laughed as he made his way inside a big white tent, Zachary and Willy right behind him.

January, 1862

Zachary had gotten up early to watch the sunrise, something he had always tied to do ever since Autumn told him she had made that her morning ritual. As he sat watching the sun rise slowly over the trees surrounding the southern camp, his thoughts turned to Autumn and the need for her. Sitting quietly, Zachary could hear men's voices drifting up to where he was sitting, clearly hearing each word in the clear morning air.

"I will be riding out this morning to Belmont, to see my girl before I leave for Tennessee in a few days. Bedford got his orders yesterday that we needed to go to Dover and get to Fort Donelson by February." The voice was defiantly Clint Reynolds', Zachary remembered it well. He had been away on a mission for Bedford and had returned sometime during the night, after everyone had bed down.

"I bet that little gal is going to be really glad to see you Clint! It's been almost a year! I sure do miss my old lady!" the other voice sounded in the still air. "I guess you've heard that Zachary Dawson is here and has been riding up front with the general."

"Dawson, here?" Clint spoke softly. "He should come with me when I go home. Autumn would love to see him after all this time and I can only imagine how that young man must be missing his woman!"

Zachary tilted his head, now unsure of what Clint was talking about. First, speaking of going to see his girl before he left for war, and Zachary, had assume he was talking about Autumn, but now, it looked hopeful again for him. "The only way I will know for sure is to confront Clint and find out just who he is going to see. He made his way down the hill and back to the camp.

"There you are, Zachary. I've been looking for you boy!" Bedford handed him a plate of bacon and eggs. "Another thing about my Calvary Zach, I feed my men well. A well-fed army makes great fighters. Right boys?" the mumbling between bites, and all the yummy noise and approval winks from the men stuffing their faces with a spoonful of food caused the leader to laugh out. "Eat up boy, you have got a long ride ahead of you this morning."

"This morning?" Zachary remembered Clint telling someone he was headed for Belmont that very morning, now Bedford was giving him some military assignment, he thought for sure, causing his heart to sink. "But I thought..."

"We were leaving the first of next week?" Bedford took another bite, then gave him a playful wink. "Relax Zachary, the Calvary is not headed out this morning, you and Clint are! I think there's a very beautiful girl dying to see the man she loves and I believe my pretty little niece has waited long enough, don't you?"

"Oh, yes! Yes, I do! Bedford, sir! Zachary ate with more anxiousness, his heart pounding with the reality that soon he would be taking his woman in his arms and feeling her lips under his again. His eyes fell on his dusty clothes. "I could use a bath sir and a clean uniform."

"I thought you would never ask." Bedford led him, himself to their man-made showers and hung a brand-new Confederate uniform out with the bars of a captain on the shoulders. "I will inform the laundry staff to clean up this black outfit of yours Zachary and store it properly until after the war.

Chapter 30

"You are really good as one of us Dawson!" Clint laughed as he rode from camp with his traveling companion. "I see the colonel has already made you a captain, like me! I am impressed!"

"How long have you been riding with Bedford, Reynolds?" Zachary was dying to ask about the girl he was referring to as his, but he would bide his time until it felt the right time.

"Ever since I brought the Forrest family back here to Belmont to stay until it was safe for them in South Carolina." The owner of Belmont kept his eyes on the road ahead as they traveled through Echo Pass. "I am told you were hiding up there in those woods when the scouting party came looking for you. You really proved to be a smarter soldier and reversed their plans to fit your own."

"My friend Bedford taught me well, Clint. From what he has told me about all you men, he has singly handpicked all of you, training you his tactics same as he did me."

"And the way we hear it, you were a better student. The apple of the teacher's eye." Clint glanced back with a smile, obviously not jealous. "Welcome aboard Dawson! It's good to know we have two great Wizards frightening the enemy."

"Clint, how is Autumn been holding up? I know she has a strong will, but to leave her beloved Laurel Grove could not have been easy." Zachary had wondered if it still stood or is Sherman had set it ablaze like many of the other old plantation mansions.

"Frederick left his trusted servants behind to take care of the plantation and to frighten the Yankees away should they start down the long drive to the manor house." Clint smiled over to the tall rider as he came up beside him when the road got wider. "Did you know all their slaves were freed on the same day Fort Sumter fell?"

"It was in Autumn's last letter to me, mailed just as the war was starting." Zachary knew now was the time to find out who Clint Reynolds was talking about. "It's been so long since I have seen Autumn. Has she changed toward me? Given up waiting, never hearing weather I am dead or alive."

"Your very beautiful Autumn knows in her heart you are very much alive, my friend. I swear that girl can feel you in her very soul.

She has never one-time lost faith that our loving God will bring you back to her and you will be in each other's arms one day very soon."

"Forgive me Clint, but I overheard you speaking to someone this morning as I sat watching the sunrise over Dixie, and you spoke of a girl you needed to see before leaving for battle." Zachary drew his attention as he slowed his horse to a stop. "For a brief moment my fears lead me to believe you spoke about my Autumn until the voice with you filled you in on my coming to join Forrest's Calvary."

"And you assumed I was speaking about your woman." Clint reached over and patted Zachary's back. "I gave up on any chance with Autumn after watching the two of you together. Never had I seen such love and devotion between two people before and it gave me a new outlook on choosing the right mate. I too found a beautiful woman of my own Zachary and I love her with all my heart. I am hoping Nellie will except my proposal and become my wife, when this war is over, if not before."

"Nellie?" Zachary smiled. "I know Nellie will make you a wonderful wife. The girl is smart and well educated, taught right along beside of Autumn." Zachary looked at the long road ahead. "Enough talk my friend! There's a long road ahead and we've got two beautiful girls waiting with open arms!"

"I am with you friend! Race you to Belmont!" the new friends laughed and took off in a gallop, leaving Echo Pass far behind.

"I just carried in another load of dry wood for the fireplaces from the woodshed in the back." Nellie dropped her armload by the door and took off her winter coat, shaking out the freshly fallen snow.

"Now Nellie, why on earth are you fetching in all that wood?" Glenda picked up a big log and placed it on the burning embers. "Where is that Willis hiding? He knows that his job keeping those fireplaces burning!" Glenda continued to mumble. "I bet when the master gets back he will tan his hide but good! Making a woman go fetch the wood and it snowing outside like crazy."

"Now Glenda, you mustn't be blaming poor old Willis. I seen him wrapping up in that big old winter coat about two hours ago, leaving with a fresh sign to put out at the entrance, warning any Yankee this place is infected with the small pocks." Nellie warmed her hands by the fire. "I wasn't out there in that freezing cold but a little while but poor Willis was going to take over for poor old Bart who was more likely a frozen ice sickle when he found him."

"Well, alright then, but you let me know when the wood is low and I will fetch it myself." Glenda walked toward the kitchen. "I will put on a hot pot of coffee to help warm you."

"Nellie, did you venture out in that snow by yourself again?" Autumn came down carrying a worn book she had been writing in. "I told you to let me know the next time and I would go get some wood for the fire."

"I cannot just sit around this big house doing nothing, Autumn! I am worried about Clint. I have not heard from him in over ten months!" Nellie walked over and looked out into the rose garden. She imagined back to when Clint had taken her out there after dark and kissed her for the first time. It seemed so long ago, now with the winter cold keeping her inside. "I was hoping he would be coming home soon."

"It has been over twice as long since I have seen Zachary. This old diary will tell you just how much I long for my dearest love and would give anything to see him walk in that door right now." No sooner had Autumn got the words from her lips, the door swung open as two men in Confederate uniforms stood observing the startled girls. Autumn rose slowly. The same long black hair, the same incredible blue eyes, perhaps a little thinner, but there was no mistaking him. Without hesitation, Autumn ran across the room into his waiting arms as Clint made his way halfway to meet his Nellie. Their men had arrived.

"You two love birds best move out of that door before you let all my good heat out!" Nellie had welcome Clint with a warm hug and long-awaited kiss before noticing the young couple, lost in one another and oblivious to the cold wind blowing through the open passage. Walking up behind them, she gave them a gentle nudge forward and shut the big outside door. Now, take off those wet coats before you catch pneumonia!" Nellie held out her arms, used to waiting on the white folks, and gave Clint her beautiful smile as he obeyed, stripping the snow-covered wool coat off and laying it gently in her waiting arms. "Now your coat Zachary."

"You heard the lady, my friend. I am sure if you go to lie in bed it won't be because you got sick, but for more pleasurable reasons.

"That pleasure will have to wait until I marry my beloved. I will never dishonor her and not use our betrothal for an excuse to make it alright." Zachary wasn't as sure about his friend Clint's intentions where Nellie was concern. "this war cannot last forever and as soon as it over, I will make Autumn my wife, but I still need to get my inheritance back from that murdering gambler!"

"Gambler?" Clint's eyes lit up. "I always fancied myself as a winner in the game of poker

Chapter 31

"Katherine, I couldn't help but noticed the affection displayed for our girls by those two gentlemen." Frederick Forrest had been observing the young couples for the past two days and they seemed inseparable whenever they were together. "In two days, Zachary and Clint are leaving for battle and only God knows if they will return and for how long."

"Frederick, what are you suggesting? Surely you are not giving those men permission to sleep with Autumn and Nellie?" Katherine hadn't shared her suspicions about Nellie making love to Clint on previous occasions, but it sounded like that was what he had in mind.

"Never would I suggest such a thing, my dear. I was referring to a quick double wedding, tomorrow, right here at Belmont." Frederick lit his pipe and sat down in the big soft chair next to their guest bed. "I ask Vera where the closest minister resided and she informed me that a Reverend Turnbull has a small parish about ten miles north of her place. It is where she goes to church when in residents."

"How convenient! A double wedding so it would make their goodbyes perhaps a bit sweeter." Katherine sighed. "I was hoping to give our girls a formal wedding in Saint Philips, after this terrible war and invite all our family and friends."

"Why not both!" Frederick stood up and took around his beautiful wife. "Give the soldiers something to take with them and our daughters the joys of knowing complete love, then as both a celebration for our son-n-laws surviving the war and giving our daughters the dream weddings they deserve, it should make everyone happy."

"My darlings, your father has something to say to the four of you and it should please you greatly." Katherine had called the family together for a big announcement. Zachary and Autumn looked at each other, trying to figure out what Frederick was going to say so early in the morning. Clint had overheard the couple's conversation the night before and had informed Nellie to act surprise when he gave his speech.

"Mother and I can see just how much you kids love one another and in a couple more days, you boys will be leaving again without knowing how long you will be gone. I know war can be hell! What with all the killing and watching your fellow soldiers get shot or blown to bits!"

"Daddy, if you are trying to warn us about what might happen to Zachary or Clint, we are more than aware, and sometimes the waiting and not knowing is a worse kind of hell than being there." Autumn felt Zachary slip his arm around her and pull her close.

"I never meant to make what is to be a beautiful surprise to all of you become the torments of battle. I speak of joining hands in marriage, this afternoon at five p.m. A double wedding, to give you two nights together as husband and wife, then later, after the war, a do over, for your mother. A proper wedding at St. Philips, in Charleston."

"Married?" Autumn grabbed Zachary, who was smiling from ear to ear. "Daddy, mama, what a lovely surprise!" she tilted her head. "Have you found a minister way out here?"

"My minister, darling, Reverend Turnbull, at St. Paul's Parish." Vera had been filled in by the parents before the couples came down for breakfast. "Even quick weddings can be made beautiful and filled with happy celebration! The cook is preparing a special meal, champagne has been brought up from your wine cellar, and I have sent for my cook, Erline, who makes a beautiful wedding cake!"

"Now, if Nellie and I had our own fairy godmother to whipped us up a beautiful wedding dress, that formal wedding could not match the pure magic the first one will have." Autumn beamed with complete happiness.

"Just being together as husband and wife for the first time, will be the only thing I require to make me completely happy, my beloved Autumn." Zachary could not resist pulling her into his arms and giving her a kiss, then whispering softly in her ear. "Tonight, our bodies will know each other as one, sweet, my darling."

"There is no need of dessert for me tonight, Zachary darling, for there can be nothing as delicious as your sweet lips upon mine nor anything more desiring than feeling your warm body next to me." Autumn felt the fires of desire sweeping through her veins, knowing that in a few short hours she would be in the arms of the man she loved, at last as his bride.

It was but a small group that gathered around the couples who had managed to find some appropriate clothes for their big event. The big house smelled of fresh cedar cutting, cut and brought in to dry from the wet snow. It rarely snowed that much in Mississippi, but this was an exceptional February, so Clint and his black driver set out in the deep snow to bring Reverend Turnbull there since his means of transportation was a one-horse cart.

The friendly preacher was handed a cup of hot tea to warm him over so he could manage asking the important questions to the brides and grooms. Smells drifting from the kitchen made everyone's mouth water and they kept looking at the big grandfather clock that sat gracefully against the parlor wall.

Autumn looked up into Zachary's alluring blue eyes when he took her hand. "Soon my darling Autumn, we will be embracing in bed, under the sheets."

"It is something I have dreamed about often," was her soft reply, then she turned when the preacher thanked the kitchen servant for the tea then picked up his worn bible. "Darling, I do believe it time. Are you nervous?"

"To marry the girl, I have wanted ever since I was ten? What I am feeling is overwhelming happiness, my darling Autumn! A joy like I have never known before! Making you my wife is the best thing that has ever happened in my entire life! I promise to make you a good and faithful husband, all my days!"

"Son, those words you just spoke from your heart, make the perfect wedding vow, there's no need for more except those to perform the ceremony, so then I turn to you Autumn, to say the words to Zachary that lie in your heart." Reverend Turnbull would give each bride and each groom an opportunity to say their own vows.

"To follow with such words of true love and devotion has lifted my spirits, so now, unafraid, I can sing of my joy and like a reflection in a looking glass, there has been no other boy in my heart but you, since I was nine. The words of love flow from my quill, written in an old worn diary, from the heart of a young girl who became a young lady, never changing, always longing, always needing! Needing to feel the warmth of your embrace and the passionate kisses that are never enough. To be your wife is what will make me complete, for at last, we are made one!" Autumn looked up into his tear-filled eyes and lifted her hand to touch his loving face as the minister softly said

"Amen. There is no doubting the deep affection between you

both." He turned to the other couple. "Who would like to begin?"

"We choose to go together." Clint took Nellie hands as they locked eyes. "Today we are made one."

"Today we began a life together as husband and wife." Nellie smiled brightly. "As your devoted wife, I promise to always be here for you and to make your days full of laughter and your nights, filled with my undying love."

"As your devoted husband, I shall always put your needs first, give you all the love you so richly deserve, to be honest with you at all times, and to never hold any secrets from the one I love most."

"The love we share has grown even greater, the truths we have already shared with each other have proved to be rewarding and I will give you children to call you papa, to climb upon your knee and learn from you."

"I will make the kind of husband to you, dearest one, to make you the mother you were meant to be, filled with enough love and spiritual faith, that our children will grow in the wisdom of knowing the Lord is to be first in one's heart if they wish to live a complete and joy filled life, such as you and I share together." Clint squeezed her hands. "Nellie, I promise to love you forever."

"Clint, my heart belongs to no one but you, forever and ever!" Nellie shut her eyes "Lord Jesus, bless both Clint and me and my dearest friends, Autumn and Zachary, with a long and happy marriage."

"And, Lord Jesus, when we are separated by war, Nellie and I pray that you will protect our husbands, keeping them in thy loving care and bring them back to us, whole, not scarred by the memories of all the killing, Amen." Autumn gave the minister her beautiful smile when he repeated her amen.

"All beautiful words from two very special couples." Reverend Turnbull noticed both couples were holding hands, so he smiled and cleared his throat. "Brides, repeat after me, I, your name, do take, groom's name, to be my wedded husband." The brides repeated their line, then the grooms, and then it came to the last statement. "In the name of the Lord God Almighty, I pronounce you, Clint Reynolds and Nellie Forrest, Zachary Dawson and Autumn Forrest, husbands and wives. You may kiss your brides, gentlemen." The preacher removed his glasses and wiped his tears away as he watched the long passionate kisses by each husband.

Katherine wiped her eyes as she whispered to her husband. "I trust by Nellie's comment, she told Clint she had Indian blood." A servant held a tray up to her filled with champagne glasses and she carefully took one and waited for Frederick to take one. "By the way darling, where did those children get those wedding rings? No one had time to go shopping for them."

"Clint is a very clever gentleman, my dear and he has trained his servants in certain skills, like iron smith." Frederick laughed softly. "His man can work wonders with straight nails. Turns out, they make pretty good rings when there's no real ones around. Zachary and Clint hope to get by a jewelry shop sometime in the near future for gold ones."

"Poor darlings, they do not know our girls will always prefer that nail ring over all the gold in this world."

Katherine reached for another glass after downing the first one to calm her nerves after losing both of her daughters in one short hour. "I feel sure we did the right thing by the words they spoke to one another and that extra-long kiss after the minister pronounced them husband and wife."

"I know we did the right thing, dearest." Frederick raised his glass as he called for a toast. "To Autumn and Zachary! To Nellie and Clint! May your life together be enriched with happiness and longevity!" With several hear-hears, everyone toasted the two happy couples then followed Clint and Nellie into the big dining hall for dinner.

After the fine meal, everyone gathered around the big wedding cake and waited to be served. After eating the delicious white cake with creamy white frosting, another round of champagne was handed out. This time was set aside to mingle and congratulate the happy couples before they slipped up to their separate rooms to consummate the marriage. Autumn and Nellie found a moment to be alone before going up.

"I am packed with butterflies invading my stomach, dear friend." Autumn had taken her sister's hands "You told Clint, didn't you?"

"I had no other choice Autumn. I needed for him to know everything to be sure his love was strong enough to handle the truth." Nellie laughed softly. "It turned out to be a blessing for both of us! Clint seemed relieved when I confessed to having a trace of Indian blood in me, then told me that he was about to tell me that a distance relative of his was Indian! Then, after a lot of kissing, he confessed that when he assumed I was born a slave, it did not matter to him because his heart already belonged to me and nothing could ever change what he wanted. To make me his wife!"

"I am so happy for you Nellie!" Autumn took around her sister in a loving hug.

"And I for you, Autumn! Do not worry about those nervous butterflies, my beautiful sister, because once you're in Zachary's arms, your life will be complete!"

"I know you are right, Zachary will make everything beautiful for us." Autumn glanced over at her new husband and saw him looking her way, the desire showing in his alluring blue eyes. Lost in her eyes, Zachary moved away from his chatting father-n-law and started across the room to claim his bride. "Well Nellie, I think this is it!" Nellie smiled as she watched the tall handsome man approaching. "Very soon from now, I will not be an innocent virgin any longer, but a very happy content bride!"

"My darling looks nervous." Zachary took her trembling hand in his steady one. "Once we are alone, my beloved, and I slowly remove our clothes while smothering you with hot kisses, then I will lift my bride into my arms and lay her across our bed. I promise to be gentle, as this will be your first experience with making love as it is with me, but I know I can fulfill both our needs. I will restrain myself from releasing my built-up need for you and hold out until I feel you are ready to meet your need for me!" Zachary knew Clint had slipped up behind Nellie to whisk her away, giving Zachary the privacy he needed to whisper these beautiful love words in his young bashful bride's ear before taking her up to his bedchamber.

The party guest gave the young couples the space they needed to leave the celebration, so they could complete their wedding vows. Katherine and Frederick stayed with the small group gathered until the party broke up, then went up to rekindle their own memories of their special first night.

Chapter 32

Autumn opened her eyes to see Zachary lying next to her, looking longingly into her beautiful green eyes. Without a word, he moved over on top of her as his lips kissed her passionately. Autumn's slim fingers moved up his strong back and through his long black hair as she whispered softly.

"Oh Zachary, I love you! I love you!" She could feel herself growing warmer as his hand caressed her round bosom and his kisses moved down her neck, her chest, until they found her breast, where they lingered, causing the warmth to become a flame of desire. Her fingers pulled him even closer as her body moved under him, wanting more, demanding more.

Zachary glanced up into her eyes, hot desire showing on his handsome face and through a teasing smile he thrust himself inside her causing her to release her desires as she quivered under him. Slowly he began moving inside her, feeling his need growing with each faster motion and when he knew she was ready to go again, he released himself at the exact moment and they both lay there wrapped in each other arms until the beautiful feeling ebbed back to normal.

"I needed this morning to be filled with passionate love, my beautiful Autumn." Zachary rolled over and pulled her into his arms. "How can I leave you now that you belong to me at last? Those years we were apart was a living hell, for I long to be with you then, and now, now that I have felt what it is like to be your husband and to make love to you, to be away from you for a single hour will seem like an eternity."

"I hated this war before, but now, I wished it would end this very day!" Autumn buried her face in Zachary's strong chest. "The thought of you being out there on some battlefield, getting shot at or attack by other Calvary men with swords, drives me mad with anguish!"

"God knows I have never been afraid to fight before, my darling, but knowing what I have waiting, I will be fighting now to stay alive, for you, for us!" Zachary lifted her tear stain face and kissed her. "That prayer you said asking God to protect me and Clint made me feel real, good, darling. Your uncle Bedford is a great leader and the casualties from his ranks are few, so I feel secure whenever I ride with him. Precious, I do not want you sitting around this house worrying about me. Keep busy doing something, anything that makes you happy."

"You make me happy, Zachary, being with you!" Autumn knew she must stay strong for him, so she gave him her beautiful smile. "Nevertheless, I promise to find something to keep me busy my darling, but you will never be far from my mind."

"I guess I better get dressed and have a quick breakfast before we leave." Zachary gave his bride one last hug in bed before rising. "We've got a long road back and the Calvary will be ready to leave for Tennessee as soon as we return."

"I wish I could come with you!" Autumn knew that would be impossible, but she could not bear him leaving for God knows how long.

Zachary chuckled as he picked up his bag and took her hand after she got dressed. "I would have to fight my own boys then too, to keep them off of you, little darling."

The long tearful farewells were finally over as Autumn and Nellie watched their men ride away, the sisters holding tight to one another. No longer in sight, the sad girls walked back inside the house and wept bitter tears, as they tried to comfort each other.

Forrest's Calvary met up with a part of the Confederate force near Fort Donelson on the Cumberland River. Brigadier Generals John B. Floyd, Gideon J. Pillow, and Simon B. Buckner were in command for securing the fort from Union General Ulysses S. Grant, who had successfully marched on Fort Henry and was deploying around Donelson.

On February 14th, in below freezing weather, Union gunboats joined the Federal forces surrounding the fort and began shelling the Confederate position. Southern artillery returned the fire, striking the ships in the small ironclad flotilla and forcing them to withdraw.

"Our guns have driven them back, General Floyd! The artillerists were a success, sir!" Clint gave Floyd his good report while the Brigadier General merely shook his head with uncertainty.

"Gentlemen, it is my judgement that our position at Donelson is untenable and our force should break through the Federal lines and force them back." So, after an early morning attack by the

Confederates, they managed slowly to press the Union forces back. Then without explanation, Pillow ordered withdrawal giving Grant the opportunity to seize the initiative and the Federals regained the ground they had lost earlier.

That night Floyd called the leaders around him. "Gentlemen, we stand no chance against Grant and the Union army at this point. Hard as it is, gentlemen, we must surrender the fort."

Colonel Forrest stepped up front, the lone dissenting voice as he spoke proudly. "These people are talking about surrendering but I'm going out of this place before they do or bust hell wide open!" Giving up was not part of Forrest's make-up, nor his men's, as they rallied around their brave leader. "Gentlemen, you have turned a favorable situation toward the prospect of surrender, by your bungling and incompetence! I can tell you right here and now, I refuse to allow that to happen to my command!" So, while thirteen thousand Confederates laid down their weapons, Forrest and his Calvary of about five hundred escaped by a flooded road.

After his determined action at Fort Donelson, Forrest had earned a recognition by the army and his actions following the battle of Shiloh, Tennessee, two months later in April 1862 cemented his reputation. Forrest had been placed screening the Confederate retreat from the battlefield and clashed with the pursuing Union column led by General William Tecumseh Sherman at a place called Fallen Timbers.

"Boys, I will only need a small group of men to come with me and Dawson to attack Sherman! We will force the Yankees to deploy so the army will have more time to escape." Forrest singled out the men he wanted. "The rest of you hold back any advancing Federals! Clint, you are in command! Will, keep the boys moving!" the small group took off and spotting a few Union Scouts to their right, Forrest gave the order for Zachary to take half the men and clean house!

Continuing ahead at a great speed, Bedford rode out in advance of his men and the brave commander found himself quickly surrounded by Sherman's Federals. As the brave man turned to shoot his way out, he was seriously wounded, but this did not stop the tough soldier. Forrest reached down, grabbed his assailant by the collar, pulled him up behind him to protect himself from being shot by anyone else, and galloped away with him. Forrest threw the man down when he no longer needed him and was met by Zachary and the rest of his Calvary. They headed for Mississippi after two operations on the bullet wound were finally successful. The legend of Nathan Bedford Forrest was born. This wound would knock Forrest out of action for several weeks, giving him time to recruit additional troops by running an ad in the Memphis Appeal, promising, "Come on, boys, if you want a heap of fun and to kill Yankees." The volunteers started pouring in and by June, Forrest assumed command of a mounted brigade of fourteen hundred men.

Zachary and Clint were placed in charge of training the new recruits to give their fearless leader the time he needed to heal from his wound. The training took away any chance the young men might have had to go see their wife's, who had received only a few hurried letters from their husbands.

"Zachary says, Uncle Bedford has got him and Clint busy training the new soldiers and any hope of coming for a short visit while in the area is very slim." Autumn lovingly held the last letter she had received before the Calvary would be headed back to battle. "My beloved says he misses me dreadfully and lies in his bedroll thinking about me and our…" Autumn blushed "our love making. He says, I was hoping to see you before years end, but Bedford is a fighter and his favorite line for us men is: "War means fighting, and fighting means killing." And that is what he expects from each one of us! I cannot believe it has been over a year since I have seen you, dearest Autumn. Spring has returned and the year has moved up to 1863. We have just had new orders to leave for northern Alabama. We will be leaving soon, and this time under Brigadier General Nathan Bedford Forrest. Clint and I was promoted to Colonel and at the rate Bedford is going he will get promoted to Major General! Dearest Autumn, I pray I can take a furlough the next time we are in the area and spend some much-needed time with my wife. The fellows like to rib me about my ear protection, but it keeps a little part of you with me and really does work to block out the loud guns and cannons firing off. Before I tie on your soft handkerchief over my head, I place two smooth-carved out ear plugs inside my ears. They can laugh all they like, but I will be the one hearing my children's laughing and calling me daddy." Autumn smiled at Nellie, who was cradling her small daughter. "Those men of ours are in for double surprises when they return. If they are away much longer, their children will be running out to meet them!"

"Mama thinks we should tell Zachary and Clint they are fathers."

Nellie looked down when her little girl giggled. "What? You think we should surprise them too, since we had to go through all the pregnancy and the labor without them?"

Autumn looked down at the playpen below her. "What do you two, think? Should we be waiting on that big porch holding your hands when they ride up at last?" the little red hair, green eyed girl and the handsome little fellow with black hair and blue eyes looked up at her with their big eyes and said, da-da."

"They finally said da-da!" Frederick chuckled as he got down to pat his grandchildren on the head. "I think surprising your da-das is the smart thing to do." He looked up at the women watching him. "Really, I do. If Zachary and Clint knew they had children waiting for them as well as beautiful wife's, they might get side-tracked in their daydreams and get in danger."

"You do have a point Frederick. I never thought of that. I see how it could change their way of thinking"

Chapter 33

General Forrest and his gallant Calvary pursued Colonel Abel Streight through the mountains of Northern Alabama in the late spring of 1863. When the two forces finally faced each other, Forrest was at the head of the force of six hundred men, Colonel's Dawson and Reynolds riding beside him. Colonel Streight had fifteen hundred men. The two leaders met under a flag of truce, and Forrest stood so the Federal commander could see his troops and artillery marching around a nearby hill. Nervously the colonel asked Forrest the question that was weighing on his mind.

"Forrest, how many men do you have with you?"

Staring calmly and answering with a smirk, the Confederate leader said plainly "I have enough men with me to handle this situation!"

Pondering the Confederate commander's response, the Federal leader was half-convinced that he was outnumbered, so he surrendered his large force to Forrest's bluff. When the deception was exposed, the tricky soldier was alleged to have said "Ah, Colonel, all's fair in love and war, you know." His method was a tactic that all soldiers wished they had the courage to try but stuck to the rules. Nathan Bedford Forrest intimidated anyone that cross him wrong, Confederates as well as Federals. And even though his troops admired and looked up to the ruthless genus, they feared his explosive temper, as did some of his commanding officers, all but Zachary Dawson and his son William.

"Bedford, you bring fear to most all your men when your temper grows out of control." Zachary had been summons to the general's tent, along with Will, to have supper with him. "They have never seen the side of you I know. Gentle and loving, treating me just as you do Will, here."

"War brings out the worse in me, I fear. I am just glad my Mary Ann is not around to see the devil come out in her devoted husband." Bedford ate his supper without feeling remorse for any of his killing. "I do not fit in with the regular army, son. The brotherhood from West Point, always treated me like an outsider and that suited me find, because I never wanted to be a part of that losing brotherhood.

205

I operate by my own rules and sometimes I make up the rules as I go along."

"I agree every situation is different and there are times when adequate does not apply to the solution." Zachary noticed how Will remained quiet, as if he too were a little intimidated by his father's ways. "I have witness many of your made-up rules in several of our battles and I agreed with each strategy, except perhaps killing a man for every horse shot out from under you."

"You might feel different if it was Midnight that was killed." Bedford knew he hit a sore spot by the dark cloud covering the usually calm blue eyes. "Yes, I thought as much," He reached over and gave him a fatherly hug. "Son, I know you pretty well too, so if every I see a mission too awkward for you to handle, I will send you on another mission while I carry out the difficult one."

"Please sir, tell me you would never stoop to killing innocent women and children, if you find them in your way?" Zachary had to ask, not knowing after seeing so much death and mangled bodies in the terrible war already, what could be too awkward for a seasoned soldier like him.

"Unless some devil of a woman or some bad seed child points a gun to shoot me or my boys, I would never harm a hair on their precious head." Bedford sipped on his brandy, eyes closed. "I grow weary boys. Go get you some rest, we got some fighting to do tomorrow."

Following the battle of Chickamauga in September 1863, Braxton Bragg failed to follow up his victory by pushing on and attacking the Union forces before they could regroup at Chattanooga. This outraged Forrest and he stormed into the general's Missionary Ridge headquarter and began threatening Bragg.

"You have played the part of a damn scoundrel and are a coward! If you were any part of a man, I would slap your jaws and force you to resent it, your actions you ordered! I say to you that if you ever again try to interfere with me or cross my path it will be at the peril of your life!" Forrest stormed back out, never to serve under Bragg again nor was his insubordination punished. Bragg knew that Forrest would have no remorse about killing him, so Bragg let the matter drop. Two weeks following the enraged General's attack on his fellow general, Forrest met with the Confederate President, Jefferson Davis and he transferred him to the West so he would feel free to command his troops around the Union lines in Northern Mississippi, near western Tennessee.

Nathan Bedford Forrest's reputation just increased and he was made major general, just as Zachary had predicted, in December, 1863. Zachary was promoted to Brigadier General at the same time, for his outstanding riding and soldiering, and quickly got the name of the Wizard Kid! Then the order came that Bedford knew would be coming, so he called Colonel Clint Reynolds and Colonel William Forrest into his tent to go over his military plan of attack.

"Gentlemen, as you can see, I have deliberately left out my right arm man. Zachary would never agree to my strategy and it will be carried out to plan. What I tell you must remain silent or you will be shot for disobeying my command. Are we clear on this?" Nathan Forrest rolled out a map when both men said, yes sir. "As you already know, Fort Pillow, once one of our supply forts along the Mississippi River was garrisoned by about six hundred Federals. What you do not know is three hundred of the soldiers are blacks, mostly former slaves, and the other three hundred white men are all Tennessee Unionists."

"These Yankee Tennesseans will pay for being turncoats!" Clint voiced his angry opinion. "They are nothing but stinking hometown Yanks and I better not see any of my Black servants in Blue!"

"We will tell the boys whenever you see anything blue, shoot at it, and do all you can to keep up the scare!" Forrest spoke softly knowing Zachary would grow suspicious having the meeting without him. "Tomorrow, we will head out and surround the fort and I will offer them a chance to surrender. If they refuse, which I am certain of, we will swarm in on them and take the fort back! I will send Zachary out to scout out any Federal scouts, giving him about ten men." Forrest smiled up at his colonels. "Remember, this is a top-secret mission and we mean to do business with that bunch of traitors!"

Zachary was waiting back at the camp headquarters when the main Calvary body rode back in, ragged from fighting, a few wounds but no casualties. He watched Bedford moved quickly toward his big tent and looking around, Zachary spotted his other friend, Clint Reynolds, looking somewhat down. He made his way over by Clint's side and handed him a drink, then joined him on a camp chair.

"Rough day?" Zachary casually asked. "It had to be hell, I'm guessing since Bedford sent me in the opposite direction, he did not want my help with this mission."

"Count yourself lucky my friend." Clint was glad for the company and a chance to finally tell what the mission was. "You are right, about the general not wanting you by his side. He knew you would be against the attack. Even I tried to convince Forrest to let me stop the boys from all their slaughtering, but he would not hear of it. He simply answered with, no, no! Shoot them down like dogs!"

"Clint, when you say 'Slaughtering,' you cannot be referring to combat. Were these Federals trying to surrender and Bedford ordered them all shot down?" Zachary suddenly had mixed emotions, glad to have missed the killing but angry that he was not there to put a stop to it before it got out of control. "I cannot believe the man I have always loved and admired so deeply could just shoot a man down in cold blood!"

"Forrest did not exactly give the order to not take any prisoners and kill them all." Clint took a big gulp, happy for the brandy. "At first, our leader offered the Federals fair treatment if they surrendered but of course six hundred Yankee's thought they could hold Fort Pillow. They weren't prepared for all the hate raging from all the Confederates that had them surrounded. Those Yankees inside that fort consisted of three hundred blacks, mostly slaves, who were begging for their lives on their knees, and three hundred Tennessee Union soldiers." Clint twisted his hat, remembering the cries of surrender. "They put up a fight at first, but all the bent-up hate and the fact our boys thought they were doing what their commander wanted them to do, they simply slaughtered most of the six hundred men."

"This will not stand with our military leaders! They will insist on a full report and even though Bedford is clever at getting away with his actions, this time he has gone too far!" Zachary looked up at his old teacher's tent and noticed his light was still on. "He is expecting me to come to him." Zachary stood up, brave and not afraid to stand for his principals. "I will let Bedford explain his rash actions, then I will tell him why I must resign!"

"I hate the thoughts of you leaving us, Zachary, when we need you so desperately." Clint looked up, feeling even more depressed about Zachary possible departure, "It just won't be the same without you. Your skills in the saddle distract the enemy for they are totally amazed with your tricks and awarding you with the nickname, the Wizard Kid! Please rethink your decision my friend. This war cannot last much longer."

"I cannot promise you anything Clint, until I have had my talk with Bedford. I will let you know my decision in the morning. Goodnight friend." Without looking back, Zachary made his way to the commanding general's tent.

Chapter 34

Zachary knocked lightly on the general's entrance. "May I come in sir. I think you have been expecting me."

"Zachary, you always did know me better than anyone else, even my beloved Mary Ann." Nathan smiled up from writing his report. "You are here about today's mission, correct?"

"Bedford, why, in the name of God, did you allow your men to massacre all those men when they were surrendering?" Zachary boldly stepped up next to his old teacher, feeling the need to get everything out in the open. "I was told the poor black soldiers were down on their knees, begging for mercy and my fellow Calvary men ordered them to stand before they shot them down in cold blood! Is that what you wanted, Bedford, to kill those men, just because of your hate for them?"

"They were damn traitors, join the Union Army to kill their fellow southerners!" Forrest answered just as angrily. "I know I will probably get the book thrown at me for what happened, but I can see no difference in what both the north and the south do to their own soldiers who run away from all the fighting and killing! They are hunt down like criminals, and executed by a firing scald, for desertion! Innocent young men who fought bravely for as long as they could endure the pain and suffering, who grew homesick for home and love ones, just like you have missed your girl!" Bedford took hold of Zachary's shoulder. "Son, this is war and war, is not pretty, but we fight to keep our rights and even though I think we might lose this war, I will not go down without a fight!"

"Even though I believe what you did was wrong Bedford, you are absolutely right to say those who lead both sides are just as bad by killing their own men for being deserters. They are hypocrites to find their commanders guilty of murder when they kill just as easily, those frightened runaways." Zachary knew what he was about to say would not be easy. "Bedford, you knew not to take me with you this morning to that fort. I would have given them a chance to surrender, which you did, at first, then you ordered the men in to take care of business after the Union soldiers refused your offer. They put up a fight at first, but they were overtaken and tried to surrender. That is when I would have stepped in to stop the fighting and order the enemy to hand over their weapons, secure them until the larger Confederate force arrived to take them as prisoners."

"Did you ever think that what my boys did might have saved those men a whole lot more suffering, if they had been taken to one of our stinking war prisons!" Nathan knew he had made a perfectly true statement. "Those men would have probably starved to death, if they hadn't been beaten to death by one of the mean wardens." Nathan gave a sarcastic laugh "Those Yankee prisons aren't any better! Our poor soldiers are given little to no rations and treated like dogs! Like I said son, war is hell on earth!"

"Yes sir, war is hell, but a soldier needs to first follow the greatest commander sir! The Almighty God has witnessed his share of wars and men killing the enemy shooting at him, but he does not approve of cold-blooded murder, as a part of war!" Zachary looked at his old friend with compassion and total sadness when he finally said. "Sir, I think it's time for me to resign and go home."

"Zachary, I will never beg you to stay. It is not a part of who I am. I will say, you are my greatest access, the best soldier I have ever trained or has ridden beside me. Do I need you to help me fight? I would feel better knowing it was you riding beside me more than anyone I have ever known, even Will, my own boy." Sadness filled his hard eyes. "But if your choice is to leave, then I will make it legal and write up your discharge papers. I would never want anyone to think you were a deserter. Could you do one thing for me first, Zachary? Sleep on this before you make your final decision?"

"Thank you for the discharge, sir." Zachary had mixed feelings when he felt his old friend touch his arm.

"I will sleep on it then, and let you know first thing in the morning." Zachary started for the exit when he heard Bedford call his name.

"Zachary, if you choose to stay with me, I will try to be a better man, the kind of man you believed me to be." He gave a soft laugh. "I guess your old hero just fell off his horse, but he is hoping for another chance to prove he is the same man that taught a young ten-year-old kid everything he knows about being a good soldier."

"Bedford, did I ever tell you I won West Point Soldier of the Year before I had to leave my freshman year?" Zachary smiled.

"I knew you were the best already, son." Bedford returned his smile. "What say, if you choose to stay, we do one more battle together, then go back to the home headquarters for a rest, and you and Clint can get a furlough and go see your pretty little women? Just an offer in case your answer is yes. Goodnight Zachary."

"Goodnight sir." Again, Zachary headed for the door when he heard Bedford's soft message.

"Forgive me! I love you, son."

Zachary paused, his heart pounding with unbelievable joy as tears filled his blue eyes and he turned back around slowly to respond to the unexpected words. "I do not need to sleep on my decision. Anyone who ask for forgiveness should always be given another chance. To be loved by you was never a doubt in my heart, Bedford, but to hear it come directly from your lips means more to me than you can possibly imagine." Zachary stepped back inside and took around the gentle giant. "Ever since my mother died then my father was taken from me, I felt like an orphan, but whenever I thought about you, I felt in my heart that you were my second father, so much like me in so many ways. I guess I was just disappointed to see your failures in my sight, but God knows, I am not perfect nor am I one to judge the man I love most in this world. So, as long as this war rages on, I will be at your side, fighting the enemy until we can lay down our weapons!"

"Sounds great! My plans remain the same though! One more fight, then take a well needed break and let you go see that beautiful niece of mine." He ushered Zachary to the entrance. "Now, get you some rest boy! I intend to do the same, now that I do not have worries to keep me awake!"

"I would not want to be the one responsible for disturbing your beauty sleep sir!" Zachary laughed when he felt Forrest's light kick on his back side and laughed all the way to his tent.

After another successful battle, General Forrest and his brave Calvary were returning though a thick row of trees when one of his scouts rode up, out of breath.

"General, we have been trapped sir! There are Federal troops in front of us and at our rear!"

"What are we going to do general?" Clint asked as he tried to see up ahead but found only the road blocked on either side by thick woods. "We are most certainly trapped inside this long road!"

"There is only one way out boys! We will split the army right down the middle and hit him at both ends! Zachary, take the back half and bust out the rear! I will take the front half and bust out the front door! Those stupid Yanks won't know what is coming for them when you start yelling like demons straight from hell! Go, give 'em what for Boys!" Bedford took off in front while Zachary flew in front of the men at the rear and took off in such a swift gallop it was hard for the men to keep up.

The Federal Troops waited silently, guns pulled, ready for combat, when they heard the sound of unnatural screaming. Their horses began balking and moving around nervously, unsure of what sort of being was causing all the noise. From the front, Bedford galloped out, hanging off the side of his big horse, causing the Union soldiers to stare at the spectacle. At the other end, Zachary's horse flew out, then Zachary did a double back flip on the saddle and stood up swinging his sword at the startled West Point soldiers. Recognizing their young award winner, the Union Calvary gave their hero enough space to do his tricks while his soldiers rode on to safety,

Zachary stopped and Midnight reared up as the young soldier yelled out to his fellow cadets, "Stay safe boys!" and over their cheers, Zachary rode away.

Both halves of Forrest Calvary reunited at Twin Lakes and rode back to their camp. They dismounted and went to pack their things. The brave group of men would be breaking camp the following morning and heading for Mississippi.

Back at Federal headquarters, things did not go as easy. General Sherman was grilling his troops. "How, in the name of God, did you miss nabbing Forrest and that Calvary of his? I made my orders perfectly clear to you, stop those men at all cost! Can you explain why you let them get away?"

"Sir, these were no ordinary soldiers you sent us after! Both their leaders are like…well…magical! These men are super-human! They can do things we only dream about!"

"So, you men are telling me you fell for That Wizard in the Saddle and the Wizard Kid?" Sherman shook his head and stormed off. In his frustration he recommended: "Follow Forrest to the death if it cost ten thousand lives and breaks the Federal treasury. There will be no peace in Tennessee till Forrest Is dead!"

But Sherman would never get his wish. Nathan Bedford Forrest had reached Mississippi and he and his loyal Calvary would be safe from Sherman's threats.

Chapter 35

"Da-da is too coming home, Winter Rose!" the young two-year-old scolded his twin sister and she started to cry. "Don't cry Winter Rose. Skyler is sorry for yelling at you, but I know da-da loves us and mommy."

"Of course, your daddy loves you both dearly, because he loves mommy dearly." Autumn squatted down to wrap an arm around each sweet child. "Your daddy is going to be so surprised when he comes home and see his daughter and son for the first time." Autumn gave Nellie a wink when she walked in carrying her dark hair, brown eyed baby girl. "I bet your Uncle Clint will be just as surprised to see his pretty Nellie holding on to his Callie."

"If those men of ours do not come home soon, they might see their children grown and ready to be married." Nellie laughed at the thought. "The least Clint could do is come home long enough to give little Callie a sister or brother. Zachary was thoughtful enough to start you out with two."

"You two are beginning to sound anxious for your charming husbands to come home to you." Frederick looked up from a letter he received that very morning. "Perhaps if I read you what my letter says it might bring a spark of glow in your cheeks." He chuckled when they both rose to attention to listen. "It is from my legendary brother, Major General Nathan Bedford Forrest."

"Uncle Bedford!" Autumn walked over and took a seat on the arm rest of her father's big chair, Nellie nestling in on the other arm. "Do read on!"

"My carefree, lucky brother, to be able to remain with your perfectly beautiful wife and daughters is a blessing indeed. I know, for there is nothing I miss more than my Mary Ann, so I am taking a furlough along with most of the men at my camp. Other than the loyal volunteers who chooses to remain at headquarters, those men who have either parent's longing to have their sons home or the luckier men who have survived this war to return to the arms of their loving wives and lovers. You may inform Autumn and Nellie that their men, who have been longing and are starved for their affection, are coming home as I write. If my calculations are correct, they should be arriving around five o'clock this afternoon. Knowing my darling niece, Autumn Rose is seated by your side at this very moment…" Frederick stopped to glanced up at his daughter giggling and shaking her head, then her father looked back down at the words. "and reading this letter along with you, word for word. Can't say that I blame her or Nellie, for that matter. They are married to two remarkable men. You should have just enough time to get yourself all pretty and be waiting on Belmont's big porch when those boys ride up. I know there will be no shortage of loving going on, so dear brother Frederick, just let them enjoy one another! This war cannot last much longer, for the south is running low on supplies and the food shortage has hurt everyone, including those stinking rat wholes they call prisons, and the damn Yankees keep blaming us for their soldiers becoming skin and bones when it's those commanders, Sherman and Sheridan that are raping and vandalizing every state in the Confederacy! The good news is, we are told Laurel Grove is one of the only plantations still standing between Charleston and Savannah. Take care, your brother, Bedford."

Autumn grabbed the letter and laid a big kiss across it and she tossed it back in her father's lap, then started for the steps yelling for the twins to play with their granddaddy. She had only one hour to get ready, and she planned to be waiting on that porch, kids in tow. Zachary was on his way to her at long last.

Zachary and Clint stopped at the entrance to catch their breaths, from riding at full speed for the last hour. Willis snapped awake, startled by the noise and the flying dust. The sign fumbled in his shaking hands as he jumped to his feet mumbling

"You can't gets down this road! There be the fever and it is real, bad! I's the lucky one!"

"Willis, it's Mr. Reynolds! Calm yourself man! We have come home to see our women!" Clint got off his horse and moved up so his servant could see him better. "Please tell us this is still just a made-up story to protect our families and the manor house and no one really has small pocks!"

"It really you, Mr. Reynolds?" old Willis relaxed when Clint gave him a positive nod. "Thank God you home sirs! We are all pretty healthy around the big house as well as the slave quarters. Everyone, including those two pretty little wives of yours, are doing their share of the work, since about two-thirds of them brothers of mine up and left. It taint been easy but we've faired pretty good."

"Well, we're here now for a while before we go back to fighting." Clint climbed up easily in his saddle. Why don't you swing on up here with me Willis and go get you some much needed rest? There are no Yankees in these parts so you can put your caution signs up for the time being."

Willis chuckled as he handed Clint the sign and with the owner's other hand assisting him up in the saddle, the cheerful black man chuckled even louder. "Yes sir, now taking that rest might not be so easy with that passel of children moving wildly around your feet every time you fix to make a step. They done went and be born when the snow covered the ground, oh, 'bout two or so winters ago, yes sir, tat they did."

"Willis, I see nothing new about your people conceiving lots of babies in the winter season." Clint smiled over at his silent friend who was taking the black man's many words in. "Willis must be regaling you with his colorful way of describing how even the slaves are stuck inside their homes during our bad winters." The plantation owner chuckled. "I add many new names to my logbook of registered blacks in my employment."

"Employment?" Zachary had been under the impression that Clint owned most all his blacks and they were truly his slaves. With these words of hope, Zachary suddenly saw his friend in a new light. "So, if your blacks are free men, those that chose to leave cannot be hold accountable as runaways, correct?"

"Correct, my friend. It was I that wrote my Nellie a letter informing her to send for my personal lawyer and have him write up papers of freedom for those slaves I had not already freed." Clint knew he did not owe Zachary any explanation, but their new bond and friendship made him seek his approval on how he ran his plantation and how he treated his fellow human beings. After hearing Zachary make a speech about that very topic to a group of men downgrading freed blacks, Clint Reynolds made the decision to free every slave he had and offer them a paying job and home.

"So, the ones that stayed have their own home and a decent salary, just like Autumn's family did for their slaves." Zachary looked anxiously down the long drive. "I do not know about you Reynolds, but there is a very beautiful woman waiting just down that drive for me and I have kept her waiting long enough!" he patted the big black horse's neck. "Midnight, your rest is over, my friend! Make fast!" with lighting speed, the horse and rider took off, leaving Clint chasing behind him laughing as Willis squeezed his big eyes shut and hung on for dear life.

Autumn and Nellie sat rocking on the long porch as their small children chased each other up and down the long space. Autumn Rose sat up and looked out the long driveway to a lone horseman coming down the road at a full gallop. Dust flew around the big black stallion as the man wearing all black, made staying in the saddle look easy. With her heart pounding with total excitement, the girl with the beautiful red hair and green eyes stood up and made her way to one of the massive pillars that went down the full expanse of the porch, and waited for the rider to reach her.

Zachary pulled his horse to a sudden stop and looked up on the porch into the beautiful face he had been dreaming about for far too many months. As he climbed down from Midnight, Autumn raced down the wide steps and met him halfway in a tight embrace. There was no need of words, for their kisses and caresses, showed their deep need for one another.

As Clint rode up, his attention fell on the love starved lovers, then up on the porch where Nellie was making her way down to him. Clint threw the reigns to his stable boy as he asked him to help Willis down, then he grabbed Nellie, kissing her repeatedly.

The couples were so caught up in their reunion they hadn't noticed three little faces staring up at them until the small boy gave Zachary a sock on his leg, causing him to look down.

"Hey little fellow, why did you sock me in the leg?" Zachary smiled down at the angry face of his son.

"Cause, you kiss my mommy, mister! My da-da will beat you up!" Skyler narrowed his little blue eyes as Zachary stared down in shock.

"Your mommy?" He took in the black hair and blue eyes before glancing over beside the small boy.to see a tiny duplicate of Autumn Rose, with red hair and green eyes. "Your mommy too, sweet baby girl?"

Little Winter Rose started crying as her little arms wrapped around his long legs. "Da-da!"

"I am…a…da-da?" Zachary finally looked over at the woman he held in his arms and found her smiling. "Autumn, my darling, did we…are these…?"

"Winter Rose and Skyler were born in November, two years ago my darling." Autumn enjoyed his happy smile as she gave him a loving squeeze before lifting up her children and placing them in her true love's arms. "When you left me to go to war Zachary, you did give me something to keep me busy."

"Why didn't you write and tell me you were expecting babies, my love. Perhaps, I could have arranged to be here when you went into labor." He remembered how they were constantly on the march and knew it would only be false promises, "I just hate you had to suffer through all those birth pains alone."

"Hardly alone, dearest Zachary." Autumn knew most men was more likely to pass out from watching their babies being born than the women who helped deliver them. "Think of it like this darling, you had your stresses with war and constant fighting. I just could not permit you to have another reason to let your mind wonder. Thinking about me was enough to keep your mind off the enemy at times." Autumn smiled at Nellie, then Clint, still unaware that he also left Nellie with a child. "We had mother, Aunt Vera, and Glenda, not to mention all those precious black ladies who assisted with love and care. So darling, you and Uncle Clint should be overjoyed you did not have to sat through the battle of a father waiting for their son or daughter, or both in your case, my dearest Zachary."

Skyler looked up at the other tall man hugging his Aunt Nellie and pulled at his coat sleeve, then waited for the big man to smile down. "You are Uncle Clint?" Clint laughed softly, patted his dark hair and nodded yes. "Hey, Callie, that is your da-da!"

Clint's eyes flew open as a small hand touched his leg. Looking down, his heart melted as he scooped the precious little girl up in his arms and gave her a tender hug. "I guess your mommy kept me in the dark just like Skyler and Winter Rose's daddy. Dang it all, I am a father!" lifting his daughter in one arm, he wrapped the spare one around his pretty young wife and gave her another kiss. "Thank you, Nellie, for giving me such a beautiful home coming gift, and just when I thought I could not possibly love anything with almost exactly the same kind of love as I do you, my darling."

The soldiers would be on leave for two whole weeks and they took advantage of every waking second. During the daytime hours, the children took up a lot of their father's time, as they showed them the things a father likes to share. Still too small for many things, like riding horseback alone, learning the art of sword fighting and gun safety, mostly for young Skyler, would have to wait, but how to plant a tree and watch it grow while they were away fighting, or how to play with each other without being a bully or a sore loser. Zachary and Clint helped with teaching the children stories from the Bible, insisting Autumn and Nellie dress up the children and all attend Sabbath services on the two Sundays they were present, promising it would become a family tradition after the war.

When the children were napping or tucked in for the night, the loving couples resumed their passionate love making. As the weeks flew past, Autumn and Nellie's parents insisted they keep the children to give their adult children some time to spend together. It was on one such morning, Zachary got a letter from an old friend and he shared it with his Autumn after riding their horses down to a private spot.

"I don't know how Abe found me here, Autumn, but he and I grew close while he arranged for my passage to Mississippi."

"The president of the United States helped you run away from the north, darling?" Autumn laid her head over on his shoulder. "Why haven't you shared this with me before, Zachary?"

"I wasn't sure how you felt about the president, since the south elected Jefferson Davis to be your president." He caressed her hair before kissing the top of her head. "I never wish to upset you and my loving Abraham Lincoln might be considered an offence to many, as being two-face or a southern traitor, neither of which I am."

"I have no hard feeling toward President Lincoln, Zachary." She sat up and gazed into his alluring blue eyes. "I find him a warm, sensitive, caring man and a devoted husband and father to his children." Autumn looked at the private stationary, not official or from the white house. "He thought of your safety, my darling, for sending you just plain stationary, so no one would see your connection to the north."

"Do you know Abe considered me an older version of his sons." He opened the letter, read the first line and tears filled his blue eyes. "The fever has no respect for someone as good as my friend Abe!"

"Zachary, what is it? Is one of his family sick? Has Mr. Lincoln took a fever?"

"It's the small boy, little Will. He was so full of energy, always wanting me to play soldier with him! Now he's dead and Father Abe and Mary are heartbroken beyond belief!" Zachary caught his breath when he felt Autumn place her arm around his shoulder. "I would like to be there for Abe but under these conditions it would be foolish, even dangerous, not only for me but for the president as well, if he is caught harboring a southern soldier, especially one they are looking for."

"Then you must find a way to send him your correspondence and let him know you too are heart broken and you will do all in your power to see him after this horrible war is over." Autumn took the short letter and helped him up. "We shall find a way together, my darling. Any friend of yours is a friend of mine. You may use some of my stationary. No one would ever expect a lady's letter to be a spy or a secret agent."

"Dearest Autumn, this is why I have always loved you so. Your 100% total devotion to me and the beautiful and perfect love we have shared for so many years." Zachary pulled her into his arms. The thought of leaving you again is bedded deep within my enter most thoughts and I pray that this war that keeps us apart will end so I will never have to leave your side again, for as long as I live!"

Chapter 36

"There's a letter from home!" Nellie ran in waving the white envelope. "It is from Big Ben and dated only last week!" she handed the letter to the head of the house and Frederick tore it open and began reading aloud.

"Greeting dear family! Good news, the Federal troops have moved out of South Carolina. It's time for you to come home and the best news is, your house is standing tall, the servants houses, barns, sheds, everything is just like you left it! You would be real proud of us, Mr. Frederick, knowing the livestock is still with us and the harvest for the long length of time you were gone, was a real bounty. You would be real proud of old Ben, I done went and took the cotton and sugar cane up to the Savannah docks and got us a fair price. Yes sir, done real, good! There is a little bad news I been treading to share with Miss Autumn. That lonely Jack done went and ran off somewhere we haven't the slightest. For almost the first year, poor old Jack would sit outside Miss Autumn's window, waiting for her to go for her morning walk, you know, to that secret place she loves so good. I felt real, sorry for poor old Jack, so Ben here started taking walks with him, trying to cheer him up, and he seemed happy enough until that stray dog came through here. Old Jack didn't like another dog sniffing around his barnyard, so he up and chased it off and never came back. Tell Miss Autumn I is real, sorry and if it would make her feel better, you know fill that empty place where old Jack was, I will buy her a new pup to raise. Well, that just about tells what's what around these parts. See you all real soon. Tell Nellie, Nora has made her some of them preserves she loves so good and she is ready for a big hug from both girls. Take care. Your old friend, Ben."

"Poor Jack, it about breaks my heart to imagine that sweet dog waiting outside my room every morning and I never came out. Why, I just bet my sweet Jack thought I forgot about him and being heartbroken, he just ran away, never looking back anymore." Autumn could not control her tears as they fell down her cheeks. "Why didn't we bring Jack, daddy" He was my pet and I let him down!" Autumn flopped down on the sofa. "I feel just terrible."

"Now darling, you know we could never bring that dog all the way from South Carolina." Katherine tried to console her sad child. "Besides, it would not be polite to bring an animal into another person's home without asking."

"I am sure Clint would have loved Jack, Katherine." Nellie flopped down next to her sister and best friend. "I feel pretty terrible myself!"

"Why, about what I did to my poor Jack?" Autumn took the handkerchief from her father's extended hand. "Thanks daddy." She blew her nose after wiping her eyes. "I'll wash it out for you before we leave."

"It is sad thinking about poor old Jack waiting up on that porch for you morning after morning, Autumn, but I was thinking about what mama...Nora said, about making me my favorite preserves. Strawberry!" Nellie started crying and Frederick looked forlorn at Katherine, knowing he had no more handkerchiefs on him.

"Nellie, sweetheart, I cannot understand why Nora making you strawberry preserves upsets you so much." Katherine wrapped her other arm around her other child. "She has made you those preserves lots of times. Why is it any different now?"

"Because I won't be going back to Laurel Grove to live any more, that's why!" Nellie noticed all three Forrest's stared at her, sadness filling each of their eyes. "I am married! I am Clint's wife and my home, is here, with him and our children." Nellie rubbed her big stomach, pregnant again, just like Autumn. "Nora doesn't know about Clint or Callie, I never wrote her because my mama...Nora never could read. She is expecting to see me, give me a hug and I would welcome it with open arms, but until Clint comes home and this baby is born I won't be doing any traveling. I must wait here for him." Nellie sniffed loudly. "That is why I am sad. Not only for Nora, but...all of you! You are my family and I love you with all my heart.

"Nellie, life without you around will never be the same for me." Autumn began crying again and she and Nellie wrapped each other in a tight embrace. "I never for one second considered you having to stay behind, but, how foolish of me to assume any different."

"It may never be the same, dear sister and friend, but we both have someone else now to fill that empty feeling." Nellie smiled through her tears. "You finally have your true love, Zachary, who will always be there for you, warming your nights and brightening your days. I got my prince charming, the man I love so deeply and he me."

"And we have our adorable children, to keep us young and active." Autumn gave a soft laugh. "We have carriages and horses and men who love us so much they would never say no whenever we wish to pay one another a friendly visit."

"Yes! I am certain we shall keep the roads between Mississippi and South Carolina quite busy." It wasn't long until both girls were laughing, which rubbed off on their sad parents, as they joined in.

After being in several more successful battles, the remnants of Forrest's Calvary were regrouping when news arrived of Robert E. Lee's surrender at Appomattox. The war was finally over. On May 9, 1865, Nathan Bedford Forrest ordered his men around him for one last time to give them a farewell address.

"That we are beaten is a self-evident fact. Any further resistance on our part would be justly regarded as a height of folly...You have been good soldiers; you can be good citizens. Obey the laws, preserve your honor, and the government to which you have surrendered can afford to be, and will be, magnanimous." Other than the farewell message given by General Robert E. Lee, the speech given by Forrest was perhaps the most conciliatory Confederate message of its kind.

The men were moved, almost to tears as they watched their brave leader enter his tent for the last time. With few things to pack, the soldiers spoke their sad farewells to their fellow fighters and rode from camp, never looking back. Only three men were left and after packing their saddles, they made their way into the Lieutenant General's Tent, to help him disassemble his huge canvas headquarters.

"I guess you boys will be going back to Belmont from here." Bedford tied up his last bundle. "Will and I will be making our way back to Crooked Creek! "The tough man picked up two large handfuls of wildflowers and gently place them on top of his saddle bag. "Flowers for my girls. One bunch for my Mary Ann, who loves wildflowers and my sweet little Fanny. Her tiny grave hasn't got any flowers from her papa for some time, and like her mama, little Fanny loved wildflowers."

"You are a good man, Bedford. I shall miss you." Zachary felt strange about the sudden stop to fighting, and the thoughts of not being around his friend and hero. "I guess you'll go back to farming, Bedford?"

"That's the plan son. Once Will and I return, the cotton fields will be getting close to harvest. I will just resume my life as a planter. A good safe occupation. Should please the wife." Bedford strapped on his last bundle before turning toward Zachary and Clint. "Clint, I guess you will resume plantation life too."

"Yes sir, only this time I too have a wife waiting for me and I am quite sure my Nellie will feel a whole lot better with me at home, being a planter." Clint reached his hand out to shake his old commander's. "I do not think I shall miss the fighting at all, but, like my friend Zachary, I will miss getting orders from you, sir."

"Then, if you should miss my orders too much, just come work for me. I give great orders to my field hands during harvest, right Will?" Bedford chuckled along with the three men.

"My father can be a slave driver to black and white alike, when he is giving orders, including me." Will shook his fellow soldier's hands before climbing up in the saddle. "Safe travels gentlemen."

"Same goes for you both." Zachary moved closer to his old commander and teacher. "Well, Bedford, this is it, for a while. Now that I am married to Autumn, I will become a farmer or more likely a horse breeder, whenever I find that murderer who killed my father and stole my inheritance."

"You are referring to that Jax Tyndall that tried to take David's property when he brought you for a visit." Bedford placed his hands on the young man's shoulders and stared into his blue eyes. "Now listen to me son and listen close. You did not just survive a dangerous war to go into some gambling hall unprepared and face a villain like Tyndall! That crooked gambler knows all the tricks there is to know about cards and he knows how to bait his mark. Are you going in with a perfect skill at playing poker and spotting a cheater? You certainly don't fit the description of a lonely man who has lost his love one, so that little bitch can move in and try to make you believe she has fallen for you..." Bedford stopped and studied the very handsome man standing in front of him. "Zachary, I suddenly feel the rules will be changed around this time. What is going through that mind of yours, boy?"

"Bedford, to begin with, I never rush into a serious situation without doing my homework first." Zachary patted the big man's back. "As for Poker, Clint has been teaching the finer points of playing and catching the best kind of cheater. As for Miss Melody Marigold, I won't be the one looking and drooling." Zachary watched the men's facial expressions for any disagreement with him referring to himself as irresistible, but saw only nodding heads in agreement, so he continued. "This is where the cards will be switched, as they say, or to quote you, Bedford, my friend, suddenly the rules have been changed and I will be playing not only for myself and Autumn, but for all the other innocent sons and daughters this murdering thud stole from."

"But, before you can go waltzing across the southern border, clever friend, you need to be absolutely sure the Federal Army has stopped looking for you." Clint knew of the old enemies Zachary had made and other than Autumn, he was the only other person Zachary had told that it was President Abraham Lincoln that helped him escape. "Maybe a good friend up north can help us get you a pardon, by President Lincoln. I hear he's a fair man."

"If the busy man has time for you kid!" Bedford grunted. "I don't hold much regards for Mr. Lincoln, cannot say I like Mr. Davis all that much either! Now, some of them lazy field workers might admire the man who is thinking about sending them back across that big wide ocean to their homeland. That's what I hear."

"I'm not too sure the black people will choose going to Africa, since America is the only home these beautiful people know. I pray President Lincoln will at least give them a choice, to stay here, in America and become citizens, or go back to the homeland their ancestors came from when the British came over and started the English Colonies." Zachary knew this would be a question he would ask his friend Abe when they got together. For now, he knew he must leave and go to Autumn, so this would be goodbye for a while. Not knowing if Nathan Forrest would except a hug in front of others watching, Zachary put out his hand. "I will see you later then."

Bedford looked down at the extended hand, then took it, pulling Zachary into his arms. "Friends shake hands boy! Family give hugs for farewell, son. Be careful, stay safe, pray hard, love hard, make babies, laugh a lot, cry only a little, remember, you have the ivory handle pistol, not Jax, the ace of jackass's, and…" Bedford pulled away, looking into his eyes, spoke softly, "never forget how proud I am of you and how very much I love you." One last smile, the big man pushed Zachary over to his horse. "Now get! Kiss that pretty little niece of mine. If I do not move my butt right this minute, I swear I will have to pick another two batches of wildflowers." Forrest swung himself up in the saddle and chuckled when Zachary did a double back flip and landed perfectly. "Not another word boy, just turn and head up that road while me and my boy head south." One click, of his tongue, Nathan Bedford Forest was gone and obeying their general one last time, Clint and Zachary raced off down the road toward Belmont.

"Not here?" Zachary stayed in the saddle as he stared down hopelessly at Nellie, holding on to Clint. "Where did she go and how long ago?"

"The family received a letter from home and left for Laurel Grove over two weeks ago." Nellie knew Zachary would find out sooner or later, so she thought it might be wise to tell him about his new daughter and son. "Autumn would have gone sooner if she hadn't been so close to childbirth."

"Another baby?" Zachary said loudly. "At the rate we're going we will have a dozen children before we reach thirty."

"It does seem like you fellows are always leaving us with a gift." Nellie laughed when Clint grabbed her and lifted her up into his arms, giving her a big kiss. "I do believe you guessed you have yourself a son, Mr. Reynolds." She smiled as Glenda came down the steps carrying the tiny baby and laid him in his daddy's arms. "Clint, meet your son. Ethan, meet you daddy."

"What should I expect to hold besides my darling wife, when I get to Laurel Grove?" Zachary climbed down to see the fine little boy, smiling up at the big man that held him.

"Another two babies to hold and love." Nellie laughed when Zachary's head flew up and stared in disbelief. "That's right, hot daddy! You are now the proud father of Nicholas and Summer Rose."

"My darling Autumn is running out of seasons to name her beautiful daughters." Zachary wiped his brow. "Thank God she didn't start naming our sons the names of the months, there would still be ten more to go!" he checked his pocket watch. "There is still a lot of daylight left in the day. If you could give me a map to Laurel Grove and enough food and water to have along the way, then I will be leaving out!"

Chapter 37

"I expect to see Zachary riding down that tree line drive any day now." Autumn had taken her usual seat on the wide porch next to her mother, as she rocked her little boy while her mother took care of the baby girl. "His letter came weeks ago stating everyone knew the war would soon be over and as soon as he could get away he was coming to me."

"If he did not get your letter about going home to Laurel Grove, how would he know to come here instead of Belmont?" Katherine smiled down at the sleeping baby.

"After receiving the news about the war ending, I thought my beloved would never receive my last letter in time to know of our return, so I had asked Nellie to give him a map to Laurel Grove. Knowing my Zachary, he probably turned right around and is headed here at this very moment."

"Then we come out on this porch every morning and plan to wait right here until we see his black horse coming down our drive, correct?" Katherine glanced over at her daughter.

"That is exactly what I intend to do mama, for as long as it takes!"

Just out at the entrance, Zachary pulled Midnight to a sudden stop when he saw the big collie standing in the middle of his way. The description fit Autumn's dog perfectly, so Zachary climbed down and bent over calling Jack by name. Tail wagging, the friendly collie ran up for a loving pat.

"Are you out here to welcome me Jack?" Zachary rubbed his head and started to climbed back on Midnight when the excited collie grabbed his shirt sleeve and pulled him back. "Hey fellow, what is wrong with you? We need to get you home!" instead of running back toward the house, the excited dog ran over to a clump of trees and gave a yelp. Then Zachary could hear what sounded like baby puppies, whimpering. "Jack, you rascal!" Zach looked in and saw a female collie feeding four little puppies. "Looks like you and I have something in common, buddy!? He rubbed Jack's head, then the mother dog. "Jack, oh boy, this is no place to raise your family." Zachary scooped up two of the pups and placed them gently in his saddle bag before collecting the other two. "Alright, Mama and Daddy, let's get you home. Lead the way Jack!" Jack gave a loud bark and waited for Zachary to climb on the horse, then both dogs ran ahead for a while, then dropped back to run beside the big black horse.

Autumn sat up and stared in disbelief as Zachary came down the driveway escorted by two golden collies. Handing the baby to her father who came out to see who had ridden up, Autumn raced down the wide, open arm steps and met Zachary in a passionate kiss. Their special moment was interrupted by the happy collie who had recognized his mistress and overjoyed to know she had come back. He jumped up and gave her a friendly lick before yelping for his mate, who ran over, wagging her tail, giving her own bark.

"So, this is why you ran off, you sly little darling." Autumn nuzzled her face up next to her loving pet, then backed away, making a distasteful face. "Jack, when was the last time you had a good bath?"

"I'd say that rascal Jack never one time thought about bathing Miss Autumn." Benjamin chuckled out loud as Zachary started handing down the puppies. "Well now, Mr. Jack, I can see you made real, good time of your run-away. Yes sir, and I thought you were just chasing that pretty little dog away when instead, you were chasing her down!" he gave another loud laugh. "You done up and got yourself some children! Sure did."

"Nellie informed me that we have a couple more kids ourselves, my beautiful wife." Zachary once again had his beloved in his arms. "God knows I have missed you, dearest Autumn. When I found out you had left Belmont, I collected a map and enough nourishment to get myself here to you."

"I guessed my sister also informed you that I did write about returning to Laurel Grove. I feared it might get crossed with your leaving headquarters and you would never receive it." Autumn sighed. "I am sorry you had to ride so far out of your way only to find me gone, my darling."

"Do not fret precious. I would have ridden a thousand miles or longer to get back to you, Autumn. You are my life, you and our little ones. Where are they hiding?"

"Mama carried Summer Rose inside right after you rode up, to put her in her crib. The poor thing was sound asleep. Daddy has your other son up on the porch. I named him Nicholas. I hope you do not mind." Autumn motioned for her father to bring the baby down as she felt Zachary touch her hair.

"Mind? My dearest one, you remembered me telling you about my grandfather Nicholas, didn't you? How I always admired him when he gave a blessing before our meals or read a passage from his old warn bible every single night before the family went to bed." Zachary gave his wife a thankful hug. "That's just one more thing I love about you Autumn Rose Dawson, you never forget what I say and the people in my life who have meant so much to me."

Autumn took little Nicholas and placed him in his father's strong arms. "Perhaps our little Nicholas will follow in his great-grandfather's footsteps and become a minister, a man of God."

"That is a far cry to what our son Skyler hopes to become." Zachary smiled down at the happy baby in his arms. "Skyler said he wanted to be a soldier, just like his daddy."

"Did he?" Autumn laughed softly as she pointed to the front door swinging open and two excited children dashing out calling, daddy!

Zachary fell right into helping around the big plantation. He and the black workers got along beautifully and his way of doing things, made hard work seem almost like fun. Like they were doing one day when Ben came down to see for himself just how they were getting their jobs done a lot faster than before Zachary showed up. Hiding himself, Benjamin saw Zachary and the workers driving their two big work horses pulling a wagon filled with fresh cut hay, piled high on top. With expert care, Zachary backed the team of horses back and the wagon made its way straight under the barn hayloft window. Zachary gave a loud whistle and a loud voice called back from the opposite side, "ready!"

Zachary called up to a couple of men waiting in the loft. "If both sides are ready, men, at the sound of my next whistle, start unloading hay! Remember, the side that get all their hay in first, is the winner! Ready!" he yelled loudly. "Set!" then he gave a powerful whistle and the two sides moved swiftly. The men on the wagon tossed the hay high in the window as the men inside kept it moved back against the far wall. As usual, both sides finished almost simultaneous and Zachary called it a tie.

Ben came out laughing loudly. "Well, I see it, but Lordy me, I ain't never seen you boys unload that hay in that barn all that fast before!" he wrapped his big arms around Zachary and gave him a grateful hug. "Boy, you done went and made working a game, yes sir, that is what you just went and did. I truly am grateful! It will be a pure pleasure seeing how you make ginning cotton and whacking down that sugar cane, then staking it all up to dry, loading tons of both for market, somehow be fun instead of back-breaking work!"

"Ben, you might be surprised how learning a few back flips, while loading wagons, can speed up the process!" Zachary laughed when the group of men looked at each other confused. "Gentlemen, it wouldn't take all of you to learn the trick, just a few limber young men. The rest will be throwing the cotton bales, or the sugar cane bundles toward the wagon, the men doing back flips would kick the bale or bundle up on the wagon and men standing there would place the produce for market."

"Zachary, could you show us how this impossible stunt can work?" one of the workers ran inside the barn for a bale of cotton. "These are pretty big and a little heavy. It takes two men to toss, two men to move it on wagon. Can one man' kick such a big and heavy thing?"

"Two of you toss it up toward the wagon, my kick will send it swiftly to the men waiting on the wagon." Zachary moved away and turned around backward before he called throw. The men tossed while at the same time the quick young man did a double flip backward and while in the air, slammed the bale on the wagon. The men watching were mesmerized over the fascinating display of talent.

Autumn stood watching the double back flip and broke into applause, causing Zachary to turn and grab her, laughing. "Darling, I do believe you have entertained these fellows enough for one day. I think it might prove safer for Ben and the boys to leave the back flips up to you, but for now, I have packed us a lovely picnic, so we can spend a little alone time together." Autumn waved two letters in front of her. "Perhaps, we can share our letters with one another."

"Sorry boys, but I would much rather spend my afternoon with my dearest Autumn." Zachary gathered her hand in his as they walked away.

Autumn led him around the manor house and up a tree covered path, Jack and Judy running ahead of them. When they reached the top of a small hill, hidden by flowering scrubs and tall trees, Autumn spread her hand across the open vista and to the open land that laid beyond it. Without looking and knowing her favorite spot was always waiting for her, Autumn took a seat on a flat rock, long enough for two people. She patted her hand next to her and Zachary smiled, then made his way to the rock bench.

"This is your special secret place, my love." Zachary looked out over the beautiful green countryside as his arm draped around her shoulders. "I can see why this place is so special to you Autumn. It sits perfectly east, so the sunrise must always be spectacular up here."

"To watch the sunrise over Dixie is just about the prettiest sight I have ever seen. The only thing better is looking at your face and into your exquisite blue eyes, my darling Zachary." Autumn took the letters out of her pocket and handed one to Zachary, addressed to him from Washington, D.C. and the other letter address to her, from Crooked Creek, Mississippi. "I will go first since it's from Uncle Bedford."

"Please do darling. I would like to know how he is faring after the war." Zachary lend back against a tree to listen.

"My sweet darling Autumn, you must be overjoyed to finally have your husband home after so many months away. I am only glad I did not have to send my favorite soldier back to you wounded or in a wooden coffin." Autumn shivered as she touched her husband's handsome face. "Perish the thought!" she looked back down to continue. "I paid the Reynold's a visit last week and found out you and Zachary are the parents of four children. As I was doing the math in my head, Nellie informed me it was two sets of twins, both times, one girl, one boy. You must come for a visit soon and bring that brood before you add two more to the fold. It is obvious there is no shortage of loving going on between my two favorite young people. I am real proud that you married Zachary so now he is a part of our family. I really love that boy!" Autumn smiled up and said. "I really love this boy too!" she kissed him, then looked back down. "I had a visit last week from the Federal Army. They have been keeping a check on some of us generals they still do not trust. I was watching from our upstairs bedchamber when they came riding up, so I call Mary Ann over to see what they were up too. Then the funniest thing happened. First, my old war horse, King Philip, rushed out at their blue uniforms and tried to bite them. As the soldiers tried to defend themselves, Theodore ran out of the house to protect my horse. Later, it was reported to me by a Yankee friend, that one of the officers in the party who came, said he understood how Nathan Bedford Forrest, had achieved his remarkable war record. My friend said, the officer looked back toward me, watching from the window and said, your blacks fight for you and your horses fight for you." Zachary and Autumn laughed as they imagined the Union Soldiers being attacked by both old King Philip and Theo. "Tell Zachary to stay safe if he still plans to take on Tyndall. Hope to hear from you both soon. Love, Uncle Bedford."

"Darling, are you still planning on taking back your homeplace?" Autumn suddenly felt anxious over the thoughts of her beloved Zachary being in danger again. "If you are set on doing this Zachary, I will not stay behind this time! I am coming with you!"

"Autumn, until I get the green light to go back up north, I won't be going anywhere." Zachary looked down at the letter addressed from Washington. "Maybe my answer lies inside the envelope. It is his writing, my friend Abe. He must have written this right before he was shot."

"A last letter from President Lincoln?" Autumn sat up and stared at the address. "I should have known. Who else could you know from D.C.? But, now it seems so strange to hear the words written by a dead man. What could he have said to you Zachary?"

"There is one way to find out." Zachary tore the envelope open. The date written clearly in Abraham Lincoln's handwriting, Friday, April 14, 1865: 7:00p.m., three hours and fifteen minutes before John Wilkes Booth assassinated him with his Derringer.

Chapter 38

Zachary sat staring at the letter, then he began reading it softly.

"Zachary, my son, I fear this will be my last correspondence to you. The bad dreams have return and now they are much too real to ignore. It is with grievous feelings that pledge the very inward parts of my mind and body, that I cannot shake the idea that this night will be my last one on this earth. Dear Mary has her heart set on a night out at the Ford Theater to see some play called: Our American Cousin and if fate plays it cards tonight as well, then my nightmares will finally come to past. It's not that I fear death, but I suppose the timing could be better if it were of the Lord's doing instead of an assassin's. The one good thing coming out of my dying is that I will live again in a world without hate or prejudice, where I can be united with my sons, three-year-old Edward, who died of tuberculosis in 1850 and eleven-year-old Willie, who past away from a fever in 1862. Willie was such a spirited child, remember Zachary? He always spoke about you as a big brother and on his death bed, Willie whispered tell Zachary I love him." Zachary paused, tears filling his blue eyes as they were Autumn's, when she reached over to touch his hand, knowing how much this family had meant to her beloved husband.

"I wish I could have been there to stop him from going to that theater. Abe would do anything to make life better for his wife. Being the wife of the president of the United States can be hard enough, but when a war is ragging on within the very country you are trying to hold together, things can be a strain for a married couple in such a high place."

"Zachary, how could you have made a difference, had you been there?" Autumn felt her heart breaking for the man she loved and hoped her choices would never put his life in danger. "President Lincoln knew Mary needed a night out, with her husband. I am certain the last thing she expected was some thug would enter a crowded theater, while a play was going on and shoot her husband in the head, when his bodyguards were supposed to be protecting him."

"I just feel so helpless, now that he is dead! I would never have let Booth near him! I would have guarded that state box with my life!" Zachary stared down at his beloved friend's handwriting and watched his tears drip on the white stationary. "I…I loved him like a father."

"Yes, you did, my darling and he loved you, like a son." Autumn reached over and he gathered her into his strong arms and they wept together.

When he had collected himself, he finished the letter. "The last time we were together will live with me in the afterlife, my son. Again, just being by your side brought out the sunshine in my dreary soul, and brightened my entire Tuesday in Richmond, this past April 4th. It is hard to believe that only ten days ago I was on top of the world with you and tonight my worse fears will come full circle. I would rather recall our short time together in Richmond when I saw you riding up on your big black horse, Midnight. I wasn't sure you could make it after I wrote you and ask if you could meet me there.

Richmond, Virginia: April 4, 1865

Zachary met up with Abraham Lincoln just on the outskirts of Richmond after getting his letter asking him to meet him there if at all possible. Making a switch with General Forrest carrier to deliver Nathan's latest battle reports to headquarters near the Confederate capital, Zachary changed into his black attire and rode swiftly out of camp while the Calvary were still out on patrol. After delivering the reports and collecting the next orders, Zachary made a detour toward the abandon town of Richmond. The only people left in town were the citizens and the freed blacks, who were cheering their hero, Mr. Lincoln, as he walked down the main street with Zachary by his side and surrounded by Union soldiers, sent to protect him from some drunk southerner who saw him as the enemy. Soon the group of men found themselves on the corner of Twelfth and Clay Streets, the former home of Jefferson Davis. Except for the black servants, the Confederate White House sat vacant ever since Jefferson and his young wife, Varina, fled with their three children.

Lincoln asked the soldiers to wait outside while he and his friend check out Mr. Davis's house, so Lincoln and Zachary stepped past the sentry boxes, grasp the wrought iron railing, and marched up the steps into the Confederate White house. A black butler smiled and gave the president a friendly welcome before he took him into a small room with floor-to-ceiling windows and crossed cavalry swords over the door. A friendly housekeeper smiled up from dusting off the big elegant dark wood desk that sat at the far end of the small room. "This is President Davis's office, sir." She said respectfully.

Lincoln nodded politely and walked over to the desk that Davis had obviously thought to tidy up before leaving, because everything was in place, and Abe let his hand run over the burgundy leather chair before taking a seat, crossed his long legs and lend back smiling. "Then this must be President Davis's chair." That was when the weight of the moment struck him and he uncrossed his legs and stared up bewildered into Zachary's eyes. Zachary called out to the housekeeper as his attention remained on his friend.

"Could you please bring the president a glass of water."

The water was promptly delivered by Davis's former butler, the black slave, now free, along with a bottle of good whiskey. Zachary took the whiskey as the butler handed the glass of water to Lincoln and he and the housekeeper left the men alone and shut the door to give them privacy. Lincoln smiled up and nodded to the chair by the desk, so Zachary took a seat. Turning the swivel chair around, the president reached for two glasses and slid them across to Zachary. He smiled, opened the whiskey and poured out two glasses, then slid one over to his friend before lending back for a sip.

"It's good Abe!" Zachary winked. "No one poisoned the whiskey."

"I guess you heard about all my southern fans that kept sending me fruit and vegetables laced with enough poisoned to kill a horse." Abe took a big swallow. "It all looked so good too! Georgia peaches, Carolina apples and pears, watermelons, all sorts of fresh produce, looks to tempt and taste to kill!"

"Some of my fellow Calvary men were happy to share that news with all of us from letters they received from home." Zachary rolled his eyes up in discuss. "There are times I have to bite my tongue and remain quiet to be a part of Bedford's Calvary." Zachary stared down in the rich drink as he asked. "Tell me Abe, have you any news about my cousins, Reid and Bradley?"

"Your cousin Reid has been a faithful soldier, under George Custer. He was wounded during the Fredericksburg's battle, the one we tried to stop but Burnside thought he knew it all, even after George Custer got tired of hearing the careful general saying, we do not even know how deep that river is, so an irritated Custer got on his horse and rode out to the middle of the river and stated, "It's this deep general!" Abraham chuckled. "Like you predicted the battle was a Confederate turkey shoot and our men were the turkeys. Reid was one of the lucky ones, his wounds healed and he is going strong. Bradley is another story." Lincoln slid his glass back across. "That man would stop at nothing to get ahead. When I heard he was heading up an investigation to hunt you down for a traitor, I put a man on him to find out why it would concern him. My man found Bradley Hastings having secret meetings with a man name Jax Tyndall, the low life gambler you told me about." Lincoln reached for Zachary's hand "Son, your own cousin was the one that set you up by sending that letter informing the enlistment board that you were a southern sympathizer and now he is setting you up against this evil murderer, informing him of your plans to get back your homeplace he stole from your father."

"I knew Bradley was jealous of my achievements, the fact that his own father was proud of me and was always throwing it into his son's face for being a failure at everything but being a playboy." Zachary poured two more glasses. "Bradley does not have any idea what my plans are for taking back my inheritance, so there is just so much he can share with Tyndall. I will meet him face to face, unafraid and with my own bodyguards. His heavy-weight goons won't stand a chance with the four men standing with me."

"Are these some of your trusted friends you speak of?" Abraham needed to know this young man would be safe. "Are they men I know?"

"Some, maybe all." Zachary took a sip before answering. "My secret bodyguards will be, Clint Reynolds, my favorite cousin, Reid Dawson, George Custer, and Nathan Bedford Forrest."

"Forrest? Custer, Hastings, and Reynolds, all very impressive." Lincoln opened the desk drawer and started moving things around as if he were in search of something. "I could bring up some charge against your cousin Bradley and this Tyndall, then have them locked up so they could never harm you, son."

"That is very thoughtful of you Abe, but I really need to carry out my plan and win back my estate in a legal poker game with no cheating." Zachary watched his tall friend scramble through another drawer. "If I find him cheating after warning him about it, I will call him out for it." he smiled when the president's head flew up, suddenly anxious. "Relax father Abe, you have never seen my fast

235

draw. It is as impressive as my double flip into the saddle trick."

"I would like to see that double flips trick for myself, but time doesn't seem to be on my side." Abraham opened the last drawer and grunted when he found it empty. "Cleaned this one completely out!"

"If you don't mind my asking, what exactly are you looking for?" Zachary watched him closed the drawer disappointedly. "If you tell me, maybe I can help you search."

"A Confederate dollar bill of some kind, to keep for myself." Abraham picked up the glass and drank the remainder as he watched his young friend reach inside his wallet and pull out a Confederate five-dollar bill, then hand it over to his friend.

"My gift to you, Father Abe, to remember me by." Zachary stood up to stretch before noticing the tears in the president's serious eyes.

"Zachary, my special son, I need nothing to remember the young man that found his way into my life and heart. I could have easily made this trip to Richmond on my own and not risk somebody possibly spotting you, but the need to see you one last time pledged at my heart and to personally tell you I have put in for your pardon, to be sent to you as soon as it is processed. You will be free then to return north at any time, no more a bounty on your head." He smiled "My gift to you."

"That is very good news! Now, I can bring Autumn Rose and the children up to Washington to meet my second father." Zachary tried to take the president's mind off his dreams becoming reality. His constant talk of dying was depressing and Zachary always had a way of getting his mind off the bad dreams. "Before we return to our escort, there is one subject I would like to bring up, if we have a few more minutes."

"I will take the time to discuss what is on your mind, Zachary and as far as a visit with your beautiful family, I wished that was something I could have done if the visions of the things that will come to past, would not have rob us of any more times spent together." Abe walked to the big window and peered out as he stated: "You wish to discuss my plans for sending the black people back to Africa."

Zachary stared at his friend's back in astonishment for a moment before joining him at the window, overlooking the street. "I can understand the first poor souls brought over in slave ships, gathered up by their neighboring tribes for money or trade goods with some white slave British merchant, who in returned sold them off at slave markets, much like someone would sale cattle, pigs, or sheep! These black people lived during the British Colonies times and all of them would have loved to return to their homeland. It was all they knew! All they loved and to be free to return to their life as they knew it would have been a welcome blessing."

"So, you cannot understand why I choose to send back this generation of blacks to Africa, the land of their ancestors." Abraham studied for the right words before responding. "There are several reasons why I think this will be better for all concern. Happiest is more than just the fact of one being free if a certain race can never feel completely free. Free to buy property and build a home, free to find a decent job, free to live anywhere, any neighborhood without being treated like an outcast, freedom without prejudice, either side, black or white. We must be one people, one nation, undivided, under one God. Can white Americans and black Americans live together in harmony, one people, one nation, and believe in the one true God? Can you promise me that there will be no hate! No bloodshed!"

"The land you just described can only be found in one place, Father Abe, heaven!" Zachary knew he must guard his words to speak his mind. "To be able to live in this great nation, we, as individuals, should always feel blessed and to uphold the sacred constitution written by our forefathers, stating, all men are created equal, and in our heavenly Creator's heart, every child is His and every child is created equal. If the Almighty God can love the greatest to the lease of these the exact same way, should we not love our earthly brothers and sisters in the exact same way?" Zachary noticed he had the president's full attention. "Why can't you give our black brothers and sisters a choice, so they can choose for themselves whether to travel back to their homeland, they have never seen or know nothing about, or let them stay in the only homeland they know and will learn to love once freed, to live the American dream once the old citizens learn to except them as human beings, friends, neighbors, and co-workers."

"Dang if you don't say a beautiful speech son!" Lincoln draped his arm around Zachary's shoulders. "You have laid out some great points to consider. But for now, I must be getting back and your general will start asking questions on why you are late from doing a job not meant for a Calvary man."

They walked out and made their way back to the presidential carriage and Midnight. No words were spoken as the two friends hugged for the last time and feeling the president's depressed mood, Zachary would give him one last thing he thought he would never witness. Giving Abe a sweeping bow, Zachary called for Midnight to start out, then raced forward, turned his back, and did a perfect double back flip.

Chapter 39

"I have included a copy of your pardon, Zachary. Now you can feel free to come back home if you so desire." Zachary stopped reading when he felt Autumn's hand tremble under his.

"Dearest Autumn, your thoughts are on what my choice will be, to go back up north or stay down here in your beloved Dixie."

"I know the choice will be yours to make, Zachary darling, and I will honor it as any good wife should. Even though my desire would be to remain in South Carolina, right here at Laurel Grove, my heart would be complete with you wherever we call home." Autumn gave him her reassuring smile and pointed to Lincoln's last page. "Do read on, so we can see what his last words were to you, my beloved."

Zachary lend over to kiss her before continuing and whispered "Abe would have fallen in love with you, my darling Autumn." Then after another kiss, he continued the letter.

"I wanted to share the nightmare I had on April 11, while waiting for late dispatches from the front. I grew too weary to wait up for more, so I went to bed and had not been there for long when I fell into a slumber and began to dream. This time, it was different. There seemed to be a deathlike stillness about me. Then I heard subdued sobs, as if a number of people were weeping. I thought I left my bed and wandered downstairs. There the silence was broken by the same pitiful sobbing, but the mourners were invisible. I went from room to room and found no living person in sight, but the same mournful sounds of distress met me as I passed along. It was light in all the rooms and every object was familiar to me. But where were all the people who were grieving as if their hearts would break? I was puzzled and alarmed. What could all this mean? Determined to find the cause of a state of things so mysterious and shocking, I kept on until I arrived in the East Room, which I entered. There I was met with a sickening surprise. Before me was a catafalque, on which rested a corpse wrapped in funeral vestments. Around it, were stationed soldiers who were acting as guards. And there were a throng of people, some gazing mournfully upon the corpse, whose face was covered, others weeping pitifully. 'Who is dead in the White House?' I demanded of one of the soldiers. 'The President,' was his answer. 'He was killed by an assassin.' Then came a loud burst of grief from the crowd and I awoke, in a sweat. After telling my dream to Mary she wailed out loudly, saying that is horrid, I wish you had not told it. But dear friend, you, of all people, know why this dream must be shared. I have been fairly warned by God, or the angels, but it will happen and it will be, I fear, this night. So, I give this letter to my bodyguard, William Crook, to mail to you first thing Monday morning, April 17, my farewell letter to the young man I love so dearly. We will be a part but for a short time when once again, we shall rekindle our loving friendship in God's Kingdom. Love forever, Father Abraham 'Abe' Lincoln."

"Oh, Zachary, what a heavy burden our president was carrying around with him for such a long time. The war must have drained the dear man of his sleep many a night and the constant weight of knowing so many young men were dying on both sides. He must have felt responsible for calling up volunteers, knowing many good men would march into battle and fewer would return unharmed, while many more would come home wounded or in a body bag." Autumn had gotten up and began unpacking the prepared picnic as her mind drifted back through Abraham Lincoln's last words to her darling husband. "Then to have those horrible nightmares return, night after night until finally the dead man's name was exposed, and to find out it was him lying there, killed by an assassin." Autumn knelt down in front of her husband and took his hands. "Your friend Abe was a strong man of faith, for this was the only thing that could have gotten him through."

"Yes, my beloved, Abe had a very strong belief in God and his holy angels, of which he claimed to have seen." Zachary got down by the spread that held their lunch and offered his hand to help Autumn sit down next to him. He bowed his head and gave a brief but gracious blessing before reaching for a fried chicken leg. "Fried chicken! I haven't had such wonderful southern fried chicken since I visited Bedford."

"Then, I shall fix you southern fried chicken anytime, anywhere we live." Autumn smiled when he raised an eyebrow, not quite sure his darling wife knew how to cook, since everything was prepared by Nora or Cora, the black twins who ran Laurel Grove kitchen. "What? You think this girl cannot cook, just because she is the boss's daughter?" Autumn laughed and handed him a small dish with potato salad, homemade roles and another piece of fried chicken.

"Everything you see on your plate, Mr. Dawson, was prepared lovingly this morning by Mrs. Dawson, with no help from Miss Nora."

"I am impressed!" Zachary laughed and enjoyed the potato salad and role. "I should have guessed my gal would want to learn how to cook and bake, if she knew how to play horseshoes better than most men."

"I am glad you figured that out, precious." Autumn glanced over at the letter, her mind obviously thinking. "Zachary, Abe said he gave this letter to a William Crook, his bodyguard, to mail first thing on Monday, April 17th. I know the mail runs slow but, it has been some time since then. Maybe, the death of President Lincoln cause Mr. Crook to put off sending it right away, shocked over losing such an incredible man so violently." She reached for the letter and pulled out the other folded paper, they had assumed was the copy of Zachary's pardon and found it along with another short note. "Darling, there is a note here from William Crook." She noticed Zachary take another bite of chicken as his eyes fell on the note she held up.

"Sweetheart, could you read it for us." Zachary wiped his lips and lifted his glass of lemonade for a swallow. Autumn looked down at the words, then began reading.

"Mr. Dawson, please forgive us for reading this very personal letter the president wrote you just before he left for the theater on Friday night, April 14th. I am sure you understand under the circumstances over the assassination, the police. had to investigate any unusual differences in the president's life prier, to his death and to find out all those who might be involved with the assassination, as well as other cabinet members being on this groups hit list. President Lincoln had mentioned your name to me on various occasions and I know how much you meant to him. The night he lay dying, the doctor had Mr. Lincoln's clothes removed and it was found in his wallet, an Irish handkerchief with the embroidered letter A..." Autumn stopped, tears filling her green eyes as she whispered "He had...my handkerchief? The one I gave you...so many years ago?"

"Autumn, for some unusual feeling, I wanted Abe to have a part of you and me, so after giving him a five-dollar Confederate bill, I noticed as we walked back to our mounts, his nose was running, from crying so I pulled out your cherished gift I carried with me everywhere and handed it to my friend. After wiping his eyes and nose, he smiled down at the A and simply said, 'Autumn! Now I have a part of you both to carry with me forever.' I assume most people

241

will think the A is for Abraham, but my daring, we will always know the truth, my little Irish blooded lover." Zachary reached over and kissed her before retrieving the letter from Crook. "Let's see if my five was in there.

"Money, both a five-dollar Confederate bill and a U.S. bill, newspaper clippings, an ivory pocketknife, and a pair of gold rim glasses whose frame the president had mended with string." Zachary stopped and looked thoughtful, as he remembered the day he and Abe entered the Confederate White House and the funny situation when the president pulled out his glasses to look at a paper laying on Jefferson Davis's neat desk, then laid them down to rummage through the desk drawers. Lifting items from one drawer and obviously not finding what he was after, he slammed a heavy book down on his glasses, and hearing a crack, looked over timid before discovering the frame had separated from the glass.

"Mary will kill me for breaking my birthday gift she had given me so happily and proclaiming, 'Now you can read without squinting when you read an important document in front of your overcrowded cabinet.'" He had looked around for anything to mend the broken glasses then noticed the spool of thread and grabbed it laughing. "Crowded cabinet? More like an overflowing cabinet. As I have said before, it's like having too many roosters under your window waiting for the sun to rise."

"Abe never tried to mend those fancy glasses with something better than a strain of sewing thread." Zachary smiled as he remembered their last day together. "To those who saw him, he appeared to be a plain simple man, but the truth was Abraham Lincoln was a remarkable genus, whose gracious words will be remembered for generations to come and a hero to the black community for finally making this great nation the land of the free!" His eyes fell on Crooks last words. "Crook finishes with, 'I look forward to meeting you one day soon. Any friend of the presidents is a friend of mine.' Then it's simply signed, William. I should be hearing from my contact soon. Until then, all I can do is wait."

Two weeks later Zachary got the news he had been waiting for. Every man he asked to help him go through with his plan to take on Jax Tyndall, excepted and would meet him just on the border of the Virginia state line. Autumn was determined to go with them, so, Zachary happily obliged her request and worked her into his plans to win back everything the murdering gambler had stolen from him.

Chapter 40

Zachary was saddling Midnight and a spotted pinto pony as he waited for his wife to get into her disguise. He was busy strapping on their overnight bundles when she stepped up behind him and said in a deep male voice.

"Is white face ready to follow Grey Wolf across the mountains of West Virginia?"

Zachary turned around with amazement over Autumn's total transformation. His very proper Irish redhead had turned into an Indian brave, stone face and long black pigtails adorned with eagle feathers.

"Why white face stare so? You no see a true blooded Indian before?" Autumn remained in her role when she noticed Big Ben walked up, looking at her with distrust. "White face, why black bear, look at me with eagle eyes. He no trust your choice of Indian Guide?"

"Zachary, you are trusting this brave to take you across an unknown mountain?" Benjamin couldn't take his eyes off the young Indian. This was the first one he had ever seen and it made him pull down on his hat, remembering hearing the red man like to take scalps off their victim while they were still alive.

Zachary laughed when Autumn said, "Why Big Ben, you really don't think I would ever harm a hair on your head now, do you?"

"Miss Autumn? Well, I be!" Benjamin chuckled out. "If you are planning on fooling everyone in that get-up, then you will be a success, yes ma'am!"

"I guess I will know very soon then." Autumn climbed up on the Pinto and smiled down at her old friend. "Clint might be easy enough to fool, but fooling Uncle Bedford might not be so easy. Wish me luck."

"I am pretty sure you could even fool yourself, if you made your way by a looking glass right now, yes ma'am!" Ben stood back to let the couple move away and waved as they galloped off down the oak covered lane.

"Autumn, I spot Bedford and Clint headed this way." Zachary took her hand "Now, remember what I told you and just follow that map George sent me. I won't let you get lost, darling." One last kiss before the men got too close to see them clearly.

"Zachary, it is really good to see you." Clint met his friend with a gentlemen's hug, while Forrest kept staring at Zachary's companion. "Did you and your guide have any trouble getting here?"

"We had a rather uneventful trip." Zachary reached out his hand toward his old teacher and friend. "I really appreciate you and Clint taking some time out of your busy season to help me."

"A— help you…" Bedford looked as though he were studying the Indian.

"I see you have noticed my guide, Grey Wolf, from the Cherokee Tribe, recommended to me by a fur traitor I once knew." Zachary motioned for Autumn. "Grey Wolf, these are my friends. They will be going with us over the mountains."

"It is good to meet you Grey Wolf." Clint started to shake hands with the Indian and noticed he only stared down at his out-stretched hand, so he pulled it down and said "I have heard Indians make the best guides. It is good to know you will be leading us, Grey Wolf."

"Cherokee? I was thinking he may be from the Navaho Tribe by his features." Nathan Bedford shook his head. "Oh well, all Indians resemble one another, but Reynolds is right, you'll find no better guide." He looked around. "Didn't you say there will be two more men making up your bodyguards?"

"I did and they decided to meet us in Eagle Nest, a small coal mining town just on the other side of Blue Ridge Mountains." Zachary mounted midnight as the others followed his lead. "You have heard me speak of both my friends but have never met either one. My cousin Reid Dawson and your old rival, George Custer."

"Custer?" Nathan Bedford Forrest pulled up on his reins. "You expect me to work along beside a blue belly Yankee, boy?"

"White hawk, man with face of wise Tribal Chief, war is over! Need not harbor bad feelings! The God of wind and rain will grow angry and make our journey unfruitful!" Grey Wolf rode ahead as Zachary hid his smile and said.

"Bedford, sometimes the voice of an Indian brave can be wise, as well as true. I need all my friends to help me beat this Tyndall. You do not have to becomes great friends with Custer, but I know Reid will be easy to like. He is so much like me." He looked up the path to see Autumn had stopped and had turned around in her saddle, waiting for the group to follow. "Grey Wolf is waiting. I will leave it up to you, old friend. Do you go home or are you coming to help the boy you wanted to be your son?"

"Try and stop me!" Nathan Bedford slapped Zachary playfully on the back. "As long as that Yankee stays out of my way, I can ride with any man!"

Zachary and Clint exchanged smiles and the group galloped off to catch the Indian guide.

As the four rode into Eagle's Nest, they all turned when someone yelled greeting. "Zachary! What a joy to finally see you, cousin!" Reid ran across the street from the two-store hotel and grabbed his best friend and first cousin when he climbed off his black horse. "I was so afraid I might meet up with you on the battlefield and was actually overjoyed when at last I did see you and at your old tricks that won you West Point's soldier of the year."

"You were among the West Point cadets I saw when I came out of the tree line road!" Zachary laughed, remembering all the applause from his should-be enemy. "I was so busy performing, I only recognized those men on the front row. I finally looked out when I heard cheers instead of gunshots! It was a damn good sight, I tell you!"

"Your soldiers should be grateful that you saved their butts that day." Reid chuckled as he looked over the rest of Zachary's group and spotted Forrest. He moved in close to his cousin. "You talked Nathan Bedford Forrest into helping you? Did he know who else was helping?"

"He does now but my Indian guide helped him change his mind and join us." Zachary had a hard time of keeping a straight face, describing his beautiful wife as an Indian. "What do you hear about Bradley, the traitor that set me up twice?"

"What goes around, comes around!" Reid grew excited. "It would appear, this crooked gambler doesn't know the meaning of loyalty. He used poor old Bradley to get personal information about you, then invited him into an 'innocent' poker game. When the foolish Bradley finally realized that Miss Melody was only pretending to adore him and only using him as a patsy, and his two-face friend cheated him out of everything him and his family owned, he got drunk, slapped around by Tyndall's bodyguards and landed in jail. Your poor Uncle Horus came to get his son and was a broken man when he left, to share the bad news with your aunt."

Zachary felt Autumn standing beside him and knew she had

heard of Bradley's fate. Knowing she could not offer her husband her wise advice as herself, she used the brave's voice.

"White face, this man, this Cousin Bradley, he, do you wrong. That is a truth that cannot be wiped away, but this man is broken, wounded! The man's father and mother, of no fought of their own, except to spoil only son, now face great loss! Man's down-cast can cause one so much pain that life holds no more meaning so they take their own life. Much heartache, much worry! Good son, you have heart to forgive! Make amend to kin and restore what is loss, as well as your own! The God of wind and rain, sun and moon, will smile down upon your kindness and make you a better life forever, with the women whose hair is as a flaming ember and eyes the color of green fields!"

"Grey Wolf makes good since Zachary. Two wrongs never make a right." Reid scratched his chin as he gazed at the Indian who obviously had the gift of wisdom. "This might be the medicine Bradley Hastings needs to realize how family should treat one another and it would help renew the faith and respect your Uncle Horus always felt for you. I know you do not expect any type of reward for restoring everything they own, but to finally have them show you the respect you deserve as an equal, not just a poor unfortunate relative."

"Why not!" Zachary noticed Autumn's big smile as he continued. "I might as well win back everything that jackal stole from my entire family!"

"Great! George said he would meet up with us in Haywood, West Virginia, the town where Jax Tyndall has chosen as he latest victim's set-up. According to George, Tyndall arrived late last Friday and plans to hang around until he wipes up on all his wealthy targets." Reid whispered "George has taken a room at the tavern where Tyndall sets up his poker games and our friend is well acquainted with all of the prostitutes working there, not that he does business with them, they all just love having their hero around. Might I add, these ladies would do almost anything for our blonde-curly hair Calvary General, still a big part of the Union Army."

"We better not share that little part with my old friend and general, Nathan Bedford Forrest." Zachary laughed when Reid stopped to study the man with the most wanted status during the war between the states. "Don't let his angry expressions fool you Reid, he is almost always of a gentle heart."

Reid watched Bedford arguing with the small man collecting luggage and bundles at the hotel entrance, then suddenly pushed him a side to enter the building, holding tight to his luggage, Forrest stormed inside the hotel. Zachary noticed his cousin trembling and gave his back a pat. "Relax Reid, the war is over and Bedford has not fought any Union soldiers since the war ended. If you just be yourself cousin, my friend will grow to love you the way I do."

"That is a hard one to believe, Zachary." Reid smiled up at his best friend who he hadn't seen him since his visit in the camp where Reid was stationed, before leaving the North to go South where his one true love lived. "I was hoping to meet Autumn Rose on your trip back up but I guess, under the circumstances, things were not safe enough to bring her along."

"That is exactly why I could never take a chance with bringing my woman. Not that she couldn't take care of herself nor the fact that she was afraid to come with us." Zachary laughed softly, remembering his wife's determination on going and the real fact that she was standing right beside him and nobody seeing through her terrific disguise. "My darling Autumn is not only incredibly beautiful, but she has many wonderful gifts to offer any man. I am only glad she chose me to live her life with and to love with undying devotion." Zachary noticed Autumn's sweet smile as she glanced down, to avoid attention. "What about you Reid, any pretty young woman stole into your heart yet?"

"As a matter of fact, there is one very sweet and charming little gal, named Belinda Lincoln, a distant relative of our beloved late president." Reid touched his cousin's shoulder. "The day you dropped by to visit me, I found out shortly after about the close bond between you and President Lincoln. I met Belinda after I was wounded in Fredericksburg, right after I spoke to you. Your friend, Abraham Lincoln made a special visit to the hospital where I was being treated, along with over one hundred other soldiers. He had brought his distant cousin Belinda to personally take care of me. I thought the other wounded men might hold it against me when we were released for battle, but they treated me more like a hero. When I ask why they weren't upset over my getting my own personal nurse, the men from West Point replied, the president was overheard telling his cousin, 'Make sure that young man stays comfortable because he is first cousin to my adopted son, Zachary Dawson.' You are still a hero to those boys from the point."

"I still have a hard time believing my dear friend Abe is gone." Zachary swallowed back his tears and forced a quick smile for his childhood friend. "We have come a long way from playing Calvary soldiers with sticks for swords, Reid. Have you asked this very sweet and charming young lady to be your wife?"

"I did and she has." Reid smiled brighter. "As of one month, two weeks ago. Belinda Lincoln Dawson is waiting for her husband on the family farm, that I inherited from my parents."

"White man, both have a squaw to keep warm at night, make the day glow with sunrise, fresh blossoms of joy and laughter. Give you much children to help plant your fields and share in your joy and love." Autumn pointed to the sunsetting in the west. "The sun, it sets! Now, go and rest! Start at first light, back into the mountain path, up and over, until we reach the place call Haywood, where silent arrows of a different war await! This one, much different! War of good over evil! The God of truth will be young warrior's shield and he will easy defeat his foe!" while Both men watched in wonder, Grey Wolf threw his bundle over his shoulder and walked toward the hotel.

"Come on Reid, we cannot let Grey Wolf try to enter that hotel without our help. Indians usually are not welcome to stay inside." Zachary dashed to catch up with his wife as he whispered in her ear.

"You are an Indian, beautiful, let me handle the doorman." Zachary towered over the very proper stiff man waiting by the door for the other two white men. He frowned down at the Indian brave.

"This one must find shelter outside! It is our policy to keep such…persons out of our fine establishment."

"That is too bad then!" Zachary waved big bills in front of the rude man before he put them back in his pant pocket. "Then I will just remain outside myself! My friend behind me can stay inside if he chooses!"

"Stay inside this stuffy hotel when I can have the stars for my roof and fresh air to breathed instead of the stale air inside this…fine establishment!" Reid turned up his nose and jumped when he heard Nathan Forrest's booming voice.

"What kind of place to you call this? Is this or is this not a hotel for anyone who needs a place to sleep and has adequate means to pay for it?" Bedford stepped up to the fancy front desk and stared down coldly at the desk clerk. "We have been traveling all day over that mountain to get here and if it was not for that fine, intelligent young brave guiding us, we might have gotten lost! He is no less important than any man in our group, so if you do not want our business mister, and it would appear we are the only guest here, we will all find shelter under God's beautiful stars!" he paused while the rest of their party waited and watched. "What's it to be? Do we stay here, and you have some business or do we stay outside, leaving your nice establishment empty for another night?"

The nervous clerk came swiftly around the desk and made his way to the door to push the doorman aside. He plastered on an unnatural smile to the three waiting outside, then turned to see Clint waiting on the bottom step with his small suitcase in hand. "Please except our apology gentlemen. Do come inside out of the cool mountain air." The clerk smiled nervously down at the serious face of the young Indian brave. "There is always room for an exception, young man."

"White face has please the God of heaven! To do good to all His children! Not to look on outside, the color of one's skin but to look on the inside, where the soul of life surely lives and swore like the great bird, even the eagle!" Autumn stepped inside after Zachary and waited as the men paid and were taken to two rooms to share. Zachary made sure 'Grey Wolf' slept next to the wall and he was the one laying, beside him.

Chapter 41

The small group entered into the town of Haywood, somewhat bigger than the small coal mining town they had left behind at first light. It was still too early for the barroom crowd to come inside for a night of drinking and gambling, so after leaving their things at the hotel across the street and Bedford's help for getting Autumn inside with them, they walked inside the swinging doors and found a table in the corner. George Custer turned to see who had walked in at that time of day and seeing his friend, laughed out as he set his half empty mug of beer down and met Zachary halfway.

"Dawson, dang if it isn't good to see you! I thought you boys got lost, with that little Indian brave guiding the way." He gave his Calvary buddy a wink, knowing the secret about the Indian's identity. "Come on up to the bar and have a beer with me while I have your friends some drinks sent over."

"Thanks, don't mind if I do." Zachary called over and told his group a bar maid would be over to take their order while he talked to his friend. "Is everything set up for tonight George?"

"I have taken care of everything you ask for, my friend. I have set up the poker game between you and cheating Tyndall, which will begin at seven sharp. I have observed little Miss Marigold. She always arrives around six to do her flirting and set up the mark for her old lover boy. Is she in for a pleasant surprise."

"That she is. This time, the table will be turned and it will be Miss Melody who will be smitten!" Zachary glanced over at Autumn who was aware of all the nights events and noticed the barmaids had brought her a beer too. "The prostitutes, do they know what their jobs are?"

"They are all excited about their rolls in this little drama friend." Custer knew how they felt about this murdering gambler and was happy to help put him away. "You can count on Tracy, Wanda, and Arlene to take care of business. It's not all paid sex where these girls are concern, they are genuine friends when it comes to righting a wrong."

"Good! We need everyone's loyalty and help tonight to finally put this low life thief and murderer in his proper place, once and for all time!" Zachary smiled down at Autumn when she walked over and handed him her beer. "Don't like white man's drink, Grey Wolf?"

"Grey Wolf can find no cause to like this beer, since tribe never has any to drink!" Autumn heard George Custer laugh and gave Zachary's friend a smile.

Speaking softly, George Custer gazed down at the perfect disguise. "I am looking forward to see Grey Wolf after Arlene talks big brave into a free round tonight and how it changes you completely." Knowing what George was referring to, all three laughed.

Six o'clock sharp, Miss Melody Marigold stepped inside the tavern and made her way to the bar. Zachary had taken a seat over at the far end of the bar, next to his group of men. He noticed, even though Melody had obviously aged, she was still very attractive as she looked around at the locals until her eyes fell on the table of strangers, then the incredible handsome man at the end of the bar, an Indian standing beside him. The gambler's lover recognized the mark, by the description given her by Tyndall. Long black hair, tense blue eyes, but she had not dreamed the one being set up would be so handsome and tall, so manly and shapely. Taking a big breath, Miss Marigold made her way over to Zachary and edged her way between him and the Indian, who seem to be a close friend. She gave Autumn her most beautiful smile before delivering it to Zachary.

"Please excuse me for interrupting you sir, but you look like a man I might trust to help me." She said innocently. "I just found out this man I have been searching for, is in this town and the mean devil is up to his old tricks, stealing everything away from unsuspecting people." She batted her eyes in distress. "The crook stole all my precious belongings and...he kicked me out, after he had taken everything my late husband had left me. I fell for his big act! Pretending to adore me when all he wanted was to rob me and leave me homeless and broke!" she worked the tears to fall as she sniffed. "Please tell me you can play poker! I can share with you all his nasty tricks for cheating everyone! I wouldn't ask you, being a stranger and all, if I did not need a gentleman to rescue me and win back my dear husband's estate he left me when..." the great actress pulled out a handkerchief and wiped her weeping eyes, "Forgive me, but when I think of my darling Henry last dying words, it nearly breaks my heart! He said he could die in peace knowing I would always be taken care of. Now, thanks to that gigolo, it's…all…gone."

"Maybe you should have remained on the stage, Miss Marigold. That was some performance!" Zachary said calmly as her jaw dropped and her eyes flew open. "You really don't recognize me, so you, Miss Melody. Way back in the small town called Hernando, in Mississippi?"

"Oh my God! That ten-year-old boy who stood up to Jax and had us ran out of town or go to jail!" Although the ex-stage actress was petrified by Zachary's revelation, she still could not take her eyes off how handsome he had become. "Look, maybe we could work something out. I am ready to stop all the cheating and stealing…"

"Don't forget murdering, Miss Marigold!" Zachary stared down at the nervous woman. "Just how many men have been shot under the pretense of self-defense?" Zachary pushed his barstool back and took hold of her arm. "Like you did my father! Does the name Jacob Dawson sound familiar, Miss Marigold?"

"I had nothing to do with any duels! I only…"

"Set up some poor lonely man in hopes of getting him to fall for your sob story like you did my father, lonely from losing his wife, my mother, or my Uncle David Hastings you almost took until I overheard you and saw you and that card thief exchanging looks and notes, and most recently my careless, stupid cousin Bradley, who's self-conceit and family's disloyalty, cost his family everything they owned!" Zachary's temper was growing stronger until he felt Autumn reached up and pull his hand away from the frightened woman.

"Friend, need to calm down! Pale face squaw, know how you feel! She, know where she, stand guilty on all white man words, this is truth. No words can she say that will make her not guilty! Pale face must face white man law." 'Grey Wolf' looked up and waved a hand over the actress' head. "White pale face squaw better be glad not judge by Cherokee law!"

"Grey Wolf is right Melody and if you wish to get a lighter sentence, then you had better start working for the right side, here and now!" Zachary looked down at Autumn and she could read thank you in his blue eyes. "Tyndall is going to walk inside this tavern at exactly seven o'clock and we are going to play a fair game of poker. He will be warned that if he is caught cheating, the game will take on a different set of rules. My four bodyguards are all well trained to both take on bullies and to see a cheating hand made. You will be watched closely and if you so much as give your lover a signal, sharing information about my hand I'm holding, you will be facing the full measure of punishment for all your part in these acts of getting rich on someone else's wealth. Do I make myself clear?"

"I promise to only help you win, Zachary, that was your name, I remember now." The older actress wished he could find something to like about her. She had never met any man this exciting in her lifetime and now it seemed hopeless that he would give her the attention she desired.

"I do not want any help Miss Marigold! That would make me a cheater then, and I will never bring myself down that low!" Zachary noticed the door opening and Jax Tyndall walking through with his beefy bodyguards. Zachary spoke softly. "I will win fair and square, everything that jackal stole from my family then I will see his cheating murdering way of life stopped, once and for all time!"

Jax Tyndall looked around the room and watched with a smirk as Zachary got up and walked over to the round table, set up with a stack of playing cards and looked down at the man he had been waiting to meet again. Before Tyndall's guards could respond, the four men with Zachary stepped over behind the brave young man.

"We meet again, Mr. Tyndall and this time it won't be a kid you are pushing around, but a man, trained and equipped for fighting the enemy!" Zachary pulled out the chair facing the gambler and reached out to brush the ready cards off the table.

"What's the meaning of knocking away my playing cards, young man? Who are you anyway? I do not remember seeing you before." The irate gambler motioned for his men to retrieve the fallen cards and noticed Zachary's smile. "Do you plan to wipe those cards off the table again boy? Are we playing poker or not? You will not waste my time!"

"We are most certainly playing the game of poker, Jax Tyndall, only not with a stacked set of cards!" Zachary lifted up his hand and Grey Wolf brought over a fresh unopened box of playing cards. "We will play with fresh new cards! A fair game between us, best man wins everything, no questions ask, unless you are caught cheating, then I will have no choice but to change the rules."

Jax stared at Zachary, mistrust written across his face. "And suppose I refuse to play you under those circumstances?" he asked boldly.

"Then that would be a grave mistake sir." Zachary took out the pearl handle pistol his friend Nathan Bedford Forrest took from the brass man and gave it to the young ten-year-old Zachary to use one day. That day had come, and at that moment the gambler remembered the young boy with the same long black hair and intense blue eyes, then he suddenly grew nervous, remembering what Bradley Hastings had told him wasn't exactly what was now happing. Zachary could read the fear that was sweeping through this overconfident thief, causing him to smile. "I can see you now remember the young boy who helped stop his uncle from being taken by you and your uncaring lover!"

"You weren't able to stop your own father though, was you boy, from losing everything your family owned and causing you to leave your precious West Point!" Jax stopped speaking when he noticed the same man that had stopped him in Hernando stand up, discussed with the mean words he was using against his young friend. One of Jax's guards started to rise off his chair, when Clint Reynolds used a headlock on him, causing him to sit back down quickly. "We play the game my way or I will get up and leave, poor boy! You cannot possibly have enough to interest me anyway."

"That is where you are mistaken, Tyndall. My cousin only knew about my salary for being the horse trainer for my Uncle Horus. Then I only received a meager salary and a room above the stables, but when I was hired to run the steel mill, my salary took an uphill climb and with the good investments I made and the money for fighting in the war…"

"Confederate money? Useless!" the gambler steered.

"Ah, but all that lovely Confederate money, except for a few bills reserved for souvenirs and one five given to a dear friend, has been lovingly exchanged for U.S. Currency, by the president." Zachary lend back and crossed his arms until the shocked gambler could respond.

"You expect me to believe the president of the treasury took a Rebels worthless money and gave him it's worth in U.S, money?"

"No, not the president of the U.S. Treasury, Tyndall, the late, great, President of these United States, Abraham Lincoln, my dear departed friend." Zachary had him speechless, so he continued. "As of my last report, I have twenty-five million dollars in my savings account."

Autumn and Zachary's friends let out gasp, not knowing exactly what the young man was really worth.

"I never thought you would actually try to beat a man as skilled at poker as myself but instead show up at the farm, demanding me to a duel to get it back." Tyndall found his strong voice, too sure of himself in the art of poker and cheating with flare. "If you are still determined to challenge me, you, stupid fool, what will be your wager?"

"I will wager my entire savings of twenty-five million dollars for everything you have stolen throughout your worthless lifetime! I have my spies also Tyndall and I am aware that after you have lavishly spent over two million of your cheating winnings, you still have Twenty-four million left, that includes the price of property and homes, filled with furnishings, and one rail line." Zachary stared back into the man's cold steel eyes. "We shall see who the fool is Tyndall! This game will be played fairly or I will take you down, in a fair sober duel. Don't expect any help from Miss Marigold, she has decided to do this one straight to avoid a longer stay in prison. Now, it is up to you! Play the game fair for once in your stinking life or die, trying to take down a calmer and faster hand."

"I can play fair and still beat you boy! I am a champion at Poker and no two-bit blue belly traitor is going to take me down!" Jax narrowed his eyes at his lover as she looked down with amazement at the handsome man and gave a sigh. "And Melody, you little cheap whore, you can just pack your things, except the jewelry, and get out of my luxury lifestyle!"

"Gentlemen, if you will excuse us." The group of men looked up to find a sexy dressed, heavy made up prostitute holding on to 'Grey Wolf'. "I just cannot stand it with grown men start gambling away their entire life, so I am taking my new friend here, big brave Grey Wolf, upstairs to my room and show him what a pale-face squaw can do in bed!" Clint, Reid, and Bedford glanced over at Zachary, thinking he would put a stop to the young Indian having to be subject to a prostitute, but noticed their young friend waved them off, saying.

"Good ideal. Grey Wolf deserves a special treat. Just remember, do not try to take his head dress off or his breast shield. It is an Indian's sacred clothing, and only taken off by their own hand." As she was leading Autumn away, Zachary called up. "Watch out for his tomahawk and war knife!" he waved off his friend's concerns as George Custer smiled, knowing why Arlene was really taking Zachary's young wife upstairs.

"Alright Tyndall, you can shuffle the new cards and deal them out! We will see who comes out the winner!" Zachary said with confidence. He had been preparing for this day a long time, and he was ready to win back everyone winnings!"

Both men had decided on one game and Zachary had warned the professional gambler if he was caught cheating, the cards would be gathered up by a man neither knew, seated at the table beside them. The gambler nervously handed the stranger the cards, not quite certain if he could trust his own cheating hands. The man, unknown by even the bar keeper, pulled his chair over between the two men and began shuffling the deck, then passed out the proper amount, of cards, then he laid the deck in front of him, declaring he would be the dealer. Both Zachary and Jax had made the same amount of changes until Zachary waved the dealer's hand away.

"I will stick with my hand." His tense blue eyes never left the gambler who gave a smirk, before a cocky smile fell on his stiff face.

"I need no more cards either, Mr. Dealer. I appear to have kept my luck! I am certain I have THE winning hand, Dawson!"

"Not when you have an Irish lass to give you a kiss of luck!" George Custer spoke up after seeing the beautiful redhead standing on the stairs. "Mr. Tyndall, you have your charming actress, but alas, all she can do is lure men to your table. Mr. Dawson has his beautiful lucky Irish charm, who happens to be a great actress in her own way, right Grey Wolf?"

"The Irish shamrock has been known to bless the finder with long lasting luck, Mr. Tyndall." Every eye was on the beautiful vision walking gracefully down the steps, dressed in a rich green velvet gown to match her emerald eyes and flaming red hair flowing down her shapely body. As she grew closer, her neckless glistened in the oil lamps, a rich green emerald in the shape of a shamrock surrounded by diamonds, a surprise gift from Zachary, as was the beautiful dress, unpacked from his bundle and gently pressed. "Far better than the shamrock's luck is the luck from a real Irish lassie kiss, to the one she has given her everlasting love. My beloved husband, Zachary Dawson."

Laying his cards face down, Zachary reached up to pull her into his lap before given her a passionate kiss while the ones watching could only sigh, the single men and some seasoned married ones, wishing this woman were theirs. And the prostitutes, barmaids, and Miss Marigold, wishing it was them being kissed by the handsome man in black. Nathan Bedford Forrest was silent and stunned, finding out he had been completely fooled about the Indian being real. Clint Reynolds was also taken back, the complete overhaul from Indian brave to an enchanting princess. Seeing them kiss, made him long for Nellie and suddenly the plantation owner could not wait to return home. Even the stranger seemed intrigued by the couple and Jax Tyndall could only pout that such a beautiful creature did not belong to him. Had he have known about her, he would have insisted she be part of the bargain. Everyone's thoughts were interrupted when Zachary picked back up his cards, still holding on to Autumn.

"Alright Tyndall, show me that winning hand, if you think I do not have it!"

"Gladly!" The overconfident gambler smiled slowly as he lowered his cards bragging. "Four perfect kings, all crowned and giving me the win!" Jax started to pull the winnings toward him when the dealer slapped his hands away with his cane.

"Not so fast, Mr. Tyndall, I think Mr. Dawson has a hand to play, right Dawson?"

"Not just a hand, sir, that lucky charm paid off, I have the winning hand, four perfect Aces!" Zachary laughed softly when everyone around began cheering for him. "It appears I left you with nothing, Tyndall, right where you started, before you went on a cheating, murdering spree. You are finished, Tyndall! No one will trust you anymore! Your bodyguards have no reason to protect a scum like you every again. You same as told your lover to get loss, and now you have nothing or no one! You sir, are penniless, alone, and soon to be a jailbird!"

The upset gambler reached for the pearl handed pistol as he slid his chair back, grabbing a barmaid to shield him. "I will not stop until I regain my wealth, Dawson, then I am coming for you! I will shoot you down like the deserter you are!" Tyndall laughed. "And get a big reward from the U.S Government for killing you!"

Without warning, the stranger slung his cane around knocking the pistol from Tyndall's hand and slapped handcuffs on him, while a swarm of lawmen rushed inside to grab the four frozen bodyguards and a willing Melody Marigold. It was obvious to everyone in the tavern, the stranger who had declared himself the games dealer, was the one in charge, giving orders for taking all Tyndall's gang in. Without a smile, the stranger asked Zachary and Autumn to step outside for a few questions while the others could have a drink on the United States Law Enforces.

"We finally get to meet in person, Mr. Dawson." The serious face melted into a friendly smile as he put out his hand. "Let me introduce myself. I wrote you sometime back to apologize for having read the president's personal letter to you. William Crook, one of President Lincoln's personal bodyguards."

"It is a pleasure to meet you Mr. Crook." Zachary was surprise that he had personally come to this small town to arrest Jax Tyndall and help him undercover. "You said you were with the president on the evening he was shot? What happen?"

"I had guarded the president all day, ever since having arrived at precisely seven a.m. in the morning and my shift was over at seven p.m. that evening. My replacement, John Parker, was supposed to relieve me three hours before, but as always, Parker was running late. My shift runs from seven a.m. until four p.m., but I was deeply attached to President Lincoln and I always fretted over his safety when I wasn't on guard. John Parker was always lazy and unaccountable! How the drunken slob was designated as the president's bodyguard is a great mystery. After the president and Mrs. Lincoln had their carriage ride, the Lincoln's had dinner with their children and then I walked Mr. Lincoln back to the War Department for a third time, this time to see if General Sherman had sent a telegraph stating the disposition of his troops in the South. After listened to a bit more information, I walked him back to the white house. My eyes were always scanning the crowds for signs of someone with means to hurt the president. A bodyguard has to be dedicated to his employer and our only job is to protect the president of the United States at all cost!"

"Did this Mr. Parker ever show up and was he sober or drunk, as you said?" Autumn could tell this man felt almost responsible for President Lincoln's getting shot by not working on, tired or not.

"Parker finally meandered in for me to brief him in on the day's events and what his duties were for the night. I insisted that he leave fifteen minutes before the president and be waiting at the Ford Theatre before the president's party got there in order to provide security the instant they arrived." William Crook looked off, as if remembering the night like it just happened. "I was finished for the night and preparing to leave when President Lincoln came to his office door with a handful of last-minute appointments that came up and he wanted to get them out of his way so he could relax and enjoy the weekend." Crook trembled as recalled their final farewell. "Just like every other night, I walked to the door and said, 'Good night, Mr. President.' And he normally would respond with, 'Goodnight, Crook' only those were not the words he spoke this time. President Lincoln said almost somber, 'Goodbye, Crook.'" The ex-bodyguard shivered. "All the way home, I felt like something wasn't right. I had the desire to change directions and make my way to Ford Theatre, but continued my slow walk home, feeling depressed and unsure of John Parker's ability to give the president the proper protection he needed."

"History will prove that Parker failed in protecting Abraham from a crazy man, determined to assassinate one of the greatest presidents this nation has been blessed to have." Zachary, once again, could not control the tears that swelled in his eyes at the thought of his most endearing friend and second father breathing his last breath on this earth. "I am not sure Mary can endure the loss of her devoted husband. If she goes on the deep end and drowns in her own dark sorrows, their poor children will be same as left orphans." Zachary let out a cry as he stated. "To God, if I had only been there to protect him! He would have invited me to sit with them inside that presidential box and John Wilks Booth could not have gotten by me!"

"If I would have followed my instants and gone on to the theatre! I knew Parker could not be dependable! I could not sleep for worrying over the president's welfare and yet I did nothing!" Crook slapped the cane in his palm as Autumn stepped in front of both men.

"Gentlemen, you must stop blaming yourself for the president's death. There is nothing either of you can do now to alter what happen and you must know, Mr. Lincoln would never hold either of you at fault for not being there. He knew, by some fate of prophecy, he was going to die! He saw it plainly in his dreams and for that reason he said his goodbyes to the both of you." Autumn felt their pain and she wanted to offer words of comfort to put their minds at ease. "Abraham Lincoln obviously thought the world of you, William. Being his loyal bodyguard while being president gave the gentle man time to know you and trust you enough to tell you about Zachary, a young man wanted by the Union Army. And Zachary, I have never seen a better relation between a real father and his son as you had with Mr. Lincoln. I finally realized just how special he was to you when I learned about you giving him my handkerchief I gave you when I was nine and you were ten. The same cherished handkerchief that had my initial embroidered on one corner. A Christmas gift from my mother when I reached eight." She reached for both men's hands and cast her eyes up toward heaven. "We all know dear Abe is well and alive in God's Kingdom, where he will be waiting to once again unite with those he left behind on earth. Until then, Abe would want us to live out our lives, just as if he was still here to help guide our way. To helps those less fortunate, to love all God's children like Jesus taught us, and to continue his legacy in making this country a place where all men are created equal!"

"Autumn, the president would have fallen in love with you!" William smiled when the young couple laughed, remembering those were Zachary's exact words. "I hope we can be friends, Zachary."

"I feel we already are William." Zachary shook his hand, then he went inside to pack for Boston.

Chapter 42

"The old farm has weathered the storm of being in the wrong hands for far too many years." Zachary had brought Autumn to the place he had called home for the first seventeen years of his life. The large farmhouse still stood proudly, missing only a few boards, nothing that could not be easily repaired. The stables, once alive with horses, cattle and chickens lay empty and the pasture overgrown. With a lot of hard work, the place could be brought back to the grander it once held and now with Zachary and Autumn's wealth, they could easily afford to have it restored. Autumn glanced up at her husband, trying to read his thoughts. Was this where she was to spend the rest of her life, raise their four children, learn new friends and hope to find some sort of connection to the place Zachary surely must have wanted. For him, she knew she would learn to love this place, even though her heart would always remain at Laurel Grove. "Autumn, you have hardly said a word since we rode up. What do you think of Dawson Farm?"

"I certainly love the name." she tried to sound upbeat for Zachary. "I can see with a little hard, work, this place can be charming."

"But, it's not Laurel Grove." Zachary knew Autumn better than almost anyone and he knew where she had rather be, even though her love for him and her devoted loyalty would do what he wanted over her own happiness. Zachary lifted his beautiful wife into his arms. "Please hear me out, my darling. I know you would go to the ends of the earth for me if that is what I wished and I know it is my final choice to make, so I have made it." Zachary looked around, rubbing his hands together. "First, we will hire some contractors to restore the house and barns. Then we will fill the barns with fine horses, a milk cow" he looked down and winked. "Everyone needs milk!" he happily went on, Autumn feeling, this is his choice! I must learn to love it for his sake, so she said.

"You are absolutely correct darling, especially growing children. Strong bones require lots of fresh cow's milk!" she tried to sound upbeat when he chuckled.

"I do not think Uncle David and his lovely wife has to worry about children's strong bones unless we pay them a lot of visits to Boston." Zachary laughed softly at Autumn's bright smile. "My beautiful southern belle, do you think for one minute that I would take you away from Laurel Grove? The home I have grown to love almost as good as you, my dearest? The wedding present, your father gave us before we left for West Virginia?" Zachary laughed even louder when Autumn jumped up into his arms laughing.

"Zachary, are you saying that daddy has given us the title to the plantation?"

"You and I are his heirs to Laurel Grove Plantation since your beautiful sister Nellie has her own big plantation in Mississippi! Your parents will continue to live on the plantation for the rest of their lives, but have turned over the business to their smart daughter and their hard-working son-n-law."

"Oh, Zachary! Never have I been more, happy…well, there was one time better. The day we got married at Belmont and you put this nail ring on my finger." She laughed happily, refusing him wanting to buy her a gold band "and you are such a dear man, to give your Uncle David a country place again after his was burnt down and everything he owned destroyed."

"My uncle has always cared for me and now that I have the means to do so, I intend to pay him back for always defending me." Zachary looked around, the memories of childhood life on the old farm, fading with the years and the loss of his parents. "As long as family is living here, this will always feel like the old homeplace, where shadows of the past still linger, faded voices in the wind, daddy calling me up from the fields or mama singing as she hung out the wash linens in the back yard." Zachary shook his head as though he was trying to shake away the loving voices now gone. "Uncle David always loved it here. He and Mama were very close and he took it very hard when she passed on. Now he can visit her grave where daddy laid her, in her favorite rose garden. I will have daddy's casket brought up from the Potters Field, the overgrown land used for the poor to be buried and bury him beside his beloved Irene."

Hiring many laborers, and doing their fair share of the work, Autumn and Zachary had Dawson Farm looking like new on the day David and Margaret Hastings drove their carriage up to the white-washed farmhouse and climbed down.

"Zachary, you sure have fixed up the old place." David gave his favorite nephew a big hug. "When I received your message that you had finally taken on that devil of a gambler and that actress lover of his, I was delighted to know Tyndall was put away for life." David looked around the peaceful country home and regretted losing his own estate, only to find himself in a small-town flat with hardly any income after everything was destroyed in that arson's fire. Zachary's uncle never regretted protecting his favorite nephew though, and was just grateful that he and Margaret healed of their wounds and found a place they could afford. David's eyes fell on the beautiful young woman walking from the house, an apron tied around her tiny waist. "Don't tell me, that has to be Autumn Rose Forrest! I could never forget that incredible red hair and alluring green eyes!"

Zachary reached for his wife's hand when she stopped next to him. "She is Autumn Rose Dawson now, Uncle David. We got married during the war, on one of my furloughs." Zachary dropped her hand long enough to hug David's wife. "Margaret, it is finally good to meet the beautiful lady who made my dear uncle a very happy man again."

"I have heard many good things about you too, Zachary. Like winning David's brother Horus' estate and business back and returning it to them, after what that spoiled cousin of yours did to you and spilled over on our life as well." Margaret reached for Autumn's open arms. "I guess we are both somewhat new to this family dear."

"It is easy to love all of Zachary's family, Margaret." Autumn gave the sweet woman a genuine smile. "My heart is so full of love for my darling husband it cannot help but overflow into all those who mean so much to him."

"Autumn Rose, even as a child you had a heart of gold. Zachary could not have found a more perfect bride even if he had the world to choose from." David gave her a friendly kiss and looked back around to admire the old farm. "I have always love it here. It is so peaceful. I almost hate returning to our town flat among the hustle and bustle."

"Then don't return." Zachary smiled at the couples questioning faces. "Just have your things packed and brought over to your new home!" tears began to swell up in the Hasting's eyes. "Autumn and I want the two of you to have Dawson farm as a gift. I could not think of anyone else I had rather visit than my very favorite uncle and his charming wife."

"Zachary, you love this place! This should be your and

Autumn's home!" David choked up. "You will need it to raise your family, son."

"My growing family of four children, already love their present home, Uncle David and it would break my Autumn's heart to take her away from Laurel Grove Plantation, not to mention my own heart," Zachary felt Autumn cuddle inside his arms. "Trust me Uncle David, my love for this old homeplace will always be bedded within me, it is where my memories will linger from my youth and the love given me by two incredible people who sacrificed a lot to give me my dream, short lived but fulfilling. I would have never received soldier of the year from one of the best Military Academies in America if it had not been for their love. I can take those best memories with me and give me a reason to return, whenever we can visit the old family farm, but my heart now belongs with Autumn, in the place we both love and intend to bring up our family and even far beyond the golden years, hand-n-hand, heart-n-heart, together forever."

"Then, we thank you both, with all our heart. How could we not?" David pulled the young man he had always loved, into a tight embrace. "Margaret and I will make it work. The sale of the flat will bring in a little revenue to purchase what staples we need to survive and a fine steed or two, to get started. I did well with horse breeding before and I can start over."

"Save your money, Uncle David. Look out in the north pasture." All eyes fell on the distant pasture containing ten fine breeding mares and one young stud. Knowing his uncle was speechless, Zachary went on. "You need not spend money on feed, tac, or anything relating to keeping up the stables. You have one stable hand to help you since you are the one that taught me how to train horses. There is a staff of ten in the house, one groundskeeper over four helpers. The food pantry is well stocked and a new bank account has been set up in your name at Boston Federal."

"Zachary, just how much money did you win from Jax Tyndall?" David asked flabbergasted over the amount, of things he had given them.

"Let me just say, besides the huge amount I started out with to even lure him into playing one game, I won enough to restore property to every man he stole from plus a whole lot extra to share with you and the men who helped me. The gentleman who owned the railroad line has given me shares and free rides." Zachary and the others looked down the long drive when they heard horses making their way at a slow trot. "Is that Uncle Horus's carriage? I've not seen another with the purple seats and canopy."

"It certainly looks like Bradley sitting in the back seat." Autumn shielded her eyes from the evening sun. The carriage pulled up and the steel magnet stepped down with the aid of the footman, who then help Horus's wife. Bradley remained on the carriage, head drooped. "So, you must be Zachary's aunt and uncle, Mr. and Mrs. Hastings. I have already met your son Bradley. Actually, some years back, at my Uncle Bedford's plantation."

"Then you must be Autumn Rose. The young girl my son could not stop talking about when he returned from…something creek?"

"Crooked Creek, Mr. Hastings, named for the creek that snakes it way around my uncle's property. The same creek where Zachary and I played and fell in love!" Autumn gave him a genuine smile and looked past them to their son, still sitting like a stone statue. "Tell me, is your son going to remain on the carriage while you obviously intend to visit your brother David's home?"

"David's? But I thought?" Zachary stepped up and pulled his wife into his arms.

"I won my farm back? I did, Uncle Horus, and knowing Uncle David lost everything due to someone burning down his estate and leaving him and Margaret for dead because he refused to tell the Union soldiers where I was, I gave them the farm They were after me because a certain family member told the enlistment board I was a Southern sympathizer, no doubt because Autumn loved me and not him! I gave them the kind of home they deserved, not just because he was loyal to me, but because I genuinely love him with all my heart as did my dear saintly mother!"

"Sweet Irene." Tears once again came into the once cold eyes, only this time, the sentiment did not fade away as Horus reached out his arms toward his brother. "David, I am not a proud man. I am guilty of a great many things I am ashamed of. One of those things is the way I treated you after you lost everything and you called on me to help you. Not for yourself or to rebuild your life, no, you never once pointed a finger toward our son, who was to blame for a great many bad needs. You were reaching out to a brother to help pay to have Jacob's body moved to his rightful place, Dawson Farm, beside our beautiful baby sister, Irene. My heart had turned to cold steel, just like the product I could not make enough of. Tyndall had moved on to his big mansion after knowing Zachary was a fugitive and a traitor, at least that's where his status ended up after Bradley faked several documents. He found out in prison that the president of the United States was on to him and having him tracked with his dealings with top generals and this man Tyndall." Horus looked sadly into Zachary's eyes. "I could have bought this farm back for Zachary. He made my horses the winning champions! He turned the mill around and saved it from a disastrous explosion that could have wiped out the entire town along with President Lincoln." Horus watched his son climb down slowly from the carriage and lend over on one of the horse's necks. "Tyndall offered to sale it to me, but Bradley would not hear of it!" turning back to David, tears fell from Horus Hasting's eyes. "Then everything changed overnight. Bradley had gambled and lost everything we owned. The estate, the champion horses, and the steel factory. We were left with nothing, not even two pennies to rub together. Then I got your letter David. You did not gloat or make fun of me, no, right the opposite. You reached out in brotherly love and sent me a check, saying you wished it could be more but that was all you had left." Horus fell to his knees, looking from David to Zachary. "Then that very week we got word that everything had been restored to us by an anonymous young man and…"

"I knew it was Zachary." Bradley stepped up, a broken man, eyes swollen from crying. "I kept saying why? Why would Zachary care what happened to us? Especially to me, after all the mean things I have done to destroy him!" Bradley dropped his head in shame. "I sat in prison trying hard to blame someone for my being there! For my bad choices and losing everything to a common criminal! Then, in a broken glass, I saw the one responsible looking back. A spoiled conceded man who had it all and wanted only what the poor cousin had." Bradley moaned. "Zachary, it wasn't just Autumn I wanted, I wanted to be you, have your ability to turn any job into a success, make my father proud of me the way he was about you. You were never afraid to do anything! Ride a horse! Swim in a murky pond, take Calvary lessons from Nathan Bedford Forrest! Fight in battles! Lead an army! Win the love of the one girl you have always dreamed of having! You even traveled with me and kept me straight! I do not deserve your forgiveness Zachary and would not blame you if you ask me to get out of your life forever! Maybe it was for my parents you won back the estate, if so, they deserve it more than I. They at least helped you a little bit, but I fought to destroy the cousin I always admired the most! A genuine friend who could give genuine love, never pretense like me."

"There is a vast difference between us Bradley, there you are right. Just like there is a vast difference between Uncle David and your father. But there is one common thing we all share, kinship. I could never turn my back on a member of my family weather they are good to me or not. I know how much family meant to my mother and father. They taught me at an early age that family was everything and we should always help a brother, a sister, aunt or uncle and as many cousins as the good Lord gives us." Zachary pulled Autumn in his arms. "They never failed to look into one another's eyes and finish with, "Zachary, little son, always show your children great love, but you will learn, to love your mate, the girl of your heart, with an everlasting love that can only be topped by your love for the almighty God. This is how I stack my love. It is because I love each one of you that I reached out to help restore what was loss. My parent's advice and the sage advice from my Indian guide, Grey Wolf." Zachary reached around and tickled Autumn's waist, causing her to laugh. To Zachary's delight, she began speaking like Grey Wolf.

"Grey Wolf knows family is blessed by love and charity of white face with good heart." Autumn spoke in her brave's voice "Now, we speak words that sit on tongue, both pale face senior and small warrior, who tremble with sorrow." She looked from Horus to Bradley, both finally smiling at her act.

"Pale face senior will go first, since I am the oldest and cause of boy's behavior." Horus echoed Autumn's Indian call. "David, please forgive me for not being there for you, both in sorrow of you first wife's death and the loss of your estate. For not honoring my beloved sister by bringing her Jacob home to Dawson Farm and laying him next to her eternal resting place." With eyes laced in tears, he added. "I need you in my life David. I need my brother."

The two-brother's whelp in each other's arms as Bradley turned to his cousin Zachary and said softly "I am truly sorry for everything I have ever done to hurt you Zachary. Please, forgive me for being a selfish, overbearing, careless, undeserving jackass!"

"Everyone deserves a second chance, cousin." Zachary laid his hand on Bradley's shoulder. "I am sorry you had to go through so much anguish and pain to finally see the light. There is no other person who could wish you a better life than I do. You do not have to try to be like me. There has always been a special person inside you just longing to come out. Just like you learn to remove your fear of horses and find comfort in their gentle touch, you too can find the ability to run a steel factory and work hand and hand with your father." Zachary lifted his fallen chin. "Be of good cheer Cousin! I forgive you, of everything. Now, all that is left is for you to forgive yourself."

"Will you help me?" Bradley looked up pleadingly.

"Bradley, there is one who can help you far better than anyone." Zachary noticed Bradley looking over those standing around. "You won't find Him among your family and you cannot even see him, but he is here and he is real."

Bradley closed his eyes, a slight smile gracing his lips. "You speak of the Lord. I have not prayed, since I was a small boy. I am not sure the Lord can hear me anymore."

"Bradley Hastings, it was you who gave up praying, most likely because it did not fit into your lifestyle. Our loving Lord never stop loving you or wanting you to turn back to Him!" Autumn took her husband's hand. "Humans may turn their backs on you but never God. You have become the lost son he spoke of in His parable about the prodigal's son and he has always been waiting for you to return to Him."

"Son, I will help you, for I too need to return to my God as well." Horus took around his son and led him around the back to the rose garden to pray. All his wife and Bradley's mother could do was look up and give God the praise, and thank him for hearing her prayers. Zachary's family was at last mended.

Laurel Grove Plantation was bustling with family when Zachary and Autumn finally rode up and looked around at all the activities taking place. Before they could climb down off their horses, Big Ben was out in front to hold the horses, in case they grew spooked by all the noise.

"Afternoon, Miss Autumn, Mr. Zachary! You is just in time for the big celebration!" he gave a loud chuckle. "Not that they could start celebrating without you! No sir re!"

"Just what are we celebrating Ben?" Zachary helped Autumn down and started untying their bags. "I know it's not one of the children's birthdays yet." He looked around and saw two little girls and one small boy chasing each other around the front yard. "We have guest! Skyler and Winter Rose is running with another little girl."

"It's Callie!" Autumn grew excited, not having seen her sister Nellie is some time and missing her dearly. "Nellie's home!" she picked up her skirt tails and dashed toward the big house.

"Yes sir, Miss Nellie and Mr. Clint done come for a visit to share a special celebration with you and Miss Autumn." Zachary took Midnight's reins as Big Ben led the Pinto Pony to the stables to remove their saddles, brush them down and give them feed and water "Them little youngsters have been running themselves ragged. Yes sir, keeping the house staff busier than they is when they be putting up wash, or canning vegetables or even giving the big house a proper spring cleaning." Benjamin chuckled "Your littlest two can get into some kind of a mess when they left feeding themselves, and the grandparents watch them laughing at their antics as they giggle and throw sticky preserves in each other's faces and hair. It's not quite so funny to Miss Nora and Dora when they're asked to give them a bath.

"I'm not sure who needs a spanking there." Zachary knew he and Autumn had their work cut out for them, calming down their little ones. Hearing the sound of men laughing, Zachary followed the sound and noted it was behind the stables. "Sounds like some sort of game going on, Ben."

"They be playing horseshoes, Mr. Zachary. Big Ben was winning when young Freddy came down to tell me of your arrival." he gave a chuckle. "We can join them for a few games before the big house rings the dinner bell."

"Sure! I might win if my beautiful wife isn't playing." Zachary followed the huge black man down the path to where Clint, Frederick, Bedford, Drake, Willy, and Ben's friend Simon had set up for another set of horseshoes.

Autumn and Nellie got caught up on all their past adventures while they had been separated. The sisters got a big laugh about Clint's description of Grey Wolf turning out to be the gorgeous red head. They could only assume Autumn felt the power of the Cherokee people through her close ties with Nellie's Indian blood while growing together side by side in their mother's womb.

The big dinner bell rang out, calling the family together to celebrate the double wedding anniversaries of Autumn and Zachary, and Nellie and Clint. It had been decided by Katherine and Frederick Forrest that both couples could have the night completely to themselves after the meal had been eaten and the large cake had been served. The six children would be tended to by their two dedicated nannies. The three girls with Buttercup and the three boys with Julip. The special guest, Bedford and Mary Ann, with son Willy, Aunt Vera and cousin Drake, Aunt Isabell and Stanley, along with their daughters, Christina and Polly Ann had all been given lovely guest rooms for their long stay.

After everyone toasted the happy couples, they departed in separate directions. Nellie and Clint went up to their big double suite to enjoy a bottle of champagne and elegant cookies before having a romantic night together, undisturbed by anyone. Autumn and Zachary had chosen a completely different way to spend their cherished alone time together. Wrapping up against the night chill, the loving couple made their way up to Autumn's secret hill, carrying one large night roll and heavy blankets, their bottle of champagne with two glasses.

Autumn watched lovingly as Zachary fixed the bedroll for later and carried one blanket over to the rock bench where his beloved sit waiting, holding two glasses of champagne. Taking a glass, his fingers brushed across her hand as a smile fell on his handsome lips.

"The daylight is quickly fading my darling and the eastern sky will soon grow dark." Zachary reached over and kissed her longingly. "I promise to keep my dearest one warm tonight within our bedroll, even though we shall be without pajamas or gowns."

"There will be no need of sleeping clothes in such a small place, my darling. I feel sure we shall keep each other warm this night with our canopy being the stars." Autumn glance out and noticed how different the sinking sun did not reflect on what the morning brought. "I guess we will have to wait until sunrise to see the magic of this secret place."

"Not anymore, my dearest Autumn Rose. It is true the sun doth rise over Dixie here, but Wherever the sun rises the sun also sets." Zachary got up and turned her around to the glorious sight behind her. Still lingering in the Western sky, the big round red ball slowly drifted down through the colorful clouds as Autumn looked on, eyes wide with wonder, a big beautiful smile forming on her lips.

"Oh, Zachary! What a special anniversary gift! "Autumn pulled him down and gave him a loving kiss. "For such a long time, this was just a special secret place for me. Then you came into my life and my whole world changed and you have made my life complete, my dearest Zachary. All I could see was the sunrise over Dixie and you have given me…"

"The promise of a lifetime of loving and sharing." Zachary gathered Autumn into his warm embrace. As they looked out at the glory of God's creation. "Yes, my Autumn, we will always have your sunrise to brighten our days, and together we can share the sunset over Dixie, our time for love and romance, for the rest of our days!"

www.ingramcontent.com/pod-product-compliance
Lightning Source LLC
Chambersburg PA
CBHW060901250626
47159CB00008B/2830